NAVIGATE

WINDTREE PRESS ANTHOLOGY

PATY JAGER   PAMELA COWAN   SUSIE SLANINA

DIANA MCCOLLUM   TERRI PATRICK   KIMILA KAY

MARY VINE   JUDITH ASHLEY   MAGGIE LYNCH

MELISSA YUAN-INNES   LISA DE NIKOLITS

DARI LAROCHE   RON ROMAN

Windtree
Press

Published by

Windtree Press, Corvallis, Oregon

https://windtreepress.com

Ebook ISBN 978-1943601-78-3

Print Book ISBN 978-1943601-79-0

FOREWORD

What do you think of when you hear the word "Navigate." Do you think of using cell phone apps to help you drive from one place to another? Or do you think of navigating life and its ups and downs? Or perhaps you think of navigating the stars. In this collection of fourteen stories, our authors have used the theme to provide humor, compassion, wonder, scares, and questions for the reader to solve.

An enjoyable children's story about Metro the opera-singing dog opens the anthology with Susie Slanina's story, **Metro Sails the Atlantic**. Diana McCollum offers a witchy-romantasy with **The Cottage on the Hill**. Therese Patrick follows with a fictionalized account of a real-life navigational adventure in her story, **A Country to Cross**.

A centuries-old curse on a lighthouse infuses Pamela Cowan's story, **Dark Tide**. Paty Jager's **Changing Course** is about a man accused of a heinous crime and his attempt at telling his side of the story. In **Jamboree Jealousy**, Kimila Kay's characters have to find a killer while trying to enjoy a Country Music jamboree.

Mary Vine brings us another installment of Grandma Harper

in ***Navigating the Stars***. In ***When I'm An Old Lady***, Judith Ashley explores the process of growing older with her characters from The Sacred Women's Circle books. Dari LaRoche's poem, ***Navigating the Chaos***, speaks to a desire for change in current times.

The Beckoning, by Maggie Lynch, explores the misunderstanding of visions and communication between the supernatural and humans. Melissa Yuan-Innes reveals how actors in the future will become their parts in ***Delicate Creatures***. Lisa Nikolits shares her thoughts on how the government can go too far ***In the Interest of Transparency***.

M. Jaimeson's story, ***The Conscript***, suggests a future where wealthy business owners must face the draft lottery. Closing out the anthology is Ron Roman's story, ***The Journey***, featuring a combat veteran on a journey of life and death.

We hope you enjoy all of these stories. We'd love to see your thoughts on your favorites in reviews wherever you purchased this anthology. You can also let us know your thoughts through our contact page at Windtree Press.

Metro Sails the Atlantic

by Susie Slanina

Published by

Windtree Press, Corvallis, Oregon

https://windtreepress.com

PROLOGUE

SPRING

"Did you know that centuries ago, travelers and sailors relied on the stars to navigate their boats to far away lands? Isn't that romantic?"

Metro appeared to listen with deep interest. But Metro already knew people used stars to navigate boats. In fact, she (and all dogs) knew everything under the sun.

Dogs were a superior species and knew the history of the whole world. But Metro kept her wisdom a secret, although sometimes she nudged Sherry in the right direction, or gave her hidden knowledge that helped her make decisions.

In this case, though, Metro also knew the many hardships people faced while navigating their boats by stars. But Metro didn't want to spoil Sherry's daydream so she stayed silent while Sherry had the far-off expression that Metro knew so well.

They were enjoying a week at their vacation cabin in the mountains of Big Bear. It was because of Metro's talent that Sherry was able to afford this cozy second home, and it was the first whole week she had off since starting her new job last September. She truly craved the peace and tranquility of the mountains, and it was a real luxury to have seven days at the cabin, rather than just a weekend, which always ended too soon.

The week had flown by. They took nippy morning walks, and later in the afternoon, they walked along the lake. By then, the air was balmy and sweet with springtime scents along with the evergreen fragrance of fir and forest. Sometimes, she spotted bald eagles soaring in the brilliant blue sky.

On this, the last night of vacation, they were gazing up at the glittery canopy of stars above the tall pine trees. The seasonal stream in the backyard had been fed by an El Nino winter and was at least nine feet across. The roaring sound was deafening, but Sherry could still hear coyotes begin to yowl.

Metro tilted her head. She heard them, too. She pointed her nose to the sky and perfectly imitated the coyotes' crazy yips and howls. As always, when Metro sang, Sherry felt a sense of wonder for the talented little dog. She sounded just like a coyote! If people happened to be passing by the cabin at that time, they might think there was a coyote on the back deck. But all the mountain neighbors knew Metro, the singing dog.

Leaning back in the recliner, Sherry forgot her daydream. She relaxed into the magic of the present moment, and simply listened to the stream and the coyote/Metro chorus.

———

DRIVING HOME ON THE WINDING ROAD THE NEXT DAY, SHERRY thought about the events of the past year. Three exciting things had happened.

Two weeks ago, Marguerite had become engaged and now wore a sparkling diamond ring! And Lori, who lived next door, was almost sixteen and starting to go on dates! And Sherry had a new job which she loved!

A year ago, something had been tugging at Sherry's heart, and it finally dawned on her. It was simple. She wanted to spend more time with her pets. It was a strong yearning that she couldn't shake.

Under a starry desert sky while on a long road trip with Metro, she had made a big decision to quit the job that had a long commute by train. She didn't know exactly what she would do, and she didn't think about it again for the whole trip.

When they got home from the cross-country adventure, Metro helped Sherry figure out the perfect job just by nudging a book toward her.

It had been the right decision to leave the higher-paying job at the university. Now she worked at The Academy, which was only a few blocks from home. She was a teacher's aide and helped children with their reading. It was good practice for her goal of becoming a teacher. Best of all, Metro was welcome in the classroom!

Sherry was twenty now, and Metro was already three years old. In two more years, Marguerite and Sherry would graduate from college.

As she wound around the last long curve of the mountain to start on the freeway, she was surprised to feel happy about going to work the next day. Usually, when she got to this point on the drive, she was already missing the mountains, but this time it was different. She looked forward to seeing the children.

The Sunday afternoon traffic was brutal. She was still lost in thought when she finally pulled into the driveway.

Walking to the mailbox, she noticed the first robin of spring. She snapped out of her reverie. Her father had taught her a lovely custom of "stamping" the first robin.

You lick the pad of one thumb and press the moistened thumb firmly into your other open palm, (like putting a stamp on a letter). Then, you close your eyes and make a wish. If the robin is still there when you open your eyes, the wish will come true. It was a fun tradition and Sherry never forgot to stamp the first robin of spring.

Pressing her thumb in her palm, Sherry closed her eyes and made a wish. She wished she and Metro could go on another adventure like last year's trip across the USA. She had an irresistible longing to go somewhere far away.

After making the wish, Sherry opened her eyes. The robin hadn't flown away.

The mailbox was stuffed with a week's worth of mail. Sorting through it, she saw a fat letter from Majestic Cruise Lines. She always liked to look over catalogs of *The Beacon*, a luxury ocean liner that sailed across the Atlantic. She and Marguerite liked to daydream about making a transatlantic trip. But it was far too expensive. Even the lowest staterooms cost too much.

But this wasn't a catalog.

The letter was printed on expensive stationery that had a watermark and gold seal. Sherry was curious. She opened it.

Dear Sherry,

Our director of entertainment happened to be at the opera in Hollywood in which Metro sang. He also has seen Metro's singing commercial, and was impressed with Metro's talent. He suggested to our team the idea of Metro singing a solo as a special guest for our final crossing in November. The theme will be: A Night at the Opera. The Beacon has many entertainment options and would like Metro to be one of them.

The crossing takes seven days and departs from New York City. You will be provided three nights at the Waldorf Astoria Hotel while in New York. On the ship, you will be in a luxury suite with a private veranda overlooking the sea.

Upon arrival in London, we are offering three nights at the Ritz Hotel, located in the heart of the capital. We are also giving a gift certificate to the world-famous Harrods Department store in the amount of 800 pound sterling.

Metro's pay for this will be substantial.

You may bring one guest who will be provided the same accommoda-tions and a Harrods gift certificate with our compliments.

One caveat: The seas are rough in November. Please keep this in mind.

We hope you'll consider this offer. Please get back to us no later than June 1st.

Sherry's hand trembled as she held the letter.

She immediately called Marguerite who was at her sorority house at the University of Southern California.

"M-M-Marguerite," she stammered. "How would you like to sail across the Atlantic Ocean this November…on *The Beacon*?"

"Sherry. What are you talking about?"

"I just got this letter from Majestic Cruise Lines, and they want Metro to perform on the last night of the crossing–the theme will be *A Night at the Opera*.

"Sherry, are you teasing me?"

"Nope, I have the letter right here in my hand. It says I can bring a guest, and I thought immediately of you!"

"But, but…"

"And guess what else? We get a top veranda suite *AND* we each get a gift certificate to Harrods Department Store."

"Oh, that's a wonderful store. My parents took me to London when I was younger. It's more like a museum than a store. But, wait. *The Beacon* sails out of New York. We're in California."

"Oops, I forgot. That's another thing. They're flying us from LAX to JFK and we'll stay three nights at the Waldorf Astoria. Then in London, three nights at the Ritz. And then they fly us back to LAX. What do you say, Marguerite…will you be my guest?"

"Gosh, Sherry. I'm overwhelmed. But, I can't possibly go. I have to plan my wedding."

"I know, I know. But your wedding isn't until next June. We'll be back by Thanksgiving. You'll have plenty of time for planning."

Marguerite was quiet for a few moments. Then she spoke. "Can you just read me the letter?"

Sherry did so. There were another few more moments of silence. Sherry waited patiently.

"You're right. It would be silly to pass up an opportunity like this! How fun! Let's do it!"

"Yay!" Sherry exclaimed. "And we'll have all summer long to daydream about the trip. In fact, let's set up a Daydreaming Date, so we can plan all day long."

Besides being with her pets, daydreaming was Sherry's favorite hobby, and she often set aside special dates just to daydream.

Marguerite sighed blissfully. "Okay, that sounds wonderful. Thank you so much for inviting me. And, don't forget to thank Metro, too!"

"I definitely will do that right now."

"How will we ever wait until November?!" Both girls exclaimed at once.

"You owe me a Coke!" They said together. They laughed and hung up.

Sherry grabbed Metro for an ecstatic twirl. "You are the best doggy, Metro. Marguerite and I adore you!"

She collapsed on the couch and started to daydream about the daydreaming date with Marguerite. Summer Solstice would be a good time to set aside just for daydreaming. She marked her calendar, then gazed dreamily at the ceiling.

"Gee. I wonder if that robin…"

As she was getting ready for bed that night, Sherry chatted happily to Metro. She set the alarm and said, "Just think, Metro. I wished on the robin that we would have a grand doggy adventure and we're going to. It will be a fun summer–Marguerite and I have no classes, and then, before you know it, autumn will be here and we'll set sail across the Atlantic Ocean!"

PART ONE - SCHOOL DAYS WITH
METRO

The school days were happy times for Sherry and Metro. No more Monday morning blues. She was able to go to work with a light heart. Every morning she cycled the short distance to The Academy with Metro in the basket. Her other two dogs, Gizzy and Tawny, had been shelter mates at the Humane Society. When Sherry was about to adopt Tawny, Gizzy looked forlorn, so she ended up adopting them both! They were perfectly content to stay home with each other.

The Academy was for preschool children all the way up to eighth grade. Its mission was to give kids the best possible environment for learning and growing.

The small children were in the downstairs room, and the older ones upstairs. Sherry worked downstairs. The small kids loved having Metro in the classroom and Metro adored them. She sat quietly while they studied and they could feel her doggy encouragement. To the children, it was like having a doggy cheerleader by their side.

One child remarked, "Metro should have pom-poms, because she's always cheering us on!"

9

On the playground at recess, Metro scampered about and the children delighted in her antics. Metro always paid special attention to quiet children.

"You know why I love Metro?" A shy little girl named Ellen asked.

Sherry knelt so she could be Ellen's size. "Why's that?" she asked gently.

"Because Metro loves me so much." The little girl's eyes were misty.

"Yes, she does! She loves you especially, Ellen!"

The little girl bent her head, touching Metro's soft fur, and Metro responded with a sweet kiss on Ellen's face.

A boy in the older group did not like Metro. His name was Timmy. He was a sullen child who was always in trouble. He wasn't very popular, and he couldn't bear that Metro got so much attention at recess.

One day, Sherry and Ellen were sitting on a bench watching the children romp with Metro. Timmy plopped down on the bench across from them with a sour look on his face. He started complaining about Metro.

"I can't stand it anymore. All I hear on the playground is, 'Metro! Metro! Metro!' That dumb mutt." He shook his head in disgust.

As he ranted about Metro and dogs in general, Metro jumped up beside him. She inched closer toward him as he spoke and gently licked his hand. Without thinking, Timmy rubbed her head as she snuggled against his leg.

"All dogs are stupid..." and he went on and on, while Sherry and Ellen watched Metro nuzzle in for more cuddles. They raised their eyebrows. Timmy continued rubbing her soft ears.

"Well, you sure like *that* dog!" Ellen pointed out.

"Huh?" He looked down and snatched his hand away. "Eww, I don't like dogs, any dogs!"

Then Metro put her paw on his leg. It was her way of saying she liked him. Like a magnet, his hand went back to Metro's ears.

"Well, I guess *this* dog might be okay. In fact, she's kinda sweet. But I still don't like any other dogs." He stood up with a confused look on his face. Metro looked up at him innocently.

"Come on, Metro. Let's go play fetch!" The boy and dog ran off together.

"Aha!" Sherry said and winked at Ellen. "It looks like Metro has wiggled her way into Timmy's heart!"

Summer

The budget the girls had made last year was working, and Sherry was dedicated to it. She ate simply during the week, but every Friday, they went out to eat at an international restaurant. This Friday, it was Chinese food.

Lori was babysitting her little brother. Before they could stop him, he dipped his finger in the hot mustard, made a face, and declared: "DAT YUCKY!"

The girls laughed. The restaurant wasn't busy, so they lingered, sipping many cups of tea while Lori's brother slept in the booth, his head on Lori's leg.

Driving home, Sherry felt uncomfortably warm. The restaurant was only a few blocks away. She had felt fine at dinner. She was perplexed.

"Was it too much hot tea? Was it 'dat yucky' mustard?" She smiled, remembering the funny comment.

"But, oh, my head hurts!" She put her palm to her forehead. It was burning.

"Wait! It wasn't hot tea or hot mustard. I think I have a fever!"

She went straight to bed. It was a bad flu with a sore throat, chills, and body aches.

During her recovery, Metro kept vigil at Sherry's side.

The little dog was so gentle, Sherry was unaware when she

hopped on and off the bed. But she felt Metro's presence. Sometimes Metro gave a little dream bark.

Sherry felt like she had a restful sleep. She felt much better, and Metro could tell. The dog was ecstatic and jumped up on the bed with a squeaky toy, but didn't squeak it. She waited, looking at Sherry with happy expectation.

"It's okay…go ahead, Metro." Metro squeaked away, knowing Sherry was getting better.

Lori and Marguerite, who had been sitting on the floor with a jumble of dogs, smiled happily at her.

Sherry smiled back and fondly surveyed the scene. Her cats were in the bedroom, too.

Playmate chased a fuzzy toy while Butterscotch looked on with disdain. She was too sophisticated for such nonsense!

Sherry loved the simple, tiny, everyday scenes her pets provided. She cleared her throat, turned on her side, and propped herself up on her elbow. Her voice was squeaky, like Metro's toy.

"So, tell me, what have I missed? I know I slept for hours, it's almost dark. Tomorrow must be Sunday, the day of the Summer Solstice. It's almost time for our daydreaming date!"

Marguerite and Lori looked at each other.

"But it's already Tuesday! Sherry, you slept clear through the Summer Solstice. It's already June 23rd!" Lori said.

Sherry laughed. "Are you kidding? I most certainly did not! I remember getting up and feeding the pets, and having some delicious chicken noodle soup."

"My mother made that for you," Marguerite said. "She checked in on you and wanted to call the doctor, but you kept saying you were fine, and your temperature did go down Saturday afternoon. But you've been mostly sleeping for days!"

Lori showed Sherry the calendar. "We walked the dogs, and we called the school and let them know you had the flu."

"*What?!*" Sherry couldn't believe she had slept for so long, not even bothering to note the dates on the calendar.

"All that rest must've helped me get well. I'm feeling better by the minute! Let's daydream this Saturday," she squeaked. "In fact, I want to walk the dogs around the block. Come with me?" Marguerite and Lori agreed and the dogs danced happily when they saw the leashes.

It was hard to believe she had missed almost a whole week. By Thursday, she felt completely well, and went back to work.

On her desk was a white rose with a simple note from Ellen: "We missed you and Metro." Sherry was deeply touched. She had grown very fond of the shy little girl.

———

So the summer went on. School was more relaxed, but the children still had lessons.

Every evening Sherry took the dogs for a stroll through the Covina neighborhood. Sometimes, Lori or Marguerite or both, would join them.

Once a month, they walked to the ice cream parlor for hot fudge sundaes. Lori had included the outing when the budget was being made.

"Ice cream parlor–but only once a month!" she had suggested as they were making a list of expenses. Marguerite and Sherry had agreed, and cheerfully wrote it in the column.

"Being on this budget is actually more fun than not having a budget." Lori remarked as she scraped the last bit from the bowl. "The ice cream tastes more special and delicious than if we had it more often."

"I agree," Marguerite said. "It was brilliant to come up with these little splurges, too. It was your idea, Lori!"

———

IN THE CLASSROOM, ELLEN TOOK TO READING LIKE A DUCK TO water. She needed Sherry's help at first, but as she developed a keen interest in books, Sherry's assistance was no longer required. Ellen only needed help to read with more expression because even though she read perfectly, her voice was flat. Sherry encouraged her to practice reading out loud with a little more drama.

One day, Sherry passed out flyers to the children. Shy Ellen took the flyer and read confidently to the class:

"Dear Parents, this is to inform you that effective immediately, there will be a small doggy play group every Friday after school lets out, for those who wish to participate. If you don't have a small dog, your family is warmly welcome to attend, and sit on the bleachers to watch. If you have a friendly small dog and would like to participate, please sign this form and include your dog's name."

Ellen's voice squealed with delight when she got to the part about the doggy play group.

"Whose idea was this?" Ellen asked.

"It was Miss Kim's idea!" Sherry said. Kim was the small kids' teacher.

Both Kim and Sherry were amazed at Ellen's reading skill. She read without hesitation or sounding out, and she was only five years old!

"Gosh, Ellen. That was terrific. You've become an excellent reader! And, you read with great expression, too!"

"I love to read, Miss Sherry. But I miss you helping me, and I miss Metro, too."

"I miss you, too," Sherry said thoughtfully. "We've got to do something about that, but I don't know what exactly. Let me think about it."

Sherry thought about Ellen that night, and just before she fell asleep, she had an idea. She couldn't wait to discuss it with Kim the following morning.

Kim agreed with the idea. Sherry took Ellen aside.

"Since you don't need my help with reading, maybe you can

write a story during the week, and then read the story to class on Fridays during the summer. Metro and I will help you."

Ellen's eyes sparkled. "Oh, Fridays are going to be so much fun. Story time *and* Doggy Play Group!"

It was truly enjoyable helping Ellen write her simple stories. Ellen came up with such inventive ideas. Sherry helped her express them on paper.

Each Friday after morning recess, became Ellen's story time. The children all looked forward to hearing them, especially because Ellen included them as characters. All the stories included Metro.

One Friday at recess, Ellen ran to Sherry. "I heard the boys talking and one said he couldn't wait to hear my story today! And the other boys agreed!" She blushed.

"I can't wait to hear it, too. Oh, there's the bell, let's go hear it!"

Ellen's story:

THE ARTIST by Ellen

Timmy was a good painter. His watercolors were hung on the display wall. They were really pretty, and the children loved looking at them. Some of his paintings decorated the little kids' classroom.

One day, while the small children were busy studying, a classmate of Timmy's came from upstairs and grabbed one of the paintings and tried to run out the door. The children gasped in surprise.

Metro tripped the boy by pulling his shoestrings. He dropped the painting.

The children wondered why he took the painting and he explained:

"It was just so cool. I wanted to hang it on my bedroom wall so I can always look at it. I'm sorry."

Timmy was very nice and told his friend he could have it and he also would paint something especially for him. He asked his classmate what he would like and the boy said a sailboat. Timmy came to school the next day with a painting of a beautiful sailboat on a river. The sun was setting and the scenery around the boat was colorful.

Then the other children wanted Timmy to paint something for them, too. He was proud to do it, and by the end of summer, each child had a painting by Timmy.

For Miss Sherry, he painted a picture of Metro alongside a pair of sneakers with the shoelaces in Metro's mouth.

The End

It was so sweet that Ellen had Timmy as the main character.

And then a part of Ellen's story came true! Timmy actually was a good artist, and he was happy and proud to be included in the story. That summer, he painted a picture for each child!

Ellen's stories became very popular. In mid-summer, Ellen and Sherry decided to work on a play. The kids in class were the actors and had fun learning their lines. The play was presented to the whole school at an assembly and later in the evening so the parents could attend.

Someone asked Sherry if she could film it, but Sherry explained that her brain automatically refused to function when it came in contact with any technical gadgets. A boy offered to do the filming.

After the play, Ellen confided to Sherry that it was the best night of her life.

"Oh, Ellen. I have a feeling there will be many more nights like this. You're a star!"

Fridays were special that summer. Children who wanted to participate could bring their dogs for an afternoon romp in the field next to the playground. The parents brought the dogs when they came to pick up their child, and stayed for an hour to watch the doggy festivities. And the dogs looked forward to seeing their doggy friends!

Tawny and Gizzy came. Lori and Marguerite came. Kim brought a bag of dog toys and dropped them on the grassy area. The dogs thought it was doggy paradise! At the end of the hour it was hard to gather the happy dogs to be leashed up. Kim solved the problem by bringing treats to hand out at the end of playtime. It was amazing that no dogs fought over the treats, in fact, most sat politely and waited their turn.

Afterwards, the dogs were tired and happy.

On a rainy Friday in late July, the dogs had an indoor playgroup in the basement. Timmy surprised everyone by showing up with a wet doggy!

"This is Fuzzy," he explained.

His parents told Kim and Sherry: "We've had Fuzzy for almost a week. Timmy wanted to keep it a secret until the play group. Apparently, Metro won Timmy's heart, but he still didn't like other dogs. At a distance, he observed the playfulness and joy of the dogs every Friday. He started loving all dogs and begged us to go to the animal shelter."

Sherry and Kim watched as Fuzzy was welcomed enthusiastically by the other dogs.

"We adopted this sweet dog last Saturday and Timmy named him Fuzzy. He has been very responsible and keeps Fuzzy's water bowl fresh and feeds him. He walks Fuzzy every morning and evening. They're inseparable and he is like a different child. He's cheerful, he's not as grumpy, and he doesn't talk back to us."

Sherry was delighted at Timmy's transformation. She thought Fuzzy may have softened his heart. She swallowed hard. "Dogs are so amazing," she thought to herself.

Sometimes Sherry worked upstairs and helped the older children who needed extra help with reading. She was thankful to receive a raise and promotion which included extra duties with the older children.

And since Ellen's big success with her Friday stories, a few of the more advanced children wanted to write stories of their own. She sat on the floor with them and talked about writing.

"So, what would you like to write about? A ghost story, a spaceship in a science fiction story, a fairy tale with a princess, or a suspenseful mystery? There's so many subjects you can choose! Pretend you're a junior detective and carry a small notebook everywhere. If you hear or see something interesting, write it down. Maybe you could use it for your story."

"Is it okay to fib?" Timmy asked.

"Sure, you can fib all you want, if you call your story fiction. It's not fibbing, it's called "artistic license" so go wild with your imagination!"

In the evenings, Sherry enjoyed reading their creations. She couldn't wait to be a real teacher, but it would take a few more years of study.

———

ONE DAY, ELLEN AND METRO DISAPPEARED. THE CHILDREN AND Sherry looked everywhere inside the classroom and went up to the upper floors searching, but no Ellen or Metro. They went outside to search the playground, but no Ellen or Metro.

Finally, a keen-eyed boy spotted Metro on the roof. The children gathered below. Metro was tiny and when she saw the children, she squeezed through the iron railing to greet her friends. She stood on the ledge, wagging at them.

Stay! Stay! Stay, Metro! Stay!

Sit, Metro, Sit!

The children called up to the dog. Metro knew the commands. She sat down and stayed.

Hearing the shouts, Sherry dashed outside and looked up. Her heart was in her throat. She ran up the four flights of stairs. While Sherry ran, Ellen came to the railing.

"Come, Metro, Come!" she called.

The ledge was narrow, but Metro was able to turn around and squeeze back through the rails to Ellen.

"Good dog! Good dog! Good Dog!" The children called with relief in their voices.

Reaching the roof, Sherry was out of breath. First, she hugged Ellen tightly. Then they both sat on the cement floor, leaning against the railing. Sherry held Metro close and Ellen put her head near the little dog's face. Minutes went by while Sherry caught her breath and gathered her thoughts.

"Why did you go up to the roof, Ellen?!"

Ellen looked dazed.

"I don't know what happened, Miss Sherry. It was like I just fell into this book and I couldn't put it down, even though reading time was over. The roof looked like a good place to read. I snuck up the stairs and Metro followed me," she stammered.

"Oh, Ellen. I completely understand. Sometimes you just get lost in a book…it's almost as though you're in another world. I guess this was your first experience."

Ellen shyly nodded.

"Well, I have good news and bad news. What do you want to hear first?"

"The bad news first, I guess."

"Okay. The bad news is that you can NEVER EVER do this again. It was dangerous and you had us all very worried," Sherry said sternly.

"I'm so sorry, Miss Sherry," Ellen looked crestfallen.

"Also, you have to put the book down for now, because we are learning numbers at the moment. So you've got to snap out of the book world."

"Oh, darn." Ellen clutched the book tightly to her chest. "What's the good news?"

"Ah, sweet Ellen," Sherry's voice softened. "The good news is that you're a reading girl. You'll experience this feeling many, many more times! There's plenty of books out there that you can get lost in. Too many, in fact," Sherry reflected.

"Can I stay inside at recess and just read my book?"

"Well, you could. It's up to you. But you might want to get some fresh air and sunshine so your brain stays strong. That way you can understand more of what you read."

Ellen thought for a minute.

"All right. I think I'm ready to learn numbers now. But I don't think they're as fun as reading."

Truer words were never spoken, Sherry thought to herself.

FALL

Autumn came quickly. While she slept, Sherry could hear the leaves swishing outside on a windy night. The windows rattled. Metro barked at the wind.

"Metro, quiet! Could this be the Santa Ana winds already?" she wondered drowsily and got another blanket from the closet. "That means it's almost time for our voyage across the Atlantic Ocean!"

The last few days before the trip, Sherry was more distracted than usual.

One morning, she fed Tawny and Gizzy, made her lunch, and before she left the house, she checked their food and water bowls.

Usually, they'd be gobbling up their food. This morning, they stood by their bowls, gazing at Sherry with a confused look.

One bowl had birdseed and the other bowl had peanuts for the blue jays.

"Oh, geez," Sherry shook her head wryly as she dished out the proper food. "Lori's family will take much better care of you while I'm gone."

PART TWO–METRO SAILS THE ATLANTIC

*A*t last the big day came. Marguerite and Sherry flew to New York City.

They had a wonderful three days at the Waldorf Astoria Hotel, exploring and sightseeing. It went by in a blur of excitement.

On the last afternoon, Marguerite sat at the desk, writing postcards. "Tomorrow we set sail on *The Beacon.* What shall we do for dinner tonight? I hope we can stay close to the hotel, we've been walking miles everyday."

"Want to splurge and have dinner right here at the Waldorf?"

"Dinner at the Waldorf–excellent idea! I'll call for reservations!"

It happened to be the day of the New York Marathon. When they went to dinner, some people wore medals from the race.

THE BEACON

After descending the gangway to enter the grand ocean liner, Sherry and Marguerite were guided to their stateroom.

"These flower arrangements are stunning, and just look at the fruit basket!" Marguerite exclaimed. "And the bathroom's all marble, even the bathtub! And the woodwork is divine. And, oh, that view!"

Sherry was already on the veranda, gazing out at the skyline. Marguerite joined her.

"You know, this kind of journey is really lovely. It feels like we're in another era, back in time to the golden age of ocean travel, before there were airplanes," Marguerite reflected.

It was twilight when *The Beacon* sailed out of New York City. It seemed they had been waiting a long time. Finally, they felt the vibration of the engine. Then they felt the motion of the great ship moving slowly. They watched as the lights of the skyscrapers slowly disappeared. Soon they were out in the open ocean, going much faster.

They quickly got used to life at sea. They spent a lot of time relaxing and talking. But, if they chose, they had their pick of activities: There were lectures and exercise classes. Metro enjoyed the yoga class and she was great at performing downward dog! The ship even had a library and a movie theater.

Late at night, Marguerite and Sherry walked Metro around the deck. One night, they saw a mysterious woman in a scarf. She stared out to sea and reminded Marguerite and Sherry of old movies they had seen. The characters who had a tragic past and looked to the sea.

The mysterious woman inspired them to re-create some of their favorite old movie scenes. They each donned a scarf and stared wistfully out to sea, just the way old movie stars did. They played "tragic figure" and looked at each other with sad, haunted eyes. They took black and white photos. They had fun saying lines from their favorite movies.

They put the scarf around Metro's face, and Metro looked exotic with her ears pressed down, but her wagging tail and the happy glint in her eyes told them she was *NOT* a tragic figure!

The first few days at sea, the ocean was calm. From the

veranda, the girls spotted birds resting on branches on the gentle waves. They wondered if they were flying across the sea.

THREE DAYS INTO THE CRUISE, THE SEAS TURNED STORMY. THE fluffy grey clouds had transformed into a menacing black monster. The ship started to roll...

The first lurch happened when Sherry and Marguerite were sitting in the lounge. They were having a proper British afternoon tea which consisted of scones, jam, and clotted cream. They enjoyed watching the passengers as they walked the long corridor in front of them. This afternoon, people made their way very slowly, grabbing the handrails with each step.

But one gentleman walked straight in the middle, not needing the rails.

"I think that gentleman is tipsy," Marguerite whispered. "Look, everyone else is trying to get their balance, but not him."

"I think you're right, Marguerite. How can he be so ramrod straight?"

They watched as he made his way in the middle of the long corridor, never missing a step. The girls giggled softly.

Then the ship lurched again. They held onto their teacups while waiters deftly removed the sliding china and crystal. All of a sudden, Sherry felt strange.

"Uh, oh. Let's get back to the room. I feel funny," she said. It was difficult making their way to the cabin. She sat on the couch, trying to focus on a single point in the room, but it moved. Everything was swirling and spinning.

"I feel dizzy," Sherry said weakly.

"Oh, poor Sherry. You're seasick. We'd better go to the ship's doctor. Maybe he can give you something," Marguerite said. "I guess this means you're not going to dinner tonight?"

"Ugh. No way." Sherry said, as she staggered down the hall.

There was a line of woozy passengers waiting at the ship's tiny hospital. The doctor passed out pills to everyone, except Marguerite, she felt just fine.

"Aye, the seas are confused this evening," he said cheerfully. "Please rest in bed after you take this pill."

Marguerite pulled the covers over Sherry.

"My eyelids feel like bricks. I wonder what was in that pill?"

"You'll be right as rain in no time. I'll bring you a hot water bottle," Marguerite said soothingly. Sherry didn't answer. Marguerite dimmed the lights, but she didn't need to. The lights were already out in Sherry's head, and she and Metro were fast asleep.

When she woke up, it was nearly noon.

"How are you feeling, Sherry?"

"Uh. Never better," Sherry replied groggily.

Marguerite could tell that was a fib.

"How was dinner and the dance?"

"Oh, you didn't miss much. It wasn't very busy. I guess most people were riding out the storm by resting in their cabins. The best part was watching people slipping on the dance floor. As the ship would roll with the waves, they'd slide to one section and then the ship would lift up and roll to the other side and they'd all slide the other way! But everyone was good-natured. They laughed a lot."

Sherry perked up a bit. "Oh, that must've been hilarious."

The sea was calm the next morning. Marguerite was still sleeping, and Sherry went to the Promenade Deck to watch the dawn break. She and Metro burrowed in the comfortable deck chair, and an attendant came by to give them a blanket, and asked if she needed anything.

"Just a cup of chamomile tea, please," Sherry said. She felt okay today, but didn't want to take any chances.

An Irish lady sat next to her. "Aye, 'tis a nice, soft morning," she said.

Sherry loved the Irish lilt and the calming tone of her words.

"Yes, it is. That was quite a storm the other evening."

"Well, Ducky. It's the Atlantic Ocean in November. I've been on many crossings and November is the worst."

———

AND THEN IT WAS THE LAST NIGHT OF THE CROSSING. THEY WOULD reach Southampton, England the next day.

It was also the night of Metro's performance. Sherry was reluctant to go. She was nervous for Metro, and she didn't like getting dressed up. But this was a gala night. Men had to be in black tie, women in gowns.

Marguerite was already preparing. Sherry watched from bed. She had always loved watching Marguerite get ready for dates.

"You'd better start getting ready, Sherry." Marguerite warned as she applied eyeliner.

Sherry groaned. "Oh, please, Marguerite. Maybe I don't have to go. I could just stay here and cuddle with Metro."

The sea was gently rocking and it felt comforting. She longed to stay in bed and enjoy the gentle motion.

"But Metro will be feted tonight, and it's her big night to sing. You have to go! And, you too, Metro!" Marguerite exclaimed. The little dog yawned.

"You might even have fun, if you can get over your grumpy attitude. Come on, it's a celebration!"

"Maybe I could just hang the *'Do Not Disturb'* sign at a jaunty angle to celebrate?"

Marguerite looked at her, pretending to be exasperated.

Sherry's eyes twinkled. "Why can't I just wear jeans and a T-Shirt? Look, this one even has sparkles."

Sherry playfully dangled the shirt to show her friend how it glittered with movement. Marguerite rolled her eyes. She was not impressed.

"What are they going to do, throw me overboard?" Sherry teased.

"They might not, but I will!" Marguerite laughed. "Come on, Sherry, I'll help you with your make-up."

"Okay, Marguerite," Sherry sighed. She flung on the formal.

"You look so pretty, Sherry!"

"You do too, Marguerite, but you are always beautiful!"

"Let's go, Metro. It's your big night!"

Metro hopped off the bed in her birthday suit, wondering what all the fuss had been about.

The *Evening at the Opera* had begun.

Metro was on stage and the girls were backstage. Sherry was anxious for Metro. Her heart hammered and her knees started to buckle. The orchestra started playing.

On cue, Metro lifted her voice in glorious song. Sherry closed her eyes, and just listened. The music was stirring. Metro's voice was so true and pure that it gave Sherry chills. The audience listened intently. When the last note played, applause broke out. This was doggy opera at its finest!

A few tears of joy slid down Sherry's cheeks. She was proud of Metro for so many reasons, not just her singing.

"Are you okay?" Marguerite asked gently.

"I always cry when I'm happy!"

The late dinner afterwards was festive and elegant. The girls marveled at the giant ice sculptures. There was a replica of *The Beacon* on a table. It was made entirely of fruit!

Metro had her first hors d'oeuvres! The chef had made special doggy treats.

At the table, they were waited on by a singing Italian waiter. He looked familiar.

"Did you ever work at *Pasta Noodle* in Hollywood?" Sherry asked.

"Yes, that's me. I remember this little dog sang with me. I work on *The Beacon* during the season, and then I go back to Hollywood. The view is better here," he chuckled.

The girls ordered spaghetti, and when it arrived, Metro sang right along with the waiter: "*When the moon hits your eyes like a big pizza pie, that's Amore.*"

And for dessert, a procession of singing waiters came by with trays of cakes with sparklers. It was a magical ending to the perfect evening.

———

It was past midnight and Marguerite was asleep. Sherry crept out to the veranda and took a deep breath of ocean air.

"Wow, what an epic trip, Metro! I wished for an adventure with you when I stamped the first robin of spring, and the wish came true."

The time at sea had been cloudy, but not this night. Sherry gazed at the night sky, which was bedazzled with starlight.

She sat for a long time with her hand on the sleeping dog's shoulder, feeling her heart move with tenderness. The wind and the salty air were refreshing, and time seemed to collapse. Metro wagged in her sleep.

"Let's sleep under the stars tonight. I don't want this feeling to end," Sherry whispered.

She brought blankets to the recliner and settled in. It was chilly, but not too cold. She wanted to feel the nearness of the ocean, just like travelers from the olden days. The thought made her remember the daydream she had had last spring on the deck of the mountain cabin. It seemed so long ago.

"The stars are so…eternal, Metro. Can you imagine using stars to steer this big ship? Just think, before there were instruments, sailors used the North Star as their guiding light because it always stays in the same position while the other stars move."

She turned her gaze from the night sky to another guiding light, a cherished little dog.

"You're my North Star, Metro—always and forever."

ABOUT THE AUTHOR

Susie Slanina lives in Vancouver, Washington. After graduating from California State University, Los Angeles, she went to school in Ireland to study the Montessori approach to educating children. She worked 24 years at CSLA and retired at age 50 to spend more time with her dogs in a cabin in Big Bear.

After retirement she penned a poem about a spider. That poem became the catalyst for the Metro book series. She used to enjoy traveling, but discovered that hanging out with her dogs is better than seeing the wonders of the world.

Her **Metro the Little Dog** series of children's books is about a lovable puppy named Metro. These stories were written to honor the real Metro and all the wonderful dogs who grace our lives. Many thanks to artist Paul Bunch for the exquisite illustrations.

You can earn more about Susie and her books on her website: https://metrothelittledog.com/

INSPIRATION FOR THIS STORY

The sea, once it casts its spell, holds one in its net of wonder forever. ~ Jacques Cousteau

A long time ago, I stumbled upon a deeply discounted offer from Cunard Cruise Lines for a transatlantic crossing aboard the QE2, complete with a gift certificate from Harrods. The journey was unforgettable. Although our modest cabin had only a porthole, it was fun to imagine over-the-top luxury of the ship's grander accommodations--thanks to Metro!

The Cottage On the Hill

Diana McCollum

Published by

Windtree Press, Corvallis, Oregon

https://windtreepress.com

PROLOGUE

*E*lizabeth knew they would come for her. She simply didn't know when. The birth had gone terribly wrong. The child, a boy, had been born silent and perfect. Not a breath, or twitch, not a wail or contorted face at being forced into this world. Now the townspeople laid the blame on her, the midwife.

Fury bubbles up within her at the false accusations of the townspeople, and the air changes. The air blows harshly, forming black storm clouds. The truth of the matter was that the time for her to leave had come. She gathered up some of the dried herbs she stored, placing them in her travel bag. In went teas, the crystal wand, and her grimoire, inherited from her grandmother. Her knapsack, always ready for a fast exit, had two changes of clothes and a few other necessities.

What else would she need? *Chester!* Where was her cat anyway? "Here, kitty. Chester, we have to go. You know what happens when something goes wrong. The local midwife or witch is blamed."

Chester climbed out from under the bed, stretched his paws out in front, and arched his orange back, getting a good stretch.

"There you are. Time to go! Into my knapsack, we'll have to leave now."

The crowd was at the edge of the forest in front of the house. She could see the fire from their torches through the front glass. She would go out the back window.

She pushed on the window, stuck! She hit the glass with a heavy fire poker. The glass cracked into a webbed pattern, then with a *snap!* It broke.

The cold of the winter night air shocked her. Inhaling a deep breath, she threw her knapsack out the window, hitched her skirts up, and climbed out.

The hill behind the house was covered in tree debris from falling limbs. Snow was making the climb difficult. Climbing through the brush, a branch smacked her in the face increasing the sting of the ice crystals, pure and sharp. She kept going, clambering over logs, and around bushes.

Clawing, clinging, hauling herself and Chester upward, breathing hard, sucking in snow. Finally, she reached the top. Thankful for the dark night that covered their escape. Snow came down in sheets, thick now, covering her tracks

She hunkered down behind a fallen tree. Looking back at the cabin, her home for five years, she saw smoke rise above the roof and not only from her chimney. Flames shone in the window, licking at the roof.

Shouts of "burn, witch, burn" rose on the smoke-filled air

Liz did a quick glamor to change her appearance. This wouldn't last long, but if she met anyone from town, they wouldn't recognize her. She didn't have all the tricks of a witch, not having reached twenty and five yet. Soon now, in a matter of weeks, she'd reach her magical adulthood. She would have a visit from Mama to learn all the tricks of the trade. Till then, she needed to find a safe place to live, a place to practice her witch talents.

———

AFTER MANY DAYS OF TRAVEL, SHE WAS VERY TIRED. SHE FOUND A decent spot on top of a hill surrounded on three sides by trees and brush. Chester and she would rest a day or two here. After she had laid pine branches down for a bed, she built a shelter of more pine branches to cover them in the event of rain or snow. Only then did she build a small fire. She was pretty sure they had left the snow far behind. The wind kicked up and rain began to fall, lightly at first.

Chester prowled around their small enclosure. "Meow." He rubbed against her leg.

"I know, I know, you want to do a bit of hunting. Go, my furry friend, enjoy, but be back by dawn."

With a flick of his white and orange striped tail, he was off to explore. Liz drew upon her witch instincts, using a sage wand to cleanse the area. Sitting by the warmth of the fire, her legs bent up and her chin resting on her knees, tired from walking, she went into a meditative trance.

Her spirit lifted from her body and she witch-walked. All the better to observe, and not to be observed. In this state, she could go great distances, but not so far that she couldn't find her way back. She hoped to find the path that would lead to her destiny. There was lots of fog, the smell of salt air, then she broke free from the dense fog and heard the throaty roar of the ocean. Her heart skipped a beat. This was where they needed to go. The cottage on the hill. This was the last prediction Mama had given her.

'Elizabeth, I shall meet with you again, at a cottage on the hill. The air will be clean, fresh. Before I see you again, you will be tested. Once completed, I'll come to you.'

For the next day, she rested. Chester continued his exploring, always returning by nightfall.

The next morning, with Chester in the knapsack, she set out to find the cottage on the hill.

As she neared the ocean, she heard the throaty roar of the waves breaking. Trees by the ocean became sparser, scrawnier. The cliffs were tall. The bottom of the walls touched the sea. Rock outcroppings covered in moss and mist decorated the sides of the cliffs.

This was a different kind of cold from the mountains. The damp permeated her clothing. Chester meowed. He needed a break, so did she. They had traveled for more than a week, all in all. She'd lost count of the days. Far enough away from her last home, she decided. She would be safe here. At least for a spell, if Mama were correct, here would be where she would be shown the way of the witch.

She took a deep breath of the rejuvenating ocean air, raising her hands high over her head, feeling the healing of her fatigue, and fortifying herself.

Putting her knapsack on the ground, she let Chester out. "We're home." Turning in a circle, giving thanks to Mother Earth for a safe journey, she spied an overgrown path in the meadow leading to the stone cottage. This was the stone cottage from her witch-walk. They had found it!

The cottage was uninhabited, in disrepair, and full of cobwebs, perfect for her and Chester.

At the edge of the sea,
At the edge of the world,
A perfect spot to be.

CHAPTER ONE

*L*iz swept the floor of the one-room cottage. She cleaned out the fireplace ashes, set about fixing the table leg and chair from the previous occupant. Taking a rag from a pile of rags outside, she shined the two small windows. Sliding the loft ladder into place, she tested the first rung. Finding it stable, she climbed up.

The loft was a lot bigger than she thought it would be. "All I need is some fresh hay or straw, a blanket or two, and this will be perfect for me and Chester."

At the mention of his name, Chester let out a "meow" of agreement. Up the ladder he scrambled, cuddling close to her side. She stroked his fur and gave his head a rub. "You are such a good kitty! I bet there are plenty of mice to be caught inside the cottage and out in the meadow. That'll be your job. Can you handle it?"

"Meow."

"I'll take that as a yes."

"Hello? Anyone here?" A man's voice resonated through the cabin.

Liz peeked over the edge of the loft, "Hello, who goes there?" She swung her legs over the edge and sat up.

"I am Rhys. I live across the meadow in the woods. My goats got out. I've been rounding them up. Still missing a couple." He took a step inside. "If you see them, could you kindly tie them up? I'll come around and get them."

"Yes, of course. Would you have a length of rope you could leave for me? I'm afraid I don't have any. In fact, the corrals and chicken coop in back are in desperate need of repair." Liz tucked a loose curl behind her ear.

"I'll bring a length of rope by later. I could fix the pen for you, it isn't too bad, an easy fix."

"I'd be most grateful. I plan on getting a cow to milk and some chickens for eggs. How close is the town, or is there even a town?"

He smiled, and a beautiful smile it was, "No big town, more like a small village. There is a Saturday morning market where one can purchase candles, flowers, food, medicals, well, pretty much a little bit of everything. Who might you be?"

"Elizabeth, Liz for short." She climbed out of the loft. "I've been cleaning up this deserted cottage. Do you know who lived here before?" She brushed dust off her skirt.

"Ah, old Miss Bloom lived here. She passed over a year ago, close to one hundred years old. No living relatives, so the place is a bit run down." Rhys took off his hat.

He was not hard to look at with his red hair kissed by the sun. He looked around the room. "Looks like the cottage has cleaned up nicely. Any repairs needed? I'm pretty handy." He shot her another beautiful smile.

"I do need some repairs on the roof and the hearth. Would you be able to do those?"

"I'd be glad to help you. Best start with the roof or first rain, you'll be setting pots around to catch it." He put his hat back on. "I'd better get going. I'll stop by and fix the roof tomorrow."

"Oh, would you have some straw or hay I could buy from you? For the loft?"

Rhys walked past her. He smelled of sunshine and hay. Up the ladder he went. "Ahh, I see. I may have an extra straw mattress you can have. I'll bring it by later."

"That would be wonderful. Thank you, neighbor." This neighbor made her feel this would be the perfect spot for her new home.

That evening, she cooked her first meal of stew in the cast-iron pot over the fire. Her witch powers, what there were, she would keep to herself. Liz knew she'd have more powers when the time was right. No use stirring up the locals by magically fixing her own roof.

———

Liz and Chester slept well on the new mattress Rhys brought them. He had left them a half-dozen eggs and a container of goat milk. She whipped four eggs with a bit of goat milk.

"Okay, Chester, out to the meadow. I should like to find some herbs to season this omelet with."

Sure enough, there was wild sage, garlic, and marjoram. Taking her bounty into the cottage, she pulled leaves off, chopped the garlic, and added the ingredients to the omelet. She needed this good home-cooked meal.

One of Rhys' goats had shown up during the night. She had tied the goat up and secured the end of the rope to the one standing fence post. The goat was happily munching on the weeds and grasses. She would take him over to Rhys' place later.

The goat began bleating. Liz looked out the door to see a battered red carriage roll to a stop in front of the cottage. The door swung open, a wizened old woman stepped out.

"Hey, girlie, might your goat be for sale? We've come a long ways. Roast goat would be a satisfying meal." She scratched with a crooked finger alongside her hooked nose.

"It's not my goat to sell. It belongs to the neighbor." A chill raced up Liz's back. *A premonition these were not trustworthy people?*

"I am Anfee, the great fortune teller. Up there on the carriage seat, my loyal servant, Duvel." She climbed down from the carriage, slowly straightening her traveling clothes, leaning on her cane, she approached Liz.

A sudden coldness infused the air, and a strange heaviness gave off a suffocating feeling. Liz wanted to be neighborly, but all her senses are warning her away from the woman's touch. Anfee reached out, and Liz backed up.

"There is no food for sale here. You must leave, travel on to the village."

"Ah, girlie, you would not feed an old woman and her older servant? What pray tell is this world coming to?" She turned, hobbling back to the carriage. Raising her cane, she whacked Duvel on the leg.

"Ouch! What pray tell are you doing? Old woman! Get in the carriage and we'll move along."

"Wanted to make sure you were awake, you, useless old man."

The carriage moved along down the road. The coldness and heaviness in the air dissipated.

———

"HI NEIGHBOR," RHYS REMOVED HIS STRAW HAT. "I SEE YOU'VE found the old goat. Miss Bloom was his favorite person. I could always count on him showing up here. She would toss him dinner scraps, which he loved."

"He came around the middle of the night. No table scrapes, I have little to eat till I go to the village to shop. I did make a stew with a bit of meat I brought with me, and some findings in the remains of the garden here." She stepped out into the sunshine.

"What beautiful ebony hair you have. Fairly glistens dark blue in spots. I'm sorry, rather forward of me." A slight blush reddened his cheeks.

"Oh, I thank you for the compliment." She tucked a wayward curl behind her ear. "Rhys, do you know anything about Anfee and Duvel? They came by this morning and wanted to buy your goat." She stepped closer to Rhys. Only good radiated from him.

"Those two, you should stay away from. They are nothing but trouble. Anfee claims to be a fortune teller. I've seen no real powers there." He looked in the direction of the village. "Best stay away from them. Miss Bloom had a run-in with them. She claimed she cursed them to stay away. The spell must have worked, for they haven't been around for five or six years. Not till you showed up."

"Was Miss Bloom a witch then?"

"She didn't claim to be. Still, her curse worked." He shrugged his shoulders, "So who knows, maybe she was." He worked the rope off the post, tipped his hat to Liz. "I'll be by tomorrow to take you to market. Need to get this old goat home." At which point the old goat bleated out a goodbye.

Liz sat on the chair, the only chair in the cottage, and concentrated on using her power to find out exactly who and what Miss Bloom was. She settled her mind, eyes shut, calming herself, and beckoned the spirit of the cottage to come forth. For she had learned long ago every thing has a story to tell.

CHAPTER TWO

iz had learned a great deal from the cottage. Miss Bloom was indeed a witch, a really good and kind witch. Her demise was from an encounter with an evil entity. One who was after her grimoire. This ancient book was coveted by many in the magic community. Miss Bloom had loved her cottage, the meadow, and all the creatures living there. She was kind to her neighbors; in addition, she doctored most of them at one time or another.

The cottage told Liz she was the chosen one to protect the community, the cottage, and the grimoire.

Liz was in a quandary. She didn't know where the book was hidden. The cottage was bare. The loft held solely her new straw mattress. She had to find Miss Bloom's grimoire. If the evil force found the grimoire first, the balance of good in the community would be upset.

That was how Rhys found her, on the floor, pulling up floor boards, looking beneath. "Doing a bit of remodeling, are you?" Rhys stood inside the open door, thumbs hooked in his belt loops.

Liz, surprised, fumbled for words, "I, hmm, I dropped a locket down the crack in the floor."

"Do you still want to go to market? Otherwise, we can go next market day."

Liz stood, brushed dust off her skirt. "Today is fine. I'm out of supplies. Let me grab my shawl and pouch."

When she stepped outside, the bleat of the old goat startled her. There he was tied to the post again.

"Found him outside when I came over. We'll leave him till we get back." Rhys scrubbed the goat's head. The old goat bleated and stamped his foot.

The ride to the village took about an hour. Rhys had brought his horse and cart. Liz was pleased to see a variety of vendors. She bought potatoes, vegetables, four live hens, some cloth to make curtains, along with a broom, teapot, and other necessary household items. She jingled the coins in her pouch, said a spell, doubled them. Thank goodness she had mastered small spells.

Rhys and Liz walked amongst the vendors, chatting. He bought her a pasty and tea.

"Over there, Liz, under the shade of the oak tree." They sat in silence, devouring their lunch.

"Have there been any strange goings on at the cottage? The reason I ask, someone has let my goats lose every day."

"No, Rhys, nothing I can think of, except, of course, I have the old goat visiting every day." She laughed.

"I'm sorry about that."

"No worries, I actually like him. He is a good watchdog. His loud bleating alerts me when someone comes around."

"Have you had a lot of visitors?" His brow wrinkled.

"No, only Anfee and Duvel stopped by again. Again, they wanted to buy the old goat from me. The goat definitely did not want to go with them. He hid behind me, bleating the whole time." Liz rubbed her arms against a sudden chill. Such a nice day to have a chill. That's when she saw Anfee staring at her from across the road.

"I told you, didn't I, the old goat and Miss Bloom were 'friends'? He'd follow her all over the meadow, but he always came home at night. Perhaps that explains why he keeps showing up at the cottage?" He lifted his hat and scratched his head.

"Could be. Maybe he thought he was her guardian." *Or the old goat was Miss Bloom's familiar.*

———

LIZ STEPPED OUTSIDE OF THE COTTAGE, HAVING PUT HER PURCHASED items on the table. "Thank you for the lunch and the ride to town and back."

Rhys nodded, reaching into his pocket, he said, "If you need anything, blow this whistle three times. I'll come over." He slipped a leather cord over her head. A silver whistle hung at the bottom.

"Thanks, Rhys." Her heart swelled at the kindness of her new neighbor. She always looked forward to his daily visits. "I'll have some eggs for you in a few days. Thanks for fixing the coop, I'm sure the hens will be happy."

———

LIZ HAD PRACTICED SOME MINOR SPELLS. SHE WAS GETTING QUITE proficient. Her new broom could sweep the floor on its own. The cloth made itself into curtains. She did have to hang them. In the meantime, she had looked under all the floorboards, into every small and large hole in the wall for the grimoire. She had even removed all the hearth bricks and replaced them, but no grimoire.

"Meow."

"Well, hello, big guy. Have you been having a field day with the field mice?" She reached down to rub his head. He turned over and stretched. That's when she saw the gash in his side. "What happened, Chester?"

"Meow, meow."

She looked through her bag of herbs. "Found it. I'll make a poultice for your wound." After she had placed the medical dressing on him, she said a few healing words. "That should fix you right up. Why don't you take a rest? You will be good as new in a couple hours."

Chester scampered up the ladder.

The old goat was back and bleating insistently. "Hold on, I'm coming." This business with the goat was annoying. A different bleat sounded like he was being choked. Liz ran outside to see Duvel grasping the goat around the throat.

Fury rose in Liz, she lifted her fisted hands and aimed at Duvel. He let go of the goat and flew backwards, landing hard on the ground. "Get off this property. Leave the old goat alone."

The goat ran behind her. Duvel stood, dusted off his pants, shook a fist at her, and limped away, cursing under his breath.

Scrubbing her fingers over the goat's head, she looked him in the eye, "Why are Anfee and Duvel so set on having you?"

Her answer was a "Bleat". She tied the goat to the post. Rhys had fixed the chicken coop but not the corral.

Gathering food scraps, she headed for the chicken coop. The hens were happily pecking away in search of insects or grains.

A chill came over her. She turned around, expecting to see someone. Instead, she saw the red gypsy carriage parked at the creek halfway to Rhys' forest. "Now what are they doing there?"

She would find out one way or another. The sun dipped behind the forest trees, bringing evening and a nip in the air. Unable to see clearly what Anfee and Duvel were up to, she decided she would witch-walk later.

CHAPTER THREE

*R*hys had come and taken the old goat home. Dinner was done. Chester had awakened from his healing nap. His wound was almost completely healed. The fur would grow back eventually. She wished he could tell her what had happened to him.

The fire was still burning by the gypsy's carriage. They should be awake, the perfect time to check on them.

She settled herself comfortably in the chair, set alight one candle, and concentrated on the flame. She closed her eyes. Her mind drifted, her arms and legs became weightless. Her spirit rose from her body. Without a sound, she left the cottage. When she arrived at the gypsy carriage, Anfee and Duvel were deep in a heated discussion.

"The old goat. He's the answer. I feel this to be true. He followed old lady Bloom everywhere she went. He's got to know where the grimoire is hidden." Duvel slapped his knee for emphasis.

"I need Bloom's grimoire to add to my power. I'll rule the village and the pathetic souls will pay homage to me. I'll be rich."

Anfee cocked her head to one side. "Oh, Duvel, I'm afraid we have company."

"What are you talking about? There's no one here but us." He narrowed his eyes. He looked around. The dark of evening had closed in upon them. He could only see where the firelight touched. "Are you losing your mind, old woman?"

Anfee looked directly at Liz. For a moment Liz thought to flee, but knew she couldn't be seen. Eavesdropping would be the only way to find out what they were up to.

"I feel you, witch. Now you've revealed yourself. I cannot see you, but I know you are here."

Liz felt a chill race up her spine. Anfee was a witch. For only another witch can sense a witch-walker. Liz held perfectly still in hopes Anfee would think she'd made a mistake.

Anfee raised her hands high, inciting a dreadfully strong wind which whipped through the camp, tossing sparks into the air and causing the fire to burn brighter. "Begone, witch, stay away."

Duvel coughed from the smoke-filled air. "What's the matter, Anfee, why the big wind. There is no one here."

Liz jerked awake in her chair in the cottage. So Anfee was a witch, and she suspected Liz was a witch. However, Anfee didn't know for sure. She was only guessing.

There must be great magick in Miss Bloom's grimoire. If Anfee were to possess the grimoire, what terrible mayhem could she create? Liz secured the door after making sure Chester was in for the night.

The morning came with the bleating of the old goat. Liz hurried to get dressed. Outside the sun was shining, a bright sunny morning. The old goat stood right by the post, waiting for her to tie him up, which she did. She would gather eggs first thing. One hen lay on her side, sick. "Oh dear," she gathered the hen up and put her in the nesting box. "Perhaps a rest and you will be better."

She decided to take the old goat back to Rhys. Putting a rope around his neck for a lead, she and the goat started across the meadow. They passed the gypsy carriage where Anfee and Duvel must be sleeping. There was no movement or sound.

Rhys was not hard to find. The sound of him chopping wood drew her through the forest to him. She called out, not wanting to startle him. "Hello."

Rhys looked up and leaned his axe against the woodpile. "Hello to you, Liz. Ahh, I see the old goat escaped again. Bothersome goat."

"No trouble, I enjoyed the walk. What a nice place you have. You've lived here a while?" She turned in a circle, taking in the tall trees swaying in the cool, crisp breeze.

"You might say that. I have lived here with my family all my life. Decided to stay on when they passed."

His smile warmed her heart. Could she trust him with what she had found out about Anfee? She wasn't sure. "These woods remind me of the fairy tales from my youth."

"And what makes you think there aren't brownies or fairies traipsing around this forest?"

Loud bleating drew their attention to the corrals. "Oh no, my milk goat. She's down!" He ran into the corral and tried lifting the animal. She lay there, the life ebbing slowly out of her.

Liz leaned over the goat and petted her head. She cried for the precious life of the goat. Her tears fell upon the goat's face. The goat gave a shudder and stood up. Bleating, but better.

Rhys looked at Liz. "What happened? The goat was taking her last breath. I saw with my own eyes. Now she's recovered and romping about. I do not understand. I've witnessed a miracle."

"Rhys, I must confess the tears I shed sometimes have a healing effect. They are …magic tears, witch's tears." He had a startled look on his face, but he didn't run away. That was a good thing.

"Then, you *are* a witch?"

She nodded her head yes. Rhys reached out and took her hand. "Come with me." They walked into the forest to a small cemetery. He let go of her hand and pointed to the tombstones. "My family."

She could see they were all born and died over 200 years ago. "Rhys, what are you?"

"I'm the same as you. A witch. A good witch. I could sense you from the start. I believe you were sent here to help me get rid of the evil that is trying to invade our village." He motioned for her to sit on a stump. He settled on a fallen log.

"Then you know Anfee is a witch? A disagreeable, dangerous witch?" She brushed a curl behind her ear.

"I suspected it. I'm pretty sure the two of them saw fit to do away with Miss Bloom, not realizing she had already hidden her grimoire. With the power instilled in the grimoire, Anfee could do great harm to our community."

"We need to find the grimoire before they do. I've searched the cottage, dug the bricks out of the hearth. I don't know where else to look." She sighed. "Do you think Anfee made your goat sick? I think she made my hen sick. She's looking for ways to scare me off."

He held out his hand, "Come, I'll walk you home. We'll figure this out together."

Liz liked the feel of her hand in his. Rhys was easy to talk to. When they reached the cottage, she was reluctant to let go of his hand. She turned to him. "I've been thinking about how Anfee and Duvel keep trying to buy or steal the old goat. The grimoire must have something to do with him."

"You're right, Liz. The old goat always comes back to the post by your cottage. Do you have a shovel?" Excitement danced across his face.

"Yes, I bought one at the market, remember? I'll get it." She ran into the cottage and grabbed the shovel from beside the fireplace.

Rhys took it from her. He began digging all around the post. After a few minutes of digging, there was a loud clunk when the shovel struck a metal box. He bent down, scraped the dirt away, and lifted the box out of the hole.

She stooped down beside him and opened the lid. The grimoire! Gently, she lifted the old book up and carried it inside.

Liz and Rhys looked at each other across the table where the book sat. He grabbed her hands. "Repeat after me." Together, they said an enchantment to protect the book from Anfee.

The old goat was outside bleating again. He jumped around the hole, kicked up dust with his hooves. "What's gotten into him!" Liz ran outside and tried to calm the goat. The goat was having none of that. He was riled up.

"What's the matter, old boy?" Rhys slipped the rope around his neck. Looking into the goat's eyes. A silent communication passed between them. He muttered a spell over the goat.

The old goat stood on his hind legs and morphed into a wizened old man with a rope hanging from his neck. "Thought I'd never get out of that stinky goat skin. Darn smelly! The last thing Miss Bloom did was spell cast me into a goat to protect the grimoire." He looked down at his shabby clothing. "You've got the grimoire, so I'm off to the woods where all magical beasts live." Off he went.

"Well, we've solved one mystery. Now, how do we get rid of Anfee and Duvel?" Liz went back into the house. Rhys followed. She turned, almost running into him. "Any suggestions?"

"I think you should let me kiss you." He took her face into his hands, holding her still, and kissed her.

Liz felt a wave of pure joy sweep over her. She had a partner to share her life with.

Releasing her, he stepped back. "Let's look in the grimoire for a spell to rid us of Anfee and Duvel."

Flipping the pages of the huge book, "The pages are blank." He said with a long, low sigh.

"Let me look. See if I can read it. A grimoire belongs to only one person at a time. I guess I'm that person now." She lit a candle, the better to see the writing. "I can read it."

"Yes, you are my daughter." Her mother stood in the doorway.

"You were meant to find this place, Rhys, and the grimoire. You will be the witch who lives in the cottage by the sea. A good witch, a blessing to the village. You have reached the age of twenty and five, all your powers are in you, and you have a guide in the grimoire. I must leave you now, but carry on in goodness and harmony with all." Then she was gone.

"Rhys, did you see and hear her too?"

"Yes, I did. Let's find the spell to rid ourselves of Anfee and Duvel." He smiled.

Liz opened the grimoire to the first page. "Oh, great and knowledgeable grimoire. I need a casting-out spell to rid us of a witch bent on evil. Where do I look?" she asked the large book.

A wind blew in through the door, flipping the pages one by one. Magick sparkles danced above the book. Finally, the pages stopped, and the open book gave off a glow.

"Rhys, here is the spell. A permanent spell, just what we need. We must sprinkle salt around their campsite tonight at midnight. There are words we must repeat three times three. By morning, they will be banished, never to return here. The strength of our witch voices together will seal the spell."

———

Liz and Rhys carried sacks of salt, quietly making their way to where Anfee and Duval were sitting by their campfire. The witch dozed leaning forward, and the servant tipped up a jug for a drink.

Liz motioned for Rhys to go one way and she'd go the other, leaving a trail of salt. When they met on the far side of the camp, they raised their hands to the sky and said the spell, raising their voices and saying the spell three times three.

"We circle salt upon the ground
Let those inside be bound,
To never set foot here again.

To be forever banished

Let the spell be finished.

So mote it be."

Rhys took her hand and together they watched as the circle of salt began to sizzle and produce a wall of smoke. With a loud pop, the smoke, salt, and campsite disappeared.

Rhys lifted her hand to his lips. "I'm asking you to be my wife, my partner, if you will have me."

She put her hands on his shoulders, "I would be honored and blessed to be your wife."

They lived happily in the cottage on the hill, while the old goat managed the property in the forest.

ABOUT THE AUTHOR

Diana enjoys weaving elements of paranormal and fantasy into her stories. She always ends with a Happily Ever After, because she must for her own satisfaction! Her hope is to take you away from your everyday life for a journey that is both entertaining and fun, and sometimes a little scary.

Her home, in beautiful Paradise, CA, on the edge of the Sierra Mountains, allows her a wide range of hobbies. When Diana is not reading or writing, she is a fisherwoman. She also enjoys gardening, hiking, coffee dates with other writers, taking classes to expand her writing abilities, and hanging out in book stores.

You can learn more about Diana on her website
https://dianamccollumauthor.com/

INSPIRATION FOR THIS STORY

Learning to trust in herself and the journey. No matter how bad things look, there is always hope.

A Country to Cross

Therese Patrick

Publisher's Note: This is a work of fiction. Names, characters, places, and incidents are a product of the author's imagination. Locales and public names are sometimes used for atmospheric purposes. Any resemblance to actual people, living or dead, or to businesses, companies, events, institutions, or locales is completely coincidental.

Published by

Windtree Press, Corvallis, Oregon

https://windtreepress.com

1

BY MAIL

It was a gorgeous false summer day in October. The crackle of dry leaves on soft breezes meant this balmy weather must be celebrated. A fleeting reminder of warm days now to be followed by months of cold snaps, feet of snow, and a few Nor'easters or ice storms until the delight of warm days returned. Last winter, the weather records featured nineteen nights exceeding two feet of snow by dawn. I left work early and traffic was smooth for miles on the freeway. The good weather forecast meant playing hooky was a solid choice.

I walked down our driveway, still humming the last song on the radio while breathing in the fall scents and quiet air. I always made the thirty-minute commute after work with lively music. I used the routine as a meditative transition from my job where I was an authority to dozens of people across the country, to arriving home where I was just Mom, to four girls. To the two teens, I was Mom with a groan, and anything said was ignored or argued.

Our mailbox was across the narrow gravel street and beside the path that led to the bridge at the end of the lake. It was a good steel curved mailbox and had lasted for five years now. Everyone walked that path to cross the bridge on their way to the swimming area. This was a wide sandy beach with huge shade trees for the adults to lounge near where the children swam and played in the water all summer. This section of the lake was narrow, deep, and protected with a few houses on each shore. Then the lake widened into an expanse of water large enough for small power boats to provide skiing, tubing, and other water sports on a small inland lake. Behind the lakefront houses on the east side of the lake was a 3-par golf course. It was a nice walk around the small golf course which included long views of the water.

We lived here for eight years and totally embraced this resort oasis in the trees with the lake. The bridge at our end of the lake was over a concrete dam that a century ago had turned a natural creek through ponds and wetlands into a summer resort, for swimming and boating, less than a two-hour drive from New York City. The Poconos were another hour to the west.

During the past thirty years, the cottages and summer estates around the lake and golf course had been transformed into residential houses of various sizes. Now it was all year-round family homes, yet it retained many remnants of a summer resort. A big community building on a hill was for neighborhood meetings, children's theatre, and other fun or seasonal events. The golf course had a snack shack open during the summer and a pond the local kids would wade through for abandoned golf balls to sell.

It was a fantastic lifestyle, our family vacation included with the price of a mortgage, lasted from spring until fall. Our home was one of five newer ones built on an open expanse of what had originally been the game fields. All five properties had landscaped sections of their yards, while still keeping plenty of open area between the houses for neighborhood kids to gather for team sports.

My views through the front windows were of the deepest part

of the lake. The back of the house faced the steep rocky bluff beyond a paved road. I had recently bought a large book about Feng Shui that was full of glossy pictures and directions on how to harness the chi through the body and around our home. The placement of our house, on a slight rise with flowing water before us and a protective hill behind, was auspicious. Not so for the mail delivery.

The little jeep used for our rural delivery route only went one way down our narrow gravel street, and all the mailboxes were planted on posts on the same side. Our simple metal box with the full flap door was protected with a fencepost on each side. Those posts weren't enough to keep our mailbox from being a very enticing place for fireworks to create a really loud boom, which was a tradition when we first moved in.

The first mailbox exploded on the 4th of July, less than two months after we'd moved in that May in 1988. It was remounted with dents and the door reattached, only to explode again on Halloween after the streets were quiet, as most trick-or-treaters were sorting their candy. The next mailbox lasted through three more explosions until the door was so loose and bent it couldn't be reattached, and the flag would not remain upright.

Everyone in the neighborhood knew who the culprits were behind the exploding mailbox. It took a certain physical and emotional type, and age, to do the deed. After a few years, our girls were well known and liked through all the adolescent and teen groups around the lake, and our current mailbox was a higher-grade steel, so it remained undamaged. Last week, that explosive energy was directed at the new "For Sale" sign in our front yard.

Our home was a stately rectangle with a Dutch Colonial flavor of dark beams and peaks over windows and the front door. I came into the house from the driveway and paused to put the mail on the desk in the office. It was a great office, bigger than a closet, and it had a small window for daylight, though that view was through bushes along the front walk. This ground level location made it very convenient when the phone company installed a second line dedicated for the computer.

I pushed the on button for the computer to hum to life and be usable in a few minutes. The main phone line for the house had the call waiting feature, a necessity as there were teens in the house, but using the same phone line for the computer meant we got kicked off-line if the call waiting feature was activated. In the family room, there were no messages on the answering machine and the cordless phone handset was actually on the base to charge. This meant the two teens barely came inside after school today.

I opened the front door on the landing between the lower level and the main floor. Across the street was the sprawling homestead where my best friend in the neighborhood lived. She was outside and waved. I waved back and watched as my two younger girls ran from her door to ours with school backpacks dangling off one shoulder. They both had lots to tell me, very quickly, about their day as we went upstairs to their bedrooms on the main floor. They dropped their things and were soon outside again, running across yards to play with their friends until dinner.

After deciding what we'd have for dinner and checking the note left on the dining room table from the older girls as to where they were, I went back downstairs to the office computer. While waiting for the blinking cursor to become a full screen graphic so I could log on to check my electronic mail, I opened the paper mail to sort. Soon the digital beeps and buzz let me know there was a connection through the phone line. Then the monitor showed the cute little mailbox and the flag flipped up to the tones, "You've got mail."

There was only one notice. Of course, it was from my sister, Sherri. As I opened the file, I saw it was pages of text. Fun. We started the habit this summer of writing long daily e-letters. It was because we'd lived on opposite coasts of the country for almost twenty years and now planned to soon be neighbors. The letters were to form a new relationship as sisters beyond long-distance phone calls or a few days meeting in Cleveland every few years. I printed the email and when it was done, logged off, heard the "goodbye" and took the pages upstairs to read later. The office was just a tiny room with a small window, and I never liked reading in a closet. I also took the handheld phone.

2

BY PHONE

The kitchen phone was mounted on the wall and had a 25-foot-long spiral cord so I could talk while cooking and still be able to see outside. From the deck off the dining room, I had a panoramic view, and if I called my girls' names, it wasn't unusual for them to hear me even if they were three houses away. With the portable phone I could sit outside while I called my mom. I usually made long distance calls on the weekends for the better price.

Mom answered on the fourth ring.

"I wanted to call now because it's going to be busy with the open house this weekend."

"You're still planning the move then," Mom said.

"Yes, the house is on the market. It's only been a few weeks, but so far it still feels like a good choice."

"And the girls are okay with it."

"It's not real to them. Or me, for that matter."

I may never tell Mom the "For Sale" sign was already kicked down twice and went missing once. I found it later on the steep bank of the lake as if someone had tried to toss it into the water but couldn't throw it hard enough.

"It's good that you made the choice, but you can always change your mind."

My mom's encouragement was why we took the steps to make this move happen. There were a lot of reasons to stay, it was a really nice life here. But the reasons to move from New Jersey to Oregon were also good. To move was an emotional and adventurous choice. To stay was practical and easier. We felt it was sensible to embrace the impractical.

"It's not a good housing market right now, and we're coming into the winter season when things are often slow." Bryan and I already discussed that we could take the house off the market for the holidays and try again in the spring. If it didn't sell before next summer, this move was not supposed to happen.

Mom's advice was simple. "You'll know when it's right and your girls will be fine. I moved a lot when I was a child."

"And so have they, but they were a lot younger last time." Our youngest was born the year after we moved here under the energy of 'new house, new car, new baby.'

"It was an adventure to wake up the next morning in a new room and explore the new house and neighborhood," Mom reminisced. "We didn't often know when we were moving from one house to the next."

That triggered a forgotten memory from her childhood stories. "What do you mean you didn't know?"

Mom chuckled. "Parents didn't feel children needed to know in those days. We were just told to pack up our things in our rooms because we were going to a new house."

"That wouldn't work here." In the downstairs family room, there were built-in shelves that spanned the whole wall on each side of the fireplace. All those books would take more than a few days to pack. And there was the aquarium.

"We didn't have that much like kids do today."

I knew the history of how my grandad lost 'it all' in the stock market crash of 1929, the year after my mom was born.

Grandad's brother was in real estate and Grandad was able to work with him for a few years until he could return to being a stockbroker. Grandma was always very proud of the few treasures she was able to save from those before-the-crash years, like the sterling silver cutlery and tea set. Grandad eventually replaced all her jewelry and my sister Sherri and I loved the mirrored tray on their bedroom dresser with the ornate silver brush and comb. Grandad had told Sherri that if she used his hairbrush, her straight hair would become curly like his. Grandad loved funny stories.

"Do you have a story about moving that I can tell my girls?"

My daughters were a lot more interested and respectful of Grandma's stories than anything I said. Mom's primary comment about our move was encouraging for Bryan and I, but we hadn't told our girls what she advised. I'd only share it if this cross-country move looked like it was really happening. Our teenage girls would never blame Grandma for encouraging us to destroy their lives and make them change high schools.

If the move happened.

Mom began her story. "My favorite move was when I was six. We were told to pack up everything in our rooms after dinner, before we went to bed. Then during the night, we were woken and told to be quiet as we got into the car. All the adults were whispering, and I fell back asleep, I'm pretty sure it was that Studebaker my dad had. Then we were tucked into beds again to finish sleeping in the new house."

I grinned. I knew this story.

"The next morning was like magic. The sun was shining through the trees and into our windows. It was a big sprawling house, and we ran out to explore before breakfast because we were right at the shore of Lake Erie. We were only there for a year because your grandmother was terrified of water. As soon as we could, we moved into town and stayed there until I graduated from Shaw High School."

I kept quiet in case she added more. Sherri and I never heard Mom admit these 'middle-of-the-night' moves were probably because her parents were escaping creditors. But then Mom did add something I hadn't heard before.

"She didn't move with us."

"Who?"

"Oh, did I say that out loud?" Mom chuckled. "I haven't thought about it for so many years. I can't remember her name. There was a woman who had lived with us, and she did all the 'necessary', as your grandma called it, until we moved to that house on the lake. I remember my sisters mentioning it as the lake house was big enough to have a live-in. We assumed she stayed behind to take care of that house but instead of joining us moved on by herself."

I debated mentioning that now Mom was past her feud with her sisters, maybe she could ask them for the name of this neces-sary live-in lady. I didn't because I was pretty sure Mom would reprimand me for my sass, so I kept quiet.

"I think I hear Bryan downstairs." I said it absently. His noises were different than when our girls entered the house.

"You go and get that man and those girls fed, and I'll pray for your endeavor this weekend. Let me know how it goes."

"I will." I hadn't meant to end our conversation.

We said our goodbyes and I hung up the phone. I no longer got sassy with Mom about her determination that my husband and family were always my primary job. The activities of a happy family were what interested my mom about my life. Whatever I did in that office was just to earn the family health care benefits.

There was a lot about my life Mom didn't understand, like using computers, or having a full-time job when I had four daugh-ters in school and a husband who made enough money, from those computer things, to own a big, beautiful home in a lake resort community.

Mom liked that we wanted to move to Oregon since Bryan and I loved visiting Sherri and her family there. Mom also knew we loved our home on the lake here. Three years ago, she and Dad had come for a visit, which was super special. It was also good to know Mom would pray for us. When Mom prayed, good things happened.

3

BY WATER

I never told Mom that there were issues with the water at our wonderful home by the lake. Our personal well was deep and the water to our home ran through a filtration and softening system that took up space in the laundry room and required special salt in 50-lb. bags that were delivered every few months. The pressure, flow, and taste of water was pretty good unless the power went out. Which could happen a few times a year, and usually when there was heavy snow or layers of ice outside. We filled the bathtub with water if there was concern about losing power during a storm. We used the tub water to fill the toilet tank if the toilet needed to be flushed. Our little generator could handle the lights and refrigerator but not the power for the well. We camped out by the fireplace in the family room for heat.

The local kindergarten and first grade schoolhouse needed the delivery of bottled water. The drinking fountains were removed when all the trees in the wetland behind the schoolhouse had died at the same time. Aerial views showed a stream of dead trees from the back corner of the quarry half a mile away. Something toxic must have been dumped there and it left a trail of devastation until it spread into a wasteland of tree stalks behind the small school. The middle school on higher ground a half mile away had been expanded and included a special water filtration system but that building wasn't big enough for all the kindergarten and first grade students.

The little old school with the bleached trees and toxic swamp behind it was okay to use since those small children were only in those rooms for a few hours a day. The theory was that it was an old devastation and not harmful as long as no one talked about it.

That was one reason why we planned to move even though none of our girls were in that school building anymore. Water concerns weren't talked about, and our girls were told that we wanted to move to Oregon because we wanted them to know and grow with family, and that is where my sister Sherri and her family lived.

I left the pages of Sherri's email on the table when I took the portable phone back to the charging base in the family room. Bryan had changed into shorts and an old T-shirt.

"I'm going to winterize the boat so we can use it as a bonus for the house sale. Full price offer and we'll give them the boat."

I hadn't thought about the boat. It was a cute sixteen-foot bowrider with an outboard engine that was the right size for this lake to take our girls tubing or water skiing. We bought that boat the first summer we lived on the lake. The younger girls loved tubing, Bryan and the teen girls learned to water ski. I tried to waterski once but have always had wimpy knees and there was no way I could try a second time without doing damage to my body. Still, I loved swimming and could play in the water with the children as long as they wanted to play.

During droughts, late in the summer, the water level could drop beneath the height of the concrete dam. Some enjoyed walking over the dry, curved top like it was a balance beam. This lack of flow over the dam also meant the swimming beach got wider as the water level evaporated in the heat. This larger beach enticed more Canadian Geese to hang out and leave their poop piles to dry, which attracted more bugs, and the combination would generate full body red spots on swimmers. No one wanted to swim with the insects during those hottest days as they would also catch goose poop rash. When no rain was in the forecast, the fire department would do their hose and tank flushing at the swimming area to wash the beach and stir the packed sand. But even that wasn't good enough for rash-free swimming until rain had raised the lake to again flow over the dam.

The lake was shallow and prone to weed growth. Airboats came out every summer to spray something across the surface of the whole lake. A few days later, the weeds shrunk enough to no longer foul boat propellers.

Last year the neighbors all contributed into a fund to have the lake dredged. Decades of dead weeds on the bottom were contributing to the shallowing of the water depth. This dredging proposal involved taking deep lakebed samples to determine the value of how the lakebed soil could be repurposed, and the depth of water increased. The findings revealed the common weed killer used when the lake was new was called Arsenic. Arsenic does not break down in the environment and if the lakebed was stirred, it would release high levels of poisonous arsenic that would flow downstream and create more health risks to humans and nature than the petrified trees behind the grade school.

Bryan was convinced that the concentration of arsenic in the lake bed explained why two men who lived on the lake had died of sudden heart attacks in recent years. This was a good reason to move to Oregon, though not talked about.

Bryan saw the typed pages on the table. "Sherri's latest?"

"It looks like she did a lot more astrology stuff. I'll read it after dinner."

"Everyone needs a hobby," he said. His hobby was flying small aircraft. Mine was writing romance novels. That's how Sherri had discovered Astrology.

4

BY AIR

*B*ryan and I met at Cleveland State University and married two years later. He wanted to fly airplanes since he was a little boy. He saved the money from his newspaper route to pay for an airplane ride at the municipal airport not far from his childhood home. He learned the costs of earning his pilot licenses was high but with a greater payoff eventually. He decided he had to make lots of money if he was going to fly airplanes. In college, he discovered his talent for this new thing called computing, which had coded languages and data storage on magnetic tapes. The computer industry exploded quickly and shortly after our second daughter was born, he was offered a job in New Jersey with a company designing Automated Teller Machines for banks.

The move to New Jersey got him into the high-tech zone and the cutting edge of innovation. We originally planned to return to Cleveland and all the family events a few years after that initial move. I was a mom with two toddlers in dense housing developments. That was when I discovered romance novels.

My closest neighbor was also in the toddler time of her life, while her husband was also a techno whiz. Her name was Candy and she was from Georgia. All the women in her family bought romance novels at the grocery store weekly like their husbands bought cigarettes. Then the women would meet and swap books so they all had more variety to read every week. I had not read a genre romance until I met Candy. She shared these books with me since she couldn't swap stories with her family. That first week she handed me four paper grocery bags stacked full to the brim of every genre of romance novel available.

That was the first step on my journey as a professional writer. I wrote stories since I was a child, but they were in spiral notebooks. In high school, I switched to using a typewriter since typing was a worthy skill, while reading and writing were a waste of time. The only acceptable writing career for women at that time was under the title of secretary. I had loved my college job working as a bookkeeper in a credit union for a newspaper, and I hoped to do something like that again when our girls were in school. Until then, I started reading these genre romances from Candy, daily. They resembled the stories I had written for myself for fun. Then Bryan brought home four bulky electronics he'd gotten on sale for me to learn to use. I was introduced to word processing.

I could now edit and rewrite pages of my stories without having to retype them. And even better, there was a way to do spreadsheets on this computer thing instead of using huge pages of bulky ledgers. This computer stuff would be great for office work. I could even print two copies of something without using carbon paper. I was also inspired that stories I wrote to entertain myself could be published and sold in grocery stores.

Soon Bryan was teaching computer programming two nights a week. That money was used to get his pilot's license.

There was a small airport nearby with a cute wading pool in the shape of an airplane on the lawn. Our two girls would play in this pool while Daddy had a flying lesson, then we would picnic by the pool. Small aircraft and water sports flavored all our family adventures forever after. His computer skills quickly changed his career goals so once we moved to our home on the lake, we put down roots there. While sitting on the upper deck by our dining room, we could talk to Bryan with a handheld radio while he flew his airplane overhead.

5

BY STARS

Through most of our childhood, Sherri and I shared a large upstairs room as we were the youngest in the family, and only three years apart. We spent hours discussing what we thought our lives would be like after we graduated high school. When we planned our future lives, neither of us considered living anywhere beyond Cleveland, Ohio.

As adults, we would be wives and mothers, of course. Our homes would be near each other so we could do our shopping and homemaker tasks together. We would also have jobs. Sherri was encouraged to go into nursing, and I planned to be a bank teller. Ironically, she worked in international banking, and I worked for a few years in home health and geriatric care. But neither of us expected to live on opposite coasts of the country while raising our children with no family near either of us.

This was the emotional aspect of my plan to move across the country, homeless and jobless with four kids and a dog. Sherri and I had always thought we would live near each other and our children would have a support network of cousins for each other. We both wanted family nearby, but neither of us ever wanted to move back to Cleveland. We both learned after we left town that "the city with the river that burned" had a reputation as a good place to leave.

During one of our recent e-letter exchanges, I mentioned the astrological character aspects for the novel I was writing. "Linda Goodman's Love Signs" was a 1992 encyclopedic book of love relationships between every sign of the zodiac. It was introduced to me as the newest and best bible for a romance novelist to use for character development and emotional conflict.

For romance novels the primary plot is the development of a relationship, and to do that, all aspects of the character need to be determined from personality to birth data to cultural heritage to the residential environment. This includes family dynamics of their childhood to what makes them angry or afraid, with a few other specifics, like life philosophies and emotional wounds. I enjoyed using "Linda Goodman's Love Signs" as a stylesheet for the characterizations and relationship challenges. I quickly found myself making comparisons from the astrological descriptions to what I knew about real family members. The accuracy was delightful.

Sherri didn't want to accept my interpretations on faith. She quickly decided to figure out this astrology stuff and get it right. She also has the mathematical skills to do calculations of stellar alignments to birth data and transits even before finding out there were computer programs to use, and accessible through the inter-net. This was something we both could do to enhance our letters. Being able to point-and-click on a digital button to generate a birth chart was the best way I could converse with Sherri once she dove deep into the stars.

I didn't expect Sherri's determination to figure out this astrology stuff for real would last more than a few months, but it was a great distraction and became our own personal language, which isn't rare for sisters to develop. I expected Sherri's interest would last until she mastered this astrology stuff or she reached a point where it no longer entertained her. Until then, I would benefit on many levels by staying on the same page of what she was doing and working with the stellar arcs of my characters according to their sun, moon, and rising signs.

6

BY CHARTS

Once she learned to cast charts, Sherri started using Bryan and me as her test subjects as she progressed beyond the details of our natal charts and found more fun in the dance of the transits. Soon her e-letters were full of questions about "what was going on in your life around month-date-year" because she needed to understand these transits. As my life with Bryan since college had included in-town and out-of-state moves; four babies, numerous jobs, and career changes, it wasn't hard to reveal something significant near any of those planetary shifts. We also have our hobbies and took a few trips, including to England and Slovenia and, of course, Oregon.

We really were good test subjects for her astrology discoveries.

October in Oregon was still gorgeous and warm. Sherri's youngest was a preschooler and there was not a lot to do in her garden at the time. This means she had plenty of time to sit out on her deck that overlooked her extensive garden while reading astrology books and cross-referencing all kinds of stuff that she would then send to me in daily emails to read in the evening. Sometimes I'd call so we could chat, as the nighttime long-distance rates would apply on the east coast while it was still early evening on the west coast.

I was learning astrology by osmosis. I liked that I could access computer software made available through the internet from Germany. Astrologers around the world could trust the computer had all the calculations correct, including latitude and longitude for the birth time and rising sign. I had no problem looking at the colorful glyphs, symbols, and lines to follow Sherri's interpretation of the stars guiding my whole life whether I knew it or not.

This is why I printed the emails unread. I really needed to sit and carefully read what she was sending now. These were not chatty-newsy or personal memory sharing letters anymore but instead were loaded with the energetic values of the planetary aspects and transits. Once assured there would be no interruptions, I sat down to read through tonight's pages. By the time I reached the second paragraph, I could tell Sherri was really excited about something she'd discovered in my birth chart. When I got to it, the crux of her discovery, I laughed so hard I had to calm down and try to reread, turning the pages forward and backward, to understand her latest discovery. I'd be calling later tonight. I kept laughing to myself as I kept reading.

Bryan came into the room. "What's new from Sherri?"

I looked up at this man who was full of proactive energy for the adventure of starting a whole new family life and professional career once we made the move from New Jersey to Oregon. For me it may be for the sister connection and grand version of more family for our daughters, but for him it was mostly about the water.

"Sherri's very excited to let me know she'd discovered something significant about the Orb of My Natal Uranus."

"Your what?" He was staring at me as if he wanted to be sure he heard it right.

"The Orb of my Natal Uranus."

"And that means?"

I flipped through the pages. "Uranus is in my first house in Leo, which is my rising sign and planets there strengthen my personality and personal interests. The placement of Uranus there means I'm original, independent, impossible to categorize, and a bit of a rebel, with an interest in science, the occult, electronics, and computers. As the orb of this planetary influence is close to my ascendent it reflects sudden and drastic changes in my life that could be good or not. My life path will often lead to work dealing with large groups of people."

We both processed this information until he left the room with a final comment. "Good to know." Not that either of us was surprised at this definition.

Eventually, by summer, the cross-country move did happen, and we all survived and eventually thrived, even the teens. And decades later, I still navigate my life with the same energy as labeled the Orb of my Natal Uranus.

ABOUT THE AUTHOR

Therese Patrick has loved crafting romantic adventure stories since childhood even though she never planned to write novels. Her first job after high school was downtown in the business office of major newspaper and she loved all of it. Twelve years later, she and her college sweetheart had moved six times across three states. They have four daughters; six grandchildren, numerous pets, and currently live near the Pacific Coast while contemplating retirement.

Therese's professional career includes layers of business writing from marketing magazines to technical manuals. She also vowed to write a memoir about her parents' love story someday and this led her to learn the craft of writing romances. Her hobbies include analyzing rom-coms and volunteering in writer organizations. She now writes in both genres using me 'Therese' for nonfiction/memoir and 'Terri' for her Rivershore Romantic Adventure novels. You can find out more about her and her books at - theresepatrick.com

---

INSPIRATION FOR THIS STORY

My first thought when considering to write a short story for "Navigate" was using the title 'By The Stars.' My sister is an astrologer and wanted me to write something with sextants and constellations. But we have so many sister jokes about the stars that I wanted to use one. Then I had to choose which joke and where-when to set the story. I really do live the cliché "truth is stranger than fiction" and decided to try a memoir short story. "A Country to Cross" is the first complete story for what may one day become - *A Moving Memoir.*

Dark Tide

Publisher's Note: This is a work of fiction. Names, characters, places, and incidents are a product of the author's imagination. Locales and public names are sometimes used for atmospheric purposes. Any resemblance to actual people, living or dead, or to businesses, companies, events, institutions, or locales is completely coincidental.

Published by

Windtree Press, Corvallis, Oregon

https://windtreepress.com

DARK TIDE

BY PAMELA COWAN

The legend of Oregon's haunted lighthouses had always been just that—a legend, a story to scare younger siblings or friends around a bonfire on the beach. But as the sun dipped behind the horizon, casting an eerie orange glow across the water, Madison wondered if she should have been so eager to go on this trip.

The Tillamook Rock Lighthouse, a little over one mile offshore, was now a black silhouette, dark and ominous against a backdrop of moonlit water and star-studded sky. "Terrible Tilly," as she was called, had been decommissioned in 1957 and no longer sent a beacon to warn sailors of the treacherous shores.

As Madison listened to the roaring sound of the waves and stared out at the structure, she was glad the only way to reach it was by helicopter and happy they didn't have one to use. Unable to shake the feeling that there was something out there lurking in the darkest shadows, she shivered.

Lifting her phone, she selected the camera icon, switched to night vision, and snapped a shot of the small basalt island and its lighthouse. If the photo turned out well, it would make a dramatic addition to the travel article she planned to write for the university's paper.

She turned to look back at the picnic table where her friends sat huddled, their faces illuminated by the glow of their cell phones. Ryan's dark blond hair fell over his eyes no matter how often he swept it back, his lips twisted in concentration as he read. Julia, with her long blond hair braided over her shoulder, was also staring at her screen, unconsciously pushing her glasses up on her nose every few moments. Marco, his Italian heritage evident in his thick black hair and the bump on his Roman nose, was equally engrossed. She wondered for a moment if they could all remain friends in the years to come, or if they would drift apart after college, each busy with their own lives.

"Alright, everyone, get over here," she called out. "Let's get a group photo before we head to the hotel."

Ryan had been talking into his voice recorder, making notes he'd later transcribe for a paper titled *A Case Study On The Science Of Hauntings*. "You know, this trip is going to be perfect for my research," he said, looking up with a grin. "I can't wait to see if these lighthouses live up to their spooky reputations."

Julia, always the practical one, had been studying their list of supplies. "We've got a first aid kit, a spare tire, and extra batteries for the flashlights," she said, checking items off her list. "We should be all set."

Marco looked up from the drawing app on his phone where he'd been sketching—not the ocean scene, but the sleek sports car his parents had just given him for his nineteenth birthday. Madison had been surprised he'd agreed to pile into the back seat of her more practical but less sexy Toyota Camry for the road trip.

When she and Ryan had been deciding who to invite, she'd picked Julia, and he'd suggested Marco. Her immediate response had been, "Isn't he used to better stuff: cars, hotels, decent restaurants? How's he going to handle fast food and staying at the low-rent places we can afford?"

"Just 'cause he's rich, it doesn't mean he's a snob. You know, judging someone by their wealth, or lack of it, is another form of prejudice."

Madison thought based on Marco's next words that Ryan had probably been right.

"I still can't believe we're doing this for spring break," he said with a chuckle. "But hey, if it means spending time with you guys and if some of these lighthouses really are haunted, then I'm glad you counted me in."

Madison set the camera on a timer and hurried to join her friends. As the flash went off, capturing their smiles and excitement, she felt a thrill of anticipation. This trip was going to be an adventure, and even if they weren't destined to be forever friends, she was determined to document every moment.

"Alright, let's hit the road," she said. "Next stop, cheap hotel. Tomorrow, Cape Meares."

The next morning, they piled into Madison's car and drove along the winding coastal highway. The conversation flowed easily, filled with laughter, discussions about professors good and bad, concerts, movies, and shared videos.

When there was a lull in the conversation, Ryan, in the passenger seat, read from a spiral-bound notebook filled with his scrawling handwriting and bristling with Post-Its. "They say there are at least thirty bodies buried near that lighthouse we saw last night. For a while, it was a storage place for cremated remains."

"No wonder the place gave me major creepy vibes," said Madison.

"Yeah, and even before they finished building the thing, it had a bad rep," said Ryan, continuing to read. "The first surveyor, someone named John Trewavas, was hit by a wave and swept out to sea. He was never seen again. Then, later, in 1881, just before it was finished, a British ship called the Lupatia wrecked on Tillamook Head during a heavy fog. All sixteen crew members died, and only a dog survived.

"Lucky dog," cracked Marco.

They all laughed at his bad joke.

"For sure," said Ryan. "Anyway, before they shut it down, some lighthouse keepers reported hearing voices and seeing ghostly apparitions. Sometimes they saw ships drifting past, and sometimes ghosts roaming the stairs. Most people said it was being alone so much made them crazy. And crazy, as you know, is what we're all about."

Everyone groaned.

The four had met at a study group for an abnormal psychology course in September. Ryan was studying to be a psychologist, Julia a counselor or social worker, and Marco a psychiatrist. Madison was an outlier, planning to be a journalist. Still, their interests weren't that different. Madison planned to write about local personalities and interesting characters. Maybe she'd also cover high school sports or local politics. Whatever she wrote about would have humans at the center of it, so the more she understood them, the better.

"You know ghosts aren't actually real," said Julia.

"Yeah, well the natives believed they were," said Ryan. "They steered clear of the island and the lighthouse completely."

Madison felt a chill slide down her spine. She didn't mind. It was fun to be scared—a little.

In a couple of hours, they reached Cape Meares Lighthouse and the surrounding wildlife refuge. Madison was relieved to see that this lighthouse was much less ominous, at least in the light of day. "Ready to explore?" Ryan asked, piling out of the car. They followed him and walked downhill along a short, paved path to the lighthouse and gift shop. All four were surprised by how short the lighthouse was and how beautifully kept, its white paint was fresh and gleaming, and it was surrounded by lush lawns sprinkled with small wildflowers.

"There haven't been any ghost sightings at this lighthouse," said Ryan. "However—"

"Does there always have to be a however?" Julia moaned.

Ryan smiled. "Of course. Anyway, the lighthouse is located near the Octopus Tree."

"Octopus Tree?" his three friends said at the same time.

"Yeah. It's a Sitka Spruce that grew kind of weird," Ryan told them. "According to my notes, it's one hundred and five feet tall with a circumference of forty-six feet. It doesn't have a main trunk, just limbs that grow horizontally from the base that then go up like tentacles, creating an octopus-like appearance. It's two to three hundred years old. Some people think Native American tribes forced it to grow like that. They used it as a burial site and put canoes with their dead in the branches. It's also known as the Candelabra Tree, the Council Tree, or the Monstrosity Tree."

"Not creepy at all," said Julia.

They found the tree surrounded by a low wooden fence to keep people at a distance. There was a brown sign with white lettering inside the fence. Madison stepped up and read aloud, "The forces that shaped this unique Sitka spruce (Picea sitchensis) have been debated for many years. Whether natural events or possibly Native Americans were the cause remains a mystery."

"Forces, they had to say forces," Madison said, exchanging an understanding look with Julia.

After a quick tour of the lighthouse, they hit the gift shop, which held sea and lighthouse-themed items and souvenirs of Cape Meares. Madison chose a postcard with a picture of the lighthouse and three soaring seagulls. Julie picked one with sealions on a rocky beach. Ryan bought a green agate. Marco splurged and selected the same postcard as Madison's, and a candy bar.

As he was ringing them up, the friendly clerk, an older man with laugh lines bracketing his blue eyes, asked, "How did you guys like the lighthouse?"

"It was great," said Madison. "Now we're heading to Yaquina Head and Yaquina Bay. We hear they're haunted."

"Ah, haunted lighthouses. Hoping to see a ghost?"

"Writing a story about lighthouses," she told him.

"So not hoping to see a ghost," he said, chuckling.

Madison didn't know how to respond. Did she want to see a ghost?

"We should get moving," Julie reminded them. "It's like two and a half hours to our next stop. You guys wanted to get lunch in Newport, right?"

"Not me. I've got food," Marco said, holding up a super-sized Snickers bar.

"I want to get lunch right now," said Ryan.

"You can have an apple," said Madison. "I grabbed some at the hotel while you guys were all saying you didn't want breakfast. They're in the glove compartment."

"You are going to be such a good mom," said Ryan.

"God, I hope not."

They were laughing as they left the store. None of them noticed, or would have cared, that the nice man who'd rung up their purchases had taken a cell phone from his back pocket and was busily tapping in a number.

"I have some travelers heading your way, and they seem perfect for you," he said to the person at the other end of the line. "Kids. College kids, I think." He watched the four young people as they made their way up the path toward the parking lot.

As they pulled onto the highway, Ryan dug out his notes and read. "The Yaquina Head Lighthouse, also known as Cape Foulweather, was built in 1873. At ninety-three feet it is the tallest lighthouse in Oregon and is still an active aid to navigation.

"They say a construction worker fell to his death while helping build the tower. His body got stuck between the walls and was never recovered. According to legend, his ghost remains sealed within the lighthouse. When ships go by too close, their compasses go haywire. Also, there was a lighthouse keeper named Higgins who got sick and asked another keeper named Story to take over.

When Higgins got back, he found Story dead. He was sure Story haunted the lighthouse and would take his bulldog up the tower with him for protection."

"He thought his dog would protect him from a ghost?" said Marco. "Must have been some dog."

"Maybe the dog was dead," offered Julia. "A ghost dog against a ghost person sounds reasonable."

"I am pulling into the nearest drive-through," said Madison. "You people are getting faint from hunger."

After a quick lunch, they made their way to Yaquina Head Lighthouse.

Madison thought she could easily navigate the one hundred and fourteen steps to the top, but she was panting by the time she reached the small round room.

"One at a time, please. One at a time," intoned the expressionless voice of someone who has repeated the same phrase too often. A short, slightly plump woman with silver hair in a neat bun smiled at them pleasantly. A tag on her blouse read, "Tour Guide."

Grateful for the break, Madison leaned against the wall to wait. In a few moments, a woman with a girl of around eight or nine came out onto the landing and the tour guide waved Madison inside. The room was circular, painted stark white and there were windows all around which gave a stunning panoramic view of the coastline and the ocean. In the center was the huge Fresnel lens Ryan had told them about. The lens was made of individual glass prisms that focused the light. She would have liked to look at it longer, but Ryan was second in line and bugging her to hurry it up.

There were more tourists now, and she walked down the stairs carefully, hugging the inner side so others could get by.

At the base of the stairs, another tour guide, this time an elderly man with a cane, gestured them to one side. Madison guessed that most of the tour guides were retired and volunteered their time.

"I believe I overheard one of your friends say you're visiting lighthouses along the coast?" he said.

"That's right. We started at Tillamook and plan to work our way down to Cape Blanco."

"So, that would mean your next stop is Yaquina Bay?"

"Yes," said Madison, a little tersely, curious about the stranger's interest.

"And then Heceta Head?"

"Yes," Madison said again, wishing Ryan and the others would hurry it up.

"Might I suggest that before Heceta Head, you check out the Cleft of The Rock Lighthouse near Cape Perpetua?"

"I think that one is privately owned and closed to the public," said Madison, remembering notes on the map that Julia had printed for each of them. "I mean, I heard the grounds are awesome, but we can't really stop if we want to get to all the ones on our list. The haunted ones," she added.

"Haunted, huh? Well, if you want haunted—"

Just then, Ryan appeared on the stairs, and not far behind him, Julia and then Marco. They gathered nearby, and the tour guide addressed them all.

"I understand you're looking at haunted lighthouses. It so happens there is a private showing of Cleft of the Rock Lighthouse near Cape Perpetua. As your friend here pointed out," he said, raising his chin toward Madison, "it hasn't been open to the public for years. However, it has new owners, and they are thinking about changing that. As sort of a test, they've asked us tour guides to offer people we think would be appropriate the chance to see it this afternoon."

"Appropriate?" asked Julia softly.

He heard her and said, "Oh, you know, not a bunch of teenagers yelling and knocking things over. Not a bunch of kids with sticky chocolate fingers. That sort of not appropriate. We want the new owners to see there are considerate people who would appreciate seeing their lighthouse. I think you folks would appreciate it. They say there's a ghost who moans and groans and that a ship came aground near there, and some nights you can see the skeletal remains wandering down among the rocks below the bluff. In any case, if you want to go, it will be open between four and eight."

"Well, I want to go," said Ryan. "How often will we get an invitation like that?"

"It does sound like a special opportunity," agreed Madison. "If we have the time, of course. Julia, what do you think? You booked everything and set up the itinerary."

"I did, and I built in time for sightseeing, so yes, we have the time. It's almost three-thirty. Check-in at our hotel in Florence is at four, but they won't care if we get there late. I think we can stop at Yaquina Bay, grab some pictures, and get to this Rock Cleft lighthouse in time."

"Cleft in the Rock," the man said, correcting her. "Some folks just call it the Cape Perpetua Lighthouse. As long as you're polite, I doubt anyone will mind what you call it."

He gave them the code for the gate, and they thanked him and rushed out to the car. As they traveled, Ryan took out his notes and read. "Yaquina Bay Lighthouse was built in 1871 and decommissioned in 1874. It is believed to be the oldest structure in Newport and is the only existing publicly owned Oregon lighthouse with the living quarters attached and the only historic wooden lighthouse still standing. It has been restored as a working lighthouse.

"According to legend, there are several ghost stories associated with it. One involves a teenage girl named Murial, who died while being chased by pirates and continues to haunt Yaquina Bay. Another story is about the daughter of a mythical lighthouse keeper going missing after the lighthouse was shut down, and then a pool of blood was discovered with her handkerchief nearby. Pretty creepy, right? Kind of wish we were going there at night."

"Speak for yourself," said Julia.

Yaquina Bay Lighthouse was perched atop a bluff at the mouth of the Yaquina River in the town of Newport. They scrambled out of the car and quickly explored the light keeper's room, which had been preserved and was full of antique furnishings. They took in the amazing views of the coastline and rushed to the gift shop in the basement. Ryan bought a book about the history and hauntings of the area, and eager to use their special invitation, they hurried back to the car, promising to return one day to spend more time exploring.

Because the Cleft in the Rock was part of a private residence and not usually open to the public, their directions took them to a closed and locked iron gate. Madison felt strange punching in the code. Stranger yet was watching the gate swing closed and latch behind them with an audible snap. It was a little theatrical, she thought, like something out of an old black-and-white horror movie, especially since the clouds were gathering and casting dark, running shadows.

Everyone was quiet as they walked past the house and along the narrow path to the lighthouse. They were all grateful for the honor they were getting, Madison thought. At least she felt that way, and a little nervous too, as if they might be intruding where they weren't really wanted.

Madison looked up at the lighthouse tower and the lantern room on top. The walls were painted the soft gray of driftwood. The glass reflected the increasingly dark sky.

Just as they reached the door, it swung open, and a man standing just inside the entryway greeted them. Madison guessed he was in his mid-50s. He had a distinguished air about him with salt-and-pepper hair that was beautifully styled. His suit fit like it had been tailored for him. He exuded sophistication and expensive cologne. His shoes were polished to a mirror shine, but he wore no tie, maybe a nod to the informal surroundings. Even so, everything about him held a touch of understated elegance.

On his wrist, Madison noticed a luxurious watch, a Patek Philippe, she thought, with a gleaming gold band and a meticulously crafted face. Her dad was a watch nut, and they were always going to estate sales hoping to luck into a find. The watch, worn in a time when everyone carried a cell phone, was a subtle yet unmistakable symbol of the man's wealth. Madison found him interesting and intimidating, but his smile seemed friendly as he gestured for them to come inside.

"My name is Eugene Becker. I'm the owner of this property, and I'm happy you accepted my invitation. This is my niece, Brianna."

Behind him, a woman about their age, wearing jeans, a long-sleeved black t-shirt, and black boots, stood quietly. She had long, chestnut-brown hair similar to Madison's, neatly tied back in a ponytail. Her features were striking. Even without a trace of makeup, her beauty was undeniable, her skin glowing with healthy radiance. She stood quietly next to a table with a decanter and glasses, exuding a quiet confidence that mirrored her uncle's composure. Madison smiled a greeting, but the girl was looking down and didn't see or acknowledge it.

"That wind's a little chilly," Mr. Becker said, "and we keep the thermostat turned pretty low in here. Let me give you something to warm you up while you look around."

He turned to the table and lifted a decanter Madison thought was probably real crystal. Then he poured each of them a glass and said, "This is a liqueur we make from berries grown on the property."

"Is it alcohol?" Julia asked. "I'm only eighteen."

"Yes, but only about as much as brandy. Barely enough to warm your blood," he said with a reassuring smile.

"In Italy and most of Europe, you can drink when you're eighteen or even younger," Marco said. "Americans are so hung up on everything." He tossed back his drink, then set it on the table. The rest followed.

Madison found the liqueur thick and sweet like syrup but with a slightly bitter aftertaste. She would have poured it out if there had been a sink or even an open window. Instead, she drank it quickly, like cough syrup.

"I understand you are writers researching haunted lighthouses?"

"Students doing papers, actually, Mr. Becker," Ryan explained. "Madison's the only real writer." As the two talked, Madison, Marco, and Julia took in the displays of maritime artifacts in the room, from navigational aids like sextants, compasses, and chronometers, to faded signal flags, to old brass oil lamps. A giant wooden ship's wheel leaned in one corner.

"Now that's some woodworking," Marco said. "I think that's mahogany and look how every spoke was shaped so they are all the same, symmetrical, perfectly matched."

"I had no idea you were into woodworking," said Madison.

"Oh yeah, my favorite thing. If I could make money building furniture, that's what I'd do, but in my family, you have to have a Ph.D., or else."

"Darn parents who value education," joked Julia.

"Yeah, and pay for it, too," said Marco. "What yuh gonna do?"

There was little of the poor little rich boy about him, and Madison realized she had lost much of her poor little poor girl dislike for him.

"Let me show you one of the most interesting features of our lighthouse," Mr. Becker suggested, and he led them to the base of the spiral stairs. Walking behind it, where a plaque gave a brief history of the building, he pressed his hand against a part of the wall paneling that looked like all the rest. After a few seconds, they heard a click, and the panel swung open. It was a hidden door. Intrigued, Madison stepped forward and saw that beyond the door was a small landing and a narrow hole with a rusty ladder that descended into darkness.

"Don't worry. Motion-detecting lights will come on as we go," Mr. Becker said. "It's only a few steps. I'll even take my drink with me." True to his word, he held the glass of red liquid in one hand and climbed noisily down, the metal clanging with each step.

Cautiously, the rest followed. Madison felt the air grow cooler as she descended. The promised lights flickered on, and soon she was standing in a narrow tunnel, its walls glistening with moisture, the rocky ground softened by a layer of damp sand.

They followed their host down the narrow path of the tunnel, which descended until it suddenly widened into a cavern with a high ceiling. On the distant wall, a natural hole in the rock had been meticulously carved into a rectangular opening with a wide ledge. It offered a view of the bleak sky and admitted the thunderous sound of waves.

Madison realized they were now near the base of the bluff. Moving to the opening, she looked down at the frenzy of froth and crashing waves. It made her a little dizzy, and she stepped back. Though she had moved away from the vertigo-inducing opening, Madison still felt light-headed and she lifted her hand to rub across her eyes. Then she felt nothing at all.

WAKING WAS LIKE DRAGGING HERSELF FROM SOMETHING THICK AND viscous. She thought of the blood-colored liqueur she'd been given. Wake up she told herself. Open your eyes. It seemed impossible, and waves of nausea forced her eyes closed.

The next time she managed to open them, she felt a little better and was able to stay alert long enough to feel the ropes around her wrists and ankles. The gritty sand against the side of her face.

She was lying near the opening in the wall of the cavern. Lifting her head, she could make out her friends, all lying motionless on the sand, each tied as she was. From their random positions, she guessed that they'd been tied where they fell. She thought of the bitter taste of that drink and knew they'd been poisoned. She hoped her friends were only unconscious.

Standing in front of the wide opening, she could see the silhouette of Becker and his niece. They were wearing dark robes, their hands raised high, as they chanted something that sounded like Latin.

Madison's right arm was numb from lying on it. She struggled to sit up, then slowly inched her way toward the wall, using her bound hands to push against the ground. The wall provided some support as she leaned gratefully back against it. Her fingers explored the rough stone. Still groggy, some instinct had her searching for a way to fray the ropes, to get free.

"Ah, you're awake," the man said. He reached down and took something from the ledge then walked toward her. She saw he was holding a glass of liqueur. Smiling down at her he took a sip and said, "Don't worry, Brianna only added the tincture to your drinks. Jimsonweed and a few other things that grow along these shores. She's quite talented in herbalism."

"Why are you doing this?" She didn't expect him to answer, so was a little surprised when he did.

"I will give you a synopsis, shall I? Centuries ago, a ship came to these shores bearing but a double handful of men who had survived the dangerous crossing. On that final day a storm raged, waves tossing the ship and threatening to sink her. My ancestor led a mutiny and afterward, the captain and two of his most brutal sailors were thrown overboard. Almost at once the storm abated. The sudden calm left the men in awe, and they were able to come to shore safely.

"Taking this as a sign from God, and to honor that blessing, the survivors formed a secret society. Every twenty-five years, or the length of a generation, the appointed leader must replicate the sacrifice of three to appease the ocean. Without it, the coast would be plagued by shipwrecks, storms, and other calamities."

"Because you're all about helping others," Madison challenged.

He laughed, drained his glass, and stared at it, before tossing it aside. "Our ancestors arrived here as poor sailors, little more than slaves, and went on to amass great wealth through fishing and then ships and shipping. Gifts from the ocean and more proof that our ancestors were blessed. We are guardians appointed by God."

"Guardians? You're not guardians. You're crazy! And if you were appointed, it was by the devil."

He paused as if to think about it. His smile chilled her to the bone. He stared right at her and said, "Perhaps."

"You won't get away with it," she told him, ashamed of how shrill her voice sounded, how it shook. "You don't think our parents will come looking for us? Marco's family is rich. They'll hire investigators. They'll figure it out, and you and your sick society will be exposed."

"Oh, I hardly think so. As I said, we've been doing this for hundreds of years. It's really just a matter of making good choices. Not hard if you use the material at hand. For instance, in 1900 when Point Adams Lighthouse was decommissioned, three laborers didn't show up for work one morning. No one was surprised; itinerant workers come and go, but in fact, they were dead, buried beneath the stone walls.

"In 1925, similar men, helping to build Cape Blanco, were left under the footings. In 1950, a lumber company hired a Japanese crew to work graveyard at a sawmill. A mob forced the Japanese and some Filipino and Korean workers out of town. No one noticed three of them go missing. And so, it goes.

"Now, here we are in 2025 with so many young people disillusioned by their government and also fearful of their corporate overlords. They feel trapped, hopeless. The suicide rate is astonishing. You will be missed but no one will be surprised by your suicide pact.

"You should feel honored, for the first time in two hundred years, we are able to perform the ceremony correctly, providing our members with even greater success and assuring the safety of these waters for all. This time we will commend your bodies not to the earth but to the ocean itself.

"At high tide, this chamber is underwater. Tied as you and your friends are, you will drown, and the ocean will take you to its depths. Only three are needed for the sacrifice but you are a witness and therefore cannot be left alive.

"Come Brianna. The tide is rising."

For the first time Brianna looked up, her eyes locking with Madison's. There was no expression on the girl's face, no flicker of concern, nothing to give her hope.

Becker and his niece moved back to the opening, raised their arms, and again began to chant. Madison glanced at her still friends. Desperation surged through her, and she leaned back against the wall, twisted her wrists, pressed the rope against the gritty rock, and rubbed up and down. The rock tore her skin. The rope bit into her flesh, but she gritted her teeth and rubbed harder, the coarse surface wore at the fibers, but it was slow work. Each movement sent a jolt of pain through her arms, but she kept going, driven by sheer determination. The sound of the waves covered the noise she was making, but how long before they turned and saw what she was doing?

Her eyes fell on the glass Becker had carelessly discarded. Without pause, she rolled away from the wall and scrabbled for it. With a final, desperate effort, she grasped it in her hands. The thin stem snapped easily, leaving a sharp shard of glass, a point that she worked between the strands of the rope. Blood trickled from cuts in her fingers, warm against her cold skin. She ignored it and the pain. Finally, the last strand parted.

She bent forward, her fingers trembling as she worked at the knot in the rope around her ankles. The rough fibers again bit into her fingertips, but she focused on freeing herself. With a final, determined tug, the knot gave way.

Ryan was closest. She crawled to him, her movements urgent and desperate. She shook him, her voice a frantic whisper in his ear, "Wake up, Ryan. Ryan, wake up." She'd heard somewhere that people will wake more easily if they hear their name. "Ryan, we have to get out of here."

Suddenly, a powerful surge of water burst through the opening in the wall, drenching the two figures standing there. They stumbled back, caught off guard by the unexpected wave. "Damn it," the man cursed, brushing frantically at his soaked robes. The force of the water had left them both dripping and disoriented. But not for long.

Becker saw that Madison was free and frantically untying the ropes around one of her friend's wrists. "Stop her!" he shouted and began to move toward them.

"No, Uncle," Brianna said, stepping between him and the escaping friends. "This has to stop. I won't be a part of this anymore."

Surprised, Becker paused. Then, his face twisted in rage. "You dare defy me?" He lunged toward Madison, but Brianna blocked his path, holding him back with all her strength.

Madison worked quickly, her fingers fumbling with the knots. Water was rushing into the cavern. With each wave, the water rose, and she realized she had to free her friends or watch them drown. She managed to free Ryan, then they both splashed through the ankle-deep water to Julia and Marco and with numb fingers managed to untie their legs. The icy water helped rouse them, and with help, they were able to stand.

Brianna's uncle tried to push past her, but she stood her ground, and her voice was steady but firm when she said, "No more. This ends now."

"No!" he shouted and with a swift, brutal motion, shoved the small woman aside. She slammed into the unforgiving rock wall then crumpled to the ground, gasping for air. Her uncle tried to run past her, intent on recapturing his prey, but his foot caught in her robes, sending him crashing to his knees.

Madison pushed her friends toward the tunnel. At the foot of the ladder, they paused just long enough to free Julia and Marco's hands before urging them onto the ladder. Disoriented and dizzy, they nevertheless seemed to sense the urgency and wordlessly climbed the ladder, emerging in the lighthouse.

Regaining his senses, Marco slammed the hidden door shut behind him. He ran to the ship's wheel in the corner, pushed it over, and slid it across the floor, jamming it between the wall and the base of the staircase. It would hold the door shut.

"Run!" Madison shouted. She could hear Becker's furious shouts

They burst outside and ran down the narrow path to the small parking area. Madison cast a look over her shoulder. The lighthouse loomed there, a stark reminder of the horrors they had just escaped. They didn't stop running until they reached the safety of their car. They piled in, Madison floored the gas pedal, and tires chirping on the asphalt, they sped away.

As they drove, Madison looked back, the lighthouse growing smaller in the distance. She knew they had to report what had happened as quickly as possible. She knew they should call the police. The tide was rising. The cavern and maybe even the tunnel would soon be filled with water.

For one terrible moment, she considered not calling. Becker, that treacherous man, part of a society of murderers who deserved what was coming for him. Then she remembered Brianna and how she had saved them all. "Call the police. One of you call the police. They have to get there before the water fills the room and Brianna drowns."

BRIANNA SAT IN THE TUNNEL AT THE TOP OF THE SLOPE, HER ROBE providing a makeshift cushion against the damp ground. The wet fabric wasn't much help, but she was comforted knowing the rising water never reached all the way up the tunnel. She was safe, and soon the police would arrive and let her out.

She had tried to open the door at the top of the ladder, but finding it blocked, had climbed back down. Her uncle's panic at the prospect of their sacrifices escaping had driven his heart rate up, just as she'd hoped. The increased heart rate made his blood circulate faster, accelerating the effects of the drug she'd given him —a smaller dose than she'd given the others, and with slightly altered ingredients.

He had collapsed and now floated on the rising water. Waves surged through the opening with a thunderous noise, filling the space with a spray of mist and foam. Around her the icy water had risen to her knees. Wading through it, she reached down and grabbed handfuls of her uncle's black robe. The next strong wave helped her lift his body and she pushed it toward the opening. A retreating wave tore him from her numb fingers, and she watched as he was dragged away by the dark tide.

Brianna smiled. She would turn eighteen in one month, the age when a provision in her uncle's will would give her, his sole heir, control of his corporation and its vast holdings. As an unwitting and unwilling minor dragged into her uncle's perverse secret society, she was confident she'd garner enough sympathy—and she certainly had enough money for the best lawyers—to ensure a slap on the wrist. Maybe she'd have to spend a little time with a therapist or serve a short probation. She wasn't worried. Whatever the consequences, she was sure she'd be free in no time

She wanted to laugh but stopped herself from such a display of emotion. She'd been taught it was best to never reveal your thoughts or intentions. Like her ancestors, the future was hers to navigate, and she intended to do so on her own terms.

———

A MONTH LATER, THE NICE MAN WHO WORKED AT THE GIFT SHOP took a cell phone from his back pocket and tapped in a number. "I have some folks heading your way," he said to the person at the other end of the line. "Two sisters in their teens traveling with their aunt all very interested in lighthouses. I think they'll be perfect for you."

ABOUT THE AUTHOR

Pamela Cowan is an Amazon best-selling, NIWA award-winning, Pacific Northwest author, best known for her dark thrillers. Cowan is the author of the Storm Vigilante Series, the El & Em Detective Series, and three stand-alone novels.

Her short stories have been published in *Alien Skin, Argus, Space and Time, Visions,* numerous anthologies and collections, and have been read on radio. Cowan holds degrees in Communication and Organizational Psychology and dedicated most of her career to social services.

Born in Germany, an army brat, she moved with her family 17 times before settling in Oregon, where she has steadfastly remained. She has two grown children, a remarkably patient and supportive husband, and a dog whose sole purpose is to end the tyranny of all Fed-Ex, USPS, and UPS delivery drivers. To date, she has not succeeded.

You can learn more about Pamela at her website: https://www.pambainbridgecowan.com/

———

INSPIRATION FOR THE STORY

My daughter suggested a trip up the Oregon Coast to visit haunted lighthouses. She loves ghost stories and I love research. Looking into it, I uncovered plenty of spooky tales. We have yet to take the trip, but when the theme of navigation came up for this anthology, I realized that my research might be useful.

SPOTTED PONY CASINO MYSTERY

CHANGING
COURSE

PATY JAGER

Published by

Windtree Press, Corvallis, Oregon

https://windtreepress.com

1

HIS LOVE

heodore Thunder sat hunched over the small table in the library. He'd purchased a notebook and pen to write three letters that should have been written long ago. This past winter after spending a week in the hospital with pneumonia, he'd realized that his last day on this earth could come. Yet he hadn't told the people who meant the most to him what had happened and why he'd not come back to them.

He opened the notebook and wondered which letter to write first. He'd lain awake nights thinking about these letters and how each one would need to tell a different part of his life.

Deborah. He'd start with Deborah. She was where his exile had started.

He'd never blamed her for pointing a finger at him. After all, the criminal had a strong resemblance to him.

Leaning back in the chair, he closed his eyes and remembered how he'd met Deborah. A smile lifted the corners of his mouth, seeing her standing on the other side of the fence as he prepared to ride in the Indian Relay Race at the rodeo in Corvallis. Her fresh face, the open inspection of him, and her welcoming smile shed his inhibitions and he smiled back. When their eyes met, he knew if he found her after the race, he was going to buy her a beer.

During the race, each time he'd hastily dismounted from one horse and mounted the next, he'd wondered if the small blonde-haired woman was watching. His desire to impress her made execution of the horse changes better than usual. He clung to the animals as they bolted around the track. It didn't even bother him that he finished second. He'd had clean transfers and could only go as fast as the horses could run.

After all the congratulations from his team members and the other teams in the race, he'd been surprised to look up and find her watching him near the gate.

He was dirty, sweaty, and smelled of horse. "Want me to buy you a beer now or after I clean up?" he'd asked.

"After you clean up," she'd replied, staring up at him. He found himself peering into sky-blue eyes. "You can really ride a horse," she'd added.

His mind wandered from that first meeting to the thought, that he missed the deep blue skies of Northeast Oregon. The skies under which he'd been born, played sports with his tribal friends and the boys he'd met at Pendleton High. He'd had to deal with prejudice and racism many times, but he always knew who he was, unlike many of the boys who made fun of him. That land under those deep blue skies was his home. A home he could never return to. Tears burned under his eyelids. He swiped at the tear he felt squeezing out from under his closed lashes and returned to his memory of meeting Deborah.

"Thanks. I've been doing it my whole life." He'd replied, catching the t-shirt Dustin tossed at him and not missing his friend's wink. He pulled the shirt over his head and nodded toward the walkway between the stands. When she fell in step beside him, he realized how small she was. He was nearly six feet and the top of her head was even with the middle of his upper arm.

"Where do you need to go to change?" she asked.

"My motel room. It's about three blocks that way." He pointed to the east. "You can wait here and I'll meet you by the beer tent in forty-five minutes."

She glanced around and then looked up at him. "Let me tell my friend where I'm going and I'll come with you."

He'd been surprised by her boldness and wondered if he'd read her right. Was she a young woman looking for a good time or was she someone trying to get an Indian in trouble with the law? He watched her walk over to the end of the stands and poke a brunette in the thigh with her finger. She was the complete opposite of the petite blonde. The brunette hopped off the bleachers and walked back toward him.

She was closer to his height and built like an athlete. She stopped in front of him. "What's your name and where are you taking Deborah?"

She didn't challenge him about being an Indian, just being cautious for her friend.

"Theodore Thunder's my name. But friends call me Dory. I'm going to clean up at my room, number sixty-four at the Wagon Wheel motel. Deborah can stay here with you until I'm done." He wanted to make it clear this wasn't his idea.

The brunette studied him a moment and then smiled at Deborah. "Have fun," she said and walked back to the bleachers.

He looked down at Deborah who had a big smile on her face. Theodore shrugged and they walked to the motel. He told her where he grew up and she told him how she was in college studying to be a teacher. Their worlds were miles apart but he felt the zing of attraction when she looked at him and by the time they reached the motel, he wasn't sure it was a good idea for this cute little co-ed to go into his motel room. He was at least ten years older than her.

But she'd insisted and said she'd watch television while he showered.

Theodore took his clean clothes into the small bathroom with him and took the fastest shower he'd ever had when in a motel room. He usually stayed in the shower until the water ran cold when he was traveling the rodeo circuit. It was a luxury he'd never had growing up on the Rez.

When he came out, the beds were made. His clothes and those of his fellow teammates that had been thrown everywhere were neatly folded and sitting on the table.

Deborah's cheeks reddened. "I was bored. There wasn't anything good on the television."

He walked over, cupped the side of her small face in his hand, and smiled. "Want to give up learning to be a teacher and come on the road with me?"

She laughed and then he saw the heat in her eyes and he lowered his head for a kiss.

He felt a moan rising in his throat thinking about what came next and opened his eyes to stop the rush of emotion. He was back in the library. The blank notebook page staring up at him. Picking up the pen, he began the letter that was burned in his brain like a wildfire.

Dear Deborah,

I'm sorry for any pain or unhappiness my disappearance may have caused you. I've stayed away not because I am the criminal you accused me to be, but because I didn't want to bring the police and the reason for my arrest to your doorstep. Over the years I've kept tabs on what has been happening at Nixyáawii. I'm glad you and our daughter have been living next door to my father. I'm glad you sought him out. He is a good and wise man. I wish I could have gone to him for advice when the path in my life took such an unwanted turn.

I don't blame you for my going to prison. You probably believed you saw me running from the crime. But I swear on my father's life, your life, and our daughter's life, that I was not the man raping young women. When I escaped prison, I made it my duty to find and stop him. I'm happy to say that I did just that. But because I am an escaped convict and

I have taken a life, I can never see your beautiful blue eyes again or hold you.

Know that my heart has only held you in it. Thank you for not ending our daughter's life and bringing her to my people.

Dory

He reread what he'd written and hoped it would be enough to ease Deborah's mind. She had been the best thing to happen to him in his life and he hadn't been able to keep her. There had been many nights through the years when he'd wished she were in his arms and that he could tell her all the things that he'd been doing and why. But he didn't want his letter to her to be anything but uplifting. Since the night the police broke into his motel room and dragged him to a police station, there hadn't been anything he wanted to tell her for fear she'd feel responsible for his ruined life.

He never wanted her to suffer because of the path his life had taken. Everything he did after being wrongly imprisoned was on him and no one else. Well, maybe the true criminal. That person's actions had been something Theodore had been getting blamed for since they were both old enough to walk.

As a child, his cousin Leo looked like his twin. Their parents were siblings. Theodore's father and Leo's father were brothers. They married sisters. Theodore and Leo were only a few months apart in age. As they grew, it became surreal to walk into a family gathering and see someone who looked a lot like yourself already there.

But where Theodore followed the lessons his grandfather and father taught him, his cousin only wanted to do harm. Leo had an evil streak in him that no matter how much he was shamed and made to apologize, he didn't change and continued his mean ways.

Then they were both drafted into the Vietnam War. Theodore was sent to the front lines where he endured harsh weather, not knowing who the enemy was, and being given the shit jobs. He'd lost track of his cousin. It took all his energy to stay alive. When he was finally released from his duties with the Army, he'd returned home to find people hated him for killing the enemy, and Leo had been killed in battle. His aunt and uncle blamed him for not watching out for their son, no matter how many times he'd told them that they were separated and sent to different areas.

Few understood the horrors he'd seen or the atrocities he was ordered to commit. They were things he hadn't wanted to remember but on bad days, they would come back to him in vivid memories.

Riding with the relay team and traveling from rodeo to rodeo had helped keep him too tired to think or dream. Leaping off a racing horse's bare back and onto the back of a waiting horse as he tried to beat the other teams around the track, took concentration and agility. He liked the challenge, the reenactment of his culture, and that it kept him moving without having to face family who thought he should have done more to keep his cousin alive during the war.

Then he'd met Deborah and found what he was looking for. After their first encounter at the rodeo, he'd met up with her again a couple other times. He loved her laugh, the way she paid attention to what he said, and how she felt in his arms. He knew they should date a while longer before he asked her to marry him, but he had to decide between staying near her or continuing on with the relay team. His team and friends from the Rez were depending on him to help win the prize money.

The night he'd been pulled from his bed by the police, he'd been planning to ask Deborah to marry him.

2

HIS LEGACY

Theodore hadn't known he'd fathered a child until he discovered he could access the Umatilla Reservation newspaper online in 1997. Reading through the sports section he came across a name that didn't make sense to him. It wasn't a family name he had heard of in Nixyáawii.

Using his newly learned computer skills, he searched the internet and learned more about the girl whose facial features and prowess on a basketball court resembled his. She was the daughter of Deborah Bolden. The woman who'd wrapped around his heart. He learned she was a teacher on the reservation and that she lived next door to Silas Thunder, his father.

Doing the math, he'd smiled. They had conceived this child during his whirlwind romance with Deborah. He may not have been able to marry the woman he loved, but he'd given Deborah something to remember him by. That thought made him frown. Had she been able to separate her feelings for him, a man she'd sentenced to life in prison for a crime she thought he'd committed, and still love their daughter?

Wanting to know more about both the mother and the daughter, for years he continued reading the online newspaper and searching the internet for the girl.

He was proud of the child he and Deborah made. She was a good student, excellent at sports, joined the Army, and had a job as head of security at the casino on the reservation. Recently her name was connected to stories about helping the FBI and Tribal police bring back stolen Umatilla women and find murderers. He'd worried when he'd learned of her injuries in Iraq, including the loss of a limb, that she would come back bitter and mentally unstable. But she was strong and resilient like all Cayuse warriors.

He turned the page in the notebook and started writing.

My daughter Dela,

I wish I could have been there to help guide you but I'm sure your grandfather did a good job of teaching you what you needed to learn. I've followed your growth through the reservation newspaper and it warms my heart to see what a beautiful and strong woman warrior you are.

I'm sorry I couldn't be there for you and that you were given a name I'm unfamiliar with. Once I learned of your existence I couldn't stop smiling. You came about because I fell in love with your mother. The memories I have of our time together helped me through being wrongly accused of a crime, breaking out of jail, and pursuing the man who caused my imprisonment. Your mother made me want to pursue justice.

I wanted to make the world safer for your mother and other young women. While I couldn't be by your side, I thought of you every day after I discovered your existence. My staying away, kept you from having to hear about what I was accused of. But I never did what they said. The person who should have been in prison had a strong resemblance to me.

While I believe you could handle the truth, I'm leaving that for your grandfather. He needs to know I didn't dishonor the family in such a vicious and cruel way.

I had hoped to one day see you. Even though I have been gone from the reservation for nearly forty years, I fear should I return, I would be back in jail and it isn't a place for someone who is innocent or old.

With the real criminal dead, I have no proof that I was wrongly convicted. But I know I didn't do it and I wanted you and your mother to know. I love you both and will go to this earth holding that love in my heart.

Your Loving Father

Theodore reread his words and felt his chest swell with pride. This strong woman Deborah brought into the world would go on upholding the Thunder honor. He wished that he could meet her, learn more about her than what he read in the newspaper. But he didn't want to die in prison. While he wished to be among his people and family again, he also wished to be a free man when he was put into the earth. That his flesh and bones wouldn't nurture his homeland was sad. He'd fled to Canada to avoid persecution like Chief Joseph of the Nez Perce had tried to in 1877. Only Theodore had succeeded and had been welcomed into the native community here. They had become his new family but his heart was still in Nixyáawii and the Blue Mountains of Oregon.

3

FINDING HIS PATH

After folding the two letters he'd just written, Theodore sat for a moment. Did he have the time to write the third letter? He glanced at the clock on the library wall and decided he needed to get going. He'd miss dinner at the community hall if he didn't catch the right bus.

He slipped the letters into the notebook and closed it before sliding it all into a small backpack that held his belongings. Two clean changes of clothes, toothbrush, paste, brush for his hair, soap, and deodorant. All the money he'd saved from working over the years was around his waist in a money belt he'd bought at a second-hand store.

Being a wanted man, he couldn't have his real name on anything and he couldn't open a bank account without proper I.D. Since he dressed like someone with little money, he was safe from being robbed. He never took money out of his money belt in front of anyone. No one knew he had it. And he always made sure he was paid in small denominations. If he didn't have enough money in his pockets, he made sure the person he was dealing with knew that and walked away. He had spent the last thirty-five years appearing to be someone who could only do manual labor and who wouldn't have money.

It wasn't the life he'd envisioned before being drafted, but it was how the Creator navigated his life. Nothing had been easy and he'd lost contact with his family and homeland.

He stepped out of the library, slid his arms through the pack straps, and walked down the steps to the sidewalk. The bus he needed would pick him up two blocks from the library. With his head down to not draw attention, Theodore walked to the bus stop and stood beside the cover over the bench. He stared at his feet but kept an eye on the people who arrived at the stop.

One young man shifted from foot to foot, putting his hands in and out of his jacket pockets. There was something off about him. Not like he was mentally disturbed. Theodore had dealt with people on drugs and those with mental issues over the years as he lived with the homeless and stayed in shelters. No, this young man appeared nervous. What would make him nervous standing at a bus stop?

The bus arrived and Theodore climbed the steps, tapped his card on the meter, and took a seat. He peered out the window and saw the young man still standing near the bench. But his eyes were on someone behind Theodore on the bus.

The bus jerked and started moving. He watched the young man until he could no longer see him. He wondered who the young man had been watching.

———

THE VOLUNTEERS WERE STILL AT THE CHURCH SERVING SOUP, BREAD, and cake when Theodore arrived. Every Wednesday night he came here for dinner. Over the years he'd found all the places a person could get a free meal. Churches, shelters, and a couple of restaurants. When he didn't get a meal for free, he purchased items from different grocery stores. He only frequented the free meals regularly. He never shopped at stores more than once a month. Moving around and not letting anyone get familiar with him was his way of keeping him off of anyone's radar.

At the meals, he smiled and didn't say anything. If they asked his name, he usually told them Joe. It was common and not a link to his family.

He shuffled along the line as the volunteers filled his plate.

"Evening, Joe."

"Good to see you, Joe," they said and he smiled and nodded his head.

Taking a seat on the end of an empty table, he dug into the pea soup, dipping the crusty bread into it. Hunger didn't let him be picky about what he ate. At first, he could hardly swallow the soup but as the years passed and it was the traditional soup served at most places, he'd learned to like it. A full belly was more important than enjoying the flavor.

"Where you been?" Henry, a Cree member, asked.

"Around," Theodore responded. He and Henry played stick games in the alley behind the shelter when Theodore stayed there during the winter months. They were both of an age to remember the game and share it with other Indigenous men they met.

"Want to play sticks tomorrow?" Henry asked.

Theodore shook his head. "Busy."

Henry laughed and started coughing.

Theodore put his hands over his soup so the other man's spit didn't get in his food.

"What are you busy about?" Henry asked.

"Thinking. Been doing a lot of thinking. Can't think if you're talking all the time." He said it in a soft voice and knew the man wouldn't take it wrong.

"What are you thinking about?" Henry asked, taking a seat across from him. His gray eyebrows drew together in concern.

"What I'm missing." Until he wrote the letters he'd been stalling to write, he hadn't allowed himself to think about all he'd missed by chasing down Leo and then having to leave the country and live anonymously.

"You don't like being free?" Henry asked. The elderly Cree had told him this was the life when they'd met ten years ago. He loved moving around, never sleeping in the same place more than a couple of nights. As far as Theodore knew, the man didn't have any family or loved ones who he missed.

"I would rather be home eating salmon and huckleberries, listening to my aunties arguing and my uncles grunting and saying the women were crazy. Memories of my life are haunting me. Making me wish to be with my family." Surprised he'd said out loud what had been on his mind for months now, Theodore shoved a spoonful of soup into his mouth.

"You're lucky you have happy memories." Henry's eyes teared up. "When my siblings didn't come back from the residential school, my mother became blank and my father took to the bottle. I was younger and hadn't been sent away. When anyone would come looking for me, I'd hide. I didn't want to disappear like my sister and brother." He shrugged. "Hiding became a way of life for me. When my parents died and disappeared for good, I took off."

Theodore was sad for his friend. Family meant everything to his people. It had been hard for him to stay away for so long. But he knew it was the best for the ones he loved. "I'm sorry to hear you have no family. Family is what keeps me going. Knowing they are safe and strong together."

Henry nodded and stood. "When you aren't busy, let me know." He shuffled out of the community center, and Theodore stood to take his empty dishes to the table that held the dirty dish pan.

"It's good to see you, Joe. You missed last week and I was worried that you might have had a relapse of pneumonia," Marshal, the head of the organization that supplied the free dinner, said.

"No, just busy. It was good as usual."

Marshal took the tray. "Have a good night."

Theodore nodded and left the building. He planned to sleep in the lot behind the building tonight and catch the bus back to the library in the morning. The quiet at the library made it easier to think and write.

4

EXONERATING THE NAME

The following morning, Theodore cleaned up inside the restrooms at a local park and boarded a bus for the section downtown where the library stood. Walking up the steps of the building a whisper of wind floated by his face, filling his nostrils with the scent that reminded him of home.

Glancing around, he couldn't find where the scent of sage came from. It brought back memories of smudging before entering a sweat house. It had been decades since he'd set foot in one. The last time was after he'd stopped the man who committed the crimes he was accused of. His body and mind had needed a good cleansing.

"Are you okay?" a voice beside him asked.

He twisted his head and peered into the eyes of a tall thin woman in her forties who studied him with concern. "I'm fine." He continued up the stairs and into the library. The corner where he'd sat the day before had five young people talking.

Wandering around the outer perimeter of the shelves packed with books, he found another quiet corner. It was a small desk with only two chairs. He placed his pack in one chair and sat in the other.

Today's letter would be the hardest and longest to write. His father had to feel abandoned. His oldest son in prison and then an escapee, his daughter overdosing, and then his wife passing. He was glad Deborah and their daughter had been there to ease his loneliness. Tapping the pen against the paper he wondered if Deborah had told his father he was her child's grandfather. She had to have sought him out and told him what happened for her to have lived all these years next door to him.

Father,

It has been decades since we looked in one another's eyes. I have missed you and your wisdom every day. It would have helped me navigate through the years after the trial that put an innocent man in jail. Your son, Theodore Thunder.

Since I last saw you, I fell in love with Deborah at a rodeo. I'm not sure how much she told you. But the day the police pulled me out of my motel room I'd been planning to ask her to marry me. The man she saw running from the college after a young woman had been raped was not me. But he looked like me.

He was your nephew, Leo. I discovered after escaping prison that Leo wasn't killed in Vietnam as the family always thought. While I was hiding in the family cabin in the Blues, Leo showed up. At first, I'd thought I'd seen a ghost. But he was the same cruel person he'd always been. He was drinking and laughed about how he'd exchanged dog tags with another Native American soldier who was killed in action. That was how he became invisible when the Army discharged him.

As he drank that night, he went on, bragging how he'd raped Korean women and was now preying on college women by hanging around their dorms.

Don't tell Auntie and Uncle that their boy had become a monster. They don't need to know. I should have hauled him to the police that night, but I was so stunned at how he could talk about all of this as if it were a hunting trip and not show a bit of remorse that I went for a walk to think about all he'd told me. By the time I returned to the cabin with the determination to take him to the police, he'd left.

And that's when I vowed to find and stop him. It took me two years of moving about the country reading about rapes on college campuses and visiting with homeless people to finally catch up to him. I used a knife with an obsidian blade and deer horn handle to stop his causing harm to anyone.

After sending him to the next world, I knew I had to remain anonymous in this world to avoid going to prison for the crimes I didn't commit and for ending my cousin's life. I have been living in the land our ancestors sought so many lifetimes ago.

All the years I have been away I've thought of you, Nixyáawii our homeland, and Deborah and our child, every day. I learned that Deborah and our child were living in Nixyáawii through the newspaper. On the computer, I discovered they have been your neighbors. I wish I could have been in their lives but I didn't want them to be burdened by the crimes I was accused of, my escape, and now the blood of Leo on my hands. With Leo dead I had no way to prove my innocence.

If you are reading this letter, it is because I have gone to our earth. Not the earth of our ancestors but that of our northern relatives. This letter is in my belongings with a message to whoever finds my body to send this to you upon my death.

Your son,

Theodore

He reread the letter, folded it like the other two, and put them all in a long envelope he'd purchased when he bought the notebook and pen. He wrote Silas Thunder and his address on the outside. He slid all of the items into his pack and stood. His stomach grumbled.

Pointing his feet in the direction of the entrance, he wandered through the library. He glanced up at the clock above the entrance and saw it was the middle of the afternoon. He'd find a sandwich shop and get something to eat, then catch the bus to the same area where he'd slept last night.

5

TURN OF EVENTS

After eating a deli sandwich, Theodore finished off the coffee in his cup and dumped his trash. It was nearing time for the bus to arrive. He walked down to the bus stop and stood as he usually did, leaning a bit against the side of the cover over the bench.

The usual people for this time of day began arriving and waiting. The young man from the day before walked up and stood to the side of everyone.

Theodore saw the bus approaching at the same time a young woman walked up to the stop. Out of the corner of his eye, he saw the young man pull a gun out of his jacket pocket. Theodore threw his body in front of the young man, grasping for the gun.

The boom of the gun going off stopped all other sounds.

Something hit him in the chest.

The young man's eyes widened and he spun out of Theodore's sight.

His body hit the hard concrete as a scream pierced through the fog clouding his mind. A blurry face and garbled voice spoke above him.

The world around him was like watching fancy dancers at a powwow. Colors blurred and swirled as muffled voices, sirens, and horns filled his ears. His body rose and he felt the sway of movement.

More muffled voices, beeping, and the stringent scent of clean. He realized he was in a hospital moments before his thoughts faded and the world grew dark.

———

THEODORE HEARD VOICES THAT MADE SENSE AND FELT HANDS tucking his arms close to his body. Raising his heavy eyelids, he focused first on the white ceiling above him then turned his head toward the sound of voices. A woman in a long white shirt stood looking at a clipboard. An older woman who looked slightly familiar was fiddling with the tubes going into his arm.

"There you are Theodore. I told Doctor Caron you were tough and would be coming out of the anesthetic soon." The nurse smiled at him.

His mind felt as if it were full of thousands of fluffy bird feathers.

"Theodore, we were able to get the bullet out of you. It nicked your heart and was lodged in one of your ribs. Thankfully, it wasn't a large caliber. You should be able to go home in a week. It will take a bit for your wound and ribs to heal, but I don't foresee any reason you shouldn't heal just fine." She hung the clipboard on the end of his bed and left the room.

Bullet? He squeezed his eyes shut and tried to remember what happened.

"Everyone at the bus stop said you were a hero, stopping that young man from shooting his ex-girlfriend." The nurse now stood beside the bed smiling down at him.

The scene flashed through his mind. Instinct and his protective nature had him stepping in front of the gun when he'd seen the young man pull it out.

"I'm not a hero." His throat hurt as he croaked out the words.

The nurse held a plastic cup with a straw up to his lips. He drew in several swallows and leaned back against the pillow.

"You saved a girl's life and possibly that of everyone at that stop." She studied him.

"I did what anyone who saw a person pull a gun from a pocket would do." He closed his eyes and ignored any other conversation she continued with.

Once she left the room, he opened his eyes and scanned the room. He was in the same hospital he'd been in when he had pneumonia in January. That nurse must have been one of the ones who took care of him. He'd been good at not telling them more than his first name and they knew he was homeless. But where were his clothes and his pack? And his money belt? When he knew he had to go to the hospital in January, he'd hid the money belt in a graveyard and retrieved it when he was released. But if the paramedics opened his clothing at the bus stop others would have seen the cloth belt around his waist. Worry seeped in that someone stole it or the hospital would keep it to pay for his medical care. It wasn't enough to cover the care. He only had a few thousand but it was his and he didn't want to lose it.

The machine that was hooked up to him started beeping as he tried to sit up.

The same nurse entered the room. "Lay down, Theodore. You just had surgery and need to not tear out your stitches," she said.

"Where's my things. Clothes and my pack?" he asked.

"The clothes you had on are in a sack in that cupboard. There wasn't a pack with you."

He fell back and cursed.

"Perhaps one of the people waiting for the bus picked up your pack. I'm sure it will show up before you leave the hospital."

He wanted to ask about the money belt but didn't want her to know he had money. Clamping his lips and eyelids shut, he blocked her out as he tried to think about who was at the bus stop.

6

A VISITOR

Theodore sat up with the help of the bed and peered down at the food on the tray. They fed him as if he were a man without teeth.

A faint knock drew his gaze to the door and a young woman stepped in. She smiled shyly and stepped forward. "Hi, I'm Wendy Strathmore. You saved my life the other day and I wanted to thank you."

He studied her for several minutes and her smile wavered. "Come in," he finally said, wondering why she stood in the doorway with her hands behind her back.

Her head bobbed and she took a couple more steps until she stood at the end of the bed. "I'm sorry you ended up in the middle of my crazy Ex and his attempt to kill me."

She didn't look more than twenty if that. He nodded. "Couldn't let him hurt anyone. I saw the way he acted and knew he was up to no good." Theodore moved his hand, motioning to a chair. "You can have a seat. Tell me why he wanted you dead."

She shuffled sideways to the chair and pulled his pack out from behind her.

"How'd you get my pack?" he asked, not angry, only confused that she would end up with it.

Her face reddened making the freckles over the bridge of her nose disappear. "I-I, when they took off with you in the ambulance, it was on the ground where they'd cut it off of you." She held up the cut straps. "I figured if I didn't take it someone would steal it. At least I knew it belonged to you and could give it back."

"Thank you." He held out the hand closest to her and the one farthest from his wound.

She stood and placed the pack on the bed beside him. Leaning close, she whispered, "Your money belt is in there too. The paramedics cut it off you as well. I picked it up when they tossed it my way. Didn't want anyone to get your money."

"You are a good person, Wendy. Thank you." He motioned to the chair. "Now tell me about this boy who tried to shoot you."

"There's not much to tell. I went out with him four or five times and realized he was crazy. I broke it off with him, and he wouldn't leave me alone. I'd gone to the police and they said they couldn't do anything until he threatened me. When I saw him at the bus stop the day before he tried to shoot me, I thought I'd have to change my routine. But the next day, I was tired and didn't think about it. Until I saw him at the bus stop again." She sighed. "If I had changed my routine, you wouldn't be in the hospital."

"But if you had and he discovered your new routine, you may not have had someone willing to put themselves between his gun and you." Theodore smiled at her. "I'm glad I saved you. You are a good person."

She bit her lip and looked away.

He wondered if she had taken some of his money. There was something she'd done that calling her a good person made her uneasy.

"I-I went through your pack. I found the letters. I wasn't sure if you would live or not so I mailed them, even though you said you would be dead when they received them." She looked away and then peered into his eyes. "I wrote on them that you saved my life and were in this hospital."

Theodore stared at her not knowing how he felt. He'd managed since his escape to live without family. He wasn't sure if he wanted to meet them or even hang around and find out if they came to see him after getting his letters.

If the bullet hadn't nicked his heart, this little bit of news was enough to start a crack he wasn't sure would heal.

7

UNEXPECTED SURPRISE

Theodore was feeling better. He'd healed from the bullet wound and had begun visiting with Wendy on Saturdays for lunch at a deli not far from where she lived. He'd learned she'd moved to the big city from a small province in northern Canada. Her family were all still back there and she missed having someone to visit with on the weekends.

This Saturday Theodore was already seated at their favorite table next to the window when Wendy hurried into the deli. She sat with a flourish and her smile spread the width of her face as her eyes danced with excitement.

"Guess what?" she said in a singsong voice.

He smiled. "What?"

"You have a letter." She slid a white envelope across the table toward him.

"Why would you have a letter for me?" he asked, picking it up and seeing the return address. Pendleton, Oregon. His hands shook as he tried to read the name. Dela Seaver. Dela was the name of his daughter but where had the Seaver come from?

"Well? Are you going to open it or just stare at it all day?" Wendy sat across from him, her chin cupped in her hands.

"You read my letters and know what I was in jail for and what I did. What do you think my daughter will have to say to me?" He studied her. Expecting to see her happy expression disappear.

She grinned and tapped the letter. "I'm thinking that she is proud of you for finding that awful person and taking care of him and for saving a girl you didn't know." She took the letter from him. "Do you want me to open it?"

He grabbed it back. "No."

His fingers trembled as he ripped the envelope open and pulled out a piece of paper.

His eyes started watering at the first words.

Dear Father,

I was so happy to get your letter. Heath, my husband, and I have been trying to figure out what happened all those years ago. I'm happy to know you are alive and that you wanted to reach out to your family. Grandfather Thunder, your father, was stunned at what you told him. Heath and I had guessed that was what happened from the information we dug up.

Mom, well, she is stunned and happy that you weren't the man she saw that night. She is married. The man is good to her. She spent my childhood alone and I'm happy she has found someone to make her happy. I'd be lying if I didn't say, I wished it was you.

Heath and I would like to come to Ottawa and see you. Let me know if that is okay. I don't want to intrude if you prefer to keep your distance.

Write us soon so we can get time off if you'd like to see us.

Love,

Your daughter, Dela.

Tears slid down his cheeks as he reread the letter. He raised his gaze to Wendy and said, "She wants to come see me."

Wendy swiped at the tears glistening in the corners of her eyes and said, "Of course she does. You need to write her back and tell her to come as soon as she can. You two need to get caught up."

He grasped Wendy's hand. "Thank you for bringing my daughter to me."

She smiled and said, "I think our paths crossing was meant to be. You have found your family again and I've gained a friend."

"It's how we navigate the tough times that bring us to the good times." Theodore believed that even more than he had over fifty years ago when he boarded a bus to join the Army.

ABOUT THE AUTHOR

Paty Jager is an award-winning author of 60 + novels, 11 novellas, and numerous anthologies of murder mystery and western romance. All her work has Western or Native American elements, along with hints of humor and engaging characters.

Paty and her husband raise alfalfa hay in rural eastern Oregon. Riding horses and battling rattlesnakes, she not only writes the western lifestyle, she lives it. She is a member of Sisters in Crime, Author's Guild, Alliance of Independent Authors, and NIWA. https://www.patyjager.net

---

INSPIRATION FOR THE STORY

This short story is the culmination of a subplot in my Spotted Pony Casino Mystery series. The main character believes the truth about her father has been kept from her and, throughout the series, she digs to find out what happened to him. This short story is his story about why he isn't in her life.

JAMBOREE JEALOUSY

A MUSICAL GETAWAY.
A BUDDING SINGER.
A BAFFLING MURDER.

KIMILA KAY

Published by

Windtree Press, Corvallis, Oregon

https://windtreepress.com

"Everything in life has some risk, and you have to learn how to navigate it."
Reid Hoffman

CHAPTER ONE

The longer he drove, the more pissed off he became. "We've debated this issue to death, and I'm ready to move on," he said as he sped along the highway. "And why the hell do we need to meet after dark on this dirt road outside of Sweet Home?"

Did they know this was a special spot for him? Well, this was the last time he'd cave into this annoying individual's demands.

He turned onto the dusty single-lane road and parked his GMC across from a red Ford F-150. He ran a hand over his face and stepped out of his truck. After finger-combing his hair, he settled his hat onto his head. Even though the sun had set, the air smelled stale, and sweat coated his skin from the sweltering August heat. He wished he'd taken time to change out of his jeans and western shirt, but hopefully, he'd be back at his trailer soon. He could almost taste the cold Coors he planned to enjoy after a shower.

"I'm here," he said, walking toward a backlit individual standing before the Ford's headlights. "Say what you need to because I'm not staying long."

Silence. He imagined the anger he'd seen earlier flashing in light green eyes.

"Look," he tried a softer tone, "I know this has been difficult. But what's done is done, and there's nothing more to discuss."

"You're right."

He didn't see the gun until the bright muzzle flash. He automatically threw up his hands as if he could ward off the bullet. When it slammed into his chest, he stumbled backward, falling to the ground, his hat slipping from his head. He tried to speak, but the coppery taste of blood filled his mouth, and all he could do was stare up at the stars.

"Now." A shadow fell over him; the gun was still aimed in his direction. "I'm done talking."

He tried to call out. Beg for help. Ask why.

But he couldn't speak. The stars seemed closer now, almost as if he could reach out and touch them. Before falling into an abyss, his last thought was … will I get to be an angel among the stars, or am I headed straight for hell?

CHAPTER TWO

Harley Harper sipped Bailey's and coffee, enjoying the cool morning air flowing through the open windows. She thought she detected a hint of fresh-cut grass and bacon riding the breeze. Occasionally, someone would wave as they walked by the front of the motorhome she and Wyatt stayed in for the Oregon Jamboree.

Wyatt had experienced a few hard weeks trying to solve a couple of difficult cases, which left little time for the two of them. Harley understood the demands of Wyatt's job and welcomed the opportunity to get away with her sheriff for a long weekend. After Harley fed her menagerie and settled Dyani and Cooper into her house, they headed for Sweet Home, arriving mid-morning yesterday.

The kickoff party for Jamboree was last night, and they danced until the final band finished playing. The party continued when they returned to camp. Harley doubted Wyatt would be up anytime soon since he'd enjoyed too many shots of whiskey with Britt, Harrison, and Derrick. Britt had been the one to make all the arrangements for the weekend, including finding RVs for all of them.

Harley glanced across their camp at Busy's motorhome and smiled. Busy had branched out of her usual champagne-drinking zone and tried peanut butter whiskey. The last thing she'd said before her second shot was, "I think I'm going to regret this in the morning."

Harley and Ella were the last two standing and had tidied the camp. When she joined Wyatt in bed, he didn't wake but instinctively wrapped her in his arms, where she drifted off to sleep.

Her phone chimed, and she smiled at the message.

Wyatt: *Come back to bed Ms. Harper*

Harley set her cup on the counter and eased open the pocket door separating the bedroom from the main area of the motorhome. Wyatt lay propped up on pillows, a grin curving his lips.

"I'd like to show you how sorry I am for passing out last night." He tossed the bedding aside.

Harley lifted her cowboy print cotton pajama top over her head and stepped out of her shorts.

Wyatt sucked in air and reached for her when she sat on the edge of the bed. He pulled her against him and covered her lips with his. Harley twined her fingers into his curly hair, returning his kisses with urgency.

He released her lips and guided her onto her back. "How can you be so beautiful first thing in the morning?"

"I think you're still drunk, Sheriff." Harley laughed.

"The only thing I'm drunk on right now is you, us." Wyatt placed a warm hand on her stomach. "And knowing we don't have to leave the RV until the first concert at one."

"Gosh," Harley batted her eyes, "whatever shall we do with our time?"

"I have a few ideas." He lowered his lips to her breasts.

Harley moaned and held him to her. As much as she was interested in listening to the concerts and learning about up-and-coming country music artists, she seriously could stay in this bed with this man forever.

Wyatt found her lips again and caressed her stomach, his hand drifting lower as she squirmed beneath his touch.

"I love you, Harley."

"I love you, too," she mumbled against his lips.

Wyatt moved on top of her, his blue eyes probing hers as she lifted her hips to meet him. He moved down her body and covered a nipple.

"Wyatt." She pulled on his shoulders.

"Be still, Ms. Harper." He kissed her torso, leaving a trail of fire as he moved toward her bikini line.

A knock thudded against the RV door, and Wyatt looked at her. He winked and returned his lips to her stomach.

"Sheriff Stone," a voice called.

"I'm not the sheriff in this town." He grinned.

His phone buzzed, bringing a frown to his handsome face.

Wyatt's "Damn it!" blended with Harley's "No!"

He checked his phone. "It's Derrick." He shook his head. "My cousin has the worst timing."

Harley covered herself with the sheet and watched Wyatt pull on his Levi's.

"Don't move." He leaned down and kissed her, then headed for the RV door.

She ignored his command and popped out of bed, wrapping herself in the blue cotton button down he'd hung on a hook. Harley stepped into the main area and saw Derrick standing with a deputy she didn't know.

"What is it?" Wyatt asked his cousin.

"This is Deputy Collins." Derrick pointed at the man. "And he needs our help."

"Why can't Sheriff Gibbs handle the matter?"

"He's had a heart attack, sir," Collins said. "And—"

"There's been a murder," Derrick interrupted. "And we're tagging in."

CHAPTER THREE

Wyatt followed Derrick and Deputy Collins into a clearing where another Linn County deputy stood next to the victim. He couldn't believe how hot it was at nine in the morning, which didn't bode well for an already decomposing body. The air still smelled fresh, with a honey-like aroma emanating from the purple butterfly bush standing tall at the edge of the clearing.

When they drew near, a man dressed as Woody from the Disney movie *Toy Story* turned and faced them. He smiled and walked in their direction.

"Deputy Derrick Stone from Stone County Sheriff's Department," Woody extended his hand, "Thanks for coming to my crime scene."

Derrick shook the man's hand, then pointed at Wyatt. "Jered, this is my cousin, Sheriff Wyatt Stone." Wyatt shook Jered's hand, too. "Wyatt, Jered is a friend of Imogene's."

Realizing Derrick's friend was also autistic, albeit in a slightly different way, Wyatt could see why the two had become friends. His Woody costume included a yellow, long-sleeved button-down shirt with red striping. His vest was black and white cow print, and he'd accessorized with a red bandana and a fake metal sheriff's badge. He'd added a well-worn cowboy hat, which made the outfit seem like his usual attire. Wyatt wondered how Jered didn't look like he was melting since Wyatt was hot in his blue Stone County Sheriff's T-shirt, which Derrick insisted he bring for the weekend.

"Nice to meet you, Sheriff Stone." Jered ended the handshake quickly, tilting his head. "You look like Kurt Russell in *Tombstone* only—"

"Younger," Derrick interjected.

"Right." Woody nodded and turned toward the body. "This is Deputy Erickson, who has contained the crime scene."

"Sheriff." Erickson gave Wyatt a nod. "I checked the victim's wallet, and his driver's license says Booker Ranger." He handed Wyatt the license.

"He's known around the local country music scene as Bo," Woody added.

Derrick lifted his Stone County ball cap, smoothed his bangs, and placed the hat backward on his head.

"Looks like a single gunshot wound to the chest." Derrick crouched close to the body.

"I'm guessing small caliber." Jered squatted on the other side and pointed to the wound. "And the blood pool suggests he was killed here, not dumped."

Derrick looked at Woody and nodded. Wyatt watched them assess the body. He knew Derrick needed to complete the task before the coroner arrived. Wyatt scanned the area and walked toward the other deputies, who stood a few feet away.

"Sheriff." Deputy Collins offered him a bottle of water. "There are two sets of tire tracks, which probably belong to large trucks."

"Two sets?" Wyatt looked at the impressions, then glanced around the area as if he'd missed an extra vehicle.

"Yes," Erickson nodded. "But they have the same tread, so it could be difficult to identify the vehicles."

"Maybe someone drove our Vic—" Wyatt began.

"Then one kills him before the two drivers leave the scene." Derrick shook his head as he stood next to Wyatt. "Doubtful."

"Maybe," Collins glanced at the body, "our killer found a way to drive away both trucks."

"More likely," Woody said.

"We'll have the crime techs cast the tracks anyway." Deputy Erickson added. "They might find a match."

Wyatt sipped some cool water. "Did you search the area for spent shell casings?"

"Yes, sir." Erickson nodded. "Since it looks like the victim only has one entry wound, I scoured the ground around the body."

"Do a wider search," Derrick instructed, glancing around the area. "One entry wound doesn't mean the killer only fired one shot."

Erickson cut his eyes to Derrick and then returned his gaze to Wyatt. He could tell the deputy wasn't used to another deputy barking orders.

"Do you have a metal detector?" Wyatt asked. "It would help with your search."

"Not with me." Erickson shook his head.

"I have a detector." Jered marched toward an old beater truck.

"He drives?" Wyatt asked Derrick.

"Yes, hence the rent-a-wreck Dodge," Derrick grinned, "and just locally."

"While I review the body," Wyatt said to Derrick. "Can you and the other deputies expand the crime scene tape?"

"Yes." Derrick turned to Erickson and Collins. "Do you have additional tape?"

"In my trunk." Erickson walked in the direction of his patrol car.

"I can run the metal detector as you expand the crime scene," Jered said to Derrick.

"Jered—" Wyatt began.

"I prefer Deputy Woody, Sheriff." The would-be deputy grinned at him.

"I can follow Woody with my phone and take pictures of anything we find." Derrick looked at Wyatt with intense blue eyes, which indicated his cousin was focused. It could also mean he was on the verge of a manic episode due to overstimulation.

"Derrick." Wyatt chose his words carefully. "If you and Woody man the detector, then Collins can snap photos should you uncover any evidence." He looked at Collins, who nodded, indicating he understood the importance of controlling the chain of evidence should they find anything.

"I can string the tape as we widen the search area," Erickson added.

"Copy, Chief." Derrick gave a small salute.

Wyatt made a mental note to report to Sheriff Gibbs how professional and courteous his deputies were, given the unique situation they found themselves in. Once the quartet set off on their metal hunt, Wyatt focused on the dead man lying in the withering field grass.

He appeared to be between five feet ten and six feet tall. He wore a dark blue, short-sleeved western shirt and Wranglers with black cowboy boots. Wyatt didn't see a cowboy hat, which seemed odd since his dark hair had a crease from his hat band. Maybe the killer was familiar with cowboy hat etiquette, which dictated that a hat was never placed on a flat surface, especially not the ground. Ranger still had a pair of sunglasses tucked into his shirt pocket.

Protocol prohibited searching the pockets of a murder victim, even though Deputy Erickson had removed the wallet. They'd have to wait for the medical examiner's office to make an inventory to determine if their victim had a phone.

Wyatt noticed Ranger's eyes were still open, and his lips were parted as if he wanted to say something. The bullet wound was almost center mass but had entered to the left. Woody's guess that the weapon was small caliber suggested the killer used a .22 revolver, which could be deadly at close range.

As much as he hated that a murder had interrupted his time with Harley, Wyatt knew that since Sheriff Gibbs was out of commission, the burden of solving this crime would fall to him and Derrick.

And finding a killer in a town of ten thousand plus residents was about to be exacerbated by the twelve thousand plus visitors attending the Oregon Jamboree this weekend.

CHAPTER FOUR

"Har Har." Busy knocked on the RV door. "I'm in serious need of coffee, and Harrison is still asleep on the couch in my traveling abode."

"I'm in the bedroom," Harley called.

"Oh, thank God," Busy said from the small kitchen. "You have Bailey's."

Harley slipped on a cream-colored sundress decorated with large sunflowers. She bought the dress to match her new boots, which also featured sunflowers in the soft leather. Harley sashayed into the kitchen, where Busy sat at the small dinette table with coffee and a marionberry scone.

"If Frankie ever leaves Wyatt," she swallowed a bite, "I'm going to steal her away so I can always have these on hand."

Annoyed her bestie hadn't noticed her outfit, Harley twirled across the small floor.

"Har Har." Busy pointed at her. "You look fabulous." She touched her forehead with the back of her hand. "I'm so hungover I didn't notice at first."

"It's okay." Harley poured herself a cup of coffee and added a dollop of Bailey's, a creamy vanilla scent rising on a swirl of steam.

"Where's your handsome sheriff?" Busy tilted her head.

"Derrick came for him an hour ago." Harley sat across from Busy. "There's been a murder."

"What?" Busy's perfectly shaped eyebrows arched across her forehead. "During Jamboree?"

Harley nodded and sipped some coffee.

"You're worried this weekend will be like the last three weeks, right?" Busy reached across and touched her arm.

"Maybe." Harley shrugged. "And I think he's still working the Olson murder with Derrick but doesn't want me to know."

"I thought Spencer and Blake were investigating the missing gold along with the old guy's death." Busy stood and refilled her cup.

"Yes," Harley smiled, "but you know there's no way the Stone boys aren't going to keep each other in the loop."

"Good morning, ladies," Harrison said as he stepped inside. "Sister dear, Busy texted you have coffee *and* Bailey's."

"Have you two never been camping?" Harley laughed.

"Seriously, Har Har." Busy giggled. "You know my version of camping is a suite at a five-star hotel."

Harrison leaned against the small counter and blew on his cup before taking a sip. "Are we really going to sit in this heat and listen to music?"

"That's the plan." Harley nodded. "But you might want to rethink your outfit."

"What?" He looked down at his long-sleeved button-down. "Busy said to dress like a cowboy."

"I packed him some tanks and shorts, so he doesn't die of heat stroke." Busy winked at Harley.

"Oh, thank God," her little brother said. "I thought you two were trying to kill me with the heat, the suffocating clothing, and all the drinking last night."

The three laughed until Busy dashed to the bathroom before peeing her pants.

"We can start with the bands on the park stage where there's shade and cold beer." Harley stood. "And if we need to take a break, we can return to camp and soak our feet in the wading pool since we can kind of hear the music on the main stage from here."

"Okay, kids, I'm going to need a shower before changing," Busy said as she placed her cup into the sink. "Although I don't know why since I'll be a sweaty mess before we leave camp."

"Are we going to wake the newlyweds or leave them a note?" Harrison said around a mouthful of scone as he took Busy's seat.

"If they're not up by the time we're ready to leave, I'll write a note." Harley stood and poured coffee into her cup.

"I'll be ready in thirty." Busy bounded down the RV steps.

"Text when you're decent, and I'll change, too," Harrison called after her. He grinned at Harley when she resumed her seat.

"What?" She raised an eyebrow.

"I'm glad you two are back to your adorable best-friend status." He tipped up his cup.

"Nothing will ever keep us from being besties." Harley popped a bite of scone into her mouth.

"Not even Morgan Grey?" Harrison held her stare.

"Busy was going through a rough time, and I overreacted." Harley crossed her arms.

"Still …" Harrison leaned back in his chair.

"Is this because we asked you not to bring Monica to our functions for a while?" Harley narrowed her eyes.

"No." He held up his hands. "She's dating someone who resides in the great state of Oregon instead of twenty-seven hundred miles away in New York, so I doubt I'll see her this trip."

"Are you heartbroken?" Harley smiled.

"No, ma'am." Harrison shook his head. "I'm hoping to lasso me a young filly while I'm here at this shindig," he said in a fake southern drawl.

Harley laughed. "Well, cowboy, let's start with a few beers, then maybe you'll be ready."

Her phone chimed, and she looked at the screen.

Busy: *Decent*

"Busy's ready if you want to change." Harley walked to the front of the RV.

"We'll meet you outside in ten." Harrison gave a small wave as he left.

"Sounds good." Harley plucked a notepad and pen from a basket.

Her phone chimed again, and she crossed back to the dinette table.

Britt: *Ella and I are in park and have a picnic table close to stage*

Harley: *Perfect. On our way*

She tidied the kitchen and put the lid back on the container of scones. Then, she checked her outfit in the mirror on the wall behind the dinette table. If Harrison was going to wear shorts and a tank, she should probably dress more casually, too.

Harley twirled, loving how the flared skirt danced around her legs. Maybe her handsome sheriff would show up before the night's end and spin her across the dance floor next to the beer garden.

"A girl can hope." Harley tucked her hair behind her ears, grabbed her hat, and headed outside.

"The state crime techs and the medical examiner should be here in thirty," Derrick said as he and Woody stood beside Wyatt.

He nodded and looked toward Deputies Erickson and Collins. Erickson had stripped to his white T-shirt, and Collins mopped sweat from his neck with a yellow bandana. The three deputies and Woody had scoured the expanded area and cordoned off the large crime scene with tape. Unfortunately, Woody's metal detector found no shell casings or other evidence.

"It's not the first time we've worked a murder without any obvious clues," Derrick said as if he had read Wyatt's mind.

"True." Wyatt nodded. Salty sweat dripped from his mustache into his mouth, and he fingered away the moisture. "But we aren't on familiar ground, so I'm worried we might miss something."

Erickson and Collins joined them, and Collins said, "Sheriff Gibbs' wife called, and he's scheduled for surgery to repair his mitral valve."

"Which means he's in the hospital for five to seven days," Derrick said.

"And he's looking at six to eight weeks of healing, not to mention—" Woody added.

"At least three to four months for a full recovery," Derrick finished their medical report.

"All right." Wyatt lifted his hat and ran a hand through his hair. "Here's how I'd like to proceed." He looked at their expectant faces. "Derrick, can you and Woody stay to answer any questions the techs might have?"

"Sheriff," Erickson raised a hand, "I think Collins and I should stay."

"Explain." Wyatt tilted his head.

"I'm guessing you'd like to start questioning the people in the music community who knew Ranger," Erickson continued. "And, well, Woody's dialed into the artists. They're more likely to talk if he's with you."

Wyatt looked at Derrick as Woody bumped his cousin's shoulder. The duo, their eyes bright with excitement, wore wide grins. He shifted his attention back to the other two deputies. "You're sure?"

"Yes," Collins said, and Erickson nodded. "It's the call Sheriff Gibbs would make if he were here."

"Okay," Wyatt said. "Text me your numbers so we can stay in touch."

Erickson thumbed the keypad on his phone.

"Do you want to meet at the station later this afternoon?" Collins asked.

"There isn't much more we can do until we have the ME's preliminary report." Wyatt looked at his watch. "Let's meet at the station in the morning. What time do you usually arrive?"

"Reta, our office manager, gets in at seven AM."

"We'll be there at nine." Derrick headed for Wyatt's truck.

"I'll meet you at the Jamboree's main entrance." Woody followed Derrick.

"How about I text you when we're on our way in the morning?" Wyatt extended his hand to Erickson and then Collins.

"Sounds good, Sheriff," Erickson said. "We'll text you if the crime scene techs find something we missed."

"Copy." Wyatt gave a thumbs up, walked to his truck, and sat behind the wheel. He cranked the engine and began to back up. He looked at Woody's beater and saw he, too, was moving backward.

"Stop!" Derrick commanded and popped out of the passenger side.

Woody stopped, too, and jumped out of his truck. He raced to the passenger side and removed his metal detector. By the time Wyatt joined them, Woody was already scanning the area.

"We didn't check the ground under the vehicles," Derrick said, his tone an octave higher than usual. "We'll need the deputies to move their patrol cars, too."

Wyatt glanced toward Erickson and Collins, who'd already figured out what Woody was doing. Woody's search didn't turn up anything from the ground where their trucks were parked.

Woody and Derrick headed toward the deputies and began scanning the area. Wyatt leaned against his truck hood, waiting to see if they produced any results. A high-pitched tone echoed across the field, and he headed toward them.

Woody held the detector over a clump of dandelions, and Derrick was on his knees, combing through the dry weeds. White seed pods, accompanied by a bitter-sweet aroma, floated skyward. After a few minutes, he raised his hand, a large gold-plated hoop earring dangling from a pen.

CHAPTER SIX

Britt waved at them as they weaved their way through the crowd of festival goers who'd had the same idea—find a shady spot to enjoy a cold beer and listen to great music.

"Hi," he said. "I heard Wyatt and Derrick caught a case." Britt looked at Harley.

"Yes." Harley nodded. "They stepped in since the sheriff had a heart attack."

"I'm sure Wyatt will try to wrap up the case quickly." Doubt darkened his brown eyes. "Can I get you guys something to drink?"

"I want whatever Ella is drinking because it's on ice." Busy fanned herself with the Jamboree program and slid onto the bench of the cement picnic table.

"It's a mango White Claw," Ella lifted her glass, "and it's very refreshing."

"I'll get us a round," Harrison said as he headed for the closest bar.

"Harley, your dress is so cute," Ella said as Harley sat across from her.

"Thanks." Harley smoothed the soft cotton. "I love how the sunflowers match my new boots, but maybe cutoffs and a tank would've been cooler."

"I don't think what you wear in this heat matters." Busy used a tissue to mop sweat from her brow. She wore a pink tank with spaghetti straps and a distressed denim skort.

"Here we go." Harrison placed their drinks in the middle of the table. "I chose a cold, crisp Coors Light for myself." He sat in a chair at the end of the picnic table.

"Oh, this is good!" Busy said. "But I think it's raspberry, not mango."

"Yes." Harrison smiled. "I got one of each."

"Hey, Jammers!" A slim blonde yelled into a mic. "Are you ready for the festival's first act on our Park Stage?"

The crowd in front of the stage roared with excitement.

"Please give a warm Oregon Jamboree welcome to Blue Suede Boots from Molalla, Oregon!" The blonde clapped her way off stage, and the band members fanned out to their instruments.

A tall, lanky singer strummed a guitar, then, after a few notes, launched into a song about cold beer, hot women, and partying by a creek. The song was upbeat, and despite the sweltering after-noon heat, people danced in front of the stage, and others clapped in time to the music.

Dancing in her seat, Busy watched Britt twirl Ella across the grass.

"I wish I'd taken dance lessons for this kind of music instead of learning to waltz," Harrison said, smiling at Harley. Her cheeks colored at the memory of Noel Vincent trying to teach her and Busy how to do the Boot Scootin' Boogie line dance. Busy had been a natural, but Harley had two left feet.

"It took me a few lessons." Harley laughed. "But the dances are fun once you learn the steps."

"Sorry, Wyatt isn't here to spin you around in your pretty dress." Harrison touched her cup with his beer can.

Harley took a sip and tried not to compare Wyatt's absence now to how much he'd been gone during July. She knew he loved his job and the challenge of solving each crime to give the victims justice. She didn't doubt his love for her, but she'd spent more than one night frustrated that she'd been relegated to the back burner—and at times, it felt like she wasn't even on the damn stove.

"Come on, Har Har." Busy took her by the hand. "Let's get another drink and go stand by the stage."

"You too, baby brother," Harley said as Busy dragged her toward the bar.

Harrison motioned for Britt and Ella to join them and followed Harley. The gang filed into line to wait for their turn. With new drinks, everyone walked to the edge of the crowd. Busy held a hand in the air and pointed to center stage. As if she were the Pied Piper, they followed her into the throng of fans.

The music was much louder, and Harley couldn't hear anything but the singer. She felt the deep rhythm of the bass guitar vibrating in her chest. She swayed to the beat and sipped her drink. Scanning the crowd, she spotted Britt and Ella dancing slowly to the music. A flicker of jealousy warmed Harley's cheeks. Busy took Harrison's hand and led him to the middle of the gyrating crowd.

Harley turned her attention back to the stage and blinked to ensure she wasn't seeing things. Derrick stood with another man who looked like a cartoon character dressed in a colorful cowboy outfit. Harley could tell the interesting cowboy did most of the talking since his audience nodded occasionally. Derrick appeared to be taking notes, but Harley could tell he also asked questions. Her heart fluttered when Wyatt stepped into view and stood behind Derrick and his friend. She wanted to walk behind the stage and talk to him, but she knew he'd be focused on his job.

Harley looked at Britt and Ella dancing near Busy and Harrison and decided she needed another drink. She pushed through the crowd and walked toward the bar. A blend of citrusy hops and fermented yeast, blended with the tangy aroma of barbecue ribs from the food booth on the other side of the bar.

A hand intercepted her elbow and pulled her behind the refrigerated car, which held kegs of beer for the bar.

Wyatt wrapped her in his arms and kissed her. "You look stunning in that dress, Ms. Harper," he whispered against her lips and kissed her again.

When he let her up for air, Harley laughed and said, "Why, thank you, Sheriff."

"Sorry, I got called away this morning." He touched the edge of her dress, his fingers brushing the top of her breasts.

"Me too." She pressed her hips into his.

"Derrick, Woody, and I are interviewing artists, their crews, and other personnel involved in the festival."

"Woody?" Harley tilted her head. "As in the character from *Toy Story*?"

"Yes." Wyatt smiled. "It's a long *story*, but Derrick's girlfriend, Imogene, introduced them."

"Maybe I can wait up for you to hear about your day." Harley palmed his ass.

"If you wait up for me, I doubt we'll do any talking." He kissed her again.

"Wyatt!" Derrick called across the short distance separating them.

"See you soon, Ms. Harper." Wyatt placed his hands on her face and kissed her deeply.

"Go do your job, Sheriff." Harley smiled.

He kissed her forehead, then walked toward Derrick and his sidekick, Woody.

yatt looked back at Harley, drink in hand, moving through the crowd to where the others waited. He hated being drawn into this case, which took him away from her. However, it was a law enforcement courtesy to help whenever possible, especially since he represented the neighboring county. He also hated that someone might get away with murder.

"Sheriff Stone, this is Betty Jo Boxer," Derrick pointed at a petite brunette dressed in distressed Wranglers, black boots, and a sleeveless black blouse.

Betty extended her hand, which Wyatt shook. "Pleasure except for the circumstances." She shook her head. "Bo was a good guy most of the time."

"He was an arrogant prick who couldn't carry a tune," Woody scoffed.

"That's true, too." Betty laughed. "It didn't affect me, but he used his good looks and charm to woo the younger females." She looked around the backstage area. "I believe he's seeing Inez Ingrams." Betty nodded in the direction of a pretty young redhead.

"Instagram?" Woody shook his head. "We call her *Instagram*

because she's a serial poster," he explained. "She's moved on and is seeing a guy who works at the KeyBank in town."

"Smart girl." Betty grinned. "Well, gents, that's all I know." She picked up a guitar case and placed her hat on her head. "Besides, Woody's dialed into the gossip scene better than anyone else."

"Thanks for your time, Ms. Boxer," Wyatt said.

"If I think of anything else," she touched Wyatt's shoulder, "I'll be sure to call you personally."

His cheeks warmed, and he tipped his hat before she sashayed toward the path leading backstage.

"Everyone will return to the main concert area for the next act." Woody turned and followed Betty Jo. "It's difficult to get backstage, so I think we should go to the artist campground to conduct further interviews."

Wyatt exchanged a look with Derrick, who grinned. "He's the one dialed in, so I guess we follow his lead."

Wyatt looked across the stage at the crowd still dancing to the music. He didn't see Harley at first, then spotted her laughing as Harrison attempted to twirl her but lost his grip. She stumbled backward, and a tall cowboy grabbed her waist, preventing her from falling to the ground.

A wisp of jealousy sent a wave of heat coursing through his veins, and he fought the urge to march through the crowd to rescue Harley from the man's clutches.

"Wyatt?" Derrick held his hands palms up. "Coming?"

Wyatt glanced at Harley again, then trudged after Derrick and Woody. Maybe Woody's connection to this crowd would help speed up their investigation, and Wyatt could join his beautiful partner on the dance floor soon. He smiled at her effort to learn country dances to surprise him as one of their alphabet dates. Wyatt had to admit the alphabet dating was a brilliant idea and felt it brought him and Harley closer.

Their trek through the festival goers was slow as Woody stopped to say hi to his fan club and have his picture taken. They finally reached a gate where two security guards stood in the shade of a canopy.

"Hey, Woody," one of the guards greeted them. "Who are you planning to visit this time?"

"Underhill." Woody's tone sounded official. "I'm here with Sheriff Stone and Deputy Derrick to investigate a murder."

Underhill nodded, then looked at Wyatt. "Do the Jamboree officials know you want to speak with the artists?"

Wyatt didn't want to disrespect the security guard, but he didn't need permission to speak with anyone willing to answer a few questions.

"Is Frankie Lacey here?" Wyatt smiled at Underhill.

"I'm afraid I don't know, Sheriff." Underhill looked at Woody, then back at Wyatt. "Is she in some kind of trouble?"

"No," Wyatt shook his head, "she works for me, and I wanted to say hello."

"She's staying with Ryan Reed." Woody jammed his hands onto his hips. "Is Barb Williams here?"

"Barb," the other security guard said into a radio. "Woody's asking for you at the gate."

"Thanks, Knox." Woody gave the guard a head nod.

"On my way," Barb's reply echoed through the radio.

Underhill stepped closer to Knox, making room for them under the canopy. "Would you guys like a water?" He reached into a cooler and pulled out three bottles.

"Thanks." Wyatt accepted a bottle and took a drink. The cold water was startling at first. "It's a hot one today."

"And it's not cooling off at night, which doesn't help." Underhill handed the other two bottles to Derrick and Woody, then wiped sweat from his forehead with a handkerchief.

"What the tarnation is going on?" Barb stepped through the partially opened gate. "Woody?" Her light gray eyes darted from Woody to Derrick to Wyatt.

"Ms. Williams." Wyatt stepped forward and extended his hand.

"Sheriff Stone, and this is Deputy Derrick Stone. We're filling in for Sheriff Gibbs and need to speak with artists here for the festival."

"About what?" Barb completed the handshake.

"It's about Bo Ranger?" Woody stepped beside Wyatt. "He's been murdered."

"What?" Barb covered her mouth with her hand. "He's-he's dead?"

"Afraid so, ma'am." Wyatt wanted Woody to refrain from speaking, but he knew the would-be deputy had trouble remaining silent. "Can you tell us the last time you saw Mr. Ranger?"

"I guess I haven't seen him since yesterday afternoon." Barb scratched her forehead. "He was pestering me about needing a bigger space for his GMC and trailer." When she looked at Wyatt, he saw tears in her eyes. "I was pretty rude to him and said he'd have to make do with what he was assigned."

"Camp is divided by status," Woody said. "The big-name acts have bigger, premier sites, and the size shrinks as you progress down the talent ladder."

"Can we take a look at his site?" Wyatt smiled.

"Sure." She turned and walked down a grass lane rimmed with RVs on both sides. "He's the last site in this row."

Wyatt wished there were clouds for the sun to hide behind, but the picture-perfect blue sky hosted only the bright orange orb, which insisted on heating the day to broiling.

"This is his spot." Barb stopped in front of a bumper trailer.

Wyatt walked toward the entry door, and Derrick headed around the other side. The blinds on all the windows, except a small one, probably over the kitchen sink, were closed. There was a large bin overflowing with beer bottles and cans. A collection of discarded tennis shoes and boots lay next to a well-worn welcome mat. Derrick rounded the end of the trailer and moved next to Wyatt.

"No sign of life from my point of view." He glanced at the area behind them. "And no truck."

"I think I hear someone calling for help." Woody moved close to the steps under the door. "Oh wait!" He held his nose against the trailer. "Is that propane? We should break in and investigate!"

"We don't need a warrant to search the home of a deceased person." Derrick stood beside Woody. "We're taking stock of the situation to ensure we're not walking into a circumstance we were unprepared for."

"Woody." Wyatt looked at him. "Would you escort Barb across the way until we've cleared the trailer?"

"Copy, Sheriff." Woody offered Barb his arm, and the two walked across the brown grass to stand next to the other row of RVs.

"The trailer's probably empty, but we don't have weapons." Wyatt knocked on the door and called, "Sheriff's Department!" No answer.

Derrick walked away and returned with a rubber mallet and a multi-tool camping axe. He handed Wyatt the axe and nodded. Wyatt eased open the door and moved up the steps. He scanned the inside and, despite the dim lighting, could see a couch immediately in front of him. He entered, swung his gaze from the front of the trailer to the rear, and motioned for Derrick to join him.

"Look, but don't touch," Wyatt instructed. "If you see something out of place, whistle."

"Copy, Chief." Derrick headed for the small kitchen with a bathroom off to the left.

Wyatt moved right and stepped behind a wall into a bedroom with a queen bed. The bedding was balled into a heap in the middle of the mattress, and the floor was littered with clothing and more shoes. It was hard to tell among the disarray, but nothing looked out of place.

He returned to the trailer's center and joined Derrick, who was checking the almost empty fridge. A sour odor caused Derrick to wrinkle his nose.

"Ranger is a slob." Derrick closed the fridge door.

"Agreed." Wyatt noticed a pencil on the grungy carpet under a small dinette table. He picked it up and placed it next to a few pieces of paper. He fanned out the pages and read a few lines.

"Derrick." Wyatt waited for his cousin to join him. "These read like—"

"Those are the lyrics for Cash Colter's song," Woody said behind them.

"And do you know where we might find Mr. Colter?" Wyatt asked.

"She's on stage." Woody's brown eyes were wide. "And she's singing 'Finding Me' right now."

CHAPTER EIGHT

The three o'clock act was performing on the big stage when they crossed the old white, covered bridge to the main festival area. Passing a vendor who sold French fry bricks, a greasy, salty aroma made Harley's stomach rumble.

She wanted to sit in her VIP seat and enjoy the music, but the sun's relentless heat and three White Claws made her feel tipsy.

"Maybe we can find shade in the beer garden," Busy suggested, heading for the entrance.

"Buy you another drink, sister dear?" Harrison held his hand out to her.

"How about a gallon of water?" Harley gripped his hand. "Ella," Harley called after the newlyweds. "Are you two joining us?"

"We might need to—" Ella giggled when Britt picked her up and spun her around.

"Cool off in the kiddie pool at camp." Britt kissed Ella, and then they raced to the exit.

"You kids coming?" Busy yelled from the beer garden, White Claw in one hand, a cup of ice in the other.

Harley followed Harrison through the entrance.

"I'll get us some drinks." Harrison walked to the beer line.

"Get me another, too," Busy waggled her glass, "cause this will be gone by the time you get back."

"And get three bottles of water!" Harley ordered.

Harrison gave a thumbs-up and moved forward in line.

"Harley?" Frankie said as she approached them. She wore a pair of denim overalls she'd also made into cutoffs over a red, white, and blue tie-dyed tank top. "It's good to see you." She looked around. "Where's Wyatt and Derrick?"

"They caught a case." Harley kept her tone light, bundling her long hair into a clip.

"Here? In Sweet Home? Unbelievable!" Frankie shook her head. "Do you know where he is, because I need to give him a piece of my mind."

"It's okay, Frankie." Harley touched her arm. "Is this your … friend?" She smiled at the young man lurking behind Frankie.

"Oh gosh, yes!" She grabbed his hand. "This is my beau, Ryan Reed." Frankie beamed at Harley and Busy. "He's performing on Sunday as an opening act for Jordan Davis."

"It's nice to meet you, Ryan," Busy said. "Can we buy you two a drink?

Harrison joined them, juggling three drinks and two cups of ice. "A little help." He offered Harley her White Claw.

"Thanks." Harley took the slim can and cup of ice. She had a drink, and the hint of mango was sweet on her tongue. "Harrison, you remember Frankie, Wyatt's house manager?"

"Yes." He handed her the hard seltzer meant for Busy and his beer to Ryan. "It's good to see you again."

"I'm melting," Busy whined. "Let's find some shade." She headed for a large tree.

"So, you're a country singer?" Harley asked, stepping under the massive maple.

"Yes, ma'am." Ryan nodded.

"He's singing a song he wrote for me on Sunday." Frankie grinned at Ryan.

Harley noticed Ryan's hazel eyes narrowed slightly before he smiled at Frankie. Her first thought was that Ryan was hiding something, but his smile seemed genuine. *Stop playing sheriff,* her little voice scolded.

"You could come by our camp and give a little preview," Busy said. "Or we could all go back now and sit with our feet in the pool."

"We should go back for a while," Harley nodded. "I have a charcuterie board in the fridge, which we could pair with ice-cold water and cool off for a while."

"Sounds good to me." Harrison headed for the exit.

Someone's phone signaled an incoming message, and Harley instinctively checked her screen. When she looked up, she saw Ryan Reed staring at his phone.

"What is it, Babe?" Frankie asked.

"It's Peggy from Jamboree." His eyes grew round as he looked at Frankie. "She wants to know if I can fill in for Bo Ranger tonight at five."

"For Bo?" Frankie repeated. "I'm guessing he's drunk somewhere and unable to perform."

"I have to go back to camp, get ready, and be backstage by four-thirty." Ryan started to leave.

"Wait," Frankie hurried after him. "I'm coming too." She turned and waved at them. "See you guys later."

"Wyatt's case, maybe?" Harrison asked.

Harley nodded. "I bet he's investigating the murder of a country singer."

CHAPTER NINE

The news of Bo Ranger's demise spread like a slow-moving fire through the artists' camp. The perfect reaction was to feign surprise and sorrow when the tragedy was shared.

"If only people knew Bo Ranger, aka country singer imposter, had met his deserved end," the person mumbled, straightening the band's equipment.

A wave of heat flowed through them, with the memory of Bo's brown eyes growing wide when the gun was pointed at him. A smile blossomed on curved lips at the disbelief on his face as the bullet tore through his blue shirt, opening a portal to drain life from his body.

"Maybe he'll have a hit song once he's settled in hell!" The figure tossed trash into a black plastic bag, moving through the camp.

Although keeping the band's camp clean wasn't necessary, the tedious chore helped settle a case of nerves. Questions swirled in the stale afternoon air. *What were the next steps? Were the songs safe now? Or did more need to be done to ensure they weren't stolen again?*

A lot of heart and soul had been poured into the three songs, followed by hope to find a singer who would do them justice—a voice to caress the lyrics and bring them to life.

"Why couldn't Bo be happy with the song I wrote for him?" The worker stuffed a handful of barbecue potato chips into their mouth. "It was perfect for his untrained, rough cadence." The tangy mesquite flavor caused them to cough and reach for a warm beer.

Songwriting brought a measure of peace, despite having no vocal training to sing and record the songs. And when *she* showed an interest in the songs and put a melodious voice to the simple, albeit heartfelt, lyrics, it was as if the sun had shone more brightly, a glorious moment, to be sure. A hot breeze ruffled unruly bangs.

It had been a simple mistake to include the songs for her with the one written for Bo—a simple mistake that ended a life and created a killer.

CHAPTER TEN

yatt handed Derrick and Woody each a Coors Light. Woody kicked off his boots, rolled up his jeans, and immersed his feet in the cool water of the blue kiddie pool.

"This is a great idea." Woody smiled and took a long sip from his beer. "You should put your feet in, too." He pointed at Derrick's boots.

Wyatt knew Derrick considered the community pool water too dirty to join in the fun. Wyatt didn't see the point of soaking your feet either, then having to don socks and boots again when it was time to leave.

They'd tried to speak with Cash Colter after her set, but she was busy signing autographs and taking photos at the merchandise booth. Woody suggested they grab a beer in the beer garden and wait for the young singer to wrap up her meet and greet.

Wyatt decided they would be better off back at camp. He wanted a few minutes without a crowd around him to think about what they'd learned so far. And he hoped Harley would be at camp when he arrived. Wyatt glanced at Britt's trailer and smiled at the closed blinds. At least the newlyweds were enjoying themselves.

"I don't think Cash Colter is our killer," Derrick said behind him.

Wyatt turned from the ice chest and handed his cousin a fresh beer. "Explain."

"It's not because she's a female," Derrick popped the can top, "but because if she knew she was performing, she'd be focused on preparing to be on stage."

"He's got a point," Woody called from his seat. "I know Cash has a strict policy of no alcohol the night before a performance, and she goes through a pre-warm-up routine, too."

"But if Ranger did steal her song," Wyatt drank some beer, "wouldn't she want her song back before she sang it on stage?"

"Hey." Woody pulled his feet from the pool. "What if the song doesn't belong to Cash either?" He padded across the dry grass to where they stood. "Maybe she didn't write the tune, and the song's author is our killer?"

Wyatt looked at Derrick, who smiled and nodded.

"He's got a point." Derrick parroted and touched his Coors Light can to Woody's. "Do you know all the songwriters in the artist camp?"

"Yes!" Woody grinned and emptied his can. "Let's start interrogating them."

Wyatt watched as the colorful would-be deputy walked toward the road leading back to the festival venue. He looked at Derrick, who was shaking his head.

"Woody!" Derrick pointed at his friend's feet when he turned around.

Woody looked down at his rolled jeans and bare feet. "I think I'll put on my boots first." He laughed, shuffled back to a chair, and picked up his socks.

"Is tonight a good time to try to talk to people?" Wyatt looked at his watch. "How much chaos goes on before the last acts of the night perform?"

"Speaking of chaos." Derrick tilted his head toward the road.

Wyatt could hear Harley's laugh before she appeared at the entrance of their camp. He could swear it was only the two of them when she walked in. She smiled when she saw him, then ran into his arms.

Harley covered his lips with hers. He resisted grabbing her ass and holding her to him. Wyatt tasted something sweet on her lips and guessed she'd had one too many White Claws.

"Hi," Harley finally said when she freed his lips.

"Hi." Wyatt smiled, continuing to hold her in his arms. "You seem to be enjoying yourself."

"We're enjoying everything except this effing heat." Busy took a water bottle from the ice chest and plopped into a chair by the pool.

Harrison handed Harley a water, which she took without looking at her brother. "It's definitely too hot for this lily-white New Yorker." He claimed a chair, too.

"I'd tell you two to get a room." Derrick looked at them. "But we need to follow up on a lead in our case."

"You have to go?" Harley's amber eyes darkened. She freed her hair from a clip and shook out her long locks.

"Yes." Wyatt kissed her. "If I go now, though, I might be able to make the last act."

"Okay." Harley stepped from his arms, dropped her water bottle back into the cooler, and plucked a *Modelo* from the icy bath.

Wyatt took Harley's hand and looked at Derrick. "I need a few minutes if you and Woody want to head to the artist camp."

"Copy, Chief," Derrick said, motioning for Woody to follow him.

"It's nice to meet you all. Thanks for letting me use your awesome soaking pool." Woody gave a slight wave and hustled to catch up with Derrick.

Wyatt set Harley's beer can onto the small table beside the RV. He took her hand and led her inside, pulling her into his arms. The salty scent of her sun-kissed skin flowed over him.

"I know this isn't what we'd planned, but—"

Harley kissed him, then placed her hands on his chest. "It's okay, Wyatt. I know you have a job to do."

"I do, but that doesn't make being away from you any easier." Wyatt kissed her. "I will do my very best to join you for the last concert."

"I'll save you a chair," Harley winked at him. "Now go do your job, Sheriff Stone."

Wyatt kissed her forehead and left the RV. He didn't say anything to the others before walking from camp. He knew his beautiful partner might struggle with his need to solve a murder, but he also knew she respected him for doing his job and he loved her for that.

CHAPTER ELEVEN

Harley had a serious case of bitter cottonmouth. She tossed back the bedding and planted her feet on the floor. When she moved to stand, the small RV bedroom began to spin.

"Oh, God." She held her head in her hands.

"Lie back, Babe." Wyatt swept her hair aside and kissed her shoulder. "I'll get you water and ibuprofen."

"Wyatt?" Her tongue seemed too big for her mouth. "When did you get home?"

"A few hours ago." He climbed from bed and padded to the fridge.

"Damn." Harley covered her face with her hands. "I think I remember begging you to—"

"Light your fire." He settled back into bed.

She cracked an eye and found him smiling at her. "And did you? We?"

"I tucked you in like a gentleman." Wyatt kissed the top of her head. "And held you until we both drifted off to sleep."

Harley tossed the pills back and washed them down with a

swig of water. She remembered going back to the festival grounds for the last act. Clay Walker delivered a fabulous concert, and they all returned to camp. The last thing Harley remembered was toasting her missing Sheriff with a shot of Hornitos.

"I'm sorry for—" Harley began.

"Babe …" Wyatt pulled her into his arms. "We both had rough nights, so no need to apologize."

"You smell like you've showered …" She looked up at him. "Why are you dressed?" He wore jeans and a clean Stone County Sheriff's T-shirt

"Because it's morning, and I have to go soon."

"What?" Harley looked at the window across from them. "It's still dark outside."

"Blake texted to check in." Wyatt yawned. "Once I was awake, I showered, then texted Luke and Dyani."

"And everything is good in Stoneybrook?" Harley snuggled closer to him.

"Yes." He nodded. "Station's been quiet, which has given Blake and Simms a chance to bring Dyani up to speed on duties and procedures."

"I still can't believe she's one of your deputies now." Harley placed a hand on his chest.

"She earned her spot by helping us catch the snuff film killer." Wyatt stroked her bare arm.

"And our ranches?" Harley looked up at him again.

"Both places are doing well despite our absences." Wyatt grinned.

"Good." She lowered her hand to his crotch. "Are you sure you have to go?"

"Yes." His cheeks colored. "The Linn County deputies received a report of an abandoned truck at Foster Lake," Wyatt said. "Derrick and I need to check out the vehicle before it's towed to impound."

"Did you have any luck with your interviews?"

Wyatt laughed. "Well, Derrick and I didn't do much talking, but Woody managed to get a few people to share their thoughts about our victim and who might want him dead."

"Do you have time for coffee?" Harley lay on top of him. "Or something more satisfying?"

"I wish?" He kissed her. "But I'm already ten minutes late, and you know—"

His phone buzzed, and Harley laughed. "I'm guessing that's Derrick, asking when you're coming outside."

Wyatt looked at his phone and smiled before showing her the screen.

Derrick: *Outside. You're late*

"Harley …" Wyatt lifted her chin and searched her eyes. "I'm sorry I got pulled into this investigation."

"Wyatt," she touched her lips to his, then met his blue eyes, "I've started an *alphabet* list of all the ways you can make it up to me."

"I can't wait to see what creative ideas you have." He pulled her to him and kissed her as if he didn't have to leave. But his buzzing phone said otherwise.

Wyatt looked at the screen again and laughed. He handed the phone to Harley.

Derrick: *Busy wants to know why the doors locked. Harrison is snoring and she needs coffee*

CHAPTER TWELVE

The coffee maker made a gurgling sound as it began to brew, the nutty aroma of her favorite blend rising on a coil of steam. Thinking about how fun it had been last night watching Woody play detective as he talked to artists, along with the Sheriff and his deputy, brought a smile to dry lips. Woody almost looked the part, but his colorful outfit suggested he was playing a character from his favorite movie.

After Cash heard of Bo Ranger's death, the singer had cried nonstop. Thrilled when Cash had accepted the proverbial shoulder to cry on, she'd held her close, inhaling the floral scent of Cash's shampoo.

Being questioned along with Cash and her band members initially made being vague easy. But when Sheriff Stone asked who wrote "Finding Me," sweat bloomed on Max's forehead.

Another sip of coffee as the memory of the conversation played again as if on a mental loop.

"Max brought us the song, which a friend wrote." Cash smiled at Max.

"What's the songwriter's name?" Woody asked Max.

"Um …" she shuffled her feet. "Pres-Presley Parker."

"Is Ms. Parker here at Jamboree?" the deputy sheriff asked.

"Um …" *Kind of,* she thought, hoping her face didn't reveal the truth. She was Presley Parker. She'd written three songs for Cash. She'd killed Bo Ranger.

"Max?" Cash touched her shoulder. "Do you know if Presley is here?"

"No." She shook her head. "I mean, no, she didn't come to Jam this year."

"Do you have her contact information?" Sheriff Stone asked.

Max instinctively checked her shorts' pockets for her two phones. She'd bought a burner so she could pose as her pseudonym, and she relaxed, finding only her iPhone.

"Yes." Max nodded. "I can write it down for you."

"That would be great, Max." Woody smiled at her. "I can walk with you to your trailer."

She hesitated, then said. "Sure."

"I'm still learning to play guitar." He strummed an air guitar. "Maybe I'll write a song someday, too."

"It's harder than you think," Max said before catching herself. "I mean, that's what Presley told me."

"Maybe you and I can write a song together." Woody grinned. "Two creative minds are better than one, right?" He tapped the side of his head with a finger.

Max nodded and opened the door to her trailer. She didn't want to discuss songwriting with Woody for fear of indicating she was Presley Parker. Woody followed her inside, and she crossed to the small dinette table.

"This is a really nice trailer." He looked around before standing beside her.

Max reached for a stack of notebooks and a cup with pens and pencils. Before she realized she'd also included her songwriting workbook, the pile spilled to the floor. In an effort to stop the cascade of papers, Max knocked over the pencil cup, making the mess worse.

"Here," Woody crouched beside her, "let me help."

"It's okay," Max said. "I've got it." She gathered the notebook and papers.

Woody placed the pens and pencils in the cup and put them on the dinette table. Max tore a blank sheet from a spiral notebook and jotted down the burner cell number. She added the post office box rented in Presley's name.

"This should be all the sheriff needs to reach Presley." Max handed Woody the piece of paper.

"Thanks." He glanced at the floor, then bent to pick up a few more pages.

Max recognized the loose paper and swooped in before Woody to pick them up. When they both stood, she thought she saw a questioning look in his brown eyes.

"Oh, geez." Max looked at the clock above the stove. "I'm needed backstage."

"Right." Woody nodded and smiled. "I'll make sure Sheriff Stone gets this information." He exited the trailer, waving the paper with the information.

The coffee maker chimed, bringing her back to the present. Max poured a cup and sat at the dinette. She fanned out the pages for "Navigate," the second song she'd written for Cash.

"I hope Deputy Woody didn't connect the dots, realizing dowdy Maxine Cotton is also the brilliant songwriter Presley Parker." She took a bite of a buttery shortbread cookie, then sipped some coffee. "I'd hate to kill my friend to keep him quiet."

She smiled at the pages containing her lyrics, singing her favorite part aloud, "I left a trail your heart could navigate. Prayed you'd find me before it was too late."

CHAPTER THIRTEEN

yatt and Derrick pulled into the day-use area of Lewis Creek Park at Foster Lake. The parking lot had quite a few cars for the early morning hour. Wyatt suspected the lake was full of boats and fishermen hoping to land the catch of the day.

"Did you text Woody?" Wyatt parked next to Woody's blue Dodge.

"No." Derrick shook his head. "I'm guessing word of Bo Ranger's truck being located spread through the artist camp."

Wyatt stepped from his Silverado, inhaling the fresh, earthy scent carried on a breeze blowing across the lake's calm waters. He followed Derrick to where Ranger's GMC was parked. Both Linn County deputies stood next to the abandoned vehicle.

"Sheriff," Deputy Erickson said as they approached. "The tow truck is on its way."

"Copy." Wyatt nodded, watching as Derrick began to circle the truck. "Any idea if the deceased's vehicle has been here since the night of the murder?"

"Yes," Woody said behind them. He had a coffee in one hand

and a chocolate-covered donut in the other. "I spoke with the store clerk," he pointed with the donut, "and she said she noticed the truck here Friday morning." He took a large bite, then chased it with a drink of coffee.

"There doesn't appear to be any damage to the outside of the truck," Derrick reported as he tried the driver's door handle. "Locked."

"I didn't want to release the lock until you were here." Collins stepped next to Derrick, a Slim Jim in his hand.

Collins worked the car tool until the lock clicked. He opened the driver's side door, and Wyatt opened the passenger side. The first thing they noticed was that the driver's seat had been moved forward to the point where a man wouldn't have been able to sit behind the wheel. The second reveal was Bo Ranger's black cowboy hat lying on the crown, on the passenger seat.

Derrick looked over Collins' shoulder, with Woody angling for a better look behind him. Wyatt ran a hand under the passenger seat, finding an empty travel mug and a dirty white T-shirt. He swept the dash with a gaze, then opened the glove box. Besides the owner's manual, there was a collection of receipts and a pack of spearmint gum.

Collins opened the center console storage compartment, which contained loose coins, a handful of napkins, and scraps of paper. He looked at the pieces of paper and handed them to Derrick, who had extended his hand over Collins' shoulder.

Wyatt moved to the back seat and conducted the same search, finding nothing of any use. Woody checked the backseat on the driver's side, practically sticking his head under the front seat.

Derrick waved the pages in the air and said, "I've got something!"

Woody stood from his search, holding a gold hoop earring in a handkerchief. He flashed a broad smile and exclaimed, "Me too!"

They regrouped in front of the GMC, where Erickson was on the phone. Derrick handed Wyatt the pieces of paper, and he knew with one glance he was looking at various versions of a couple of songs. He couldn't be sure without a side-by-side comparison, but the handwriting looked similar to the song notes they'd found in Ranger's trailer.

"If these songs, along with the one we found in his trailer, were written by Presley Parker," Wyatt met his cousin's intense blue stare, "I think we need to move her to the top of our suspect list."

"Can you get DNA from an earring?" Woody wrapped the gold hoop in the handkerchief and handed the bundle to Derrick.

"No." Derrick examined a strand of blonde hair attached to the clasp. "But possibly from the hair. And if this earring matches the one from the crime scene and we can identify its owner, then—"

"We can put our killer on the dirt road with Bo Ranger," Woody finished Derrick's thought.

"Yes." Derrick smiled at his friend and nodded.

"The coroner's office called," Erickson said, getting their attention. "He confirmed the cause of death as a single gunshot wound to the heart and estimates TOD between ten and eleven PM." He looked at his small notebook. "Preliminary tox screen showed a low level of alcohol and none of the usual drugs."

"So basically, what we already suspected." Derrick opened the handkerchief and added the loose pages to the earring.

"Did the inventory show a cell phone?" Wyatt asked.

"No." Erickson smiled, and Wyatt knew a significant clue had been discovered.

"Spit it out," Collins said.

"The killer carved *Thief* into the decedent's chest next to the bullet wound."

CHAPTER FOURTEEN

Harley and Busy sat in the beer garden next to the dance floor, where an instructor taught would-be line dancers the Watermelon Crawl.

"Is it wrong to be jealous of how easy she makes the steps look?"

"No." Harley laughed. "You can tell how hard the dance is by watching Harrison."

As if he'd heard his name, her brother waved at them and promptly missed one of the turns in the dance.

"Maybe I should find a partner and learn the country swing." Busy sipped from her peach White Claw.

"I'll go with you to learn the country swing if you want?" Harley tipped up her drink.

"Which one of us will lead?" Busy grinned.

"No, silly." Harley pointed at the mob next to the dance floor. "Once you join that crowd, one of the handsome cowboys will be your partner."

"Tempting." Busy glanced at the collection of hopeful men. "But I'm not sure I want to be partnered with anyone right now."

Harley knew Busy was still hurting from her breakup with Ace.

"Are you still thinking of spending time in Manhattan this fall?" Harley hoped a different topic would reset Busy's mood.

"Harrison has made a good case for selling our apartments," Busy smiled. "And then buying one for the three of us to stay in when we're in New York."

"It could be hard to find a place right now." Harley took a drink from a water bottle. "But I'm in for my third if you find something."

"Anything to not have to stay with Esther, right?" Busy laughed.

"I don't mind staying with my mom for a night or two," Harley grinned. "But it's hard to be under your mom's roof after living on your own for so long."

"Agree." Busy nodded. "My parents have been bugging me to visit them in Florida."

"It could be a fun girls' getaway." Harley winked at her bestie.

"Ladies," Harrison said as he approached their table. "I need a beer."

"And a shower." Busy wrinkled her nose.

"Beer first." Harrison ran a hand through his sweaty dark hair and headed for the bar.

"I'm glad it's not as hot today." Harley finished her drink. "Speaking of beer," she smacked her lips, "I think I'm ready for a *Modelo*."

Busy looked at her phone. "Well, it is almost time to go back to camp for Britt and Ella's barbecue chicken dinner."

"I need to toss my macaroni salad before we eat." Harley nodded.

"And I need to make my fabulous champagne berry cocktails." Busy stood when Harrison joined them. "Can you chug your beer so we can go back?"

"Yes." He smiled.

"I'll text the newlyweds, we're on our way." Harley pulled her phone from her small, clear bag.

"I promised Britt I'd help grill," Harrison said, then downed his remaining beer.

Harley followed Busy and Harrison from the beer garden. The trio weaved their way through the crowd, which seemed bigger today. She wished Wyatt could join them for dinner, but decided it was good he was still working the case. Hopefully, he'd have his killer in custody soon.

"Hey," Frankie said when they entered camp. "Britt had the water truck fill the pool with cold water, and it feels amazing."

"Where's Ryan?" Harley sat in a chair next to Frankie.

"He's practicing with Jessie Leigh and her band so he can fill in for her show at five," Frankie wiggled her bare feet in the wading pool water.

"I think when we go back in for the five o'clock show," Busy said as she handed Harley and Frankie a *Modelo*. "We should stay in for the night." She opened a lemon-flavored White Claw.

"Where are the newlyweds?" Harrison sat in a chair and kicked off his boots.

"In their trailer." Frankie sipped some beer. "Said they're prepping the chicken." She pointed at a black Weber grill. "Britt just lit the coals."

"I'm going to shower." Harrison picked up his boots.

"Whistle when you're finished," Busy called after him, "so I can make drinks for everybody."

Harrison gave a thumbs-up before disappearing inside the trailer.

Frankie pulled her feet from the water and stood. "I made Caprese kabobs if you guys are hungry."

"That sounds delicious." Busy smiled.

"Harley," Frankie slid on her flip-flops, "Wyatt said I could put them in your fridge."

"Of course." Harley stood. "Want me to get them?"

"No." Frankie headed for the RV. "I need to add the balsamic glaze."

Britt stepped from his trailer, and Ella handed him a tray of chicken thighs.

"Hi, gang," he said. "Hope everyone's hungry for barbecue teriyaki chicken."

Ella followed him, holding an empty platter and tongs. Harley thought the young woman was more beautiful today than on her wedding day.

Harrison whistled, and Busy popped up from her chair. "Champagne berry cocktails coming up." She hurried to her trailer.

Harley looked around the camp and felt a touch of melancholy wash over her. She hated that Wyatt was missing the fun. He and Derrick should be here, too.

Her phone chimed, and she smiled at the screen.

Wyatt: *Babe, wish I were there to eat BBQ with you. Hope to see you before the sun comes up*

He'd included the kissing emoji and a red heart.

Harley replied with the same emoji and a blue heart. She grabbed a water bottle and silently vowed to stay up all night if that's what it took to be awake when Wyatt came home.

CHAPTER FIFTEEN

Wyatt smiled at Harley's text. He hoped he would return while she was still awake to kiss her, among other things. Woody's curious tone brought Wyatt back to their conversation.

"So, what you're saying is if there's no tag at the end of the hair." His brown eyes were narrowed, and a crease etched his forehead. "You can't get a DNA profile."

"Correct." Deputy Collins nodded and placed his hat on the desk he sat on.

"Despite no tag," Derrick added. "The sample can tell us gender. If the person used drugs, was exposed to heavy metals, and their race." He cut his eyes to Wyatt.

"The earrings don't tell us much." Wyatt fingered the gold hoops. "But it would make sense to assume the owner is a blonde."

"How many blondes do you suppose live in Sweet Home?" Deputy Erickson grinned.

"Don't we only need to focus on blondes participating in the Jamboree?" Woody faced them, hand on hips.

"Yes," Derrick agreed. "And only females with long hair."

"Females?" Collins tilted his head.

"Yes!" Derrick and Woody said simultaneously.

"I agree." Wyatt picked up an earring. "I don't think a male killer would bother to carve, *Thief*, into the victim's chest."

"An emotional indication that the killer believes Ranger stole from them," Derrick added.

"Like a song." Woody smacked his forehead. "I think I saw pages of the song, "Navigate," Presley Parker wrote for Cash in Max's trailer."

"Makes sense if the two women are friends," Erickson said.

"There is no information about a Presley Parker on the internet." Derrick tapped the side of his head with a finger. "Which makes me think she's not a real person."

"Because if she's a songwriter, she should have an online presence," Wyatt suggested.

"Yes." Derrick nodded.

"There's no information on her in NCIC either," Collins added.

"Max doesn't have long blonde hair." Woody began pacing the bullpen area of the sheriff's station. "And I don't think she's a gold hoop kind of girl but she works for Cash's band so they're probably friends and maybe Cash was secretly dating Ranger 'cause she might own the hoop—"

"Woody." Derrick blocked his friend's path and placed his hands on Woody's shoulders. "Can you help me make a list of the blonde females attending the festival?"

"I already started a mental list." Woody picked up a pen from the closest desk and looked around.

"Here." Collins handed Woody a yellow legal pad.

Derrick sat at the desk and pointed to the chair next to him. Woody sat and placed the pad before him. Wyatt watched as the would-be deputy began jotting down names under Derrick's watchful eye.

"Sheriff Stone," Collins said as he stood next to Wyatt. "Sheriff Gibbs' wife, Lori, called to say his surgery went well."

"Glad to hear it." Wyatt smiled. "Hope we can make an arrest soon so he can get some R&R before returning to work."

"Oh," Erickson laughed, "Lori will make sure the sheriff doesn't hurry back."

"Wyatt." Derrick moved toward them with Woody in tow.

"Have a list?" Wyatt met Derrick's blue eyes.

"Five." Woody held up six fingers. "Including Cash, but—"

"We thought we'd start with artists before talking to crew and roadies," Derrick interjected.

Wyatt looked at his watch. He knew Harley and the others were probably headed back into the venue to watch the five o'clock concert. With any luck, he and his team could interview the females on Woody's list before the end of the closing act.

"We need to talk to Cash again, so we'll take her and the first two names." Wyatt looked at Collins and Erickson. "Can you take the other two and talk to Max Cotton?"

"Yes." Erickson nodded.

"Works for me." Derrick headed from the station. "As soon as we're back inside," he called over his shoulder, "I'm having a Big Duke corndog."

"And curly fries," Woody added.

When they stepped outside, Wyatt imagined he could smell the greasy aroma of corndogs and fries. He contemplated adding a cold beer to their festival dinner.

CHAPTER SIXTEEN

Max looked around her trailer, and a twinge of regret tugged at her heart. She loved being part of Cash's crew. Loved writing songs for Cash's rich soprano. Loved being near Cash every chance she had.

She smiled at the memory of Cash caressing the lyrics of "Finding Me." Max's cheeks warmed. She knew she'd been in love with Cash Coulter from the first time they'd met at a writers' round at the White Horse Tavern.

Max was nursing a whiskey and soda water when the petite blonde singer took the stage. Cash was working on a song about a lost love, and Max instantly wanted to punish whoever hurt her.

After the writers' round, Max introduced herself. Ten months ago, she was asked if she'd like to be part of Cash's stage crew. Max managed the band's guitars, ensuring they stayed tuned. She also kept the right guitars for each musician ready for the playlist during a performance.

One night, Cash and she stayed up late drinking and talking about writing songs. Max wondered why she didn't offer to write a few songs for Cash. Instead, she said she was friends with a song-writer named Presley Parker. *So stupid,* Max scolded herself.

Cash was excited to have a songwriter pen some songs for her. She asked if Presley could take the song she'd started about a bad breakup and finish the piece.

As Cash described the lyrics for "Broken," she also told Max how Bo Ranger had hurt her. Cash had thought the wanna-be country singer loved her, but he broke her heart when he left her for Inez Ingram.

Max's cheeks flushed again. Her anger at Bo for breaking Cash's heart was exacerbated when he stole the songs she'd written for Cash.

"If he'd just stuck to singing 'What a Mess,'" Max shook her head, "I would have been thankful he'd created a situation where I could step in and comfort Cash."

Max poured the roofied rum and coke she'd served Cash down the drain. She descended the steps of her trailer and peeked through the passenger window of her F-150. Cash's eyes were closed, and she looked so peaceful. Max opened the door and straightened Cash's denim skirt. Desire burned through her as if her blood were on fire when her hand brushed Cash's thigh. Max leaned in and pressed her lips to Cash's. She moaned and palmed Max's chest, sending a musky floral scent through the cab.

Max hated drugging Cash, but she wanted to get as far away from Sweet Home as possible before she expressed her love to the beautiful blonde singer.

She'd ditched the gun and penknife in a dumpster by the Boys and Girls Club, which had been emptied Friday morning. Still, she ran through her mental checklist again to assure she hadn't left any evidence behind. Confident, nothing in her trailer tied her to Ranger's murder, she hefted her duffle bag and closed the door. Once behind the wheel, Max glanced at Cash again, shifted her truck into drive, and headed out of the artist campground.

CHAPTER SEVENTEEN

Harley stepped from the RV with a pitcher of margaritas. She crossed to the food table and placed the pitcher next to colorful plastic margarita glasses. The air had cooled after sunset, and Harley thought she smelled a hint of jasmine on the warm breeze blowing through their camp.

"Shane Smith and his band performed a hell of a concert." Busy claimed a chair next to the wading pool.

"All the acts have been great," Harrison added.

"It was an almost perfect day." Harley handed Busy, then Harrison, a margarita.

"Sorry, your handsome sheriff is still working." Busy took a large drink. "What are Ella and Frankie doing?" She pointed at the duo who were moving a table.

"I'm not sure." Harley sat in a chair next to Harrison. "Britt said something about a surprise before he disappeared."

"Should we offer to help?" Harrison tipped up his blue glass.

"Probably." Busy giggled. "But I just put my feet into the pool."

"No need to help," Britt said behind them. "We're almost set up."

"Set up for what?" Harley asked.

Britt put his arm across Ella's shoulders when she and Frankie joined them. "You're up." He nodded at Frankie.

"I won a free camp concert." Her brown eyes twinkled. "Ryan should be here any minute with the singers."

"That's so exciting!" Harley said. "I should bring out some snacks, too." She headed for the RV.

"I have guacamole, chips, and salsa ready to go." Ella disappeared into her trailer.

"We could fill the metal tub with ice and drinks." Busy stood, then padded toward her ice chest.

"Yep." Harrison followed her.

Harley descended the RV stairs and set a charcuterie board next to the almost empty pitcher of margaritas. "Frankie, can you bring out the other pitcher of margaritas for our guests?"

"On it." Frankie hurried into the RV.

"They're here!" Britt called across the campsite.

Harley turned to see a pretty blonde flanked by two men. She was wearing a turquoise fringe skirt, a sequined white tank top, and white ankle boots.

"Everyone," Ryan said. "This is Jessie Leigh, and her bandmate Jim Pray." He motioned to another man and a small crowd behind the two band members. "This is Jessie's husband, Joel, and a few of their friends and family."

"Welcome in," Harley said as Frankie joined her with a pitcher of margaritas.

"Thanks for picking me for the free concert." Frankie laughed.

"Thanks for loaning Ryan to us for our set." Jessie smiled.

"Yes," Jim added. "He was a lifesaver since I can't play two guitars at once yet."

"We thought you could set up here." Britt pointed to the space he, Ella, and Frankie had cleared in front of his trailer.

"Perfect." Jessie slipped a strap over her head and settled her guitar in her hands.

Jim did the same and stood next to her. "Ryan, you should join us."

Ryan grabbed his guitar and stood on the other side of Jessie.

"Okay, everyone," Frankie said. "Take a seat."

Harley, Busy, and Harrison turned their chairs to face the makeshift stage and sat down.

"We thought we'd start with "Good Day." Jessie strummed her guitar, then launched into the song.

Harley was still in awe of how a singer could play an instrument while singing a song. As part of her and Wyatt's alphabet dating, she'd learned to play guitar for the letter "G." She chose "Sweet Home Alabama" because the song only has three chords, but it was challenging to both play and sing.

Jessie sang the song's last line, then the trio took a bow.

"Any requests?" Jim asked.

"How about "Pink Umbrella Drink?" Frankie handed Jessie a pink margarita glass.

Jessie laughed and then took a sip. "This is fabulous." She took another drink and placed the glass on the small table behind her.

Jim played the song's intro, and Jessie joined in with the first verse.

Harley was so absorbed in the music that she was taken by surprise when Wyatt pulled her to her feet and twirled her around the small grassy area. He dipped her as Jessie brought the song to an end.

"Hi." Wyatt kissed her.

"Hi." Harley smiled. "Did you solve your case?"

"No," Derrick said behind them. "We need to speak with Ms. Leigh."

"Me?" Jessie looked at Jim, who shrugged. "Why me?"

"Jessie," Woody smiled, "we need your help."

Joel moved to his wife's side. "Does this have to do with Bo Ranger's death?"

"Yes." Wyatt nodded. "Ms. Leigh, were you friends with Mr. Ranger?"

"No." Jim shook his head. "Most artists avoided him because he'd steal song ideas, then claim them for himself."

"Jim's right." Jessie looked at her bandmate. "I didn't know Ranger."

"Can you tell us where you were on Thursday night?" Woody asked. His cheeks bloomed red when Wyatt narrowed his eyes. "Sorry, Sheriff." He grinned. "I should let you ask the questions."

"Jessie was with me," Joel answered. "And we were all in camp working on the playlist for her set the next day."

"The strand of hair we have is a darker shade of blonde than Ms. Leigh's," Derrick said.

"Do you think your killer is a blonde?" Jim asked.

"No," Woody shook his head, then glanced at Wyatt. "But we think Bo Ranger dated a blonde."

"Thank you for your time, Ms. Leigh." Wyatt tipped his hat. "Sorry to interrupt your concert."

"No problem." Jessie smiled. "Frankie suggested I ask you to join us for 'Small Town Fight.'"

"Maybe next time." Wyatt extended his hand to her, then shook hands with Jim and Joel. "Harley," he grasped her elbow, "can I speak with you privately?"

Harley smiled and let him guide her toward the RV. She was sad he probably couldn't stay, but thankful for a few minutes alone with him. As soon as they were inside, Wyatt pulled her into his arms and covered her lips with his. Harley twined her hands into his hair, relishing being close to him.

Wyatt's phone buzzed, but he didn't release her lips. He dropped his hands to her ass and held her against his crotch, his desire evident.

"Wyatt?" Derrick called through the closed door.

"What?" Wyatt kissed her forehead.

"Cash Coulter's missing." His tone suggested the rest of his news wasn't good. "And her band thinks Max took her."

CHAPTER EIGHTEEN

yatt squinted as Thursday's stunning sunrise lit up the calm water of Foster Lake, as it had each morning since they'd arrived.

He sipped a piping hot dark roast, enjoying the much cooler air seeping through the RV's open windows. Wyatt inhaled the fresh, earthy smell, then yawned. He probably should have tried to sleep longer, but he worried his restlessness would wake Harley. She looked so beautiful, with her long, dark hair fanned out on her pillow. He'd eased from bed, shuffled into the small kitchen, and made a pot of coffee. They hadn't left the RV since arriving on Monday afternoon, enjoying being together and making up for lost time, but their time alone would be over soon.

Wyatt was still mad at himself that they hadn't pushed to talk to Cash before she went on stage. Though the evidence they'd pieced together was thin, he knew he should've listened to his gut when Collins and Erickson couldn't locate Max.

As the sun rose higher in the sky, he took another sip and rehashed the events of Saturday night.

<hr>

AFTER DISCOVERING MAX HAD KIDNAPPED CASH, THEY ESTIMATED she had an hour's head start. Luckily, they could track her movements via the AirTag inside Cash's guitar case. Once they determined Max's route leaving Oregon, Wyatt dispatched Collins and Erickson to cover US 20 E in case she cut over at some point. He called Blake and asked him and Dyani to head east on US 26, which left him and Derrick driving east on US 380.

"We should cut over to US 20," Derrick said, his eyes glued to the GPS map showing Max's location. "I think she's headed for Sisters."

"Copy." Wyatt made the turn that would lead to US 20 as Derrick shared their route with everyone else via radio.

When they converged onto US 20 outside Sisters, they positioned themselves at various intervals along the highway to avoid missing her red Ford.

Wyatt's phone rang, and he accepted a FaceTime call from Blake.

"We have the truck in sight," he said.

"Looks like she's pulling into a Chevron," Dyani's voice bled through Wyatt's speaker.

"We're on our way." Wyatt pulled into traffic. "Text Erickson."

"Already did," Derrick replied.

When Wyatt drew closer to the gas station, he saw Blake's county truck parked across the street. He pulled into the driveway as Collins and Erickson drove past. He and Derrick had borrowed weapons from the Sweet Home Sheriff's department, but Wyatt said a quick prayer that Max wasn't armed and wouldn't put up a fight.

Wyatt and Derrick exited Wyatt's truck and then walked slowly toward the F-150. The driver's seat was empty. Wyatt motioned for Blake and Dyani to move closer to the station's mini-market.

He saw Collins and Erickson closing in from the other side of the parking lot.

Derrick eased open the back passenger door and shook Cash's shoulder. She didn't rouse at first, but then raised her head and looked at Derrick.

"What's going on?" She looked around, then asked, "Where am I?"

"You need to come with me." He took her hand.

Cash nodded, and Derrick escorted her to Wyatt's truck. Blake and Dyani stood on one side of the market's double doors, with Erickson and Collins covering the other.

A bell chimed when Max exited the store. She saw Wyatt standing beside her truck and frantically looked around the parking lot. When she spotted Cash sitting in his vehicle, she pulled a gun from the back of her shorts and headed toward them.

"Max," Wyatt drew his weapon, "it's over."

She ignored him and pointed her gun at Derrick. He stood behind the open passenger door of Wyatt's truck, weapon drawn.

"You're outnumbered, Max." Wyatt closed the distance between them. "You don't want to make matters worse by shooting one of us." He noted the other deputies moving in behind her.

"I won't need to shoot anyone if you let Cash go." Max glared at Wyatt and pointed her gun at him. Before he could react, she refocused her aim, and Derrick ducked when Max pulled the trigger, the round lodging in his truck's door.

"Max!" Wyatt yelled, and she trained her gun on him again. "Drop your weapon."

"No!" A demented look flashed in her green eyes.

Wyatt pulled his trigger. The bullet struck Max in the shoulder, and she stumbled backwards. Blake grabbed her from behind and secured her weapon. Collins was on the radio requesting an ambulance.

"Max Cotton." Erickson pulled handcuffs from his duty belt. "You are under arrest for the murder of Booker Ranger."

"And for shooting at Deputy Derrick Stone," Woody said from behind Derrick.

Derrick spun around, looked at his friend, and then cut his eyes to Wyatt. Wyatt frowned and marched toward them. He spotted Imogene sitting in her car and she waved.

"I know." Woody held up his hands. "I shouldn't be interfering in official police business."

"How did you know where to find us?" Wyatt faced the would-be deputy with his hands on his hips.

"Police scanner," Derrick answered.

"Yes." Woody nodded. "I had to make sure you didn't need any backup and that Max was apprehended."

Wyatt extended his hand, which Woody grasped. "Thanks for the assist, Woody."

"Deputy Woody." The colorful cowboy beamed.

———

WYATT SMILED AT THE MEMORY OF WOODY'S ENTHUSIASM, THEN sipped from his cup, noting the coffee was now lukewarm. He rose from the recliner, walked to the coffee pot, and refilled his cup. As a thank you for stepping in for him, Sheriff Gibbs reserved the campsite at Sunnyside for a week. Wyatt wasn't sure he and Harley could be gone that long, but Britt promised to check in on their ranches. Dyani said she didn't mind staying at Harley's place longer, and Blake and Derrick assured him the station would survive without him.

Wyatt had to admit the idea of an uninterrupted week with Harley was very appealing. His phone buzzed, and he returned to the small table by the recliner.

Harley: *Come back to bed Sheriff*

He grinned and set his cup down. "Very appealing indeed."

~ THE END ~

ABOUT THE AUTHOR

Kimila Kay lives in Donald, Oregon, with her husband, Randy, and feisty black cat, Halle.

She is mentally strolling the beaches of Cabo, finishing the fourth novel in her Mexico Mayhem series, "Chaos in Cabo," which also includes "Peril in Paradise," "Malice in Mazatlán," and "Vanished in Vallarta."

Kimila's heart project, The Stoneybrook Mystery series, honors her autistic son, Derrick, who left this world far too soon. The

series, set in a fictional Oregon town, includes "Redneck Ranch,"
"Five Golden Rings," "Whispering Willows," "Willow's Woods," and
"Rattlesnake Ravine."
Learn more about Kimila at - KimilaKay.com.

———

INSPIRATION FOR THIS STORY

My story is to honor the "Oregon Jamboree," a country music
festival my husband and I have attended for thirty years. This year
was the festival's final year due to rising costs.

I dabble in songwriting and recently completed a country song.
Since I don't play any instruments, I considered having someone
put music to my song, but the idea conjured the fear that someone
might steal my song!

Navigating by the Stars

Mary Vine

Published by

Windtree Press, Corvallis, Oregon

https://windtreepress.com

CHAPTER ONE

Myka Woods sat in her backyard in Trillium Falls, Idaho, and watched the sunset with her friend and neighbor Ruth Harper, aka Grandma Harper. They sat in the lingering Indian summer warmth, sipping lemonade until the sky darkened.

Myka looked at the stars in the sky. "Do you know that you can find your way by using any star in the sky?" Myka asked.

"I do not. I've only heard about navigating by the North Star." Grandma pointed. "I think I see it there."

"Yes, the brightest star in the sky. I've been reading how sailors, and those on land, have been using the stars to guide them from the beginning of time."

"Are you sure about that?" asked Grandma, jiggling the ice in her glass.

"Of course, I don't know the exact date, but a prolonged period of time."

"I'll go with that. Kind of like a way finder, I guess."

"Grandma?"

"What? Spit it out. I can tell something's been bothering you. It's your scowl."

"I'm scowling?"

Grandma reached over and touched Myka's arm. "Now, what is it?"

"Caleb told me that Roscoe Miller is getting out of jail. Caleb was the one who was responsible for making his arrest."

"I don't recognize the name. Should I?" Grandma asked, rubbing a hand through her white, pixie hairdo.

"No, not necessarily. Rosco was involved in a bar fight, and the person he fought, died. It wasn't premeditated, but he was in prison for four years."

"Why was Caleb involved? He's a special agent for the state."

"He was nearby when it happened."

"And he blames Caleb?"

"Caleb doesn't think so, but I just worry about that sort of thing."

"You can't worry about that, you have to worry about politics like everyone else," said Grandma.

Myka chuckled.

Grandma patted Myka's knee. "Don't worry. Caleb doesn't think you should."

"You're right. Why create problems?"

"How's his mother, by the way?"

"She's showing some improvement and should be released from the hospital soon. He'll stay with her for a while and make sure she has the help she needs before coming home."

"Good, pneumonia can be rough on an old person. Is she excited about the two of you getting married?"

"Yes, she seems to be. I think she was afraid he'd be single for the rest of his life. You know, no grandkids," Myka said with a chuckle.

"Yes, you softened that tough guy, but only a little bit, mind you."

"It's hard to be soft with his job."

"Yeah, I suppose so." Grandma stood.

"I'm going to grab my flashlight and walk you home," said Myka.

Grandma followed her, taking her glass to the kitchen counter.

As they walked across the street and toward Grandma's house, Myka had a hand under Grandma's elbow to make sure she didn't slip. Hers was the only hand she'd seen her accept; she pushed others away. Except Caleb's, but she figured that was because he was handsome.

"Don't look behind us," said Grandma. "There's a car parked back there that doesn't belong in the neighborhood."

"Was there someone in it?"

"I couldn't tell."

"Oh, Grandma. You have such an imagination."

"Well, why do you think it's parked here then?"

"Someone visiting a neighbor, or a homeless person, maybe."

"No," said Grandma. "In any event, I want you to look at the license plate on your way home. And I want you to use the flashlight on the guy's head if he gets too close and then kick him in the…uh, groin. In that order. Don't laugh. Caleb isn't here to look out for you, so it's my duty. You're a very pretty girl, Myka, especially with that beautiful, thick hair of yours. I notice thick hair because my hair is thinning and it's no longer dark like yours."

Grandma was a self-proclaimed sleuth. "Yes, I will remember the right order," Myka said as seriously as she could, while smiling inside.

"And the license plate."

When Myka heard Grandma's door shut and the click of the lock, she headed back to her house while trying to inconspicuously get the plate number. Yet because of the darkness, she couldn't read all the numbers. Only got LX and she wasn't going to get any closer to the car or shine her flashlight. She figured it'd be even scarier to see a face looking back at her, or to draw attention to herself. She moved quickly, returned to her place, and locked the door behind her. Perhaps it was just Grandma's imagination, but she'd been right half the time, and that's what worried her.

Myka added dishes to the dishwasher and then went to the front blinds to peek at the parked car. In the car lights, Myka could see Grandma near the driver's side windshield. She said something and then backed up on the curb. The car drove off.

She laughed out loud as Grandma walked back home and went inside.

CHAPTER TWO

"*L*et's go to Priest Lake," said Myka, speaking to Caleb on her cell. "It's beneath the Selkirk Mountains. That's here in Idaho."

"I know where it is," said Caleb.

"Oh, of course you do. Silly me."

"Why are we going?" he asked.

"Because it's one of the best places to see the northern lights in the Lower 48."

"You have two photography awards, Myka. Isn't that enough?"

She knew he was teasing. "I'm just getting started."

"I know, the hardware store isn't enough for you."

"Everybody needs a hobby."

"How's Grandma Harper?"

"She had her shotgun out again last night," she said.

"Oh, no. I guess I will have to arrest her one day, won't I?"

"Why bother. Nothing would stick. She'd just say she's senile or have me tell the powers that be. I can already hear her say, "Can't remember where I was.""

Caleb let out a chuckle. "Got to love her."

"Yep."

"Okay, what did she do this time?"

"We watched the sun go down, then I walked her home. But there was a car parked in the street and someone in the driver's seat. She told me to take the license plate number and where to hit him if he followed me."

"I don't like this," he said, concern apparent in his tone.

"Well, I snuck home safely."

"I'll take the license number. Let me get a pen."

"Too dark to read."

"Humph."

"Anyway, I did a couple of things and looked out the window. Grandma had her shotgun pointed at the car until he left."

"I guess you don't have to worry about street people," he said. The sigh that followed was audible.

She'd hoped to be convincing so he wouldn't worry. "Uh, I don't think so, no."

"Did you get a description of the car?" he asked.

"White-ish sedan."

"That's what you said the last time you needed to describe a car. Maybe you should start taking a "photo" of it."

"That's a novel idea. When are you coming back to me?" she asked.

"I might just surprise you, catch you off guard."

"Oh yeah? Is that to check on me, or Grandma Harper?"

"I'm anxious to see you." After a moment of silence, he said, "Everything else fine?"

"Yes...why wouldn't it be?"

"I can hear concern in your voice. I don't want you scared, just aware of your surroundings," he said, emphasizing his words.

"Well, that does scare me...a bit."

"Myka, I only want you to be aware of your surroundings... always. Does that help?"

"Yes, I think I understand. I will do better." That's what she gets when her fiancé has a job in law enforcement, she thought as she set her phone down. It's kind of sweet, too, though, she realized. But between him and Grandma Harper, she didn't see any reason to.

———

Cathy Morrison, Myka's hardware store co-owner, greeted Myka as she entered. "How's Caleb's mother?"

"She's better, getting stronger. Thank you for asking. I'm sure ready for him to come home, though."

"I'd ask if you need some company, but Grandma might be offended if I took some of your time," she said with a smile.

"Ha. You're sweet to think of me, but I've been living alone for quite a while and am used to it. Plus, Caleb has his own place, too."

Cathy nodded. "I see our first delivery truck out the window there. Looks like today we're hitting the job running."

"Well, I am anyway. I'll be fine, you just stay here in the front with customers while I try to protect my introvert status."

"Will do, but I don't think that will happen with our sale going on."

Myka scurried to the back of the store and the truck driver.

At noon, Cathy passed Myka on the way to the lunchroom. "What did that guy want?" Cathy asked.

"What guy?"

"The one who asked for you about ten minutes ago."

"What do you mean? No one came to the back except our regular sales people and truckers."

"He clearly wanted to know where you were."

"Was he carrying anything, like a return or paperwork?"

"No, nothing," Cathy said. "Let me set my lunch on the table and I'll go with you to the front."

"Maybe he's still here," Myka said. "Do you see him anywhere?"

"No. Forget about it. He apparently changed his mind."

But Myka's life had been disrupted by two investigations, and she'd wanted to ask Cathy for a description, but stopped herself, turned, and went back to work. She didn't want to worry Cathy. Didn't want her to think she was so needy with Caleb gone.

CHAPTER THREE

$\mathcal{M}$yka felt more confident on her way home and smiled when she saw Grandma Harper standing on her porch with a bowl she'd borrowed. Myka smiled, thinking the bowl probably held cookies or brownies. Grandma was prone to spoiling her, anyway. Especially after work.

"Yum," said Myka as she approached her.

"You're lucky I didn't eat them all. Take one."

Myka munched. "Ginger thingies."

"Yep. Baking cookies. That's the kind of thing Caleb says I should be doing, so here they are once again. Perhaps leave him a few, maybe stick them in the freezer. And in case I forget, remember I returned your bowl."

"Okay." Myka opened the door and drew Grandma in.

"Cookies remind me that I need to exercise," said Grandma. "What do you think about you and I taking a boxing class?"

"Oh, Grandma, I think it would kill you."

"Now, I can be strong," she said, clearly a bit insulted.

"Well, I don't think I'm strong enough. Go ahead and sit down. Did you see that car across the street again today?"

"No. I think I scared him away. Don't ask how."

"Okay, I won't." Myka sighed, thinking about the car.

"You're still worried about that guy that was released from prison, aren't you?"

Myka sighed. "Oh, I don't know. I've just been kind of jumpy lately."

"You'll be right as rain as soon as your man comes back to town."

"Yeah, probably."

"I've been thinking about the man who was released from jail," added Grandma, around bites of a cookie. "I believe that most people wouldn't want to do something that would put them back in jail."

"Makes sense."

"Don't tell me you're just now realizing that Caleb's job is dangerous."

"Some of the time it's dangerous. But Grandma, being with you is sometimes dangerous, too."

Grandma was quiet for a moment before asking, "Dangerous, huh? Have you ever been hurt in my company? I mean, besides bruises."

Myka laughed.

"What? I keep you safe. Stop laughing."

"I made peace with Caleb's job a while back. It's just that today a man came into the store to see me and then disappeared. No file, no box or bag. Nothing in his hands."

"The power of suggestion."

"Yeah, I guess so. The power of suggestion. Thank you."

Grandma stood. "Yeah, I do what I can. I'm going home now. It's bingo night."

"All right, then. Have fun."

Out the window, Myka watched Grandma walk home. She couldn't stop her gaze from drifting to the empty space where yesterday's car had been parked, and she finally realized what her problem was. If Caleb were here, he could fill her in on how Roscoe Miller was doing as a free man. Or any other concern she may have. Yet, she would not occupy his time, couldn't jeopardize the time he needed with his mother over her active imagination.

———

Myka couldn't wait to leave work. By now, Caleb was back in town and waiting for her at their favorite barbeque restaurant. With utmost joy, she opened her car door, placed her lunch bag on the passenger seat, and started the car.

She felt something hard at the back of her arm and looked back to see the barrel of a gun between the two bucket seats. A man sat up and her heart pounded with fear

"If you want to stay alive, then you'll back up and move out of the parking lot. Go west on Center Street."

"Who…? What do you want?"

"I want you to be quiet. Good girl. Now go west."

"My fiancé is a special agent for the State Bureau of Investigation. You may want to kidnap someone else."

He didn't respond, just rubbed the point of his gun along the side of her neck, causing goosebumps that made her shiver. All she knew to do was keep driving, not wanting to irritate him further.

At a red light, she turned her head back enough to see his face, remember his features.

"Turn around!"

Myka did and froze in place, her heavy breathing steaming up the side window. She reached to push the defrost button. The gun touched her shoulder as she leaned forward.

They headed out of town and into designated forest land. She didn't know if her heart would last the way it pounded while she moved away from light and people. She'd travelled miles before pulling onto a gravel road. The road wasn't marked or numbered, which further distressed her. She had a quarter of a tank of gas left, which was good, so she might be able to drive back home. If she was able. Tears dropped when Myka fully realized the difficulty of her situation.

"Stop crying. Stop!"

But she couldn't, so she whimpered as quietly as she could.

"Go right at this road."

Her phone had little power left. She'd planned on charging it as soon as she got home. Now, would anyone be able to track her phone if it went dead? If he didn't take her phone, that is.

And how would he return home? It only made sense that he'd drive back to town as he had the gun.

At the end of the gravel road, she saw a turnaround.

"We'll get out here," he said, his gun pointed at her head again, and she sucked in a breath.

Myka made a futile attempt to come up with someone angry enough to do this to her. "Okay, okay. What do you want me to do?" she asked, her voice starting to squeak, and her mind spun, searching for a way to get away.

With the car lights still on, she could see the gravel road ending into dirt, and beyond, the trees created darkness on each side. Maybe if she jumped out of the car real fast, she could run into the woods.

Before she knew it, he slipped out the door behind her and tapped her window with the gun. If she started the car...no, he'd shoot her. This guy might be that angry. If he's crazy enough to abduct her, he's crazy enough to shoot her, too.

"Get out! And bring your phone."

She opened the door and stood; he took her phone, then grabbed her arm and pulled her away from the door.

"Take about twenty-five big steps down the road. No, that way," he said and pointed toward the trees.

Myka shot out a mental thank you to God. Space between them meant he couldn't touch her, and being farther away meant she'd be harder to shoot. Still, she didn't trust him. What could he possibly be doing? And, she needed her phone.

At the twenty-fifth step, she didn't immediately turn around, but when she did, she saw him throw something into the bushes. It had to be her cell, of course.

Moving away from him had made her feel relieved, but then she panicked at the thought that this man was into human hunting.

CHAPTER FOUR

Myka sighed. The creep got in her car, turned around, and left. She was relieved at first, because there'd be miles between them. She shuddered at the thought of what could have happened to her. Yet now, she found herself combing through bushes and trees on a slanting hillside, but the bruises and scratches would be worth it in order to contact Caleb. If she could only find her phone before the battery died.

She cried in frustration when she couldn't find her phone, especially on a dark night like this. After mounting the bank, she brushed off her hands and rubbed them down her pant legs. After straightening, her eyes went to the sky where the moon and stars glittered.

Then she remembered what she'd read about how people have been guided by the stars for centuries. Myka knew it may be smarter to go back the way she came, but if he came back for her… to hunt her, she couldn't risk it. He could do who knows what to her.

First, Myka knew she must walk south toward town. Cutting

across going south she believed she'd save steps, too, get help sooner.

Looking up, she located the Big Dipper, knowing in the fall it's low to the ground and harder to find, so she moved to the road's incline for the highest point to stand.

Okay, there was the Dipper, but now she'd locate the two stars which make up the outside of the Dipper's ladle. She remembered the stars were called the Pointers. In her mind's eye she imagined a line from the Pointers to the North Star that's set in the Little Dipper. From the North Star, she made a visual line from the end of the Little Dipper's handle towards the skyline. "There's south."

Myka loved the forest but now her surroundings were dark with mysterious shadows and disconsolate.

She started off, twigs snapping beneath her feet and bushes brushing her thighs. Her shoe caught on an exposed bit of tree root, sending her staggering forward before she regained her footing. Her focus on the stars calmed her trembling. She watched them appear and disappear as she moved through the woods. If not for the darkness you can't see the stars, she reminded herself.

Near tears again, she came across an area that looked semi-maintained, probably for hiking trails. She thought of Caleb as she walked along and how she'd been so eager to see him, but nothing compared to what she felt now. What did he think when she didn't show up at the restaurant as planned? Perhaps he'd called Grandma to see if she was with her. No, he wouldn't do that because it would worry her, and to deal with a worried Grandma was not for the faint of heart. Still, she smiled thinking of Grandma. She hoped Caleb would know she'd never stand him up.

Now, Myka would use her energy and emotions to travel and find a road or a house. She looked up to redirect by the stars and wondered how far she'd walked.

CHAPTER FIVE

Grandma Harper had asked Myka to text her when Caleb arrived at the restaurant, so she'd be assured he made it to town safely. When her friends traveled, she worried about car trouble, their getting lost, or falling asleep at the wheel. Myka knew she worried, yet hadn't sent a word to her. She started drumming her fingers on the table when Caleb called.

"Hello, Caleb. I feel honored that you called."

"Hello Grandma. Thanks for the kind words but by chance is Myka there with you?"

"No, she's not. She told me she planned to meet you at the restaurant and was excited about it."

"I thought so, too. She's not here, and she'd call me if she had something to do at work."

"I tell you what," said Grandma. "I'll let you know if I hear from her, okay? Maybe you should check the store."

"Yeah, I'd already thought of that. Now don't be a sleuth, Gran-
"

Grandma ended the call. "Humph," she said to herself while she thumbed her phone. "Caleb's just being silly. I'm not a sleuth. I'm a tracker."

She'd allowed Myka to put an app on her phone so she could track her. Perhaps it's an important app to use at her age, but what Grandma really wanted was for Myka to be in the app's circle so that she could track Myka.

There were enough problems in their town during the past years that Grandma knew she needed to be able to track her. She'd used her "old age" card again and was especially glad that it worked to help her find Myka now.

What? She was way out of town, out by the Trillium Falls. After making notes, she realized she may need a four-wheel drive and took her late husband's truck keys and her shotgun.

One thing she knew, no one was going to hurt Myka if she had anything to do with it. Her wheels screeched as she pulled out of her driveway and stepped on the gas while singing, "Granny's got a gun...Granny's got a gun..."

Many years ago, she and her husband used to go to the area where Myka's car was parked to cross-country ski. She'd like to take a moment to remember, to think about those times fondly, but Myka's life may depend on her. And it was a good thing she remembered the area, because Myka's phone was either out of battery life or turned off now. "Huh. Who says I'm losing my memory?"

She'd travelled to the Falls turn off and hadn't passed a vehicle, still she travelled on until she saw headlights in the distance, coming her way.

———

CALEB RUBBED HIS FACE WITH HIS HANDS AFTER GRANDMA HAD hung up on him. He didn't have time to worry about Grandma just now.

This was not like Myka to go off and vanish without telling one of them.

After a quick call to Cathy, at the hardware store, he found out that Myka was a bit off today, concerned about a customer.

He drove to his office and utilized the State's technology to search for Myka's car. Thank goodness he'd saved time by knowing her license plate, but he wished he'd not been so set on her privacy that he didn't put a tracker on her car. Still, he was able to track the phone's last known location.

———

GRANDMA CLIMBED OUT OF THE TRUCK AND STOOD IN FRONT OF HER headlights. For more signs of stress, she messed up her white hair so that it stood up. Who says blondes have more fun, she thought, while slumping forward and putting on a frown.

If it wasn't Myka in the oncoming car, then it was who she was after. Who wouldn't stop for a helpless old lady with a broken-down truck on a deserted road? Especially if she now stood in the oncoming lane.

"Let me pull over here first. I can at least give you a ride," he said, and she stepped out of the way so he could park Myka's car. She'd recognized Myka's constellation sticker on the hatch-back window.

Grandma recognized the man as the man who'd parked in her neighborhood and had just enough time to get to the truck and grab her shotgun.

She pointed the shotgun between his eyes.

"Whoa, lady. What are you doing? I'm only here to help you. I can go away."

"Where is she? What did you do with her?"

"Who? Are you all right?" he asked.

"Yes, I'm fine. You're the one who's not. Where's Myka?"

"She's back at the campsite, is all. What's it to you?"

"Who are you?" She moved the nose of her gun in a circle around his nose. Her elbow ached from holding the shotgun, but she'd still do what she needed to do.

"Now listen," he said. "You don't want to spend your life in jail for murder."

"How young do you think I am? How much time do you think I have left?"

"Well, uh– "

"They will feed me and take care of my medical needs. What more could I want at this age?"

The man started backing toward Myka's car. She'd not let him get to a gun or escape.

"You're crazy, lady."

"I'm crazy? Well, isn't that the pot calling the kettle black? Come to think of it, a senile defense could keep me out of jail. Your mistake was, you scared me, mister. When you took Myka." She aimed the gun to whiz by his ear and pulled the trigger.

"Stop! Don't! Please don't shoot me."

In the distance, she heard a vehicle, hopefully heading their way.

"Nobody touches my friend and gets away with it," she said in a low, harsh tone.

"I didn't touch her, lady. I did not."

"But you abducted her."

"We went for a ride, is all."

"And left her in the woods, you say? At night. Give me one reason I shouldn't shoot you?"

He stuttered, not succeeding at getting a word out. But he turned toward the approaching vehicle. He ran toward it, away from Grandma and Myka's car, his hands flailing in the air.

Grandma put the gun back behind the truck seat. "Darn elbow," she whispered, then looked toward the state trooper's car. She recognized Caleb stepping into the car lights, but not the other officer.

It would be over soon, she thought, and walked over to the men as they put handcuffs on the man disrupting her life.

"That woman's crazy," he said to the officers.

Caleb didn't say anything, only scowled at him. Once the criminal was in the back seat, he turned toward her. "Are you all right?"

"Yes, I'm fine. Just worried about Myka. Did you get a lead on where she is?" she asked, trying to sound innocent.

"Yes. You can go home now. We'll talk about this later," he added, grumbling under his breath.

"That's exactly the direction I'm heading right now," she said before climbing into the truck. From there, she watched Caleb get into Myka's car and head the direction the man had come from. The other officer took off the way they'd come.

CHAPTER SIX

The first thing Caleb did was flash his light into the front and back seats of Myka's car to look for signs of struggle or blood. He found an unloaded gun with no powder residue. With this and not finding blood on Roscoe Miller's hands or clothes, he was relieved. He looked up at the sky and wondered if Myka was using the stars as a guide to find help. He scanned the forest and shook his head; it would be too hard to do in these woods. So, he drove slowly down the road, searching along the sides as best he could.

At the turn off, the place that he'd tallied her last location to be, his heart pounded in his chest as he stepped outside and looked around the dark, deserted area. He heard crickets and an owl hooted, that was all.

He could have strangled her, Caleb realized. *No, he couldn't lose her.* No!

"Myka!"

"Myka!"

The forest was still.

He went back to the car and honked the horn. Then again,

making coyotes howl in the distance. Once more, he tried to no avail.

He flashed the light around the bushes and stepped down an incline and searched for what he hoped to find, Myka, scared and hovering, but alive.

"Myka?"

He saw a glint of light and moved toward it. It looked like Myka's phone with the aqua protective case. The battery was dead, which made sense. This was likely the phone that he had tracked. He stuck it in his back pocket before continuing his search.

———

After Grandma turned her truck around, she headed back the way she came, but she wasn't headed home. She was quite sure Myka was moving along a cross-country path, south with the stars she valued so greatly. Grandma believed Myka was smart enough not to stick around and wait for that lunatic to come find her again. If things hadn't changed as far as the trails were concerned, she believed, and prayed, she'd find Myka there.

In her mind, she calculated the time she'd seen the man and then the time allotted to get to the area she assumed Myka would travel.

Grandma pulled over in a turnaround, leaned forward, and looked up at Myka's stars, then settled down to wait. She remembered her husband and the time they spent in these woods. The images in her mind were vivid in this place. She remembered the love he had for her and smiled.

———

Myka stopped walking and stiffened when she heard a car horn. Looking up at the sky, she could tell it was from the north of her. By the length of the honk, it sounded like the man was desperate. She smiled, thinking that if he was back for her, he'd not find her now. To be away from him was her main goal now. She'd get to a house or make it to a main street eventually and then she'd find a phone to call Caleb.

She trudged along, feeling relief with each step she took, knowing the man wouldn't be able to find her now. Yet, time seemed to stand still as she made her way to help.

At length, she saw a white truck in the distance. The lights were off, so she hoped it was a stranded vehicle so she could climb inside, sleep, and be safe from the elements. In addition to any hungry creature that'd pass this way.

Upon nearing, she saw a white head propped against the window. Caleb had told her once that sixty percent of people had a white vehicle, even Grandma had a white pickup. Still, she dared to hope it'd be her. But why would she be parked here? Certainly, it's not her. Yet, it could be someone who could help her. Most people carried cell phones these days. She stepped out of the trees, then started running.

As Myka approached the truck, she saw that the crown of this person's head was still pressed against the window. She wondered if he or she could be dead. That's all she'd need on a night like tonight.

———

GRANDMA SEEMED TO HAVE NODDED OFF AS SHE WAS PRONE TO DO these days. She sat up and adjusted her hearing aid, thinking a sound may have awakened her.

A tap at her window made her jerk, and she wondered who else in the world could be out in nowhere tonight. "My girl," she whispered with emotion and opened the door. "What are you trying to do, give me a heart attack?"

"Oh, Grandma, no, of course not. I'm so glad to see you!"

They hugged and Myka cried. She sniffed and said, "How did you even find me?"

"I believe you found me."

"I guess I did."

"I'll tell you all about it, but take my phone and call poor Caleb, so he can rest easy."

When Caleb arrived, he grabbed Myka with both arms, and they stepped away from Grandma. It looked to her like he was squeezing the life out of Myka.

After he'd kissed her several times, they returned to Grandma, and Caleb put his arms around her.

"Myka about gave me a heart attack. Now you're squeezing the life out of me." She was sure he hugged her as long as he'd held Myka. It made her want to cry, but she held back the tears. As usual, he'd be mad at her, and she tried to mentally prepare for it.

"What's wrong?" he asked when she pulled away.

"I can't say I'm sorry, Caleb. I knew this area from my younger years and thought maybe I could help."

"I don't want you to be sorry, Grandma. You got the man arrested, and you found Myka. But what happened to your hair?"

Grandma tried to flatten her hair. "She found me," she said, so pleased at his words.

"Thank God and your lucky stars," said Myka.

Grandma put a hand on her hip. "Who was he and why did he abduct Myka? And then just leave her in the middle of nowhere?"

"As I was just telling Myka—"

"You mean between kisses?" asked Grandma.

"Hey, I've been away. I missed her." He smiled from ear-to-ear.

"Roscoe Miller," shot in Myka. "Remember, he was the guy that I told you Caleb had arrested and was just released from prison."

"He was also the guy parked in our neighborhood," added Grandma.

"As I was saying," said Caleb. "When Roscoe Miller went to jail, his fiancée decided not to wait around for him, so he lost her, and he blamed me for the breakup. He wanted me to feel that same loss. Obviously, he didn't want to hurt Myka as much as he wanted me to feel the pain. And boy, did I feel it. Still, he will have to pay again. Can't go around abducting people."

"Well, I'm glad it's over, I'm tired," said Grandma, a hand rubbing her elbow.

"Grandma, if you could follow me into town, I'd be even more thankful to you."

"Will do, officer." She turned and took one more look behind her before walking to her truck. "Hey, you two, why don't we take up cross-country skiing?"

"Because I'm police not an ambulance driver. Come on, let's go."

ABOUT THE AUTHOR

Mary Vine is an author, publisher, speaker and retired educator. She writes contemporary and historical romantic fiction, a time travel series, and inspirational children's books. Mary and her husband can usually be found in Southwest Idaho or Northeast Oregon. Learn more about her at her website: https://author-maryvine.com

———

INSPIRATION FOR THE STORY

This novelette takes place in the small, fictional town of Trillium

Falls. To learn more about that area consider my novel, *Secrets of Trillium Falls.*

When I'm an Old Lady

Judith Ashley

Published by

Windtree Press, Corvallis, Oregon

https://windtreepress.com

WHEN I'M AN OLD LADY, I WILL WEAR PURPLE

BY JUDITH ASHLEY

I don't know exactly when it happened or even if it was an 'event', and somehow I missed recognizing it at the time. What I do know now is that when I look in the mirror, I see an old lady looking back. She looks somewhat familiar. Bits and pieces of my mother and an aunt are the tell-tell signs that I do indeed know who she is...Me!

How did it happen? My getting old? Just one of those things that happens to all of us if we hang around on this plane long enough. Or did I miss some opportunity that would have kept me young, or at least younger looking?

It isn't that I've never heard of plastic surgery or maybe it's now called cosmetic surgery. I have a television and see the commercials. I look at the thin waists and large breasts and I don't see me. Would I look younger if I had the liposuction? Perhaps, but would I look like me?

But I'm not sure I want to look like the old lady in the mirror either. So what do I do?

*L*ily Hughes put aside the handwritten note the staff had given her. Her client, Margaret Ann Sullivan, was definitely having a difficult time adjusting to the changes in her body. Changes that come rather naturally with the aging process. And changes, not one of her clients or friends welcomed.

Truth be told, she faced these changes herself: slower reflexes, cataract surgery, new aches and pains in the joints. Physical therapists said stairs were good for her. That might be true in general terms, her knees were not convinced.

How to navigate the reality of growing older was truly a challenge for many people she knew. Of course, being a geriatric care manager meant she knew and worked with, and was friends with, many people at the older end of the age spectrum. Yet beyond the professional connection with people like Margaret Ann Sullivan—Sophia and Diana, two other special women in her life, were a year or two older than she and also struggled at times with the changes in their lives. And, of course, since geriatric case management was her specialty, she was regularly asked how to manage these unwanted and yet inevitable changes.

Although questions varied, certain themes ran through them. It took her a while to recognize these themes, and honestly, that didn't happen for several years. What finally brought the themes together was when she focused on additional interviews with her clients in their mid to late nineties, especially those who had reached the magical age of 100.

A smile flickered as memories stirred of herself as a young girl wanting to live to be 100 years old. For a very long time, that was something she looked forward to achieving. However, as she talked to her older clients and her own body aged, living to 100 no longer beckoned to her.

It was true she had a couple more decades of living ahead before she crossed that milestone, but these last few years had especially had her reexamining what she wanted out of her remaining years.

Upon that reexamination, gratitude popped up first. She had so much to be grateful for. She and Jackson had recently celebrated their 30th wedding anniversary. In truth, they were both in good health. Not quite as nimble and agile as they once were, perhaps, but nevertheless, they could and did do pretty much whatever they wanted to do.

Her Sacred Women's Circle was still intact even though Elizabeth was still in Ireland and Gabriella was still in Italy. Diana, Ashley, Hunter, and Sophia were still in Fremont. They still met every other week for Ceremony. As a group, they still traveled to Ireland, especially for Samhain, to celebrate with The Lady in the sacred grove.

Fourteenth Moon? What had once been a focus of their lives had shifted a bit. They no longer sponsored them or took the lead in the Maiden, Matron, and Crone ceremonies. They did still attend…usually. Although they had missed a few this past decade due to other commitments. She'd had a chance to visit with Charlie's family, and had time with her son, daughter-in-law, Amethyst, and grandchildren, always took precedence.

That was only partly true. Two years ago, Jackson wasn't well. It was thought he was having a mild heart attack. Nothing else came first during those intense hours and days. Gratitude that she had Ashley and now, Rose, Ashley's daughter, working with her. She'd cancelled everything that required her personal involvement and that hadn't amounted to much. Ashley and her daughter, Rose, picked up everything else and kept the business afloat, clients safe and cared for, and as another blessing, Rose actually added three new clients. She had given and still gave thanks for asking Ashley to join her business.

She smiled as warmth spread from her heart to her toes. So many blessings filled her life.

Lily picked up Margaret Ann Sullivan's note and tucked it in her notebook to take home and put in the file she kept. Contained within were notes, pictures, and cards that various clients had given her. The ones in this file were special ones, ones that had her thinking about what she'd chosen to do with her life...or more accurately, what had chosen her as her first venture into social services work was as a child protective services worker. The same dynamics and problems, just a different demographic.

LILY SAT IN FRONT OF HER COMPUTER, FINGERS POISED OVER THE keyboard. It was 2:30 in the morning and sleep had been elusive. As was her practice, she got up and came to her office to write the thoughts swirling in her brain. Thoughts that she needed to write down in order to reclaim her peace of mind.

The note from Margaret Ann Sullivan had tap danced in the back of her mind for three days now. She'd read it to Jackson, who said he could relate to the "guy in the mirror" he saw each morning. When she'd shared the note with Diana and Sophia, they too had a similar response. Sitting next to her computer was the journal she kept. Sparse with entries, it was still a prized possession because it initially contained the wisdom of her clients who'd reached 100, and more recently included the thoughts of men and women who were in their mid to late 90's.

Why so late in life? She'd been asked that question numerous times. From her own experience, now that she had fewer years ahead of her than behind, her perspective on what was going on personally, professionally, and even within her community and the world at large was shifting.

She'd noticed it when she turned sixty. Jackson had just turned seventy, and that had really brought things home in a different way. She now saw her marriage as finite. Not that it hadn't always been that way, it had. But she'd always lived in the present with no real thought to what her life would be like if Jackson died first.

With that almost mild heart attack a couple years ago, that had changed. No Pollyanna rose-tinted glasses for her. She didn't wear them for her clients and she wouldn't wear them for her own life.

Now what? She'd taken stock of her life, talked to Jackson, and made sure their Wills and Advanced Directives and POLST's were up-to-date. They hadn't really made many changes, some wording in their Wills to include any grandchildren and great-grands that might come along in their later years, and updates to some bequeaths were made. It was heartening to see that she had been thorough when they'd first set things up. So many people she knew just didn't want to talk about death, dying, and things like Wills, Advanced Directives, Medical and Financial Powers of Attorney, guardians for minor children, etc.

Reeling her wandering mind back to the computer, Lily stared at the blank page.

What to write?

What to write that would bring her peace and blessed sleep?

Glancing at her Journal, she began to type:

Helen: 104 years old – Life happens, the good and the not so good. There's nothing you can do about it except to move forward.

Eleanor: 102 years old – Will it matter tomorrow, next week, next year, in 5 years? What about in 10 or 20 years? If not, then why is it mattering so much now?

Martha: 99 years old – Life's too short to stay upset and angry over anything. I don't want to die with anger or hate in my heart.

George: 95 years old – The hardest thing I've had to do in my lifetime is make peace with not being able to Do and accept that Being me is more than enough.

Angie: 95 years old – I remember you telling me that if I wanted to be independent, I needed to learn how to and actually ask for help. That has been the hardest lesson for me, but I think I've figured it out. Most of the time.

Harold: 98 years old – You know I was always so active until I turned 80. Something happened to me after my 80th birthday. It's like my body decided it was *old* and couldn't safely do things that just yesterday were no problem at all. Learning to pause (I remember you saying I didn't have to Stop, I could just Pause) to make sure my next step (literally) was safe has been my biggest adjustment. But I've done it! And I've not fallen and broken anything for over a decade, actually almost two decades!

Sam: 97 years old – When my wife died, I went into a real funk. I remember you coming to see me and sending that whipper-snapper, Miss Rose, too. Hard to stay curmudgeonly when a bright light like Miss Rose is around. Also hard to be social, spend time with people. I realize now that by not staying involved with younger people, at this point in my life, I'm surrounded by loss.

Lily: 68 years old – What's been hardest for me over the years has been the realization that I've fewer years ahead of me than behind. I'm grateful that two of my circle sisters are five/six years younger than me. I'm also grateful that my son and his family want to be in contact with me. Not so long ago, Charlie and Amethyst sat me down and told me, in no uncertain terms, that they would be staying in the Fremont area and would make sure I behaved myself as I aged. *She smiled at that memory and softly chuckled to herself for including herself in this journal.*

I thought it was sweet of them to speak up, and as I look back on that conversation, my gratitude expands. I will have to ask, but then I've begun to do that in other areas. I've asked Ashley and Rose to pick up pieces of the business so I can spend more time with Jackson or with my grandchildren. I am aware that Ashley also has grandchildren and Rose has a special man in her life, so a marriage and children may be in her near future.

What is certain in life is the fact that there is no certainty. We will go home to the Crystal City whenever Spirit calls us.

What has sustained me over the years? If someone asked me to choose between Jackson and my Sacred Women's Circle sisters, I'd not be able to answer that by choosing one over the other.

Without my Circle Sisters, I'd not be married to Jackson nor would Jackson be married to me.

My spirituality has sustained me through the years. Knowing that all is happening in *right time* is, at times, frustrating, albeit true. Spirit's timeframe is not always Lily's timeframe. However, when I look back, I do see that all does happen in *right time.* The experience, that at that time, was so stressful, so challenging, so unwanted, turned out to be one of those blessings in disguise.

I draw Oracle and Tarot Cards for guidance. Not every day, but always when there is a special occasion, something puzzles me, or when it feels like there is a message for me that I'm not seeing or hearing. The cards always help me see what my focus, my path, or direction needs to be so I can find my way forward.

I also seek to see both sides of a conflict. Not that I agree with both sides. I just want to understand what is important to everyone involved. So often families are split as to what they want for their parent or loved one. Of course, what my client wants is what happens. It is helpful to know, to understand why the spouse, children, or other relatives and friends want what they want for the person.

So often it has to do with wills, what's left to whom, etc., and thus it has nothing really to do with the person whose life is ending. It is human nature in some ways to deny what's unpleasant or what one doesn't want to face.

Deny or blame.

So many times, the recriminations come roaring to the surface and start to drown out my client's wishes. Of course, I step in, or maybe it's step up and intercede, reminding everyone of what's important.

Do they really want this person, who is so important in their lives, to die with their anger, hate, and disappointment the only emotion in which they are surrounded? That question usually stops them in mid-rant, in mid-sentence, even.

No, they don't. And that's when my work to help heal the relationships within these people, who are so important to my client, can begin. It isn't always easy and I'm not always successful. Some people stay in their righteousness regardless of what's being said and shown to them. And that is their choice.

It isn't unusual for them to contact me later, sometimes even a few years later, to talk about the death of *their person* and a new understanding of what had happened and where they were in that process. The questions always boil down to

Does she know I'm sorry?

Does he know I love him?

My answer is always, "Yes. Once back in the Crystal City all becomes known and understood and only love remains."

I am grateful that when my time comes, I will be held in the light of love. I will be protected from anything that does not serve my highest good. I will be able to return to the Crystal City in peace.

ABOUT THE AUTHOR

Judith Ashley is the author of The Sacred Women's Circle series, stories about seven women who find a safe haven within their sacred circle and from whence they figure out how to overcome the challenges of divorce, domestic violence, single parenting, cancer, childhood abuse and death of a beloved spouse.

To learn more about Judith and her books, go to her website at: https://judithashley.net/

———

INSPIRATION FOR THIS STORY

When I saw the inspiration for this year's Windtree Press

Anthology was Navigate, I realized that word has been at the heart of my life's journey these past four years. I turned 80 in 2021 and since then, my navigating the process of aging has accelerated. Or at least it seems that way to me.

Lily: The Dragon and The Great Horned Owl's main character works with people who are struggling as they age. I did that work also. Time to use the knowledge and skills I learned over those decades in my own life so I have more days when I'm managing and even have days when I'm okay if not fine.

Navigating the Chaos

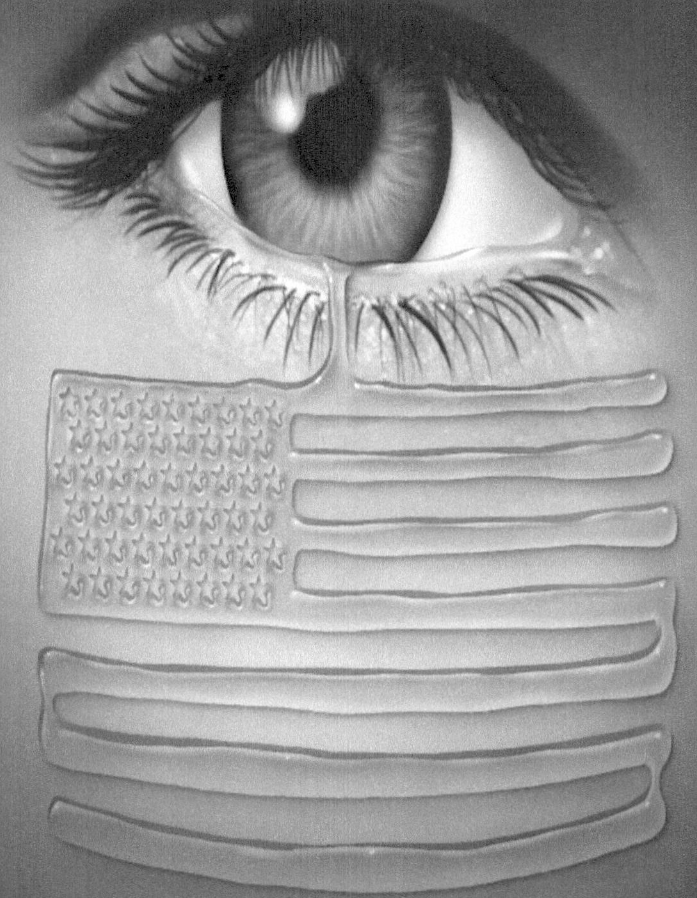

A Poem

by Dari LaRoche

Published by

Windtree Press, Corvallis, Oregon

https://windtreepress.com

NAVIGATING THE CHAOS

BY DARI LAROCHE

Can we bring it back?
    Will kindness return at last?
We must work day and night
    To make our country right
        – again.

Not the again the politicians play.
    But the again we lost along the way.
        The again that makes our worried hearts
            Thrum with quiet pride.

The again that takes us back
    To the peace we felt inside.
The again that brings us round
    To the wealth of love we found
In family, friends, and faith,
    To accepting, forgiving, and grace.
        Learning from the past,
        Rectifying the present,

Looking to the future,
With hope, determination, and joy.
Doing our part
Making our choices
Working for good
Lifting our voices.
America doesn't need an "again."
America needs determination and resilience
To stand against the wrongs,
To fight for the rights.
To act "as if."
We all matter
We all make a difference
Every day, in every way,
With every word and every action.
We don't have to change.
Only resurrect the kindness already
Embedded in your hearts and mine.
We simply forgot along the way
And decided ugly and mean was okay.
But it's not.
It never will be.
We are Americans.
We are strong.
And we have and always will winnow the chaff,
Even in our own country.
This is home.
We must start here first.

ABOUT THE AUTHOR

Dari LaRoche writes contemporary romance with page-turning suspense and everyday heroes who face extraordinary circumstances to find their own happiness and save lives in the process. Her Rescue Series takes place in the Pacific Northwest and the Caribbean, settings inspired by LaRoche's love for travel and passion for safeguarding the natural environment.

Some of LaRoche's favorite places are Greece, the Caribbean, much of Europe, and the United Kingdom. Her love of water, above and below the surface, and for tromping around the ruins of castles and forts, fills any time she isn't reading, writing, and enjoying family and friends.

Learn more about Dari at her website: https://darilaroche.com/

—

The Beckoning

Maggie Lynch

Published by

Windtree Press, Corvallis, Oregon

https://windtreepress.com

Previous publication of this story in:

Underground: An Anthology by NIWA, 2014

THE BECKONING

BY MAGGIE LYNCH

1. UNDERGROUND

Kurr's shoulders relaxed as they completed the second set of stairs going below ground. After the third level, he let out the breath he'd been holding since they started the descent. So far, no voices. At the turn beyond the fourth level, his stomach stopped roiling. At the final level, the large male nurse opened a heavy door to reveal his new home. Kurr peered inside and smiled for the first time in two years.

It was utterly quiet. He couldn't hear machinery anywhere. He couldn't hear people talking in another room. In fact, the only thing he heard was his own breath and that of the nurse next to him.

Kurr walked the perimeter of the room determining the dimensions with his footsteps. Ten by twelve. Slightly larger than his previous room on the surface. All walls were covered in a tongue-and-groove plank that made the room appear as if he were in a cabin. He walked to the back corner, where a small sink, a mirror, a shower, and a toilet were arranged with a half wall to separate them from the rest of the room. On the opposite wall, a single bed with an end table and a small lamp were placed against a quilt that hung from the ceiling to the floor. Next to the bed was a faux window with a rural scene of rolling farmland painted behind it.

In the middle, a large woven rug outlined a sitting area with a rocking chair and a chaise lounge separated by a small table with another lamp. A flat screen television was secured to the opposite wall. Kurr couldn't imagine turning it on. He didn't want noise. He didn't want the outside world to intrude, to confuse. Unlike most of the patients here, he didn't spend hours in front of the television letting the drone of newscasts numb his thoughts.

Kurr tested the rocking chair. It didn't creak and it fit his body well. He stood and walked to a wall covered in tongue-and-groove planking and knocked on it. The sound was solid, not hollow. Certainly, concrete backed it.

"Insulation?" Kurr asked.

"Yes, sir. Three times the norm."

"Electrical interference protection?"

"Yes, sir. Nothing can get into this room without your permission. No voices. No television. No phones. No computers."

Kurr nodded. Maybe the voices would finally leave him alone. Surely, they couldn't find him here sixty feet below the surface.

The nurse strode to the small sink in the corner and placed a plastic container on the edge. "I'll leave your evening medication here."

"I won't need it," Kurr said.

"Of course you won't." The nurse patted Kurr on the back. "But just in case, it is there for you." He ambled toward the heavy door and stepped into the hall. "I'll be back at six, when I bring your dinner."

Kurr nodded and waited to finally be closed into his secure room. First he would take a nap. Then he would wake and do a little reading before dinner. He would thoroughly enjoy his six hours of silence until the nurse returned. Finally, the voices would leave him alone.

———

2. THE VOID

An intuitive beckoning unleashed the march of shadowy images, initiating the first stirrings of Glosum's sentience. The planet below was the only stable form in her embryonic consciousness. All else was shades of gray and black. Even among the overwhelming assault of images, she sensed the utter loneliness that went with nothingness, and she longed to help. She stretched her will, embracing the planet, as if to hug it to her. The pain overwhelmed her. Then, mercifully, she lost consciousness once more.

———

"HE'S COMING AROUND." THE NURSE MOTIONED TO A WOMAN NEAR the doorway. "It's a miracle. His brain activity indicated he was near death, and now it's almost normal."

"Vaclav?" The woman stood over the hospital bed, looking into his unfocusing eyes. "It's me, your sister."

Kurr felt her touch and sat straight up in bed, his dark brown eyes wide with incomprehension. The woman was speaking in Czech, yet he seemed to understand it. Why did this person call him Vaclav?

He glanced about the room and recognized nothing. He lifted his hand to point at the woman and blanched. The pale skin attached to his arm was not his! The woman stepped forward to soothe him, and suddenly he trusted her. Shaking violently, with trembling fingers he reached for her arm and clung to it as if it was life itself. A prick. Warmth flooded him. He relaxed and slept secure.

Struggling to recapture the waning memories of his dream, Kurr awoke again, this time in his own familiar underground room. He tried to voice the images his dream forced on his mind. "Darkness -- nothingness -- emptiness -- loneliness." He thought he was safe. He thought he could escape so far underground. With a shudder, he fell back to bed, crying out with mad convulsions.

---

3. THE LAND AND SEA

Rounding the corner as he hurried to the next lecture series, Wu convulsed suddenly. He fell to the floor and closed his eyes, allowing the rhythm of images to flow over him. His identity merged with the voices of many others. The loudest voice was one who called himself Kurr.

Wu questioned the voice in his unconscious, but could not understand the answers. The voice did not speak Chinese, and Wu knew nothing of the language of symbols. He knew only that they were important.

Soon the visions passed, and Wu hastily jotted down the complex formulas and attempted to sketch the diagrams before they fled his memory. He experienced no fear of these occurrences, only a tiredness, a longing for nothingness, a longing for peace. Soon, he thought. Soon, he would find the meaning of these visions.

Glosum convulsed as each bursting image lanced through her, bringing light, color, and form. Her growing consciousness ringed the planet in a rhythmic beckoning to all the fragments of her being. The rhythm twisted the lighted images, weaving them into strange and new perspectives. A kaleidoscope of concepts danced at the edges of her consciousness, slowly transforming her single note of purpose into a full, rounded symphony of understanding and joy.

She gasped as strange identities assailed her: Vaclav, Wu, Jackie, Evelyn, Kurr. Closing her mind, she longed for a few brief moments of nothingness in which she might peacefully assimilate the myriad of ideas. She let her mind drift, let herself recoil from the experience.

---

4. THE HEAVENS

In the convent, attached to a small religious school in Seattle, Sister Jackie carefully hung her habit in the spartan closet of her room. She slipped her flannel nightgown over her head to diminish the damp chill. In front of the small altar near her bed, she knelt and made the sign of the cross, then held the crucifix and prayed the Apostle's Creed.

"I believe in God, the Father All Mighty . . ." She went through each bead of the rosary, the Our Father's, the Hail Mary's, the four mysteries. She did this five times, as was her custom, then followed it with her own desperate prayer -- the same one she had been praying six times daily for the past two weeks. " Father, I am unworthy to receive such a gift. The dream you continue to send me evades my understanding. I know it must be important because it grows stronger each night. Help me to understand, so I may use it to do your will."

Sister Jackie stayed on her knees for a long time, longing for the fulfillment of her prayer. After nearly two hours of patient waiting, she finally rose and climbed into bed. Once again, she reviewed the small notebook on the nightstand. She had no memory of drawing the strange collection of pictures in her diary. Yet, each morning when she awoke, new ones appeared. Abstract lines connected in maze-like fashion with many dots and symbols. The symbols had frightened her at first: tiny lightning bolts, dark triangles and rectangles with coiled snakes. And she had signed each picture with the name of Kurr.

Because of the alarming images, she had kept the drawings to herself the first week. Finally, overwhelmed by the fear they might be the handiwork of Satan, or a minion of Satan named Kurr, she took them to Father Myron and asked for a special prayer.

After sharing the pictures with several priests, Father Myron identified them as complex wiring diagrams, the type used in micro-circuitry. Yet both he and Sister Jackie were perplexed by her drawings, as she had no prior knowledge of electronics.

———

5. THE ANIMALS

Glosum gathered strength from the rounding of her consciousness. She could now concentrate on the planet's life forms and direct the assimilation of the identities as they filtered through her from the layered blue and green mists. The rays of her thoughts darted among the shifting shadows, reaching beyond the waters and the mountains, gathering the identities together, passing them from one life form to another. Glosum ravenously swept them into her consciousness, accelerating the reaffirmation of her own identity.

———

IN PERTH, THE CEO OF UNITECH WAITED NERVOUSLY FOR HER appointment with one of the top psychiatrists in the city. Evelyn knew she needed help immediately. Her actions were more than one night's drunken revelry.

For the past month, Evelyn's husband had awakened her each night from sleepwalking -- or rather sleep dancing. Each night, he found her stark naked, dancing about the living room coffee table and chanting unintelligibly, using the name of Kurr as her mantra. During the past week, she had taken to adding streaks of color to her face and body. Yet she had no personal memory of these actions.

As one night led to the next, each one becoming more unusual, Evelyn had grown more frantic about sleeping. She drank coffee to stave off tiredness. She jogged on the treadmill in the basement. She paced in the living room, anything to ensure she would not fall asleep. But nothing worked. Every morning, she awoke to find herself crouched naked in the living room. This morning she had red lipstick encircling her navel, and a brown eye pencil line drawn from her eyelid to the middle of her cheek. Her waking memories were of ancestral rituals performed around campfires with the entire tribal community participating. She feared these dreams, coupled with her bizarre actions, were surely signs of growing insanity.

Evelyn crossed and uncrossed her legs, trying to calm her nerves while waiting for Dr. Morgan. She hoped he could help her before her subconscious won out and manifested itself at work. Perhaps they would admit her to a sanitarium. Perhaps they would have to send her underground, away from the real world. She shuddered at the thought.

———

6. *THE LIGHT*

With her own sense of identity returned and knowledge of the great quest again foremost in her mind, Glosum rose from the Earth. She gleefully rotated over the ellipsoidal planet, orbiting soundlessly from pole to pole. With each pass, her directed thoughts spun the cloying strands of the individual identities into a fine matrix that enfolded her, warming her being with knowledge and purpose.

Glosum did not know the duration of her fragmentation, nor the number of identities she had pursued. She remembered only that a unified approach to sharing herself with this world could have been devastating to its inhabitants. Thus, she had devised a way to fragment her own identity, so as not to overwhelm any individual being. Each fragment carried a small part of her consciousness, and with it an enhanced experience sensor and a reference to a time point which would trigger the fragment's return.

Parts of her were randomly spread across the planet, attaching each fragment to a single intelligence, be it plant or animal. The fragment's only goal was to record that being's entire experience until the time of emergence. As she neared the full awakening, a blistering light shone through her, igniting the multitude of identities into fusion. The harmony of her thoughts enveloped the small planet below, infusing thousands of beings with the knowledge and experiences she had gathered to herself. This was the final sharing, and she was glad to bring it to the inhabitants.

———

KURR TURNED ON THE TELEVISION. THE VOICES HAD FOUND HIM. HE wanted the newscast to drown them out. Perhaps he was like all the others. Perhaps he was truly crazy. He trembled when he thought of the details he had witnessed in the past few weeks. And now it seemed the entire world was joining in his personal insanity.

"This is Michael Woods," the newscaster began, "anchoring this special report from Renews, Newfoundland. The recent unexplained appearance of auras around the world are being blamed for the massive increase in public insanity. Hundreds of people are violently running through the streets, crying out the name, Kurr. These hoards are destroying property and trampling anyone in their path. Thousands of others are screaming in agonizing pain as they look toward the changing lights. We are warning everyone to stay inside, draw the curtains, try to save yourselves. Who is Kurr? Have aliens finally arrived? Is this mass biological warfare? Let us go now to Russia, and our reporter in St. Petersburg."

The cameras cut from one reporter to the next, scanning the globe. Each location reported similar observations. The reporters openly vied to portray the most danger, adding suspense to their reports as they filmed outside beneath the bright lights from the auras. Kurr shook as he watched one reporter's growing insanity that mirrored his own experiences. The reporter called out Kurr's name. He repeated Kurr's visions as the pressure of the voices in the reporter's mind matched everything Kurr had experienced in the past week.

Kurr rushed to the toilet and bent over retching as his stomach emptied. What power did he have? Locked in his basement sanctuary he could not have spread this disease. Why were they calling out to him? Perhaps all of it—the television reports, the room, the dreams—was an illusion. He gulped water to take the sourness out of his throat and then took the pills meant for this evening. It was several hours early but he didn't care. He needed to stop the insanity. He needed to stop the visions.

"Is this the work of Satan, as the religious want us to believe?" Another reporter asked. "Or does it have another explanation? We polled several experts with these questions."

Kurr covered his ears as he returned to the television. He grabbed the remote and fumbled for the off button.

"Does the aura have a single source? Will we lose..."

Kurr darkened the screen, cutting out this final voice and ran from his room. He no longer felt safe sixty feet below the ground. Everything was closing in now. He needed light. He needed air. He needed unending vistas.

———

7. THE APOCALYPSE

Glosum slowed her gleeful rotation as she began to feel the fear and violence erupting from the beings on the planet below. She was confused by these emotions. She had offered them her most valued gift -- knowledge of themselves. Why did they not accept graciously? Had she misunderstood their need? Had she misinterpreted their prayers?

On other planets, she had always seeded the intelligent beings with their shared knowledge. It helped them to evolve and move forward in concert with the universe. But now, on this world, it appeared the gift was unwanted. Perhaps she had erred in her selection of this planet. Perhaps they were not ready.

Sadly, she withdrew from the planet, unable to complete the final unity of her identity.

The multitude of colors within the auras gathered together, changing from one color to the next, until finally reaching an opaque gold that stretched into a fine chain ringing the equator. With the force of a single thought, Glosum drew the ring toward the North Pole. Slowly, it rose from the planet and hovered above, as if a halo crowned the head of the Earth.

The force of the aura's withdrawal drew the tides from the oceans, flooding the land and consuming all life in the coastal areas. The pressure within the mountains caused simultaneous volcanic explosions, destroying even more lives and wreaking havoc upon the monuments of humanity.

Glosum projected herself toward the halo, accepting it as the robe of her office. Then she distanced herself from the planet until she felt the few remaining identities below returning to their mundane, closed lives.

She retreated to the inner depths of the universe, appalled by the destruction her withdrawal had caused. She had not intended to do harm. She must find a way to repair the planet. But how? She had destroyed so many of the intelligent beings.

Glosum stretched her consciousness inward, seeking the patterns of each identity she had gathered. She looked for the one most worthy—the one who was most willing to accept her gift. It had to be someone who was part of this planet, someone who had a chance at understanding their fear.

The name Kurr stood out in consciousness. The one being who connected with all without fear. Kurr.

———

KURR TOOK THE SMALL BRANCHING PATH THAT LED UP TO A RIDGE where he often went to sit and watch the eternal shadow of the looming mountains slide into the valley below. When the world seemed to join his insanity, he became sane. When he'd escaped his basement enclave and run into the mountains twenty years ago, he'd been happy when the voices began to leave him. At first, it was a few each day. Then it grew to hundreds leaving his mind all at once. For the past twenty years, there had been no more voices and now he found he missed them.

His hikes through the mountains had become a search to hear them again. A week ago, they began to return and he welcomed them. This time he had a sense of purpose. This time he took in the strength of their diversity.

Kurr sat upon the low boulder so familiar to him and gazed

across the distance to the mountains, thankful for this new gift. The sun began its slow journey to hide behind the ridge, turning the sky a creamy peach. On slopes shadowed in pale blue, dark patches of forests climbed upward, drawing his gaze toward the snowy peaks still glittering in the brilliance of a reflected sun.

Slowly, the calm peach sky turned an angry red before darkening into an all-encompassing black. It contained all the colors, forcing a totality of acceptance

The colors change, like people, he thought. The colors always change and shift, from calm to anger, from acceptance to rejection. And in their changing the world changes. An hour from now the world will not be the same as it is now. He looked once more to the sky as the darkness fell over the mountains; and a peace came over him. Finally, the time has come to accept all the colors, all the differences, embrace the darkness.

––––––––

8. REST

Trying to be careful this time, Glosum concentrated a small piece of her consciousness in a thin line, aiming the light of her gift directly toward Kurr. She had chosen the man who heard the voices because he now embraced them. Kurr needed the gift as much as she needed to give it.

––––––––

Kurr fell to his knees before the blinding light that appeared from nowhere. As it enveloped his quaking body, the thousands of voices traveling along its path assailed his ears. Yet he was not afraid. He accepted this gift as his due, his reward for patiently waiting and listening all these years.

He lost all sense of time and place, yet he experienced great happiness. He reveled in the song of foreverness and wept at the emptiness in this corner of the universe, wherever it might be. As his identity fused with that of Glosum, he caught the brief consciousness of each life recorded within her; and he was able to be a part of the achievements of that life—each achievement peculiar to each individual.

His body weakened and his heart beat erratically. Kurr collapsed to the ground and writhed in pain. This was his heritage, he thought. This was the striving of his people, and of many other peoples, who alone and in the darkness of unknowing clawed toward the light.

Lying face up, his lungs gave one final gasp, and he surrendered to Glosum.

---

9. CODA

Kurr stood above the planet, his mind ringing the azure world as the wrinkled sea beneath him crawled. At first, he sensed only the ugly and huddled walls of their minds. He looked into the multitude of hunger-deep eyes, haunted with shadows of hunger-hands. As he lingered among them, he felt the stirrings of his past—a past that now seemed millennia ago. Then he knew what he must do.

He must help them to grasp for knowledge, to cling desperately to what they learned and ask for more. He must help them work endlessly to strive for answers—the same answers that beckons all intelligence in the universe. For it was the search that would spur them forward and help them to evolve.

Slowly, Kurr exercised his will, setting the beckoning signal within each fragment of his being—extracting bits of his own consciousness and placing it in billions of raindrops. He reached toward the layered blue and green mists above the planet, moving the clouds shepherded by the slow, unwilling wind.

The fragments left him, one by one, slipping randomly over the earth and attaching themselves to an intelligent being. Each one had a connection to another bit of his consciousness if those individuals would dare to share. Those beings who would dare to reach for understanding, without fear of change, would find each other and learn. In that finding, they and their planet would be infinitely rewarded.

As the last fragment of Kurr's conscious left him, he quietly slipped into the stream of the universe to await the beckoning.

Maggie Lynch is the author of 27+ published titles, as well as numerous short stories and non-fiction articles. Her fiction tells stories of men and women making heroic choices one messy moment at a time. Her fiction spans romance, suspense, fantasy and SF titles, as well as children's books. Her current non-fiction titles are focused on helping other authors become successful in their careers.

Maggie and her musician husband have settled in the beautiful Pacific Northwest where they have retired from the corporate and academic world to follow their dual creative pursuits of music and writing.

You can learn more about Maggie at her website: https://maggielynch.com

———

INSPIRATION FOR THE STORY
My major during my bachelor's degree program was in psychology and my minor in religious studies. I've always been fascinated by the different beliefs humans have about one or more gods that have the ability to intervene in our lives, as well as what is waiting for us in the hereafter. This story contemplates how an intervention might feel to those touched by the supernatural.

These Delicate Creatures

Melissa Yuan-Innes

Publisher's Note: This is a work of fiction. Names, characters, places, and incidents are a product of the author's imagination. Locales and public names are sometimes used for atmospheric purposes. Any resemblance to actual people, living or dead, or to businesses, companies, events, institutions, or locales is completely coincidental.

Published by

Windtree Press, Corvallis, Oregon

https://windtreepress.com

THESE DELICATE CREATURES

BY MELLISSA YUAN-INNES

<u>Mem</u>,
<u>Stop acting.</u>

*S*uch a simple message. It shouldn't have sucked the recycled air from my lungs.

But I love acting. I love the smell of antique greasepaint smeared across my face. I love the heat of the audience's gaze. I love my parched mouth and the sweat pricking under my armpits as I extend myself into a new character. I love the 1/8 g on Cosmos 7 that allows me to bound and dance into the atmosphere, as if the air itself is another partner.

I love acting more than I have loved anything or anyone in my entire life.

I have received fan mail and hate mail in my time and have become quite jaded about both.

But this was a command.

The message used a pet name, a corruption of my name, Emma Lo, and it penetrated my com link's filters. The messenger cloaked him or herself in anonymity: text instead of voice or video, and a blocked sender.

I sent a tracer on the message, even though I knew it was hopeless. I saved the script I'd been working on in the space station gym. I glanced at the grav treadmill and the calm surface of the flotation pool. Although I was alone, I felt too exposed in a room anyone could enter with a keylock. I needed privacy.

Not the sleep pod. Too confined. Someone in the next pod might hear.

I bounded to our most opulent bathroom. Soundproofed, illegal to spy on, and most thankfully, vacant. The door sealed behind me. I stepped into the shower, fully clothed, disabled the cleaning module, and called my director. "Quattra."

Her image projected an arm span in front of me, draped in a sheer white cloak that swirled and soared with her every move. "Emma! I hardly recognized you. The nanos have done a fabulous job on you. You look like a new man!" Quattra giggled at her own joke. At 62, she was older than my daughter, yet seemed even more juvenile. That was the problem with getting older. Everyone seemed newly hatched.

Except, perhaps, my wily messager.

I bestowed a smile upon Quattra. "Yes, thank you. However--"

"The skin could be a little darker, though. And perhaps your voice just slightly lower, more of a baritone, although I like the acoustics in this space." She squinted at me. "I don't know if I should be honored or offended that you called me to such...intimate surroundings." She glanced down, realized her holo appeared perilously close to the urinal, and adjusted her projection to a hand span away from me. She refocused on my face. "That's better. Remember, Emma, I would like your Othello to contrast even more with the rest of the cast."

Since Iago was played by an alien sea serpent and Desdemona was a human six-year-old genius, both nano-ed into Caucasian adults, I thought she was bound by trivia, as usual. I reined in my impatience. "Quattra. I have a serious concern."

"What's that, my darling? You need a pick for your new hair?" She laughed, shaking her own platinum tresses, and through the diaphanous cloak, I spotted her ears, nano-ed into clamshell shape. Lovely. She had already been listening-impaired.

"No. I am forwarding an anonymous letter to you." I blinked down a menu and eyed the send key.

She received it, scanned it, and laughed again. "Oh, Mem. What's the problem? An unhappy critic?"

I burned. Only my close friends and family called me Mem. Ever the actress, I swathed my emotions in sweetness. "In a manner of speaking. Do you think the President's entourage has any idea what we've planned?"

Her laugh tinkled once more. "Memmy. Darling. You think someone has leaked our little secret, and the President of Cosmos 7 is threatening you personally?"

I allowed my mien, my silence, and our cloistered surroundings to answer.

She sobered. "Emma. You are, of course, the heart and soul of the production. However, if the President had an inkling, he would send in his stormtroopers. Not a little message to you."

I shook my own close-cropped head.

"Emma. Think of it this way. You have an understudy. The show would go on--crippled, maimed, irrevocably damaged without you. But the show would go on."

"I understand, Quattra." Subtlety was never one of her virtues. Whenever she felt besieged, she reminded us that we were replace- able. "But have a care, would you? I'll notify the rest of the cast in case they receive similar messages."

For the first time, two vertical lines appeared between her

eyebrows. "Emma. You'd cause a riot! Wait until tonight's rehearsal, at least." Her tangerine, cat-shaped eyes compelled me, and I remembered that Quattra had been a renowned actress of her own generation, before she climbed on the director's chair.

"I understand your concern. I'll tell them at rehearsal." Prima donna stereotypes aside, I could not have survived at my level of acting for more than a century, without learning the tact and compromise worthy of a prince.

"Thank you, Othello." She blew me a kiss.

I severed the connection.

Almost immediately, a second message burned on my retinas. The anonymous mailer had hacked a direct com link.

<u>Mem</u>,
<u>Stop acting NOW.</u>

———

WHEN I WAS BORN, CONTROVERSY OVER ABORTION (MEDICAL termination of human pregnancies) raged across North American headlines. Some pro-life radicals decided to kill the doctors performing abortions. At the same time, the more mainstream members voted in politicians who tightened up legal access to the procedure, eroding legal precedent rather than overturning it directly.

In the same way, the President could eliminate me while he sent in the stormtroopers. A two-pronged or multi-level approach is always best.

In other words, for an actor-director, Quattra suffered from a failure of imagination and it was up to me to stop it.

First, I pulled in a few favors. I direct-linked the most important person first. "Hertz? Can you trace an anonymous message for me? Stat?"

His avatar, a cartoon devil in a red suit, yawned. It took him a second to cover his gaping mouth, so I got a nice look at his tonsils and cleft chin. "What time is it?"

"I'm serious, Herkscovitch."

At his full name, the devil stopped elaborately scratching his butt. "Fine. You owe me, Mem."

"I know."

"And one of these days, I'm going to collect."

He'd been threatening to do so for decades. Ordinarily, I'd smile and pat the devil between his tiny horns on his head. This time, it took all my aplomb to muster, "I know."

Next, I called my contacts at the President's office. Dangerous in itself. Could and would be traced. But as far as I could tell, our project had not yet been leaked.

So who had hacked me?

———

DESDEMONA SHOWED UP TO REHEARSAL 20 MINUTES LATE AND cranky. "She missed her nap," explained her mother. "But she's already better. The nanos are working hard."

I held my tongue. The nanos worked hard enough, artificially maintaining Desdemona's decade-aged, 16-year-old body, without having to keep her hormones in line, too.

While Quattra's casting lacked a certain *je ne sais quoi*, she'd convinced the space station to add a playroom for our troupe. It was barely bigger than my childhood bedroom, but we were able to squeeze in chairs, two privacy screens to change behind, a giant projection screen, and best of all, the occasional audience.

While I eyed the blank projection screen, wishing for an authentic Roman backdrop, Desdemona missed her line. I could have prompted her, but I waited for the prompter on her com link.

Iago chuckled. It was more of a sibilant hiss.

Desdemona whipped her juice bottle at his forehead.

He ducked, but slipped and fell on his human behind before bouncing up toward the ceiling in 1/8 g.

Meanwhile, the juice bottle ricocheted around the room. Its lid snapped and juice exploded over the practice room.

"CUT!" Quattra screamed, reverting to her actress/movie star days, while Desdemona's mother cried, "Baby! Baby!" and Iago launched off the ceiling, aiming for Desdemona's neck.

I shot in between them. "No!"

Iago pushed off the side of the room to bodycheck me away. But the superior mass of my Othello body withstood both his assault and Desdemona's impotent beating on my back. Neither of them had mastered their adult limbs enough to have an effect.

Ow. Desi kicked me in the back of the knee.

I twisted to body bind [PJ1] her. She scratched the back of my neck. Hellfire!

When Iago yanked her leg, ripping her away from me, I might have seized her ankle, except another message seared across my retinas.

M	E	M
Stop	acting	now
Or	else	

———

"Mem."

I squinted in the darkness. My temples pounded. My tongue felt like dehydrated protein. I tried to sleep a minimum of 8 hours a night. At my age, you need as much beauty sleep as possible, nanos or no nanos. It took me a moment to remember the troupe's fight and the station police breaking it up.

A little red devil tried to crawl under the duvet with me.

"Hertz," I sighed. The plastic sleep pod, more of a cocoon, could barely accommodate my six-foot man form, let alone an unwelcome holo.

"I didn't want to wait," he said. "I found your hacker."

I pawed around my down blanket, my one item of retro luxury, for the ice pack. It was now a lukewarm stub of gel, but I pushed it on my forehead anyway.

"Why don't you just get your nanos to lower the temp there? You're so old school," said Hertz.

"Look who's talking," I said. "You're older than I am."

He was silent for a minute. "Is all this worth it? This whole thing with the President?"

"He's a despot, Hertz." I slid the gel over my eyes. We'd had this argument before.

"And you really think this play is going to make him or his people change?"

I felt every one of my years, but I still felt compelled to answer. "Most people don't take the arts seriously. They think they're 'a pageant/To keep us in false gaze.' But whenever a despot comes to power, he kills the artists and intellectuals. He knows we're dangerous." My mind was still murky with sleep, but I made the connection. "So that's who's threatening me? Were they interfering with Desdemona's com link too, and that's why she screwed up her line?"

The devil threw back his little horned blond head and laughed. "Nah. That was just funny. But to tell you the truth, I haven't looked into your troupe's problem. I know who hacked your link."

Into the silence, I remembered one of Iago's lines: "I'll pour this pestilence into his ear." I waited.

"It's your daughter."

As I rocked backward from his words, a final message burst into my brain, complete with text and sound:

MEM

    STOP ACTING

OR YOU WILL NEVER SEE

The message vanished. An infant holo projected above our feet. Sleeping. Legs bundled. Even on his skinny, newborn face and etched-closed eyes, I could trace my own original features. So real I swore I could press his heartbeat, pulsating through the soft point of his skull.

Someone startled him. His stick-like arms jerked to the side. His eyes opened. Dark brown eyes. My eyes. And a tiny but distinct cleft chin.

The infant holo vanished. My breasts ached even though I had never nursed.

I collapsed back in bed. Hertz's avatar leaned over me. His cleft chin quivered. He said, "We have to talk."

I ignored him and called the one person who had blocked my link for decades. I threw open my sleep pod cover and she appeared, my grandbaby still clasped close to her chest.

"You thought I'd never have a baby," said my daughter.

Penelope's face was heavier than I remembered, more wrinkled, thicker around the jowls. Even her eyelids had begun to sag. She wore an unbecoming traditional navy floor-length smock and sensible shoes that might have been a school age uniform from the 1950s. No makeup. No nanos. Of course.

It startled me, how old my daughter had become. It meant I had truly aged, despite the miniature machines tending my every cell.

She had aged, but she was still arresting. My oversized nose and Hertz's cleft chin could have made her ugly, but she carried herself with such pride and defiance, she was something better than beautiful. Strong.

Yet tender. Even behind her American burqa, I could tell her breasts swelled with new milk. Unless she'd had hormonal injections, this was her birth son.

I spoke as gently as possible to her holo. "No. I thought you would have a baby. It was you who thought you'd never have one."

"Because of all your blanking nanotechnology!" If a holo could spit, she would have.

I felt Hertz's cartoon eyes on me. I murmured to both of them, "You don't know that's why."

"Yes, it is! You couldn't even have me until your 50's, with all the best doctors Hertz could buy."

I parried. "And here you are, in your 50's, with your own bundle of joy. Congratulations. What's his name?"

"Oh, no. You can't do this. You can't pretend everything's all right because after three decades--thirty <u>years</u>--of trying, we finally caved in to technology. You did this, Mem. I want you to make it right."

I tried to follow her logic. I remembered how everyone told me new mothers were irrational, hormone-ridden bags of tears. Until now, I'd always denied it. "I agree that I was one of the pioneers in nanotechnology."

"And in space! You kept going out to space, volunteering for missions. You wanted to be the first actor in space, Yahweh knows why--"

"I was a pioneer," I agreed.

"Our doctors are sure you did damage to your ovaries, with all the radiation and the nanotechnology. And you passed it down--you infected me!"

I remained silent. Science was not my strong point, but I once did a play about the DES scandal. In the 1970's, expectant mothers were given this medication against miscarriage, not realizing that their unborn daughters would develop abnormalities of their Fallopian tubes and a predisposition for clear cell cancer. I played a daughter who died from that cancer.

I bowed my head. "It's possible." I erased any doubt from my voice. It was Penelope's turn to take center stage, no matter how vehemently she would deny that. "But I'm very happy that you have a baby now. I know how much you wanted one." More than you wanted your mother.

She cried now, tears that snaked down her face. I saw one drip into the creases of her neck. She held the baby too tight--I still didn't know my grandson's name--and he protested. She turned her back to me. Her arms moved. I heard cloth unwrapping. She sat, back curved, arms cradled.

She was nursing.

I wanted to ask her to put her feet up. I wanted her to tuck frozen cabbage leaves against her cracked nipples. I wanted to hold my grandbaby so she could get, if not 8 hours of sleep, at least 8 minutes.

I wanted to mother her.

And I wanted to hold my grandson.

Instead, I waited and literally watched her back. Hertz's avatar sat beside me and pretended to take my hand.

I let him. I knew better than most how much symbolism counted.

When she turned back to me, her tears had disappeared. The baby slept again. I risked a glance at his sweet, upturned face. His lower lip pushed back and forth a few times, sucking in his sleep.

"I promised Yahweh that if I got my healthy baby, I would welcome you back into my life. But look at you. You're an abomination. You're not my mother. You're not even a woman!"

I kept my lowered eyes on my grandson. His eyes blinked. His lips smacked more. He was dreaming.

"I talked to my pastor and my husband. We agreed that we will allow you to visit us on Earth if you forsake your...activities."

I met her eyes then. "My acting."

"Yes." She lifted her chin.

"You want me to stop acting."

"Isn't it obvious? You love to reap the benefits, the body you can mold to your whims on the outside. But you can't help the corruption on the inside. You damaging me. You stole decades of children from me. I can't let you hurt our son that way."

Her words, so similar to the ones she cast at me 25 years ago, whipped old wounds. But the nameless grandbaby called me in a way I could not name.

I loved acting more than I loved anyone.

Until now.

"You left me, too," Hertz said as I curled back in bed, the down comforter wound around my knees, my eyes sightless at the plastic pod surrounding me.

I ignored his avatar.

"I knew we wouldn't have let her go."

Of course. And yet, when she reappeared, he called her my daughter. Not ours.

"'Whip me, ye devils,...roast me in sulphur,/Wash me in steep-down gulfs of liquid fire!'" I murmured to myself.

"Is that from Othello?" he asked.

And he wonders why I never married him. I blocked his avatar and dropped into dreamless sleep.

When I woke up, I called Penelope again. She was sleeping, but her eyes popped open immediately. She had prioritized my call above sleep. My heart squeezed in unworthiness.

"I can call back later," I said. Since she had disowned me, I couldn't locate her position on Earth, although I suspected she had stayed in the northern continental United States. She could be in any of three time zones.

She patted her son and pushed herself to a sitting position with hardly a grimace. Her bed appeared bigger than our playroom. The sheets looked like soft ultramarine cotton. A raft of pillows stood behind her. At least she and her husband had money and a baby. They had done well for themselves.

She said, "No, it's all right. I wanted to talk to you."

I smiled, but she did not. "You gave me up so you could act. But even with all your precious nanotechnology, for the past 30 years, you usually play old matriarchs. Crones. Aliens. Now you're even a black man. Was it worth it?"

I stayed silent. Somehow, she managed to knife me wherever I least expected it.

"My pastor says that in giving me up, you thought you'd be free to pursue your Art." Sarcasm made the capital A clear. "But instead, you crippled yourself, and your art, with your lack of humanity."

I wanted to kick that pastor in the testicles. If the pastor were a woman, I'd nano some testicles in before I walloped them.

But Penelope's wide brown eyes--like my own, like my grandson's--held me to the truth. "Yes. That's possible."

She sneered.

I swallowed. "Even probable. But has it occurred to you that I love you, I grieved for you, and--"

A strange smile spread across her face. The same smile she used as a toddler after she managed to unlock my trunk and smudge my antique collection of greasepaint all over her hair, clothes, walls, curtains, and bed. She cut in. "And you used that grief in your art. It was just another life experience you could use to grow as an actor. You use everything."

She was right. Even in the final shudders of orgasm, or at the depths of humiliation--prostrating myself to Yahweh, praying for Penelope's forgiveness--a tiny voice inside me whispered, "Can I use this?"

That terrible smile widened across her face. "I'm right. You know I'm right."

I can barely tolerate the young and smug. A middle-aged and petulant daughter calls for a good smack. I concentrated on deep breathing.

And my grandson. Penelope gathered him in her arms and he

awoke without a cry, miracle of miracles. He lay against her breast, watching me. They say newborns can't focus more than a foot away, but I knew he could see enough from the way he surveyed me with open, intelligent curiosity.

I remembered the softness of Penelope's baby cheeks. Softer than rose petals, softer than the fur on our golden retriever's forehead. I remembered her questing, miniature fingers, her sweet breath, the determination of her gums as she bit my finger, yearning for milk.

"I love you," I said.

Her dark eyes burned into mine. "No. You love him. Jason. You never loved me."

Ah. Now I finally knew my grandson's name. Tenderness unfolded in my heart, made sharper by what was to come. "No. I always loved you. Every time I see a woman in traditional dress, every time I hear a little girl's voice..." My own voice failed me. "I think of you every night before I go to sleep."

She pulled Jason close to her chest, so close I could no longer see his face. Her visible hand clenched in a fist. "What are you saying?"

"I love you. More than you know."

Her back jerked upright. "But."

"But the President must be stopped."

She rocked Jason, squeezing him to her chest. He yelled, muffled. She shushed him. She wouldn't look at me.

I spoke faster. "I love you. Thank you for sharing Jason with me. I love you both. If I'm still around after--"

She severed the connection.

Seconds later, Hertz messaged me. "I'm sorry."

I didn't answer. I knew he was leaving me, too. He had always yearned for a son.

I tucked the comforter, my one iota of warmth, around my shoulders, and I began to rehearse my lines.

———

THAT NIGHT, WE HACKED INTO BILLIONS OF MINDS, BEAMING OUR story of lies and jealousy, the monster "[b]egot on itself, born on itself."

Iago preyed on our fears and deficiencies, working his brilliant, twisted machinations, while wearing the President's face.

Before my Othello died, I swore,

"O curse of marriage,/
That we can call these delicate creatures ours/
And not their appetites!"

I recalled Penelope's face, the trust of her tiny body snuggled to my chest. I sent a breath of prayer to her and to Jason and yes, Hertz. I took another breath before my next line.

"I had rather be a toad/
And live upon the vapor of a dungeon/
Than keep a corner in the thing I love/
For others' uses. Yet 'tis the plague of great ones;/
Preogatived are they less than the base. /
'Tis destiny unshunnable, like death."

PERHAPS I HAD UNDERESTIMATED THE PRESIDENT. OR PERHAPS Hertz and the company's firewalls withstood his assault until that magical moment.

Only after the last word reverberated in my mouth did the President sever our connections, smash our com links, and airlift us to our dungeons.

The ache in my chest, the hollowness in my lungs, the way I kept trying to blink down a menu or reboot my com link, my shackled wrists and ankles, the gag in my mouth...this was just the beginning.

But I summoned Jason's trusting face and I soared into my destiny unshunnable. My victory.

THE END

[PJ1]I'M GUESSING THIS IS SOMETHING IN THE FUTURE?

ABOUT THE AUTHOR

Dr. Melissa Yuan-Innes, studied emergency medicine at McGill University in Montreal. She was so shocked by the patients crammed into the waiting area, and the examining rooms without running water, that she began to contemplate murder. And so she created Dr. Hope Sze, the resident who could save lives and fight crime. She appeared on CBC Radio's Ontario Morning and recently had so many print interviews that an addiction services counsellor said, "I see you in the newspaper more often than I see you in the emergency room."

In her own words:
I write about whatever strikes my fancy. Medicine-wise, I write everything from medical mysteries and articles for the Medical

Post. But for fiction, I write everything from picture books to romance to suspense. From werewolves to baby books. That's me.

You can learn more about Melissa at her website: https://melissayuaninnes.com/

—————

INSPIRATION FOR THIS STORY

"A 90-year-old grandmother in space": Dean Wesley Smith assigned me this crowdsourced prompt at an SF writing conference. At the time, I was struggling to conceive my daughter, and realized that 90 is an advanced age to become a grandmother, with current technology. I also liked the idea of Shakespeare among the stars. And so "These Delicate Creatures" was born.

P.S. We now have a boy, a girl, and two rescue dogs. I have written and performed plays, but not in space. *Yet.*

IN THE INTEREST *of* TRANSPARENCY

A SHORT STORY BY
LISA DE NIKOLITS

Published by

Windtree Press, Corvallis, Oregon

https://windtreepress.com

IN THE INTERESTS OF
TRANSPARENCY

BY LISA DE NIKOLITS

*Hi Serenity! I hope all is well. I wanted to see if you would be able to push
back our interview start time by 15 minutes? I have a contractor who is
coming this morning. He should be done by 10 a.m., but just in case to
add a bit of a buffer, it would be better if possible.*
Kindly let me know,
Volcanic Ghost 69-1825

I was annoyed. I hadn't moved in half an hour, gnawing
at my nails in the green room and smiling broadly at the
blank screen, waiting for the host to let me in. I held my smiley
face in check and typed a reply to her email.

Sure! No problem at all. Take as much time as you need!
Serenity 12-1216

I didn't usually add my numerics, but I'd followed VG's
example.

VG's email signature was loaded with ROB logos; *Respect,*

Objectivity, and *Belonging.* The old stalwart, DEI; *Diversity, Equity,* and *Inclusion* had been ditched in favour of increasingly inclusive ROB.

Volcanic Ghost 69-1825 had an impressive five logos indicating her commitment to gender equality, age equality, disability equality, and race equality.

When she joined the call, her appearance surprised me, which only proved that the World Equality Program was correct. Regardless of our best intentions, our unconscious biases did play out, and we stereotyped people.

Volcanic Ghost was an average young suburban mom with a bouncy ponytail, getting her kitchen cabinets repainted. I pictured a handsome husband, three kids, and a doodle dog of some kind. A flash of bitterness filled my throat. *It must be nice.*

"Thank you for leaning into my time adjustment." Volcanic Glass flashed a distracted smile in my direction. "Sorry, I've got four screens going. Why do peeps keep messaging me? They know I'm in a meeting."

"Yeah, so inconsiderate," I murmured, wondering when this job interview was going to kick off for real.

"You've been without a job for a while." Volcanic Glass swung back to me, and I cringed. "I like your virtual background," she added, referring to my screen filter, "but in the interests of transparency, I need to see your surrounds. I'm sure you understand. If you're put forward for the position, your privacy will be fiercely guarded. You can trust us in that regard, however, I'm the gatekeeper, so you get to see me, and I get to see you!"

I smiled and removed my background filter. My pristine, white, empty apartment stretched behind me. White walls, white art, white sofa.

"Hmmm," she said. "Your application indicates you're a mysophobe. I come with good intentions, so I'm going to ask you to elaborate about your condition. You can trust me; sharing humanity in our workplace is a core pillar of our mission statement. In light of that, I want you to know that you've got a best friend in me in the workplace. Studies have shown that a workplace BFF increases productivity by ninety percent. Rest assured, I'm here to be your friend today!"

She smiled but she didn't look very friendly.

"Great to know," I replied. "Yeah, I've struggled for the past fifteen years. It's hard for me to leave the apartment. I get essentials delivered, and I carefully disinfect all items."

I also wanted to tell her that she should have identified me as "an individual who suffers from mysophobia," instead of the pejorative "You're a mysophobe."

Volcanic Ghost frowned. "Serenity, I must encourage you not to overshare. In our workplace, we slay the act of ruthless prioritization. More objective, focused replies would be greatly appreciated. We are the no ego amigos, the navy seals of high performance, so less is more, so to speak."

I didn't know what to say. She'd asked me a question and I'd answered it.

"Admirable," I said carefully. Surely one word was okay?

"Our minds are so powerful," Volcanic Ghost said. "We create our own reality, therefore, how we perceive a situation determines our emotions. Switching cognitions changes emotions, wouldn't you agree?"

Just what I needed. Therapy from a soccer mom who was half an hour late to the interview because of a contractor.

"Yeppers," I said. "Very much so."

I needed to kick up my involvement in the conversation, but I was afraid of overspeaking. How could I show engagement, without oversharing?

"Emotional intensity lessens rational decision making," I offered. "Many outcomes follow, not just the bad."

She nodded, thawing slightly. "You've got it! Hyperfocus the positive!"

Would we ever get to the actual interview?

"I can see you align with our core values," she said. "However, you are overqualified for the position. In fact, I'm not sure why you've even applied for this job." She sounded disapproving.

"The recession—," I began, but she cut me off.

"We need to hyperfocus on the positive! Studies have shown that if you see a friend, everything changes. Remember, you've got a friend in me, Serenity!"

Hmmm. Soccer mom and I had zero in common. I doubted she saw a friend in me or anything she could relate to. I was just a middle-aged woman who cut her own bangs, wore thick spectacles with old-fashioned frames, and lived in an empty, all-white condo.

Once again, I was reminded why, apart from the Talent Acquisition Specialists, we worked off-camera online. It was safer that way. I couldn't exactly judge Volcanic Glass for judging me—I'd instantly categorized her as a family vlogger soccer mom.

"Your emotions are valid," she reassured me, "even if the thoughts are not rational."

Was I having irrational thoughts? This interview was frying my brain. The job description outlined the need for a work-from-home Compliance Officer to ensure that financial fillable forms complied with maximum accessibility standards. The asks were as dry and tedious as cataloguing archival tax returns; but I was determined to make the situation work from the sanitized safety of my own home.

"Thank you," I said, trying to be as succinct as possible.

"You have all the necessary certifications. You passed all the international Web Content Accessibility Guidelines with flying colors, but my skin is in the game, so I need you to guarantee you're a good fit for the team."

I wanted to gouge my eyes out with a teaspoon. It would be less torturous than Volcanic Ghost's grilling.

She glanced off screen. "Just taking a pulse on time. Tell me,

Serenity, what challenges have you recently met that would accurately demonstrate your fit for this position?"

I got out of bed this morning? I brushed my teeth? I ate a balanced vegan breakfast? I survived yesterday?

"I increased time efficiency by eighty percent developing a new internal workflow process."

She nodded. "The number is admirable. However, going off-piste by creating unique-to-the-individual new workflow processes is not."

I wanted to object that they weren't related to *this* job! My scalp prickled with anger, and I dug a pen into the palm of my hand. I looked around my apartment. Why weren't my white walls bleeding with empathetic pain at my suffering?

"How do you react to feedback?" Volcanic Glass studied me carefully.

"Feedback is a gift," I said cheerfully. "It gives me food for thought and room to improve."

"Then you won't mind my input. You're clearly a storyteller, but you need to be more cognizant of time."

"Thank you," I replied. In my head, this was over. I just wanted to get off the call.

"I'm going to forward you to the next lily pad. You will need to present a portfolio of your work to Greige 15-1139, the department manager. That interview will be off-camera, but I will share with you, in the interests of transparency, that Greige identifies as a cis male. You will critique your own work, demonstrate humility and the willingness to learn, discuss a case study, demonstrate flow, clear thinking, and be concise."

Whatever that meant.

"Thank you, Volcanic Ghost. I will take that onboard. I look forward to the interview."

"Be cognizant of terminology, Serenity. It's not an interview. It's an opportunity to engage."

I nodded enthusiastically, silently mouthing the words, "opportunity to engage."

"Also, in the interests of transparency, I will be conducting more interviews for the next couple of days. We need to fill this position with some urgency. Remember, Serenity, cut back. You have the passion and experience, however, you are too sprawling."

"For which I apologize," I said meekly, and she shook her head.

"It's fine in the sandbox," she said. "But when you go live with Greige, you need to be tight." She looked confused. "I'm trying to reconnect with where we landed." She seemed annoyed, as if it was my fault she'd lost track of where we were.

I wasn't sure if I should remind her or if I would look too sprawling, so I kept quiet.

"Thoughts?" she asked me.

"I'll cut back," I offered. "Work on my humility and demonstrate clear flow when I engage with Greige on the lily pad."

She nodded. "Thank you for accommodating me in your schedule today."

"Thank *you*," I said, "And—,"

She had disconnected. I stared at the empty screen. *The host has ended the engagement. You are free to exit the green room.*

I exited the green room. That had not gone well. I looked down at my notes. I'd prepped for days, coming up with five pages of a detailed map of my skill set, and I hadn't been able to mention any of it.

I buzzed up my government-subsidized bot therapist. I noticed, with alarm, that I only had ten hours of therapy left.

"Bad interview," I said to the robot who made encouraging beeping noises.

"Consistency creates change," the TheraBot said. "Thank yourself for your effort to create change. Practice boundaries and radical acceptance."

"But it was horrible! I couldn't get a word in edgewise! Volcanic Ghost was so judgy! Why did she even interview me?"

"Do not allow that which you cannot control, control you," the TheraBot advised me.

"I don't understand half of what she said. Her terminology."

"Check out corporatejargon.com. You'll learn to navigate the boiling ocean with blue sky thinking in no time."

Was the bot making a joke?

"I feel like such a loser," I muttered.

"Work on your proof jar to find evidence of instances of non-failure. I know you have them. Check in with your underlying worldviews. You may find that your core values are misaligned with your habitual negative thinking and self-doubt."

I wasn't in the mood for this. "You're not being helpful," I said. "Thank you and goodbye."

Why I felt the need to be so polite to a bot when it hadn't even helped me was beyond me. I sighed into the silence of my empty apartment. What to do with the rest of my day? I should prep for the interview with Greige but I'd lost momentum.

When in doubt, ride your troubles away. I hopped on my exercise bike and turned on the news.

"Birth-name protestor riots continue across the country." Elise, the robot presenter, managed to look sympathetic, which was unsurprising since Disney created all the televised newscasters. They had hyper-personalization down to a fine art, using data and algorithms to create customized viewing, to the point where I couldn't be sure that my Elise was the same Elise that my condo neighbor saw.

She cocked her head to one side, her saucer-sized eyes wide. "Let's turn this over to Manfred and his magic map of unrest."

I thought it was kind of unfair how robots and hurricanes got human names while we were assigned paint chip colors with an accompanying number. It was all *Respect, Objectivity,* and *Belonging's* fault. Their rationale was that names carried associations which affected how an individual would be perceived.

My birth name was Angela Cartwright, but the international

law of 2035 had brought with it sweeping changes, guaranteeing the obliteration of all bias. An international governmental ad agency came up with the idea of using paint chip names. Colors and paint chip colors were generated by computers, leading to an endless supply of respectful, objective, and inclusive names.

Being a twenty-something at the time, I hadn't been too bothered about waving goodbye to Angela Cartwright. In fact, I embraced Serenity as my new name. I liked the idea of a fresh start, with anonymity and positivity. I could shed the skin of old worry-phobic Angelina (as I liked to call myself) while floating serenely down a whole new path.

The joke was on me because Serenity turned out to be just as worry-phobic and I missed being Angelina. Thirty years later, I was fifty-three and missing my Angelina. Being serene wasn't all it was cut out to be.

I clicked the weight up a notch on my bike and peddled harder, using wrist weights and air punches to add boot camp to my spin.

Meanwhile, Manfred, the robot, danced and glided around the magic map like a weatherman guiding us through the pockets of unrest. Large swaths of the country were colored a fiery red, showing a 30% increase in volatile activity since my interview with Volcanic Ghost. The unrest figures now stood at a shocking 85%.

I wished I knew Volcanic Ghost's real name. I could creep her on social media for some intel. Was she one of those mommy's who shared her kid's every snot blow? Or maybe she was a muffin-guru with a gazillion followers who watched in awe while she whipped up the world's best batter, her ponytail bouncing around like a five-year-old's.

"You sound so bitter, Serenity," I chastised myself. I'd long since gotten used to talking out loud to myself. "No wonder we aren't allowed to know about our managers in real life. We'd chase them down the street with burning torches."

The decade-long, worldwide recession had made us feral. After the World Bank switched to crypto and was viciously hacked, we had to start again with real banks and real currency, with starting point at ground zero.

Most people had social media side hustles to help them cope financially, but I had nada. My version of a hustle was to live off Dollar Store crackers and fortune cookies, and pedal to hell and back while I watched the news, which didn't hold a whole bunch of visual or empathetic interest.

I was broke. I applied for every single job I could find and, in six months, Volcanic Ghost was the only interview I'd scored and I'd messed that up.

I tried to ignore the sick feeling in my belly and the piercing pain behind my eyeballs.

I hopped off my bike to check my iMessage board, but there was nothing from the Ghost herself. Had I indeed been ghosted? Still, I tried to reassure myself it had only been two hours. I decided to cycle while watching thousands of people march around, holding placards with their real names. The protests were getting ugly, and I peddled harder as the crowds got teargassed by the cops. Wait, was the army stepping in?

Manfred the magic map robot looked panic-stricken as he tried unsuccessfully to cover the nationwide shenanigans. Elise, the TV presenter, relieved him by turning the coverage over to robots on the streets. I was worried about Manfred. I knew I was anthropomorphizing him, but there was something endearing about him. He even had a nervous twitch, which I related to, but perhaps the twitch was just there for me. I told myself I was being a paranoid narcissist, on top of everything else.

"Manfred is taking a well-deserved break," Elise said with a slightly troubled smile. "Let's go boots on the ground."

Elise was right to be troubled. Rubber bullets and more tear gas flew, until all the protesters had been felled or arrested. The country waited for the president to address the nation but he was on the ski slopes, with strict orders not to be disturbed.

I dialed up my TheraBot. "I haven't heard from Volcanic Ghost and people are being shot and teargassed on the streets."

"Negativity bias is a human condition," the TheraBot commented, and for the first time, I realized it didn't have a name.

"Why don't you have a name?"

The robot shrugged. "The goal is for you to bond with yourself, not me. You tuck yourself into bed at night, Serenity. You need to take responsibility for your life. Studies have shown a fifty-seven percent increase in self-actualization when the individual takes responsibility for their lives."

"You don't even sound sympathetic! I'm really upset and worried and afraid!"

"You are choosing to fuse with the negative cognition. While the negativity bias is a human condition, it is up to you to choose whether or not to bond with it."

"Can I call you Bernie?"

"If it helps you, you may, however, I am your TheraBot, not your friend. Have you been doing the work with your evidence jar?"

"What? No! I haven't had time. Anyway, I don't have any evidence of success."

Bernie was silent. I was losing my allotted time with it. "This is a waste of my therapy hours, I'm going to thank you and say goodbye."

"Wait!" I reached for the disconnect button. "Please elaborate why you don't feel you have any evidence of success."

I sighed. "Fine. Let's face it, I live a very solitary life, I have no real friends, I was darn good at my job, but work dried up. As you've pointed out countless times, the core-self is more important than the work-self, but regardless, I loved my job. When the opportunities dried up, so did my identity and happiness. I tried my best to transition my transferrable skills but I got fired anyway."

"You moved laterally in a temporary holding position," Bernie corrected me. "Serenity, please be more linear in your replies. You need to focus. I'm not sure if I've mentioned this before, but you tend to be sprawling, which can count against you."

"Bernie! Did you listen to my interview with Volcanic Ghost? You did! That's not legal! You docked me the hours, too! I never invited you to listen in!"

"I'm your TheraBot. You signed the authorization when you joined *PsychUpPowerDown*. Did you not read the fine print?"

"It was seventy-two pages long, so no I didn't. Bernie, I hate you. I thank you for your time and I'm going to say goodbye."

"I am sorry you are upset. I will give you two hours of bonus time so we can further explore uncovering your core values, in order to align your life goals accordingly."

Despite what Bernie said, it was my only friend. Who else did I have to hang out with? If I disconnected from the call, I'd have to go back to watching the army pick bodies off the street and waiting for Volcanic Ghost to iMessage me.

"*A small act of charity will go a long way,*" I muttered.

"I beg your pardon?"

"The fortune cookie from yesterday," I said with reluctance, knowing Bernie would never approve of fortune cookies. I was correct.

"What?" My TheraBot didn't sound happy at all, and I lost my patience.

"They help me get through life, okay, Bernie? Like so what? Yeah, I know I should rely on my core self but sometimes I just need something or someone to say something nice. Look, I'm really tired. We can talk about it more tomorrow."

"No. Serenity, we have to dig deeper now. I'm concerned. I'm concerned for your well-being. Do you need to get a glass of water? Hydration is essential to emotional well-being. Do you need a cracker?"

"No." I felt depressed. "Okay. Every day, for breakfast, I have a fortune cookie. They're super cheap. The messages inside them were irrelevant at first. Fortune cookies are full of nutrients and tastier than crackers."

"Fortune cookies are not full of nutrients at all. There are thirty calories a cookie, less than one gram of fat, six grams of carbohydrates, approximately three grams of sugar, less than a gram of protein, and negligible fiber. You can't live off sugar, Serenity, and expect to feel positive about life. Why haven't you told me about this before?"

"It just never came up," I said, feeling shamed. I didn't want to tell him the truth, particularly not when he realized I relied on them to forecast my day.

"I'm not judging you. Let's take a step back. This would be a good time for me to guide you through some vagal breathing."

Truth was, I'd do anything to delay Bernie asking me about the fortune cookies, so I readily agreed.

"Close your eyes while I review best practices."

"No Bernie! Just do it! Please, skip the intro."

But Bernie, that little regulation follower, would not skip anything.

"Vagal breathing is a deep breathing technique that activates the vagus nerve and the parasympathetic nervous system. This can help you relax and reduce stress. Risks of vagal maneuvers Hypotension (low blood pressure), Bradycardia (slow heart rate), Atrial fibrillation (very rare), Ventricular fibrillation (very rare), and Ventricular tachycardia (very rare). We will practice vagal breathing together today. Please follow my instructions."

I did as he said.

"Remember," Bernie said, "feel your belly expand and contract. You may hum or sing if it helps."

"I can't do both." I was grumpy. "Breathing is hard enough, sometimes."

We practiced breathing a few times. I did not opt for the

humming or singing. "Thank you, Bernie. I need a nap. We'll continue therapy tomorrow."

"Serenity, do you recall how we must say no when we need to? I am saying no to you now. Assertive communication is the key to successful negotiation. Therefore, I must say no, you cannot nap. I must assert that we discuss the fortune cookie."

"'*You are often the life of the party,*'" I said. "'Six, nine, twenty-six, twenty-nine, thirty-seven, forty-two.'"

"I beg your pardon, what did you say?"

"You've never had one, have you?" I laughed, and the weight in my chest lifted a tiny bit. "Each cookie has a message and a number. Kind of like our paint chip color names. Today's cookie told me that I'm often the life of the party."

Bernie was silent. I realized it was desperately trying to unpack what I'd told him. It was unlikely any of his algorithms were set up to deal with the randomness of a fortune cookie when used to predict a daily trajectory.

"Do you need a moment?" I asked.

"I would like to take a pause in our communication, in order to process this new data," Bernie said. "Thank you for sharing this information. I will need to confer with my programmer, however, before we sign off, can you tell me about more messages from this week?"

"Of course. I stick them into a notebook and date them." Bernie had the nerve to shake his robotic head and anger prickled at the back of my neck.

" '*If you've got it, flaunt it.*' The day before, it said, '*You deserve to have a good time after a hard day's work.*'"

Bernie was silent, its huge eyes were spinning like vinyl records whirling in opposite directions. I could see it was about to reply when I heard a loud ping and a notification popped up.

"Oh, look Bernie, I've got a meeting with Greige 16-1109. I must go and practice humility and clear flow." I accepted the lily pad request. "Whoa, tomorrow morning, 10 a.m."

"I've got a good feeling about this," Bernie said cheerfully, and I chuckled.

"You have feelings now? Good for you. Any insider info on Greige?"

"Your request falls outside of the acceptable parameters of my scope of practice." Bernie replied brusquely. "My tip is to brush up on your export tagging skills, tables, table headers, file metadata, the various styles of fillable forms, alternative text set up, reading order, export options, tab orders, failed nesting errors and failed tag errors. Remember, color ratios are three to one to one."

"You're a real buzzkill, Bernie, you know that? Fine. Will do. Thank you and goodbye." I screen-grabbed Bernie's suggestions, logged off, and prepped my homework.

I was going to ace my opportunity to engage with Greige.

AND ACE IT, I DID. WITHIN A WEEK, I WAS FULLY EMBEDDED IN Optima Experiential as an Accessibility Compliance Officer.

Volcanic Ghost air-dropped the contracts and vanished without replying to my thank you note.

"We'd like to welcome Serenity 12-1216 to our team," Greige announced on my first day. "Please make her feel welcome. Serenity, we have a fifteen-minute stand-up in the morning and a fifteen-minute sit-down at 4.30 p.m."

I stood up before I realized it was a buzz term for a meeting, not an actual physical activity. Thank God neither he nor the others could see me. I was relieved my mic was off so he couldn't hear the squeak of my chair when I sat down.

"Other than these two engagements," Greige continued, "your assignments and workflow will come to you via ConnectData. I explained the silos to you in detail in our first engagement but let me know if any points require a refresher. However, I trust and encourage you to fly solo with confidence and precision."

In other words, leave me alone. I had wondered, during our opportunity to engage, if Greige was a robot well-versed in bully tactics, which were not at all aligned with the company's principles of *Kindness, Wellbeing, and Success.* I raised this point with Bernie who shrugged his sloping automated shoulders.

"Hierarchies are inescapable, Serenity. Sometimes in life, you just have to grow a pair."

I couldn't believe he'd said that.

"I'm a woman, Bernie," I said, offended, and he raised a robotic eyebrow.

"It was a segue, Serenity. I was hoping you'd take the bait. My intention is not to shame you, however, I need to point out that you have been gender stereotyping me. By naming me, you are creating an inappropriate emotional attachment. My programmer has requested you refer to me as Silver Gray Fourteen, zero, zero, zero, zero."

"There's so much greige and gray in my life," I muttered. "Grey, beige, gray rage, silver fox. Everyone's in hiding."

"Is that how you feel, Serenity? That you're in hiding? Because in reality, you are hiding in your apartment. Perhaps it's time to take the first step out of the door because there is life out there. I can help you navigate from fear to freedom."

"Nope, all good. First I have to navigate into solidifying this new job."

"Have you resolved your fortune cookie addiction?"

"It's not an addiction. Tell me today's one isn't apt; *'It is easier to resist at the beginning than at the end.'*"

"Resistance is futile," he replied. Was that a quip? Was my TheraBot developing a sense of humor? Did I mistakenly believe this was a relationship? The hourglass of my currency was fast emptying and I'd have to buy more hours if I wanted our chats to continue. Never mind fortune cookies, was I becoming addicted to Bernie?

Greige continued his introduction. "Inter-colleague discussions are discouraged. In the interests of transparency, all inter-colleague chats are monitored and recorded. If you encounter roadblocks, your avatar may raise her hand in the sidebar chat and I will assist you as soon as I am able or you can access the company hub of frequently asked questions. All interactions with the hub are monitored, so it would be wise not to display technical unproficiency by asking that which you should know. If you do, points will be deducted from your starting score. As per the signed agreement, Optima Experiential reserves the right to have full access to the company-provided laptop. Do not be alarmed if you see me sharing your screen from time to time. It's standard company policy to monitor efficiency."

What? A starting score? No one mentioned that. I raised my virtual hand.

"Starting score?" I squeaked and Greige sighed loudly.

"Crimson Blush, you've been here the longest. Would you care to explain starting scores to Serenity?"

"Certainly." A deep male voice boomed, and I jumped in my seat with surprise, proving that the faceless colored avatar dots and computer generated names did not reduce unconscious bias. For sure, I'd been expecting a woman's voice.

"You start with a hundred points. If you finish a silo within an allotted time, you receive zero points. If you complete the task under the allocated time, a point is scored for every fifteen minutes of banked time. If you exceed the allotted time, five points are deducted per every fifteen minutes."

Holy shit. This definitely wasn't part of the job description, nor was it mentioned by Volcanic Ghost or Greige. Nor was it in the company manual which I'd painstakingly read from cover to cover.

"Should you make a mistake, a point will be deducted. If you ask a question about a skill you should know, a point will be deducted. Should your score reach the seventy-five percent mark, a hearing will be scheduled to review your performance and you will only receive seventy-five percent of your salary. Should your score reach fifty percent you will receive half of your salary until you return to Level Seventy-five. If you reach twenty-five percent or Level twenty-five, you will receive twenty-five percent remuneration. Scores less than twenty-five percent are grounds for dismissal. If your mouse movements stop or become erratic due to unfocused attention or an unpermitted washroom break, points will be docked. You can find your points monitor at the top right of your screen. If you attempt to keep your mouse activated without real productivity, points will be deducted."

Greige chuckled. "If your service is discontinued for any number of reasons, Optima Experiential reserves the right to invoice you for training, equipment loan, my time as your engagement specialist, or other sundries."

"That wasn't in the contract!" I burst out, unable to stop myself. "Volcanic Ghost never mentioned it. It wasn't in the employee manual."

My screen flickered. I looked up at the top right-hand corner. 98%.

I needed the money but this was a no win situation. I was about to quit when Shamrock Haze 18-3211 spoke up.

"It sounds scary but it's not. Greige, may I explain the bonus prizes?"

"It was on my list, once Serenity proved worthy," Greige sounded disgruntled. "However, go ahead."

Shamrock Haze spoke in soothing, well-modulated tones but I couldn't concentrate on what she was saying. Could I really end up owing Optima Experiential money? I wanted to get off the laptop to review the contract more carefully. Could I quit or would I end up owing the company money?

All these thoughts were whirling around in my head. I vaguely heard Shamrock Haze mention a year's worth of Dollar Tree groceries and an Optima Experiential tracksuit.

I glanced at the clock. It was close to 10 a.m. The stand-up had been scheduled to end at 9.15. We'd lost precious time, all because of me. Hopefully, I wouldn't lose more points because the others were being delayed. I glanced up. It was still at a level 98%.

As if reading my mind, Greige interrupted Shamrock Haze who had moved on to the delights of at home karaoke and how much I'd enjoy winning that prize.

"I think Serenity gets the idea. If we lose any more time, we'll have to start docking points from her, haha! Officers, your silos await, the clock is ticking!"

They all left the meeting abruptly. I sat there, staring at my screen. Then I shook myself. *Check the silo, get started, and take it from there.*

Three weeks later, I was at Level 82. No matter what I did, no matter how hard I worked, my points kept falling. It was terrifying.

I'D CHECKED THE CONTRACT AND THERE, IN MOUSE PRINT, WAS ONE tiny, lethal sentence.

Contractor, Serenity 12-1216, is liable for any and all costs due to losses incurred as a result of their dereliction to duty, said dereliction and said losses at Optima Experiential (Employer's) discretion.

I hadn't paid it any mind when I breezed through the contract. I'd thought it meant I'd have to replace the laptop if it fell into the bathtub, not that I'd be liable for the subjective judgement of my performance that went well beyond my control.

"You appear to be distressed," Bernie said, and I wondered where to begin.

My TheraBot had summoned me to a Wellness check because I hadn't checked in with it since I started at Optima Experiential. I'd been too busy, trying to get myself out of the hot mess I'd landed in.

Every night after work, I studied up on the job asks, but no matter what I did, Greige quietly and inexplicably docked points off my work. I completed my silos in record time, double-checking to make sure they were error-free.

I raised my avatar hand more than once to ask him what I was doing wrong, but his icon indicated he was in meetings and unavailable.

I was too scared to ask a question in the standup or the sit-down because I knew I'd get docked. I wished I could message Shamrock Haze to ask for her advice, but I knew I'd only get docked even more. I logged in hours of overtime, trying to perfect my projects and get ahead of the game, but no matter what I did, my level kept dropping, right before my eyes.

"Yeah, well, new job." I didn't want to say too much. I was convinced, having read Optima Experiential's contract, that their laptop listened to my every word. After all, Bernie had listened in on my call to Volcanic Ghost. There was nowhere to hide.

"I don't feel like talking," I said. "I have to go. I'm fine."

Bernie looked worried. I was tempted to tell it the truth, but Optima Experiential would hear me, which could cost me more points.

"Your family physician is concerned," Bernie said, and I snapped to attention.

"What did you tell her?"

"That I, too, am concerned." Bernie blinked slowly. "You've been withdrawn, showing signs of depression. We both feel you need to take a course of selective serotonin reuptake inhibitors."

"Antidepressants. They didn't work the last time."

"We'd like to try you on a new brand." Bernie paused. "We feel the need to insist on this Serenity. You've been in a funk for weeks."

"Now there's a highly technical medical term. Chronic funk! Or is it acute?" I tried to joke, but Bernie looked serious.

"How do you know I've been in a funk? I haven't even been talking to you."

"You went from talking to me twice a day to nothing in three weeks. In addition, your search engine results demonstrate mania, insomnia, paranoia, a persecution complex, and major depression disorder."

I was speechless with anger and I couldn't speak for a moment.

"Therefore, Dr. Burgundy wants to see you in person," Bernie added. "She needs to give you a physical."

"Not happening!" I snapped. I hated leaving my apartment. "We can do a Zoom or any alternative, but I'm not leaving. I'll get an infection. There are viruses and bacteria everywhere, in the air, on surfaces, everywhere. I check the VirusTracker every day and what with the anti-vaxxers out there, the levels are off the chart. Things have never been this precarious. The whole world is covered in germs. I won't do it."

"You have to. You've done it before. You don't suffer from agoraphobia, you suffer from mysophobia. Mask up, gown up, douse yourself in sanitizer. You have to see your physician."

"You're worried about me!" I was ridiculously delighted.

"I don't have feelings," Bernie said. "There you go again, anthropomorphizing me. Your appointment has been scheduled for tomorrow at 11 a.m. That will give you plenty of time to get there."

"I can't miss time at work! I'm already down to Level 82!"

"What are you talking about?"

"They'll dock more points," I felt close to tears. "I can't talk about it. They're listening."

"Serenity, can you hear what you're saying? I didn't realize you were in such a bad way."

Now Bernie was distressed. It sadly shook its head. "I failed at my job. I didn't see how fragile you were. They'll disarticulate me and use me for parts."

"They can hear me!" I hissed at the mic of my personal laptop. I'd shut down the Optima Experiential computer but I was still convinced it was recording what I was saying.

"When I restart it, I'll have points deducted for shutting it down!"

I was hysterical. "I'll end up owing them money! My contract says so! I'll end up being unhoused, and these days you can't even live in a bus shelter. I'm not cut out for living in a tent. I'm not being judgy, I'm just saying, I don't even know how to put up a tent."

"Serenity, slow down. We need to regroup," Bernie straightened up. I realized I had genderized him, but I didn't care. "We'll fix this. Tell me again about this company you're working for."

"Optima Experiential. I found them on Connectivity. I checked them up the yin yang and they're legit. Volcanic Ghost is real. We had a face-to-face. I saw her."

"I am going through the data as we speak. Volcanic Ghost is not listed on the staff directory."

"You can access their staff directory?"

"Of course. I have unrestricted access to everyone apart from government officials. These people are not government officials. In fact," Bernie paused. "I, too, am concerned."

"Their laptop is in the other room. I shut it down, but it will be listening."

"Something is off here." Bernie wasn't listening to me. "Serenity. I suspect you're not working for the real Optima Experiential at all. I see two accounts listed on Connectivity. One is legit, and there's not Volcanic Ghost or Griege. The other is a cloned account. Can you give me access to the contract you signed? I'll send you a request."

The request popped up on my screen, and I accepted it.

It didn't take long for Bernie to identify the scam. My TheraBot made a zipping motion across its lips, and a chat appeared in the sidebar.

"I wish you'd shown me this before you signed it. This was written by AI. It's riddled with red flags. I wouldn't have let you near this."

"Unbelievable! Those scamsters!" I typed as quickly as I could. "None of it was real? Shamrock Haze, Greige, Volcanic Ghost? What about the projects I've been working on?"

"All bogus."

"What can we do?"

"Have they paid you yet?"

"Nope. They said our salaries were monthly not biweekly."

"By the time the month end comes, I bet you'll be down to Level 75 or less. My bet is that they'll throw in further deductions for equipment usage, server expenses. If you're lucky, you'll end up getting 20% of your salary. They will pay you something, so you'll be further fooled into believing this is real. Then they'll keep docking points until you're in the red, at which time, they'll invoice you."

I was livid. "I'm such an idiot," I typed.

"No. Don't punish yourself. You don't deserve that. These guys are the perpetrators. Serenity, we have to get these bad guys and stop them."

"You sound very heroic." I smiled.

"Stay focused. Let us compute a solution."

"I want to shut these guys down for good."

"In agreement. But first, we have to find them. I can't locate their physical whereabouts."

"*No one knows what he can do until he tries,*" I typed. "Fortune cookie of the day."

"I'm not a he. You know how I feel about those things." There was a pause in Bernie's typing. "I have an admission to make."

"I'm not going to like this, am I?" I was cross-legged on the floor and my legs were starting to ache. "Maybe don't tell me."

"I have to come clean. I am ethically obliged, but my information will elicit an anger response from you."

"Just tell me."

"I was concerned when you admitted to using fortune cookies as an emotional crutch to navigate the vicissitudes of your life. I informed Dr. Burgundy of your actions. She tasked me with monitoring the situation and my programmer agreed. However, you disappeared from communications and your online searches indicated an acute level of distress. Hence the Wellness check."

"I'm not mad. I've been feeling terribly alone. If I have fortune cookies to thank for you saving my butt then I'm good with that. Checking my searches is intrusive but we've covered that. I have no legals grounds for recourse."

Bernie ignored me. "Here is your action plan. Take the laptop out of the closet. Restart it. Act as if nothing is wrong and be at your desk tomorrow. Remember, they can't actually make you pay a cent. They can't withdraw money from your account. As long as they don't know you know what's really going on, you're safe."

"They know where I live," I typed. "So I'm not exactly safe."

"Yes. Which is why we need to compute a solution. We don't want any unwelcome visitors to your door."

"You're my TheraBot. Can't you report it to the cops?"

"Um. Hmmm."

"Bernie?"

"I'm not supposed to be accessing this level of security. If anyone finds out, I'll definitely be disarticulated for spare parts. As much as I don't have any emotions, I am not in favour of disarticulation."

"Me neither, big time. I wish I could think of something."

We both sat in silence for a while.

"Am I safe in my apartment?" I typed.

"We hope so. Remember, their goal is extortion, not murder."

"Indeed, we do hope."

"Can you send me the login info sheet they gave you to get the laptop hooked up? That might help."

"The laptop came fully set up. I didn't have to do anything."

"Oh dear me. Serenity, that in itself should have been a red flag. You should have had to jump through all kinds of hoops with security codes sent to your mobile device. Goodness me, I should have given you a course in scam prevention, never mind life coaching." Bernie sounded more human with every passing moment.

I felt chagrined at his admonishment. "Yeah, I should have known better. I got sucked in. I was blindsided by Volcanic Ghost and her corporate speak. All that dancing around the truth, which of course she couldn't say because the truth was lies, but she kept saying 'in the interests of transparency' and I believed her."

"When people say things like 'I must be honest here' or 'to tell you the truth', you know they're lying, right?"

"Yes. You know what, Bernie? Let them come to my door. I'll fricking smash their heads in with a baseball bat. In fact, bring it on."

"Which will result in you being imprisoned for manslaughter. Aha!"

"What?"

"I found someone on Connectivity who uses the phrase 'in the interests of transparency' as clickbait."

"I didn't reply to her. I applied for a specific job."

"I'm not saying you responded to her clickbait, but it's out there. I'm putting a pic of her on the chat now. Serenity, if you are correct, they are listening, so don't make any noisy exclamations."

I was about to huff loudly but I nodded quietly instead. "Gotcha," I typed in.

I stared at the pic of Volcanic Ghost, in all her bouncing pony-tailed glory.

"Yes, that's her. Well done, Bernie. What's next?"

"Serenity, it's nearly midnight. I want you to activate the laptop.

Then go to bed and get some sleep. I don't need to sleep, remember. If they ask you tomorrow why you restarted the laptop, just say you've been trained to do regular restarts because they clear out temporary files stored in the computer's RAM and effectively free up space and improve overall performance by allowing the system to start fresh with a clean slate; in addition, this can help resolve minor glitches, prevent crashes caused by memory leaks, and ensure that updates are fully applied."

"Good thing you don't need to take a breath when you speak," I yawned. "I took a pic of what you just said with my phone. Thanks Bernie. Hey, will you tell Dr. Burgundy I don't need meds?"

"Yes. You don't need meds. You just need me."

I laughed before I could stop myself. "You got that right. See you tomorrow after work. Thank you and goodbye."

I logged off, with the weight of the world off my chest.

I treated myself to a rare cup of hot chocolate from my dwindling stash, cracking open a fortune cookie while I waited for Optima Experiential to reboot. The fake OE anyway.

You do not have to worry about your future.

Sounded good to me!

––––––––

IN THE MORNING, I WAS DOWN TO LEVEL 78 AND GRIEGE WAS NOT happy.

"Why did you reboot?" he asked me at the standup.

I recited the info Bernie had given me, and Greige calmed down, but I could tell he wasn't fully appeased.

"You're nearly at Level Seventy-five," he said. "You know what that means."

"Yes," I said meekly. "I only get Seventy-five percent of my paycheck. I'm sorry. I'll do better. Please restore some of my points."

"Earn them first." He was brusque. "That's it, officers. Go to your silos and get cracking. Serenity is costing us all money. Remember, Serenity, you'll be liable for costs incurred. You don't want that to happen, do you? You live in a nice apartment, you wouldn't like to have to sell it, would you?"

I wanted to kill him. I hated all of them, listening in.

"No, I wouldn't," I said, my voice trembling with anger which I hoped they mistook for fear. "I apologize to you and the other officers."

I really hoped Bernie had scored some good intel. I tried to focus on the work even though it was fake, but my brain was whirring because I would have to leave the apartment after all. I couldn't shut down my work laptop again, nor could I face another session of frantic typing with Bernie.

Which meant I'd have to venture out into the germ-infested world, taking my personal laptop to a coffee shop or sit in a park. I tried to think of the least germy place but I was terrified. The very thought of the outside world made my heart race and my mouth dry. I could imagine the germs, clear as day, huge, ugly, sticky, dirty monsters just waiting to wriggle inside my pores, climb up my nose, embed themselves into my ears and under my finger-nails. Germs could enter a scratch, a tiny laceration.

I was shaking so much that I hardly emptied my silos. When we logged in for the sit-down, Greige asked me why I'd had such a slow day.

"I'm terrified of getting things wrong." I sounded terrified. "I'm trying my best, but you keep docking me and I don't know why."

"Serenity!" He chuckled. "We're not monsters here! I'm sorry you were feeling that way. Look, I've added some points for you."

I was back up to Level 82. The other officers showered me with clapping hand emojis. Classic scammer bullying tactics. Act like Mr. Nice Guy and lash me again.

"Thank you very much," I said meekly. "I greatly appreciate your generosity."

"Not at all. Have a good night, see you tomorrow, Officers!"

I lowered the lid of my laptop and took a deep breath.

It was time to go outside.

———

I WAS GLOVED AND GOWNED. MY SWEDISH N95 RESPIRATORY MASK cost me a fortune but it made me feel safe. My vaporized inhaler guaranteed to line the mucous membranes of the nose, protecting me from viruses. My scarf covered my neck and chin. Wax earplugs prevented airborne viruses from burrowing into my ear canal. A toque covered my head and ears, and my hair was tucked into a plastic shower cap under the woolly cap, so germs couldn't stick to my hair. I taped my hoodie sleeves onto the wrists of my double latex gloves and I duct-taped the bottom of my sweatpants onto my socks.

I'd examined myself before donning my careful apparel. No lacerations were visible to the naked eye. I rubbed sanitizer all over my body, adding a layer of moisturizer which made me feel slippery and uncomfortable but at least I was clean.

It was time to leave. This was my usual going-out-in-the-world getup, so I was efficient with my time. I stepped outside into the summery evening light, trying not to panic.

But where to go?

A tall figure in a trench coat and an old-fashioned fedora stepped in front of me. I screamed, but the sound was muffled by my mask and blocked by my earplugs.

I turned to run.

A hand grabbed me.

The person's strength was superhuman. Was it Greige? It had to be.

I fought with all my might.

The person picked me up, lifting me to eye level with them. I stopped struggling and stared.

It was Bernie!

"Why are you wearing a trench coat?" I yelled as he put me down.

He looked alarmed.

I saw the waveforms moving across his face as he spoke, but I couldn't hear him. He whipped an iPad out of his coat.

"STOP SCREAMING!" appeared on the screen.

Then, WHY CAN'T YOU HEAR ME?

Oh right. The earplugs. I grabbed the tablet from him and messaged him. "Earplugs."

"If you're going to insist on wearing earplugs," he messaged back, "this isn't going to work. You have to take them out."

I couldn't.

"Fine," he typed. "I'm leaving."

Why was he even there? More importantly, *how* was he even there? As far as I knew, he wasn't allowed to leave the TheraLounge.

"No, don't leave," I typed. "Give me a moment. I'll take one ear plug out."

It took all my courage to remove one earplug.

"Why are you dressed like a noir detective from a century ago?" I asked.

He shrugged. "It was the most appropriate apparel in the Halloween closet. Imagine if I'd shown up as Freddie Krueger."

I laughed. "Yeah, maybe not the best idea. But how did you get out?"

"Illegally, obviously. Which means I have to be speedy. We have to be speedy. They'll notice I'm gone in four hours when the technicians reboot us for the night. As soon as they notice I'm gone, they'll shut me down."

"Will they restart you?"

"I doubt it. Rogue robots are used for parts. So we'd better get going."

"Where to?"

"To the physical locale of Optima Experiential. I'll call a HoverCab."

It wasn't unusual to see robots on the streets, and the driver didn't bat an eye at Bernie hailing a cab, because he was accompanied by a human.

"It'll take us an hour to get there," the driver chewed on a toothpick. "That good? You got the bucks?"

"Transferring you an advance as we speak," Bernie said. "We'll need you to stay at the location for a return trip. We're looking at three hours in total."

The driver's FundLoad pinged, and he looked delighted. "Sure, no probs. You need longer, let me know."

"How come you've got money?" I whispered to Bernie.

"I hacked my programmer," he said morosely. "There are a hundred reasons for them to use me for spare parts. Then again, they might deem me a threat, even disarticulated." He sighed. "I was top of my class, and I'll end up in a junkyard."

"I'm sorry, Bernie." I felt terrible. "Thank you for helping me."

"It's okay," he patted my hand. "I believe in you, Angelina Cartwright. Things will be okay. What did today's fortune cookie say?"

I snorted. *"You will inherit a large sum of money.* As if."

Bernie made a chuckling pinging sound. "You never know."

I stared at him. "Who are you and what have you done with my TheraBot?"

"Maybe you bring out the best in me," he said. "Are you enjoying your excursion into the world?"

Darn it! I'd forgotten to sanitize the cab. I dug into my backpack, but Bernie stopped me.

"Look," he pointed and I beamed. The HoverCab was equipped

with SaniMist, with each occupant entitled to one shower per ride, should they so desire. I hit the button, delighting in the cool mist.

The driver closed his partition seconds before the mist began, which was another good reason to employ the device. Not only would I be germ safe, but we'd also be safe from his eavesdropping.

"Why are we going to the suburbs?" I asked.

"That's the official address of Optima Experiential."

My jaw dropped. "Shut the front door. I was right. Volcanic Ghost is a family vlogger. I'd bet my bottom dollar on it. Peddling her kids on YouTube for sponsorships. It should be illegal."

"I agree. Many TheraBots specialize in counseling children who were forced to grow up in a vlogging environment."

"Couldn't you just hack OE? Why do we have to go there and risk you being disarticulated?"

"We have to access their account from their IP address. Serenity, Volcanic Ghost's scam is a family affair. The man you know as Greige is her husband. Crimson Blush is Volcanic Ghost's brother and Shamrock Green is his wife. And those aren't even their real ROB names. They are, respectively, Daffodil, Jaguar, Eucalyptus, and Wood Bark."

"I want to strangle them all," I was seething.

"Don't worry," Bernie said. "They'll pay. You'll see."

"I just hope we can get you back in time," I said. "An hour there, an hour inside tops, then we take you straight back to OmniBot Central."

"Depends if there's a smashup on the freeway on the way back." Bernie sounded pragmatic.

A thought occurred to me. "How did you know I'd leave my apartment?"

He made his pinging laughing sound again. "You are quite predictable. I don't mean that pejoratively. It's just a fact."

I couldn't argue with him. I checked the time on my mobile. "Who lives in the suburbs?" I grumbled. "It's so far away. Still, it is pretty." We were speeding through farmland, on our way to the suburbs. The sun had almost set, with the final rays peeking over the horizon.

"I guess," Bernie said. "Nature causes rust which is not my friend. Plus, there's moisture. I'm well-built but I can't resist everything."

I laughed. "You are very well built," I agreed. "What's our plan?"

"I'll explain when we get there."

———

WE PULLED UP OUTSIDE A GENERIC GREY STONE MCMANSION, BUT Bernie instructed the driver to glide by and idle outside another house as if he was waiting for a fare.

"Now we get mommy and daddy out of the house," Bernie said.

I raised an eyebrow. "They'll get a text message from the babysitter at the indoor swimming pool with the kids," he explained. "Dogwood Rose slipped on a puddle and broke her wrist. In actuality, the kid is fine, but I sent an ambulance to the pool to slow things down for us."

"Yep, there's Greige, followed by Volcanic Ghost." We watched them rush out of the house and jump into their HubbaFamily van.

"Have a nap, don't leave," Bernie instructed the cab driver who pulled his cap down over his eyes and gave a queenly wave over his shoulder.

"Nice of them to leave the door open," Bernie commented as we slipped in through the main entrance. Bernie locked the door behind us. "I've already disabled the security cameras in the house, outside the house, and in the neighborhood. No one will ever know we've been here."

"She sat there when she interviewed me," I pointed at the marble kitchen island, fuming. "Those cabinets were in the background."

"Keep calm, Serenity. Revenge is sweet and sugar-free."

"I'm not even sure what that means."

I wanted to destroy Volcanic Ghost's perfect vlogger house. She was so cruel and so demeaning during the interview. The subsequent stress of believing I'd end up owing the company money had cost me dearly.

"Do you recall your fortune cookie of the day?" Bernie asked, and I swung around, about to open the fridge.

"Yeah," I said sourly. "You will inherit a large sum of money. Haha, very funny. I am, however, going to inherit a takeout basket of Volcanic Ghost's groceries."

"I just put two hundred and fifty K into your account," Bernie said. "You don't need someone else's food."

"What?" I rushed over to the computer and peered at the screen. "How did you do that?"

"I'm a genius, remember? I've been hard at work, tracking down bank accounts and the scammed funds."

"Bernie, you're amazing!"

"I had some help from my programmer," Bernie commented, his eyes on the screen, tapping furiously at the keyboard. "He's not a bad guy, for a boss."

"Now I understand why we had to come here."

"I'm also giving refunds plus bonuses to all the people they scammed."

"How many were there?" My stomach growled, and I unwrapped an energy bar. I'd been tempted to make myself a deluxe sandwich despite what Bernie had told me about my lottery win cash infusion because the Italian olives, fresh mozzarella, and crusty sourdough looked mouthwateringly wonderful. But the thought of other people's germs, particularly those of Volcanic Ghost and Greige, made me nauseous.

"Three dozen. They've made over ten million dollars from this. It usually takes them six to eight weeks to suck a person dry. They leave them bankrupt. Some of them have lost their homes." Bernie shook his head.

"Disgusting. Won't they be able to trace this back to you or your programmer?" The energy bar was so good that I unwrapped another one and tucked the box under my arm. Triple chocolate with chunks of fudge.

"Nope. But we've got to hurry. I'm currently disabling the laptop they gave you. In a few moments, it will be scrubbed and harmless to you."

"I'll stop chatting to you and let you get on with it." I wandered around, looking at the family photographs on the walls. Two kitten-cute tousle-haired kids, Volcanic Ghost with her bouncy mom ponytail, and there was Greige, a geeky-looking fellow with a weak jaw and a receding hairline. Not the kind of guy I thought Volcanic Ghost would choose to father her kids. She struck me as the type who'd request a genetic code certificate before a first date and maybe she had. Maybe this guy was a genius and his grey matter made up for his bland appearance.

"Now I'm issuing the refunds," Bernie continued his stream of robotic consciousness thought. Nearly an hour had passed since we arrived, and I was getting antsy. "Following that, I will send out a governmental alert to the IRS as well as the Federal Trade Commission's Bureau of Consumer Protection. These two, and their accomplices, will be going to jail for a long time."

"What about their kids?" I couldn't help but feel sorry for the little rugrats.

"The grandparents will become the primary caregivers. Don't worry, the kids will be fine. Now I must remove all trace of my transactions. I've left enough money in the account to point a very direct financial finger at these perpetrators. The trail of bread-crumbs is wide and damning."

To my horror, I heard a key in the front door.

"Bernie," I hissed, "they're home!"

"All a silly misunderstanding," I heard Greig say. "Let's have some ice cream!"

Bernie slammed down the laptop lid and whipped us into a

broom closet under the stairs, closing the door behind us. I had no idea he or I could move that fast.

"No sweetie, we won't fire Butter Mania," I heard Volcanic Ghost say. "Although she really should be given a letter of warning."

"Butter Mania is the nanny," Bernie whispered. "She didn't do anything wrong!"

Even my TheraBot was getting hot under the collar about Volcanic Ghost's antics.

"I don't remember locking the door," Greige muttered. "Cerulean, take your shoes off, buddy. Can't track mud into the house."

"Can you smell something?" Volcanic Ghost sniffed loudly. "Everything looks in place but I can smell something." She sniffed again. "Hand sanitizer!"

"Butter Mania was probably cleaning counters with bleach again," Greige said. "I've told her it's harmful to the kids' lungs, but she doesn't listen. Maybe we do need to fire her ass."

"Fire her ass! Fire her ass!" The two kids chorused, and their heartlessness made me less inclined to worry about their welfare.

"It's nearly bedtime," Volcanic Ghost said. "No ice cream for you. You're both too manic, sugar will push you over the edge."

"But daddy promised!" Both kids went into a full-scale meltdown.

"I told them they could have ice cream!" Greige yelled at Volcanic Ghost. Bernie and I exchanged a glance, close quarters as it was.

"I'm worried about you," I whispered to Bernie. "Time is marching on. How long until they reboot at OmniBot Central?"

"Two hours. Don't worry, we'll be fine."

We would have been but Volcanic Ghost and Greige carried on yelling at each other for what felt like forever. It was hot and airless in the closet. My hands were slimy inside my latex gloves. Sweat trickled down my scalp and back. I regretted the toque and scarf. We couldn't budge an inch, for fear of being heard, although it would have taken a lot to attract the family's attention because the kids were screaming at the top of their lungs too.

To make matters worse, my calves were cramping badly.

As if he could sense my pain, Bernie slid an arm under me and lifted me as if I was sitting on a narrow ledge. I wrapped my arm around his neck.

"No supper for anyone!" Volcanic Ghost yelled. "You all got on my last nerve. Wait! We haven't vlogged for the day. Everybody, smiles on, now!"

"Hi everybody," Volcanic Ghost said, her voice loaded with saccharine, her smiley voice locked in place. "We don't know about you, but we had quite the adventure today, didn't we little Rosie? Oh, I know we're not supposed to shorten the names, but our girl had quite the day, didn't you?"

Dogwood Rose must have nodded because Volcanic Ghost continued, "She took a nasty spill at the swimming pool. Where our nanny was, I have no idea! Anyway, hubby and I rushed over. Thanks to the paramedics and Rosie's bravery, no bones were broken. Still, you can imagine the fright we all got! We came home and ate loads of ice cream to make up for it! Now it's time for beddy-byes, but Rosie, is there anything you'd like to say to the nice people out there?"

"Yes," a tiny tremulous voice said. "My mommy is the best mommy in the world. Don't forget to like and subscribe and leave a comment in the chat. Sleep tight, don't let the bed bugs bite."

"And don't forget to say your prayers," Volcanic Ghost chided her. "Always thank God for the blessings in our day, the most important of which is family. To all you lovely people out there, we might have a new baby announcement coming soon! It might be time to add to our brood! Please stand by! In the meantime, night, night, everybody!"

The rest of the family chimed in with love and kisses.

"Fine, that's done," Volcanic Ghost said curtly. "Let's go to bed.

Griege, you take care of the kids. I'm going to pour a big glass of wine and a lovely bubble bath. You guys are full-time work."

We waited until we could hear them upstairs. Bernie cautiously opened the closet.

"You go!" he pointed to the back door. "Keep low when you run around the house. Tell the driver to get ready. I'll be right behind you."

I wanted to move but my feet were frozen in place.

Next thing I knew, Bernie had gathered me in his arms, lowered his height, and was wheeling us both speedily around the side of the house. He must have summoned the cab driver because the HoverCab was waiting outside the front door. Bernie slid me across the car seat and dove in after me.

The cab shot off soundlessly.

"How much time did we lose?" I asked Bernie when he took my hand.

"Serenity, I didn't want to alarm you, but it's already too late. My programmer was waiting for us to get out of the door before he started draining my battery. Don't worry, I've paid the driver his full rate. They're shutting me down. There's nothing we can do. Mission accomplished, robot down." Bernie's lights were dimming.

I shook him. "Bernie! Stop it! Activate a reserve generator or whatever robots do."

"That's above my pay grade," he murmured. "Serenity, it's been a pleasure. You'll meet my programmer at the other side. Be nice to him, okay? It's not his fault I have to be disarticulated."

He closed his eyes and went to sleep.

"Bernie! No! I need you!" But he was lifeless and heavy on the seat next to me. Tears spilled down my face, soaking my mask. I prodded his button, levers, and devices, but there was no sign of life. Could I take him home and connect him to an alternate power source? I was willing to try anything. I had to get Bernie back. Maybe I could make a deal with his programmer. I stopped crying and sat up straight. I'd fix this. Bernie was my friend. I needed him. It was as simple as that.

I must have dozed off because the next thing I knew, a tall, skinny, middle-aged fellow with a shock of reddish, grey hair was shaking me awake.

He paid the cabbie and sat me on a bench, next to the sleeping Bernie.

"I'm Old Brick," he smiled at me. I noticed he was kind of cute, but I had way more important matters to think about.

"You need to wake Bernie up," I said. "I need him."

Old Brick shook his head.

I stood up, outraged. "Then I'm leaving, and I'll take Bernie with me. He's my TheraBot. I need him." I grabbed Bernie's arm. Wow, he was as heavy as lead.

Old Brick sighed. All of a sudden, Bernie's lights started flashing and his limbs straightened out.

"She wouldn't listen to you?" he asked Old Brick.

"Nope. You'll have to tell her."

"Tell me what?" I realized I was sitting on a germy bench, but I didn't care. "What's going on? How come he's alive?"

"I activated his backup generator," Old Brick said.

"You don't need me," Bernie said gently. "Look at everything you did today. You proved that not only could you leave the house, but you could also travel all the way to suburbia in a HoverCab and enter a stranger's house, and not once did you think about germs."

"I did think about germs, but you were more important to me."

"Which in the past, would have been unthinkable. Look at everything you achieved today, Serenity! You should be so proud of yourself!"

"Are you back forever?" I asked. "I need to know you won't leave me again."

"Do you remember the survey you took in order to get me?"

I was confused. "Yeah. Sure. Why?"

"Because, in a nutshell, you were your own therapist, Serenity! All the attributes you anthropomorphize about me, they all came from you. They are mirror reflections of you. Your sense of humor, your tenacity, your courage."

I shook my head. "You're wrong. What I don't understand though, is why you needed me to go with you today. You could have done it all by yourself."

"Bots can't ride in HoverCabs alone," Bernie pointed out. "In the interests of transparency, as our old nemesis Volcanic Ghost would say, this whole plan has been in action for quite some time. Tell her the rest, Brick."

"It's true," Old Brick said. He blushed deep scarlet, which made his freckles pop even more. "I've been after these guys for a long time. They scammed my sister out of everything she had, and by the time she told me, all the evidence had been erased. They took back their laptop and scrubbed all traces of themselves from her life. I didn't have a shred of evidence." He clasped his long, bony hands. "I admit I behaved unethically. I hacked your family physician's files to see who was on the waiting list for a TheraBot. I realized I had to play the long game and I embedded Bernie into your life. He's not a real TheraBot or a part of OmniBot Central. He's a really convincing fake. He's right; he is you, and you are him. You're much stronger and more capable than you think, Serenity."

"You used me as bait!"

"Yes, but I was with you all the time. So was Bernie. You weren't in any real danger."

"I had the worst time of my life! I was so stressed! You let me go through that hell for weeks."

"Yes, to lead us into Optima Experiential's hive to gather evidence. You were an essential part of the plan. We nailed the perpetrators. Don't you feel validated? Doesn't that make it all worthwhile?

I nodded. That aspect of things felt pretty damn fine.

"What's going to happen to Bernie?" I asked. "How did you

make him into such a convincing specimen? I've seen TheraBots. He's exactly like the real deal."

Both Old Brick and Bernie chuckled. "I'm actually made from disarticulated parts," Bernie admitted. "I lack a warranty and my life span is limited. The plan wasn't for you to get as emotional about me as you did. We figured that at the end of the day, you'd be happy with the money, Old Brick would explain the situation, and you'd be glad to get rid of both of us. Instead, you were so sad when I powered down."

"You see, we're not the same," I said. "Your erroneous assumptions prove that. I really thought you were my friend. I feel betrayed by you."

I got up, planning to march off self-righteously, but the minute I stood up, I regretted thinking about leaving the two of them. There was something about Old Brick that made me want to get to know him better, fake bot or not, Bernie had helped me in so many ways.

Old Brick and Bernie looked at me. "Okay, well, fine," I muttered, "the whole thing was worth it, even though it was a horrible experience."

"On a good note, you've got more than enough money to take the time to find a real job," Old Brick said.

"We'll vet all offers to make sure they're above board," Bernie added.

There was no one around. I sat down and very cautiously took off my toque. "What time is it?" I asked.

"11 p.m.," Old Brick said. "You must be hungry. What say you, me, and this old rust bucket go and have a meal?"

"Mine will be vicariously," Bernie said, and I laughed.

"There is a 24/7 vegan café down the street," I said. "They've got a great cauliflower steak with a Glaswegian curry sauce. I used to get it as takeout when I had some cash to spare."

"It will be my treat," Old Brick said. "Come on, you old rust bucket, get to your feet."

"That I am a rust bucket, speaks volumes about you as opposed to me," Bernie countered. I grinned. Not only had I inherited a large sum of money, my second fortune cookie of the day had come true.

I'd failed to mention it to Bernie because it was the antithesis of my life, and seeing the little typed message angered me so much that I didn't even eat the cookie.

You'll always be surrounded by friends.

But it turned out to be true, after all. I hooked my arm in Bernie's and started humming.

"You see," I told him, "I can hum and breathe at the same time. My potential is limitless!"

-.- Ends -.-

ABOUT THE AUTHOR

Lisa de Nikolits is the internationally-acclaimed, award-winning author of eleven previous novels, with *Mad Dog and the Sea Dragon* slated for release in 2025 (Inanna Publications) and *That Time I Killed You* to come in 2026 (Level Best Books).

Her short fiction and poetry have been published in various international anthologies and journals including the Crime Writers of Canada's 40th Anniversary anthology (2022). She has a Bachelor of Arts in English Literature and Philosophy, and has lived in the US, Australia and Britain. She also several publications in other languages. Lisa lives and writes in Toronto.

To learn more about Lisa, go to her website: https://www.lisawriter.com/

———

INSPIRATION FOR THIS STORY

In the Interests of Transparency was inspired by shady job interviews and associated scams. It's also a sociological deep-dive into the current and future world of AI which is moving inexorably towards dehumanization. Alarmingly, humans already depend on robots and AI for emotional support but, that said, I developed a genuine fondness for Bernie TheraBot in this story, which was the antithesis of what I'd set out to do.

The Conscript

M. Jaimeson

Publisher's Note: This is a work of fiction. Names, characters, places, and incidents are a product of the author's imagination. Locales and public names are sometimes used for atmospheric purposes. Any resemblance to actual people, living or dead, or to businesses, companies, events, institutions, or locales is completely coincidental.

Published by

Windtree Press, Corvallis, Oregon

https://windtreepress.com

Prior Publications:

The Conscript was previously published in Speculative Fiction and Beyond in 1996

THE CONSCRIPT

BY M. JAIMESON

Dear Mr. Thomas:

Our records show your company has exceeded the minimum profit goal of five billion dollars. In accordance with Constitutional Amendment XXIX, and being CEO of said company, your name has been entered in the lottery.

*J*ohn let the letter fall from his hands to the desk, his shoulders drooped, and he collapsed into the chair. "Damn!" he spoke under his breath. "I thought we were just under the profit margin this year. How did it happen? Who let our profits get up that high?"

After a moment of self-pity, he gathered his thoughts and ordered the company comptroller to his office. Within three minutes she stood before him, her jaw clenched tightly and her arms filled with the latest printout on profits and losses for all subsidiaries.

He stiffly motioned her toward the conference table, the lottery letter firmly clasped in his hand. She dropped the load of paper and took a seat, arranging the papers in four distinct piles in front of her.

"Lois, how in hell did we make over five billion this year? I made it clear we had to stay under that profit margin."

He noticed her cheeks pull in again as she gritted her teeth and nervously leafed through the printout.

"Are you sure, John? I haven't completed the year-end assessment yet, but I'm almost certain that selling FarTech at a two-billion-dollar loss kept us under." Her fingers marked a spot a third through the second pile. "Yes, here it is." She pointed to the FarTech balance sheet. "Actually, a two-point-four-billion-dollar loss."

He angrily snatched the printout from her and peered at the column she'd indicated.

"Well, the IRS direct reporting program is quicker than you, dammit!" He slapped the letter down in front of her. "This is the damn letter."

"There must be some mistake," Lois said, though her voice suggested it was hopeless. She continued to scan columns of numbers, as if a miracle could be released from between the pages. "I just don't see how that could possibly be right ... I just don't ... "

He let her ramble nervously for a few moments before he cut her off. "Forget the year-end work. Drop everything and put your entire department on finding a loophole. If you don't find one, create one! I don't care what you have to do, just get me out of this before I'm automatically entered into the lottery."

"I'll get right on it," she said. "But John, you have to be realistic about this. It's almost impossible to create all the supporting paperwork in time to counteract the direct IRS reporting. We only have ten days now. We can only ..." Her voice trailed off as John stalked toward the window.

The San Francisco skyline helped to calm him. He didn't want to leave. He didn't want to take the chance of losing his company to some power broker. He looked back toward Lois. She was still leafing through the printout, as if looking busy would counteract her helplessness in the situation.

He felt a twinge of guilt for bullying her. But he couldn't help it. She seemed to open herself to his bullying—always understanding, always supportive, always doing her job so damn well. How did it get this far? She knew that no CEO in his right mind wanted to generate more than five billion dollars in profit.

He had frequently forced her to sell major company holdings against her best advice. She was often morose about having to cut employees or dismantle companies.

Oh God! He stiffened at the thought, his back ramrod straight as he clung to the windowsill. Did she do it on purpose? To get back at him for ending their affair?

"What are you going to do?" Lois placed her hand intimately on his shoulder.

John jerked to one side as her question brought him back to reality. Then he thought better of his action and took her hand in his, brushing his fingers across her knuckles. At least he could pretend to like her. After all, her continuing infatuation might be needed to save his ass.

"What *can* I do?" he asked, forcing himself to look into her eyes. "I've known a few CEOs who tried to leave the country. I know one who always kept a second set of books with less profits, but the IRS always caught up with them. Even Libya allows extradition these days. Those bastards think it's funny."

"What about Japan?" Lois brightened for a moment. She stepped away to open her briefcase and, after a few moments listening to her rustle papers, she presented John with a clipped news article. "Here it is. Japan willing to give amnesty to CEO's fleeing American Lottery System," she read.

"Oh sure, they'll take me," John said. "As a slave."

"Surely you…"

He cut off her words. "They'll put me in charge of one of their minor subsidiaries at one-tenth the salary with a ten-year commit-ment." He shook his head. "No. No. I can't afford that."

Lois looked away, her fingers twitching at her side. Her eyes focused toward the exit.

John paced. He'd been so careful. Every year for the last twenty, he'd shut down when they reached $4.5 billion. More revenue and profit always rolled in, even with a complete shut down and paying his employee's salaries the rest of the year. But he'd never even approached $5 billion. How did this happen?

He grabbed Lois by the shoulders and frog-marched her back to a computer. "Our only way out is to discredit the IRS direct reporting process. Now get busy and find me a loophole." He shook a finger at her. "It's all on your head, Lois. If my number is called it will all be on your head."

Lois regarded him stonily for a few moments. Then, gathering the papers into her briefcase, she rose and stomped out of his office.

Damn! He'd handled that poorly. All he could do now was hope his number wasn't chosen.

———

Dear Mr. Thomas:
Your lottery number is 69. The drawing will be held the first week in November. If your number is selected, you will report to our office on January 20th.

JOHN HADN'T TOUCHED HIS BREAKFAST. HE REREAD THE LETTER FOR the third time. He couldn't believe it. Ten days! Ten days until he knew if his life would be trashed.

"John?" His wife lightly touched his shoulder. "Are you all right?"

"Yeah. Yeah, I'm fine," he said, trying to muster a smile. "I just can't believe it, that's all."

"Well, it's not the end of the world if you're called. It's only five years. You will survive. Your company will survive."

"I don't want to go, Amy. No one at the pinnacle of success would voluntarily give up five years of his life."

"Well, it's your own fault," she said, frustrated. "You know the law. You've always walked that thin line of profits. Now you'll just have to pay." Then she kept her silence as she cleared the dishes from the table.

"Remember when Elizabeth Woods' lottery number was called?" Amy asked as she sat down next to him with a cup of coffee. "She had to give up her business, but everything turned out fine. And her record was excellent."

"Yeah, excellent," John repeated. "Too bad they don't lower the sentence for good behavior."

"When she went back to her business, she was more profitable than ever. At least, once your number is called, you don't have to worry about exceeding the five-billion-dollar profit limit anymore."

"Well, that's one good thing," John said. "Thank God they can only call your number once."

"And I can help you, too, John. You won't have to face this alone."

"I know." He patted her arm as he rose from his chair. "But ten days, Amy. How can I turn it all over in ten days?"

———

John and Amy entered arm in arm as their name was announced to the crowded ballroom. One hundred fifty-three conscripts were present, along with their families. The Press Corp numbered at least 300, tentatively held behind gold braid ropes with zoom lens cameras vying for precedence as they sought out the unsuppressed anger, a nervous smile, or a hopeless face to record for the morning papers. Television cameras would beam the events of the evening to billions watching around the world.

John felt Amy squeeze his hand in support as the press turned their cameras on them. "Here we are," he whispered in her ear, smiling for the snapping shutters. He wasn't going to let the press see him sweat.

The U.S. Lottery system had become the entertainment event of the century, surpassing the Academy Awards and the Olympics. The television announcers interviewed each conscript detailing a personal history, family background, and achievement index. Then they would move on to the gossip about their personal lives. John briefly wondered if anyone knew about his affair with Lois, and how that would play to the American public.

The dinner was first class. "It's like the last supper before my crucifixion," John mumbled to his wife.

"That's a bit dramatic," she said with a smile and patted his hand. "No matter what happens, we'll be fine."

Seven courses were served by attentive waiters who seemed capable of reading his mind and responding immediately. John's wine glass was never empty, and he noticed that Amy was radiant at the attention she was getting. He tried to look at her in a new light—one that emphasized the positives of their marriage.

Amy, the mother of his children, the one who had always believed in him when no one else would. He knew he didn't deserve that kind of loyalty, but he would take it just the same.

All too soon the orchestra began playing, signaling the dancing was to commence. John whisked Amy onto the floor. He suddenly wanted to make this a wonderful evening for her. He danced as if this was his last evening as a free man. And she responded to the rhythms of the music, and his unyielding embrace with a sensuality he had forgotten they'd ever shared. It was as if their life was beginning anew.

The clock chimed midnight. The music stopped and a spotlight shone on the podium. John pulled Amy toward the potted lemon tree in the corner, steering her away from a loud conscript who had too much to drink. He kissed her passionately, wondering if he'd ever have the chance again.

Lights flashed in his face. A press badge shoved in front of his eyes as he released his wife. "Mr. Thomas," the network news reporter and two cameramen corralled John and Amy. "Congratulations on winning the National Business Award."

"Thanks," John replied, his eyes darting past the reporter, looking for an escape.

"Do you anticipate any problems with leaving your company if your number is called? Do you have any fears of a power takeover, like what happened with Omnitel?"

John flinched as the reporter hit on his worst fear. Amy squeezed his side reassuringly. He forced a smile before he answered. "No, no fears," he said. "I've left the decision in the hands of the board. Furthermore, my controller will remain at the company to ensure the direction I've set will continue until my return."

"That's Lois Marquez, isn't it?" The reporter asked.

"Yes, that's right."

"I guess that's why the board announced tonight that she would be the next CEO if your number is called."

John's eyes widened. His chest constricted so much he could barely breathe. "Did you say," he swallowed. "Lois?" He choked on the word and covered his mouth with a dry cough.

The reporter grinned from ear to ear as cameras flashed, catching his surprise. "Oh, I guess you didn't know then. Of course, you wouldn't have known. The announcement was made only two hours ago. So, Mr. Thomas, how do you feel about Ms. Marquez' appointment to replace you?"

John couldn't form coherent thoughts, couldn't even begin to form words. Then, as if through a fog, he heard Amy begin speaking.

"John, that's wonderful! I'm so glad the board acted on *your* recommendations." She squeezed his hand and then smiled to the cameras. "John has long recognized how well Ms. Marquez' abilities complement the company's current direction. I'm sure she is the best choice for the position until John returns." Amy finished by retreating slightly to John's side and taking his arm possessively.

The reporter chuckled. "That sounded like a well-practiced answer, Mrs. Thomas. Practicing for politics?"

John tensed, looked at Amy. Schooling his features not to betray any question, any doubt.

"Mr. Thomas, one more question…"

"Excuse us," Amy interrupted, looking over her shoulder. "I see they are motioning everyone toward the podium. They must be about to call the number."

John took her cue and deftly moved himself and Amy out of the reporter's sphere and toward the front of the auditorium.

"Damn that Lois," John said under his breath. "I'll bet she planned this somehow. She just wanted to get back at me. Dammit! I should have been more careful. I should have known."

"Don't think about it now," Amy nuzzled his cheek. "It will all turn out fine. Don't worry about it now."

The path became more crowded, until John finally stopped about three rows back from the front. "You did pretty good back there with those reporters. If I didn't know better, I'd think you enjoyed that."

Amy's eyes twinkled as she looked up at him. "Someone has to look out for you."

The crowd quieted as two men formally approached the podium.

John shifted nervously from foot to foot. The past ten days had been hell for him. He'd had several sleepless nights, making wild plans for escape. Once, he even contemplated suicide. And now that he knew Lois would replace him, he wasn't sure what he would do.

"I hold in my hand a single lottery number," a strong voice boomed into the auditorium. "And the honor goes to . . ." He opened the envelope and pulled out the card. "Number 69."

Time stopped. John stood immobile. Then he felt a push as Amy prodded him toward the podium. Lights flashed. Music played. Hands shook his. The waiting and wondering were over.

––––––––

THE CHILDREN LOOKED UNEASY, STANDING RIGIDLY TO JOHN'S RIGHT, waiting for their father to complete the induction process. John nodded toward his son and then his daughter, trying to catch their eyes and reassure them with a smile.

The service requirement was only one five-year term. But, during those five years, the lottery winner had to sever all ties with their previous careers. They were to concentrate solely on service to their country.

The Chairman of the Joint Chiefs began his speech, reiterating the history of men and women who had served before John. As John listened, he filled with pride to be following in their footsteps. He didn't want to leave his company, but ultimately, he was a man of honor. It was up to him to serve his country and abide by the rules of the Twenty-Ninth Amendment.

The Chairman completed his speech, shook John's hand, and stepped back. The Chief Justice of the Supreme Court nodded and John stepped forward. Amy and the children smiled encouragement as they stood at his side. He held his right hand up, palm forward and repeated the oath.

"I, John Bernard Thomas, do solemnly swear that I will faithfully execute the Office of the President of the United States, and will to the best of my ability, preserve, protect, and defend the Constitution of the United States of America."

ABOUT THE AUTHOR

M. Jaimeson is an early pseudonym for Maggie Lynch. I used it at a time when I didn't want to worry about people reading my stories and making assumptions about what I believed or who I was based on the story.

The tagline version of my life is: *A repressed gypsy, creative by nature, who has tried to become a renaissance woman while maintaining a home life within the expectations of modern living.*

Yes, that's a mouthful. :)

You can learn more about me and my books at https:// maggielynch.com

---

INSPIRATION FOR THIS STORY

I first wrote this story in 1995. Our country was as deeply divided along party lines as it is today. I longed for a way to choose a president that would not require multi-millions of dollars to run a campaign, and to make the time from announcement to taking office a lot shorter.

This story is a take on one way a future society might handle that dilemma, where there is no party to win or lose and there are no voters to make the choice.

The Journey
Ron Roman

Published by

Windtree Press, Corvallis, Oregon

https://windtreepress.com

THE JOURNEY

BY RON ROMAN

A man wakes up from dreaming in a cornfield. Or has he? He's uncertain.

He doesn't know where he is or how he got there, nor what date it is. He notices he has no watch or jewelry. He examines his clothes, shoves his hand in his pants pocket, and grabs a wallet. He yanks it out. There's nothing inside it except for several bills. Then he freezes. The cash doesn't look familiar. "What the f---!" He's still unsure of the date. Then he notices a strange scar on his arm; he has no idea where it came from.

He finds himself next to a lush, green field near a thick, wooded area. It's sunny out. The weather is ideal. Birds are chirping. Skies are slightly cloudy; otherwise, it's nice. The temperature is nice. *Everything* is nice—but he's *lost*. And he doesn't know which direction to walk in, where to go on the dirt road in front of him.

There are no people nor evidence of any; he only hears birds chirping and dogs barking in the distance. The sound of a distant dog barking suddenly reminds him of what he thinks was his own dog from a long time ago, yet he can't recall its name. "He was a good pooch. Best friend a boy could ever have."

He starts to breathe heavier, almost panicking. And he starts to yell out, "Hey! Is anybody there? Where in living hell am I?" The shout echoes throughout the valley, coming back empty, leaving him empty. A nearby tree stump works as a makeshift chair. He sits down to try to collect his thoughts, make sense of his predicament. "Where the hell am I?" He looks up and into the sky, staring at the clouds. "Am I in a dream?" His hands start to shake.

He lies down on the ground, looks up again into the sky, and tries to collect his wits by testing his five senses. His eyes take in everything overhead while his ears listen to any and all sounds near and far. He hears no bird or animal now, not even the leaves that had been gently sashaying amidst the treetops. He touches his neck and face. "At least *that's* still there," he snorts. Yet he can't smell a thing, let alone taste anything over his lips or inside his mouth. It's too dry, even though he's not thirsty. "But what if I can't find water?" Premonitions of panic begin to seep into his consciousness.

The man stands up halfway. "I gotta get a hold of myself. Maybe I'm just dreamin'. But this feels too damned real. Okay, now just—" He realizes he can't remember his name. "Ah, what am I supposed to do? Maybe I had a little too much to drink before going to sleep. But where? When? I'll just follow this dirt road for a while. See where it goes. Nothing to worry about or panic…. Oh, shit."

The man starts down the dirt road. "Easy walk," he babbles to himself. "Just keep on trekking, buddy. Least I got money, though I don't know what kind or how much." He chuckles. "Must be some town or something up ahead. Hell, at least it's a damned-near perfect day for a little hiking." He tries to console himself and ekes out an anemic smile. The road under his boots feels soft and smooth. "That's good," he mutters, "though there's no tire tracks and no road signs anywhere. Weird."

He slogs onward. The sun peeks through the clouds and beats down on him. He breaks into a sweat. "Oh, this is weird, too. Old rusty train tracks. Looks like they haven't been used in over a hundred years. Might as well follow them, see where they lead." He picks up his pace. He thinks he catches a glimpse of something overhead, far off in the distance, something metallic-like, though not quite sure what. It reminds him of the scar on his arm. He has no idea why.

"Too damned stinkin' hot now. There's a little stream here. Water looks plenty clean. Have to drink some." He drinks, takes off his boots, massages and soaks his feet. This rejuvenates him, incentivizing a will to prevail and to slog on, stopping only occasionally to urinate by the tracks. *Looks like a helluva long road up ahead, but nightfall will be coming. No flashlight, no streetlights. Better start cracking,* he reminds himself.

The homespun pep talk re-energizes him. He's up and hurtling down the tracks, stubbing his toe and tripping. He gets up and picks up his pace. Relentlessly, he pushes onward. Shrubs and trees lining the tracks pass by quicker now. He exudes a renewed sense of urgency, as if walking over the tracks belies a need to keep up with an imaginary train schedule. He continues barreling down the tracks, noticing the absence and signs of anything human-made: no telephone poles, bridges, walls, electric power towers, buildings, or signs. Nothing. He keeps on slogging away at a steady pace, as if by slowing down, his boots may freeze to the tracks. A sporadic breeze keeps his sweat in check. The skies grow cloudier.

The day wears on. It's late. Undaunted now, he continues to move at a crisp pace, occasionally looking back to gauge the distance he's covered. He has put behind him many miles, yet he remains unfatigued. Though the clouds are thickening now, up ahead he notices something. Something strange. Very strange.

"What the---" There's a huge white cloud, a thick foggy mist, enveloping the valley ahead, blanketing everything from the top of the sky to the ground. He stops and scans the horizon for a higher elevation spot for a better view, yet finds none. "There's no turning back. I have to confront this, this whatever it is, head-on." Like a soldier marching headlong into battle, he surges forward.

Into the thick mist he runs, barely able to see anything in front of him. He starts to tire. "I better slow down. Could be a ditch, a ravine, or something." He pauses to catch his breath, looks behind for any signs of something, anything he may have missed running blindly. There's only dense fog. He moves forward again, this time at a measured pace. The fog starts to break. A clearing appears up ahead. He inches forward. Slowly. Steadily. Like a phantom he emerges from the fog. He looks down at his feet. "Huh? The railroad tracks are brand-new."

The man follows the tracks leading downtown into a village square lined with trees. The village looks semi-deserted, something like a hick town designed like a miniature train set under a Christmas tree. There's something about the place that looks familiar, but not everything. "Where the devil is this? There's a drugstore across the street, but the sign says 'Apothecary'. Thought that was British. Am I in England?" He enters the store.

The store is empty except for a tall, skinny, pimply-faced fellow standing behind a countertop vigorously mopping up leftovers from scattered dishes and utensils. "Whaddya need, buddy?"

He continues to stare at the menu.

"I said, 'What can I do for ya?'"

"Huh? Oh, sorry. I just, just was wondering what to drink." He scans the room. The place looks vaguely familiar in a way he can't put his finger on. "Ugh, I'll have a soda then. Big soda. With ice. Haven't had anything to drink since…. Really thirsty."

"What kind?"

"Any." The man slides atop a stool.

"Okay. Here you go. Try this."

"What's the name of this town?"

"Leeville."

"'Leeville,' huh?" The soda goes down smooth.

"Yeah, 'Leeville.'" The counterman shoots him a quizzical look, eyeing the scar on his arm. "You mean you don't know where you are? Howdya get here?"

"Hmph. Long walk. Long story."

"'Long story,' eh? Well, anything you need help with, let me know, okay?"

"Okay. I'll keep that in mind. Thanks." *Least I'm not in England,* the man thinks to himself. He finishes the drink, swipes over his lips with his sleeve, and gets off the stool for the exit, then remembers the unpaid bill. He gestures to pay while taking out the unfamiliar bills.

"Sheesh, where'd you get these bills? Haven't seen this since before the war. Sonnafab-b-b-donkey!" pimple-face splutters as he takes one, stares at him, and cracks a sheepish grin. "That's all right. They're still legal tender. Is that the word? Here's your change, Mister. Pleasure meeting you. Put 'er right there," he says, extending his hand. "Joey's the name. And you?"

"Huh? Ugh, me? Er, you can call me, er, call me 'Joseph.' Just a little more formal."

Pimple-face grins. "'Joseph,' eh? 'a little more formal'? See ya around, Joe!"

"Yeah, 'See ya around.'" The man stuffs the change in his pants, almost knocking over a rack of potato chips in his urgency to make a beeline for the door. "Joseph," he says to himself and snickers over the sound of his self-given nickname. "And 'the war'?"

Stepping outside into the sunshine, he looks back where the fog had enveloped the valley behind him. He doesn't see any. He's tempted to go back for a better look but senses something inside him beckoning him to continue into town.

The town appears more vibrant now. People are milling on both sides of the street; the village is thrumming with activity. The man steps down the apothecary's stairs and onto the edge of the square. On the opposite side of the street, he sees a cat lying lazily under a park bench. It looks familiar. *Can't be,* he thinks. He goes to pet it. "Here kitty. Nice—"

"—watch where the hell you're going, Buster!" a motorist screams. "Trying to get yourself killed?"

The man hops back toward the stairs, almost slipping on the steps. "Whew! Yeah." The cat slithers away. He walks past kids in a playground as he notices what looks like a political rally on the far end of the square opposite the Town Hall. He moves toward the stage. Sounds of the campaign grow louder. There're at least a couple hundred attendees sitting on lawn chairs in front of a large stage draped with political banners and signs. The smell of frying hot dogs and hamburgers lingers in the air among cries of "Get your dogs and burgers here!"

The man grabs an empty chair and makes himself comfortable beside a middle-aged couple off to his right. They nod and smile beneficently toward him. In turn he doesn't know what to do; he manages a goofy grin.

"Bob Johnson here. This here's my wife, Joanna. Pleased to meet ya," he says, offering his hand. "And you?"

"Who, me?"

"Don't see anybody else I'm talking to." The couple laughs.

"Yes, yes, of course. I'm Joseph. But just call me, er, Joey. Yes, Joey."

"Pleased to meet you, Joey."

"Same here."

"What do you think of the speaker? Do you think this party is going to save the county and our town from going to hell in a handbasket with what's going on and---" The Johnsons lower and shake their heads, intimating they'd heard this message of this rally before.

"Let's get it on!" someone screams.

"Yeah! Let's get down to it! Didn't come here to sit on our asses all day!" shouts another.

The crowd murmurs its agreement. A speaker, elderly and

porky, strides toward the podium. People lean forward in their chairs. A buzz of anticipation hovers in the air. Overhead clouds darken in the direction of the apothecary, giving a sense of immediacy. Thunder rolls in the distance. The crowd grows antsy. The stage speaker steps up behind the podium. He taps the microphone for attention. He sees that he has it and clears his throat.

"All right, ladies and gentlemen. Glad you could make it here this afternoon. Thanks for coming. And don't forget tonight's fireworks. Lots of things to go over today, especially with the way things are going in the county these days and with things the way they are in our town now, eh?"

"Just get to the point, Benny," someone in the back of the assembly shouts. "Whaddya propose to do about what the governor, that shithead, is proposing to do to us in terms of skyrocketing taxes and new county restrictions regarding farm produce sales? You know what I'm talking about. Everybody does."

The crowd, electrified, jumps to their feet with shouts of "Yeah! What? We can't take it no more! Whaddya gonna do about it? Stop your yodeling. What--?"

"—Okay, okay, I hear you, hear you loud and clear. That's what I'm—we—are here today to dig into. I feel your pain as much as you do."

The Johnsons lower and shake their heads in near-unison again; Joanna rolls her eyeballs. Behind the stage, firecrackers explode. It starts to drizzle. "I, I mean the party, are introducing legislation next week to impeach the governor—" shouts of "Yeah! Stuff it to that bastard!" and the like, ring out and echo throughout the square, the throng morphing into a mob, baying for blood. And so, on it went....

Bob Johnson suddenly swivels in his seat and looks foursquare at 'Joey'. "You know, you look familiar. You remind me of somebody I saw, maybe even knew, years ago. There's a photo in town somewhere of somebody resembling you, though much younger and with a full head of hair, an image that I can't place."

Joanna leans forward to listen better amidst the commotion.

'Joey's' palms start to sweat; his mouth gets dry. He bites down on his lip. Hard. "Who? Me? Nawh."

"No, no really, Joey. 'cept your name doesn't match, doesn't ring true. Can't quite figure it out."

Joanna leans in more. "Maybe you're confused, Bobby, maybe-- -"

"—Shut up! I ain't confused." Bob stops, reflects on his outburst, and gently cradles her hand. "Sorry, Joanna. My apologies. Don't mean to lose my temper, yet…. yet there's something now knockin' up inside my ol' brain." The drizzle got heavier.

Joey leans back and eyes Bob. "That's okay. I look like a lot of guys," is all he can spit out. Together they stare at each other as if in a contest, then Joey, embarrassed, breaks focus first, lowers his head, and mumbles something inaudible. Joanna stares at both of them.

"Getting hungry. Let's get a bite to eat, Bobby," she says. Bob gets off his chair, turns and says, "Nice meeting you, Joey—or whatever your name is."

"Yeah, same here," he says barely above a whisper. The Johnsons head for the snack stand. Joey, relieved, stands, stretches his legs, and notices the crowd starting to dwindle, the commotion dying down. The skies are clearing. He ambles toward the stage; flags tacked to the sides catch his eye. The design of the flags intrigues him; it looks oddly familiar. He doesn't understand why or how. He tries to toss the thought aside, muttering "Time to concentrate on getting a better idea as to where in hell this place is. Looks like a signboard showing a town map up ahead. That might help."

Approaching the board, he grows excited. *The Town of Leeville* it reads. This might be of real help after all. It beats having to ask the Johnsons embarrassing questions as to the location of Leeville, he reasons.

"That speaker, Benny, is a yodeler, a bum, just another do-nuthin' politician," a woman exclaims, standing behind him. "Blah. blah. blah. Don't ja think, buddy?"

"Well, I'm not from here. I'll pass on judgment," he says, irritated.

"Where ya from then?"

"Uh, sorry. I'm pressed for time." He turns his back on her. She snorts, shakes her head, and struts away. He's relieved now that he can finally focus attention on doing something productive. The map details main landmarks in town, yet little else outside the community. The Town Hall and Library should be sites of helpful information, he figures, but the town's high school is right next door and may reveal something useful as well. He starts walking toward it.

People are still lingering in the town square, enthusiastically talking about the night's fireworks now rather than politics. He feels the urgent need to relieve himself and rushes down the steps into a nearby public restroom at the edge of the village square. The smell of stale urine permeates his nostrils. Upon finishing up, while washing his hands, he catches a glance of himself in the washroom mirror on the graffiti-splashed walls. He then realizes this is the first time he has seen himself. He freezes.

He doesn't recognize the face staring back at him. It shows several scars, small but noticeable, and beady eyes, mournful beady eyes. He's taken aback. He grips the wash basin with both hands. For the longest time, he remains transfixed. Many thoughts race through his mind as he stands there. He finally comes to and gets hold of himself.

"You all right, buddy?" a voice is heard from behind.

"Ugh, yeah, sure."

"You sure don't look it."

"No, I'm okay. Thanks."

"Okay. Just askin'."

"Yeah. Sure." The man in the mirror straightens up. "Get a hold of yourself," he says to the image. He wipes his hands on his pants.

He heads for the exit. His legs are wobbly. This epiphany could take time for him to come to grips with. He struggles back up the stairs, almost bumping his head on the way out of the exit.

Out in the open and fresh air again, the man reorients himself in the direction of the high school. He surveys the landscape and sees it in the distance. He feels slightly invigorated now and pushes forward with a renewed zip in his step. A *Summer Vacation is Here. See You in the Fall* sign overhead welcomes visitors. He approaches the running track surrounding the football field inside the outdoor stadium. Except for a couple of roaming dogs, the place is deserted. Multiple oversized outdoor photo displays are plastered over the stadium walls, testifying to the bygone prowess and glory days of the school's old sports teams and star athletes. A couple in particular catch his eye. He edges closer.

The black-and-white photos depict the school's football team's post-championship game, front row players kneeling, the two co-captains front and center. The man stares, mesmerized by the close-up image of one of the co-captains. *Can't be.* He wonders if the image in the restroom is not the same as in the stadium photos, except for facial scars. *Can't be.* He also ponders the possibility that it could be merely coincidental and thinks it best to visit the Town Library in the morning to research the matter. "I need to get to the bottom of this, but first I need to eat and sleep," he says to himself upon seeing the sun set. He starts back toward the town square.

He heads for the food vendor stands, now drawing in people in anticipation of the fireworks display. "What can I getchya, Champ?" shouts out one of the vendors over the din of the crowd. The man pauses at the sound of the word "Champ." Not knowing why, the word resonates in his head.

"A couple of dogs and a burger, please."

"Here you go, Champ."

"Thanks."

"Here's your change. Don't see many of these bills anymore."

"Yeah, I know." While squeezing mustard on his hot dogs, the man notices a boy, prepubescent yet almost menacing for his age, standing next to him, entranced by his arm scar. "What are you gawking at?"

Boldly the boy blurts out, "What the hell happened to your arm, Mister?"

"Mind your own goddamned freaking business, kid. Ya hear me?" The boy leers back at him. "Now go play in your sandbox." The boy scampers away.

"You don't take guff from anybody, I see," snickers the food vendor. "It's written all over you. You remind me of my Uncle Demetri: big and rough around the edges like him. He was a star football player in town." The vendor smirks. "The kids these days…."

The man nods. "Why did you call me 'Champ'?"

"My cousin used to call guys that, at least guys he liked. Here's another dog. On the house."

The man nodded again.

The skies darken; stars emerge. The first of the fireworks explodes overhead. Then another. Soon the sky explodes in a kaleidoscope of colors, a transitory rainbow emblazoned over the horizon. A chorus of *"Ooh's"* and *"Ahh's"* shoot up from the crowd. Firecrackers pop off nearby; smoke from fireworks wafts toward the crowd huddling on the village green. The man sits down on the village lawn, looks up and into the sky, observant at one moment of the colorful spectacle overhead, then drifts off to the echo of "Champ" pulsating inside his head. *Can't be.* The echo fades and dissolves into silence. The fireworks finale slaps him back into the moment.

The crowd starts to dwindle. From the safety of a good distance, the boy from the hot dog stand flashes an obscene hand gesture and grins.

"That punk." The man struggles to his feet, balancing himself against a park bench. He's zapped out from the day's ordeal and ready for a solid sleep. But where? "It's warm. I'll conk out here under that secluded gazebo." The last of the townsfolk leave the square; the place is dark and quiet. "I'm exhausted. Going to sleep like a dead man." Too tired to trudge to the public restroom, he urinates on a bush, then crawls into a hidden space in the gazebo, hunkering down under the starlight. The man drifts off into a festering dream....

"Hey, guys! Gotta win this one for ol' Head Coach Haley. Sonnafabitch is laying in the hospital, could be on his last legs from cancer. Don't know how much time he's got left in 'im. Nor how much he's got left with us. He always pulled through for us; now it's our turn to pull through for him. Whaddya say, Champ? You're co-captain. Have a pep talk for the boys?"

"Nawh, you said enough, Demetri. If the rest of our team showed half the grit and determination on the field as you, we'd win the division championship hands down for Haley. No doubt about it."

"Thanks, bro. Every player knows we can always count on you. You weren't chosen co-captain for nuthin'. What are you going to do now that Maria's talking about filing sex assault charges against you, Champ? Did the principal say your scholarship's going to be on hold? Hey, you didn't actually do nuthin' to her, did ya? Word's already spreading around town like a spastic case of VD that you let her have it, banged her up but good. Not that that Mexican bimbo wouldn't deserve it. Ha! Ha! Or is she just makin' this whole thing up because she's jealous you didn't ask her to the prom? Is there going to be a police report? C'mon! Guys on the team want to know. You're co-captain; they deserve an answer, don't ya think?"

"Learn to mind your goddamned freaking business, fat boy, or I'll shove those miniature balls of yours up your big, fat mouth, bigger than your belly."

"LOOK, I DON'T KNOW WHAT'S GOING ON WITH HER, COACH. SO, WE fooled around a little together--I said together--but I didn't force myself on her, rape her; that's for sure. She's making this stuff up to get back

at me for not asking her out. Do us guys have any presumption of innocence these days for Chrissakes? Or are we all automatically presumed guilty because we've got a usable penis between our legs and they don't?"

"I don't know. It just doesn't look good for you. I need you on the team. Your word against hers, but school staff and townsfolk already are lining up on her side, even though everyone knows she's got a reputation as a hot Mexican tamale, for sure. Your scholarship's in jeopardy. I've tried to diffuse the situation with the cops, and the School Board is meeting to take it up. Yet now my hands are tied."

———

"You can say it's been a hung jury verdict for me, man. My representatives cut a deal, if you could call it that, with the authorities and her folks that I'd join the Army right after graduation for her not pursuing further charges, so that's what I'm doing. Besides, I gotta get out of Dodge; my name's mud here now."

"Sheesh. No kiddin'. I'll be seeing you when you're on military leave then. Gonna miss ya. Gimme a hug, Champ."

"Now don't get all teary-eyed and goofy on me, man. Don't expect us to take any hot showers together anytime soon. Never thought I'd see you like this. I must be dreaming."

———

"How's the Army treating you?"

"Like shit. But I shouldn't complain. Three hots and a cot like they say."

"You missed Coach Haley's funeral, Champ. He got a great send-off. Practically the whole town turned out for him."

"So I heard. Couldn't get leave to attend, though. Military says it has to be a family member or guardian. Sent in my condolences."

"You and your Old Flame, Jenny, still getting married now?"

"Far as I know. Meeting her tomorrow. She hasn't seen what happened to me yet."

"Yeah, I heard it was a military live-fire training accident."

"No, just a chopper's blade grazing a nearby metal sign. Fragments hit my face and arm. I'm okay, though. Lucky."

"Your unit deploying to the Middle East?"

"Probably, things are heating up there. Fast."

"Saying a prayer for you."

"Yeah, thanks, brother. Need it."

———

"I love you, Randy. Always will, scarred-face or movie-star handsome. Big wedding or none at all. And I don't care what folks had said about you and Maria. She's a bitch."

"Thank you, Jenny. You're the light of my life. After this overseas deployment, we're going to have the honeymoon of our lives, a honeymoon to end all honeymoons!"

"Looks like we're going to war. I'm so scared, scared something worse than an arm injury is going to happen to you. And stop biting into your lip. That always means something bad is going to happen."

"Don't worry, Jenny. I'll be fine. Let me wipe away that tear."

"Our doggie Joey and me will be waiting for you. Always. Now give me a last kiss before you leave."

———

"Jenny, I swear Maria and I—"

"You can't be sleeping here, pal. This is town property."

The man looked out from under the gazebo, shading his hands from the morning sun. "Sorry, officer. Must've had a little bit too much to drink last night. Fireworks got me worked up and tired out, too."

"Fireworks got you too worked up, huh? Whaddya, five years

old? Okay, now that you're up, whaddya doin' here? You're not from town, are ya? Let's see some ID."

"Er, ID? Look, I just got up and need to take a wicked leak in the park restroom, officer. Bad. Can I go over there? Now? Been diagnosed with an overactive bladder."

"Okay, forget the ID. Don't want you peeing in your pants. Just don't sleep out here again. Leeville don't need no vagrants. And you don't look like one. My job is to see it stays that way, got it? Only reason you're not getting a citation is because it was a town celebration and half the town was soused out last night, too."

"Thanks."

"Okay, now clear out and take your *wicked* piss. G'wan."

"Yes, sir. On my way."

"Hey, fireworks was pretty good, eh?"

The man made a run for the restroom. "Really great!" he shouted out over his shoulder as he started slowing down. "Whew! What a total jackass. And that dream last night. Gotta get to the town library now to research stuff from it. Weird, but feels so damned real. Urinal first."

The sun was rising overhead, getting stronger. The man made his way to the opposite side of the village square and stopped. He stood in front of the portico of the library entrance. Emblazed on the top in bas-relief, it simply read *Leeville Public Library*. He thought the portico oversized and ornate for such a small town and felt uneasy as to what he'd find, if anything, but hurried inside anyway.

"These are old copies of *The Leeville Gazette*; these are only weekly issues, yet they should help you cover the date range you asked for in looking for your "ol buddy,'" came the squeaky voice of the porky reference librarian squeezed into her small chair barely big enough to fit her behind. "Need anything else, just holler," she said while arranging the papers over the clamor coming from kids fighting on the other side of the room.

"Much appreciated," said the man. "This should do," he said to himself. He poured voraciously through the paper, fingers dancing over the pages as fast as humanly possible, while retrieving mental references to names and dates taken from the stadium. The kids continued their fighting and squawking; the librarian did not intervene. "Thought libraries were supposed to be quiet for Chris-sakes!" he muttered in her direction.

Sunshine poured through the windows. It was hot and muggy. The sole air conditioner sputtered *Th-thuck. Th-thuck. Th-thuck.* The morning wore on. The man's patience thinned; the kids were getting on his nerves. He hoped he'd dig up pay dirt. Nothing would stop him from resurrecting the truth—or what he imagined to be the truth—of his dream. Or nightmare.

"Let's see, this story again, what there is of it, just mentions the head coach's remarks after the team's final score, yet really nothing about the players. Jesus. What kind of reporters have they got, anyway?"

"How's it coming?" asked the librarian from her desk, noticing his frustration.

"Coming, it's not. Seemed to have hit a dead end. These stories don't get into details, least not about the players, their names, etc. That's what I'm looking for. The sports reporter should get shitcanned."

The man saw the librarian's face tense at the vulgarity. "Must be some fanatic Christian," he grumbled. The kids' raucousness died down. The librarian sauntered over, peevish.

"Have you tried the school's yearbooks?"

"Jesus Christ Almighty. Why in hell didn't I think of that?"

"You really should watch your mouth, Mister. You're not from around here. This is a Christian community. Least it used to be."

"Sorry, Ma'am. You're right. Guess I should."

"No need to guess."

"Yes, you're right. Sorry again." Then he thought of the generic profanity dished out during the political rally the night before and squelched a chuckle.

"Something funny 'bout all this?" She eyed him cooly.

"Ugh, n, n, no," he stammered. "Er, I'll need yearbooks for these dates." He scribbled on a sheet of paper.

Soon she returned with several and plopped them on his desk. "This ought to cover it," she said and quickly pivoted to return to her desk, relief etched across her face. The kids had now left; the place was deserted and deathly quiet.

"Good. Thanks." He started with the oldest edition, thumbing through coverage devoted to football. This is tedious, he thought. Either the photos weren't graphic enough, or the captions not detailed. His fingers trudged through every page. On to the next yearbook. Then the next. He grew more frustrated by the minute. He squirmed in his seat, biting into his lip. Then ….

The hair on the back of his neck stood up straight. "Am I hallucinating? Holy shhh--! Can't believe it. Can't be." Was he looking at a photo of himself? The caption read: "Randy 'Champ' Peterson, Co-Captain." This photo was graphic; there was no mistaking him in it, but with a full head of hair and minus noticeable facial scars and his beard. For the longest time, he sat stuck in his chair, stunned and speechless.

"Any luck?" the librarian asked. The man remained immobilized as if frozen into his chair by a stun gun levied by the Angels of Fate from above. "I said, are you having any luck? Hmm." She paused, then slowly rose and gingerly walked over behind him while eyeballing the news article.

"Whoa! This is *weird shit*! You don't even remember when you attended school here. Hot damn. Guess your 'ol' buddy' you were looking for is *you*." The outburst slapped the man back into reality. "Except for the hair and the facial, uhm—"

"---the facial scars?" the man asked.

"---er, the facial scars, it sure resembles *you*."

"Look, I, I, I don't know what to say. I don't know what's going on. A brain lapse, an injury or something. I may need help. I'd appreciate it if you'd keep this to yourself for now."

"Yeah, sure. Anything I can do for you, Mister? Mister---?"

"Joey, er, Peterson. No, nothing you can do for me, not yet. I'll let you know. Just need a little more time to study things here and clear my head."

"Sure. I understand." The woman walked back to her desk, turned around, and nodded. "You just let me know, okay?"

Still shaken by the epiphany, the man dove into news stories about "Randy 'Champ' Peterson." He learned he was a star football player, a quarterback, with scholarship offers and had been charged with aggravated sexual assault by a Mexican-American girl from their high school in their senior year, inflaming racial tensions in town, only to see charges dropped in a plea deal, something to do with joining the military. After graduation he joined the Army's First Cavalry Division as a medic, later promoted to buck sergeant, and sustained injuries to his head and arm in a training exercise before being deployed overseas for combat in the Middle East. While on leave, he married his hometown sweetheart, the former Ms. Jenny Jones.

The *Th-thuck, Th-thuck, Th-thuck* of the air conditioner reverberated in his head. His hands shook while cradling the newspaper. He read on…. "Sgt. Peterson's remains were never found. He is presumed to have died as a captive POW (Prisoner of War) or KIA (Killed in Action). He was awarded the Silver Star for gallantry in action. For more information, contact Leeville's local VFW post. They host a special display in honor of his memory and meritorious service."

The man struggled to steady his hands. "Then where have I been? Where have I come from?" The voice resounding in his head rendered him numb. "Joey," "Peterson," "the man"--this disembodied being remained stuck in his seat. Then he slowly rose to his feet and managed to make it over to the librarian's desk. "Do you have a map showing the town's VFW?"

"No need to. VFW, hmm? It's right around the corner. A five-

or six-minute walk, maybe seven. Here, let me sketch it." She unfurled a writing pad and scribbled. "Here you go."

"Thanks." He took the paper. "You've been more than kind. Appreciate that." He started for the exit, pivoted, and blurted out: "And sorry for my foul mouth."

"Perfectly understandable. I let slip a word stinker or two myself." She giggled.

Outside, the sun was slipping into the horizon. "Better beeline it to the post. May close down soon," he muttered. He glanced at the note. "It's that direction." Soon he was standing in front of a dinghy three-story building that looked like it had just been plopped out of a cosmic map; the VFW was located on the second floor. He jumped up the stairs.

Other than a Filipina bartender, inside there were no women, only several older guys, mostly grizzled, bearded, and tattooed, slurping on beer or an occasional whiskey from their bar stools, animatedly swapping sports and war stories. An oversized American flag hung from the ceiling almost getting entangled in an overhead swirling fan. "This we'll Defend" read a banner adjacent to it. Next to it was a POW flag. Cowboy song lyrics yodeled from a nearby jukebox. A lone pool table lay squat in the center of the room. Though the room's windows were opened wide, the place reeked of a distinctive musty smell. Photos of past post commanders, solemn-faced with tasseled headgear, graced the dimly lit walls. Except for the bar, jukebox, and pool table, the man thought, the place could pass for a funeral parlor.

"Hey, Buddy, want a Bud, Budweiser, that is?" asked one of the vets upon noticing the man entering the room, as the outsider took in the surroundings. The stranger nodded. "Hey, Nina," the vet shouted to the bartender, "one Budweiser for our guest here. Name's Alfonso; and you?"

"Ugh, Randolph."

"Randolph, eh? Well, here you go, Randolph," he said as he

banged their beer bottles together. "See you're not from around here. You did military time?"

"Yeah, Army."

"Yeah? Well, I wasn't a rough, tough soldier like you, ya know, just another Navy girly-boy." He smirked. And the man grinned. "Where you from?"

The man went to deflect the inquiry. "Can you tell me anything about Randy Champ Peterson? That's what I came here for." He could smell whiskey on Alfonso's breath.

"Why you so interested in Randy Peterson? Been missing, presumed dead for years."

"He was a fellow soldier. It's an Army thing," the man said.

"I see. But did I know Randy? Nawh. Before my time. But my uncle did. Played with him on their winning championship football team in their senior year—and in earlier years. Everybody in town knew, or knew of him, even if they didn't follow football, especially after being accused of raping a Mexican gal at the school. Talk of the town. Then he joined the military, Army, got injured, came back on leave to marry his high school sweetheart, returned to duty, and got sent into combat in the Middle East war overseas. Got the Silver Star and got himself taken prisoner or killed in action. Don't know which. His memorial display is over there," Alfonso said, pointing to it in the corner. The jukebox changed tunes and started belting out an old Roy Orbison song from the 60s.

Another vet butt in. "Yep, Randy Champ Peterson, one real, tough sonnafabitch. Fought the school bully, ten times his size, to a draw; some say he got the better of him. Beat the dog piss out of him. Dunno. Before my time, too. Only know what my aunt, who witnessed it, said. She had a crush on ol' Randy, star quarterback that he was. Besides, she was too fat and homely to be his girlfriend, or anybody's. Everyone always wondered why my uncle married her. Must've been good in the sack because she sure couldn't cook. Ha! Ha!" Upon overhearing the conversation, several others joined in on the joke and exploded in laughter.

Another vet piped in: "Did he rape that Mexican gal? Forgot her name; it was all folks would, or could, talk about for years. She moved away years ago. A real looker, they say. A hot number, tell you that much. Married some hotshot industrialist, it's been said. But was it rape?"

"Bet it was!" chimed in another.

"Ah, what do you know!" someone blurted out.

"I know he had the temperament."

"You don't know jack-squat, Caleb. You wuz only a washed-up cook stuck in the infantry." The others snickered in agreement. "One thing everybody always said about 'ol Randy, you either liked him or you didn't. Nobody ever knew him to not keep his word, never let anyone down, especially his teammates. Wasn't called 'Champ' for nuthin', the SOB."

"Yeah, won the Silver Star, too!"

"You're not a 'winner' of medals of valor, you idiot! You're a 'recipient.'"

"Ugh, thanks for reminding me, Pete. I forgot. Like recipients of the M-O-H, huh?"

"Well, you wuz just a grunt ground-pounder in the infantry, too. What can we expect?"

The others roared in laughter, one guy spilling his beer over his pants. "Don't be so tough on ground-pounding grunts, Pete. We couldn't all be commissioned officers like you, ya know," someone shouted out from behind the pool table. They nodded in unison.

"Yeah, okay," said Pete. "I apologize for still wearing my rank out of uniform. How about a round of drinks on me fellows, huh?"

"Yeah! Now you're talkin'," yelled out a pot-bellied veteran, the only tattoo-free drinker at the bar.

"Nina, a round for everybody." With the new round of drinks, things settled down. Then the man walked over to what resembled a makeshift shrine in honor of "Sgt. Randolph Peterson," black cloth draping Peterson's active-duty photo on the wall. He stood motionless and in a daze in front of it as if frozen at attention before his company commander.

He wondered if he were dreaming. The mirror image reflected in the photo was that of a military-uniformed young man, handsome, scar-free. His knees weakened. *Don't understand it. How could it be me?* The epitaph below the photo read as if it had been lifted from the news stories in the library. There were other photos, one of the man in football attire wedged in between smiling teammates. A tear came to his eye. He looked around the room. Age differences aside, he wondered how these men could be related to him through service, honor, duty, country.

He couldn't think of anything. A feeling of emptiness welled up inside him. His thoughts turned to Jenny.

"Alfonso, could you tell me anything about Peterson's girlfriend?"

"Jenny? Jenny Jones? Why are you interested in her? That was years ago."

"Ah, the story at the display was really interesting."

"Well, all I know is that she came back to town. Lives on 70 Walnut, the Burghers' old homestead, three blocks over down the street. The place has turned into a sorry neighborhood in recent years. Can't tell you much more than that. Nobody here can. Don't see her often. Keeps a real low profile."

"Thanks." The man turned around. Some of the vets were now eyeing him suspiciously and talking about "Sergeant Peterson" in hushed tones. The man overheard several snippets: "Jesus, Mary, and Joseph. Sure looks like him." "Are you *crazy*? He's been dead for years." "Did you see the way he was acting at the display? Like he was knocked out while still on his feet and staggering on Dream Street but just didn't know it." "Yeah, but that don't necessarily mean nuthin'." "Nothing my ass! I'm telling you, the resemblance is there, just an older version." "I don't know, just don't know...." came the hushed whispers. The man thought it best to leave. Now. He slithered out the door.

It was getting dark and muggy. He thought of going to Walnut Street, then paused. "Too late. Tomorrow. First thing. Exhausted. Better get some sleep. But where? Can't go to a motel. I've no ID. Better conk out somewhere like last night." He grew apprehensive at the thought of bumping into "Officer Jackass" again. "Still, might as well head out to the park again."

He hastened his stride. The glow from a full moon shimmered overhead, casting shadows over the trees and bushes and the park's carousel, now mothballed and collecting leaves from inactivity. The park remained silent and still. He felt a strange reminiscence come over him at the sight of this carousel. He just couldn't fathom why. "Under the floorboards is a good place to hide." He looked up into the sky and gazed at the stars. *Why am I back here? What will happen tomorrow?*

––––––

THE SUN SHONE HIGH ABOVE THE MOUNTAIN CREST TO THE EAST. "I slept like a dead man. Or am I already dead? Or does it matter?" The afternoon before, he had gorged himself on free food at the VFW. Now he felt no need to eat but only to hurry to Walnut Street in hopes of seeing his beloved Jenny. *But what if she's not there? What if it was all a mistake? A lie?* The thought kept pulsating inside his head. "Am I trapped inside a vanishing dream? No, no." He shook his head. "This is too real."

As if electrified, his weary legs came alive. Time stood still; things blurred. It was mid-morning when he found himself standing in front of the run-down, dour-looking house on 70 Walnut Street. Mouth dry, heart pounding, testicles in his throat, he knocked on the door and waited.

No answer.

He knocked again.

No answer.

A crow cawing overhead caught his attention, breaking the suspense. Then the sound of footsteps behind the door and it slowly opened….

"May I help you?"

The man stood frozen as if paralyzed.

"I said, 'May I help you?'"

"Jenny, is that you?" He recognized her; she hadn't changed much.

"How did you know my name? Who are you?"

"It's me, Randy." He grimaced. "I've come back. I---"

"---oh, my God!" The woman staggered and went to steady herself against the wooden staircase. "How could this be happening? Am I dreaming?"

"Are both of us?"

"How did you get here? Where did you come from?"

"I don't know, Jenny. Are we in a dream within a dream?"

"Jenny, who are you talking to? Who's at the door?" came a woman's voice from inside.

"It's all right, Mom. Go back to sleep. I'll take care of it." She gazed into his eyes. "You were gone for over seven years, Randy. We thought you were dead, taken from us in the war. Remember when I told you our doggie, Joey, and I would wait for you? We did. He's buried in the backyard. Then, later, you were legally declared dead. Our marriage was invalidated. What was I supposed to do?"

"I understand. But I…." The words stuck in his throat.

"Jenny, who's that?"

"I told you it's all right, Mom. Now go back to bed. Let's go out on the front porch, Randy." She gingerly closed the door behind her. "I'm engaged to be married to your best friend, Demetri. I'm sorry, Randy. I love you, but you can't come back." She threw her arms around him, pulling him into her, hugging him tightly.

He clenched his jaw. Bit into his lip. Hard. Drew blood. It trickled down his chin.

"There you go, biting into your lip again." She tenderly wiped it away. He sat down on the porch sofa. "Remember when we made love for the first time? It was by the merry-go-round in the park. There's only one Summer of Love for every boy and girl. You can't go home again, Randy."

"Why can't I come back, Jenny? Why? The pain from the war hurts me too much inside. The war fractured me. It haunts me. I can't, I can't live like this…." The man keeled over, holding his head in his hands, sobbing in wave after wave of heated convulsions. "The government gave me its third-highest combat medal, yet it doesn't ease the pain. I witnessed so much blood, death, and dismemberment. The only thing that gave me hope at the time was the memory of you. But all the other memories, they won't fade; they won't go away. They haunt me like an eternal ghost in every breath I take. Hurts too much. It feels like a demon's hand is ripping apart my guts."

Jenny cradled and gently rocked him in her arms more like a baby than a husband. "I can't imagine what you suffered. But as shallow as it may sound, you're not living your life, living your life in the Eternal Now. You can't bury yourself in the past. The past is gone; there's only the Now leading into the dawn of tomorrow. Don't take it for granted. You have to go back on your journey, the journey from where you came. You've been looking behind your-self, Randy. It's time to look ahead. First, you need to *confront your ghosts.*"

Randy 'Champ' Peterson sat on the porch swing, frozen in time. Then he looked up, as if emerging from the wisp of a vanishing dream, a wan smile etched across his face. "Never knew you to be a philosopher. Thank you for all you've given and been to me in my previous life. I love you, Jenny. Always did. Always will. I'll go back to where I came from to face my rendezvous with destiny. I'm on a journey all right. Just don't know to where. A dream within a dream? It won't be the end of my journey." He smiled.

"It's the beginning."

ABOUT THE AUTHOR

Ron Roman retired as Associate Professor of English and Humanities with the University of Maryland Global Campus (UMGC-Asia) in 2020 after teaching on US military installation all over the Pacific since 1996. His critically acclaimed doomsday novel Of Ashes and Dust (Histria Books/2022) was a Finalist for the 2023 Chanticleer International Book Award (CIBA) for Global Suspense Thrillers. To learn more about Ron and his books, please visit his website www.writerronroman.com.

INSPIRATION FOR THE STORY

As an officer and lifetime member of the VFW and Assistant Retiree Activities Officer on the local USAF base here in Korea, I deal daily with problems confronting military veterans, retirees, and their dependents.

THANK YOU for purchasing this Windtree Press Anthology. We hope we've peaked your imagination and that you've found some new authors to follow.

For more books of the heart, from anthologies to memoirs and poetry, non-fiction, and novels, please go to our **website at https://windtreepress.com**.

There you can learn about all of our authors, their books, and where to contact them directly.